I0536180

LIV, AGAIN

Tracy Dale

Flying Feather Publishing
2024

This is a work of fiction. Names, characters, places and events described herein are products of the author's imagination or are used fictitiously and are not to be construed as real. Any resemblance to actual events, locations, organizations, or persons, living or dead, is entirely coincidental.

ISBN: 978-0-9992098-7-5

Liv, Again
Copyright © 2024 by Tracy Dale

All rights reserved. Except for use in review, the reproduction or utilization of this work in whole or in part in any form by any electronic, mechanical or other means now known or hereafter invented, is forbidden without the written permission of the publisher.

Warning: The unauthorized reproduction or distribution of this copyrighted work is illegal. Criminal copyright infringement, including infringement without monetary gain, is investigated by the FBI and is punishable by up to five (5) years in federal prison and a fine of $250,000.

Published by Flying Feather Publishing

Visit us at http://www.flyingfeatherpublishing.com

CHAPTER ONE

"Think you can keep your mouth shut during the interview?" Connor's new partner briefly took his eyes off the road to glance meaningfully at his wide yawn.

Shame they weren't friendly enough yet for Connor to give him the finger. "Bribe me with caffeine and your odds improve."

"Heard that about you." Fernando turned into the Dunkin' Donuts parking lot. "You're bribable."

Couldn't be helped, Connor shot his middle finger at him.

Fernando laughed. "Just jokes, partner."

They were ten years apart in age, but Fernando acted like it was a generation, maybe because Connor had been with the police force for seven years to his twenty. He'd take the ribbing if it meant the Old Man routine was on the way out. It's not like Connor had been playing video games until twenty-five and suddenly decided to become a cop.

"Pretty sure I've heard this one before," Connor said. "Two cops walk into a donut shop..." "I love to make stereotypes come true."

They grabbed two cups of coffee, which Fernando insisted was the best around.

Not really, and not strong enough, but Connor chugged it like a frat-boy, hoping it would get his mind in gear. They were on their way to interview a psychologist regarding a suspect.

Fernando had started working the case before he and Connor teamed up, and he had an undeniable *this is mine* attitude about it. Connor had no problem. He could sit quiet, absorb, and wake the hell up while Fernando did his thing.

The office building looked worn and outdated, not too far from where Connor grew up. He'd driven by it a hundred times, never really noticing it. The courtyard had a couple benches and basic greenery. In the middle of it all stood an old, dried-up fountain with rusted scale hardened on it like oozing lava.

Inside, the office had a Zen Garden feel to it. While Connor strolled the waiting room, Fernando spoke to the receptionist, a burly guy who looked out of place amidst the tranquil music and muted paintings of still lakes and barely blooming flowers.

After a brief phone call, burly guy stood. "The doctor will see you now," he said, and escorted them to her office

Connor had two seconds to process the name plaque on the office door before the receptionist pushed it open. Mind suddenly blank, he walked in and looked at Dr. Livia Jones— *Liv*—for the first time in thirteen years.

When she saw him, her mouth dropped open, and out of nowhere, "Just saw a *really* big bug," tumbled out of him. She gasped and her mouth snapped shut, making it clear the long-ago joke was not lost on her. How he used to tease her when they were kids.

"Know each other?" Fernando looked from Liv to Connor and back again.

"Yeah," Connor answered.

At the same time, she said softly, "We did."

Fernando sighed and rubbed the back of his neck like, *these damn kids always make life difficult.* "I'm Detective Fernando Velez and," he threw an arm out, "You know Detective Connor Peltier. We're here about a kid that's disappeared, a patient of yours."

In that brief speech, Liv collected herself. She stood with remarkable poise, while Connor stared. She looked elegant now. As teens she'd been gangly with flowing everything: hair, clothes, jewelry...but now, the blond hair that he'd privately thought looked like gold silk was held back in a contained twist. The trim blue suit she wore outlined how the lankiness that made her downright bony in youth had changed to a sleekness that reminded him of a ballet dancer. As teens he'd told her she'd be hot one day. His prediction had been more accurate than he'd ever anticipated.

Oblivious to his attention—because she hadn't looked at him again—she made a graceful gesture to her counseling area, replete with two comfortable chairs and a sofa. They all filed over and sat.

"I'm sure you know that patient/client privilege means there's little I can divulge to you," Liv said.

Fernando dipped his head. "What can you tell us about Jeremy Olawale?"

Liv showed no surprise at the identified patient, but then she'd shown no emotion whatsoever since the initial shock of seeing Connor. Her hands though, they shook the tiniest bit, and Connor watched with a satisfaction he had no right to feel, as the graceful flow of her fingers linked together to hide it.

"Probably very little that you don't already know," she said. "He's a child—"

"Sixteen," Fernando interrupted.

"Yes, a child under the law."

"Depending on the crime."

Liv paused and seemed to concede the point with a barely perceptible dip of her head. "He's seen me weekly for the last number of months by order of the court, and he's been a model patient."

She fully stopped. The set of her lips tight to signal she was done speaking.

"Anything else you can tell us?" Fernando said. "Anything off in his behavior recently?"

She shook her head.

"Alright." He settled deeply in his chair, the leather groaning as he got comfortable. "You don't seem surprised he's disappeared. Or concerned for that matter. Is this a common occurrence for him?"

"What kind of reaction from a medical professional would be appropriate, in your opinion, Detective?"

Fernando held his hands up in surrender. "Look, we're not the bad guys here. I'm trying to help your patient."

"Then you would know from his record he's run away at least twice."

"Has he ever told you where he runs to?" Connor said the first thing he could think of to get her to look at him.

A flush swept her cheeks as she looked at his chin. "I can't divulge anything that's not already known to you."

"This kid's dangerous, Dr. Jones," Fernando said.

"I understand you think so."

"But you don't. Why?" Fernando pressed.

Connor would swear a gleam of steel entered her eyes. *Interesting.*

"Because I know him in a uniquely individual way. He's been my patient long enough I know the likelihood of what he would or wouldn't do. You only know him based on his record, which tells you very little," Liv said.

"It tells us he was criminally violent and made credible threats."

Liv looked utterly unimpressed and then gave Fernando the most articulate slow-blink Connor had ever seen. "What you have on his record tells you very little."

"His record tells me he's been convicted of assault, theft, making violent threats... And now? Jeremy's father turns up murdered. Shot. With his mother unconscious next to the body. Where's the kid? All the signs point to he's taken off. So, from where I'm sitting, he's looking like an armed and violent criminal."

A beat of silence passed.

"I wish I could help you, Detective, but I'm confident you know that I can't."

Fernando sighed, did a rolling tap of his fingertips on the chair a couple times, and then stood.

Connor followed suit, willing Liv to look at him, but she kept her gaze locked on Fernando as she stood and then escorted them to her office door.

"If you'd like to leave a card at the front desk, I'll contact you should any non-confidential and pertinent information come my way."

"Thank you, Dr. Jones." Fernando shook her hand.

With ridiculous anticipation, Connor reached his own hand out, but she pointedly ignored it, ignored him, and then swiftly shut the door as he left.

* * * *

Once the outer door closed, and the fading murmur of their voices had gone, Liv's posture crumbled. She breathed hard against the burning pressure squeezing her chest and wrapped her arms tight around her middle to still her trembling.

Long minutes passed. She reached deep to find ease, taking slow, quiet breaths before she went back to her desk.

Picking up the phone, she dialed the receptionist. "Patrick, please call Greg and let him know I can't make lunch. Tell him something's come up. Call Dr. Meadows and see how soon she can meet me." Hardly anything in her voice gave away her turmoil.

"Sure thing, doc," Patrick said.

Twenty minutes later, a short knock and Dr. Meadows—Holly—came striding in, a mischievous smile on her heart-shaped face. With her artfully highlighted hair bobbing around her shoulders and the lively sprinkle of freckles across her nose, everything about her looked cute, always had. In college, they couldn't walk anywhere without some guy trying to get her attention.

"This is completely inappropriate," Holly said quietly, "but do you think you could impose a no-shirt rule for Patrick? I'd like to add—again—that hiring him was one of your best decisions."

"I'm sure Patrick wouldn't mind, but your husband might."

Holly's smile fell. "What's wrong?"

"Connor—" *Damn it!* She tried so hard to speak normally. Instead, it came as an uneven, raspy whisper. "He was here." Tears welled faster than she could fight them back. They dripped down her cheeks, collecting under her chin in an irritating tickle.

"*Here?* In your office?"

Liv visibly trembled, but when Holly moved toward her, she shook her head. Grimly, she grabbed a tissue and pulled the fraying pieces of her self-control back together with each aggressive swipe of her face.

Holly stepped to the window, gazing out. "Since you didn't tell me about it beforehand, I'm guessing you didn't know he was coming." A quick glance over her shoulder at Liv. "I hope to God he came to apologize."

"No," Liv said, sounding more even. "He was as shocked at seeing me as I was him."

"God, I hate him," Holly muttered. "Give me a minute alone with him, and I'll show him a whole new meaning to Special Forces." She looked over her shoulder again, noted Liv's composed features, and turned to face her. "Can you tell me now?"

Liv described the meeting, how *unmoved* he was by seeing her. "Literally half my life, he's affected me. After seeing him today, after all these years, I don't think I affected him even a fraction as much. If at all." It had been devastating to see the non-reaction, other than brief surprise perhaps in his hazel eyes, framed with thick black lashes that somehow weren't feminine on him. His sharply angled features revealed absolutely no emotion, his sculpted lips showed no softness. He was all hard lines and strength and so attractive in his adult masculinity that it made her stomach clench.

"I always thought because he was out of the country, doing whatever he did in the army, it was easy for him to put our relationship away. He was good at that, compartmentalizing. To now know that he's been a cop in the city I've always lived, that we both grew up in… I can't think what compartment that would fit in."

"You've long believed he didn't love you as much as you loved him," Holly said gently.

"But to experience it." Liv briefly closed her eyes. "And maybe I didn't truly believe it." For three years after he slipped out of her life it had hurt every-single-day. Another two before she stopped thinking about him regularly. Every single one of those days, she'd fought the hold his devastating betrayal had on her, but it had changed her. That it affected her for so long caused a burning humiliation deep inside.

"After today, I have tools for closure I didn't have before. So, I'm grateful for that." Pulling open a desk drawer, she took out her handbag, and gathered her composure around her like armor. "Have time for a latte?"

CHAPTER TWO

"I bet she knows something." Fernando handed him the case files. "I should have given you these Monday. Had you read them, you would have been prepared for meeting the good doctor."

"I did ask for them," Connor said mildly.

"A lot of times new kids walk into homicide, thinking they've got something special, and then they go and say some dumbass thing at the worst time, and it sets progress back. I was trying to circumvent that."

Right or wrong, Connor could appreciate his frankness. "Is everyone a kid to you?"

"Anyone younger than me is," he said with a quick grin. "What's the story with you and Dr. Jones?"

"We dated in high school."

"How badly did you treat her?"

Heat raced up Connor's neck. "Who says I treated her badly?"

"I have five baby sisters. I know what being hurt by a boyfriend looks like on a woman. For it to last this long, means you hurt her bad."

"*Five* younger sisters? No wonder you act burdened by us all."

Fernando chuckled. "My sisters are amazing. It's my baby brother that did it."

"Good God, how many of you are there?"

"Seven. Every one of us was planned."

"You have a bunch of kids yourself?"

"Two is good for me." Fernando smiled wryly. "Two was good for my wife." He tapped the files. "Try not to make any dumbass comments with this info."

It was a relief when he walked away. Certainly, he clocked Connor's subject change and was savvy enough to go with it. The guy was sharp, and Connor guessed he didn't miss much. Not exactly ideal when you've just taken a very personal hit.

Liv. To see her for the first time, after what he'd done all those years ago. And he was a worthless piece of shit, because for the thirteen years since, he'd wanted her. He was disciplined though. When thoughts of her surfaced, shoving them right back down again wasn't that hard to do. Life was busy. He went deep in the army. Followed that right up with the police force and buried himself in the drug world.

Didn't look at a single picture of her in all that time. Never a conversation about her; even lapsed his high school friendships, so she was never brought up. He'd been fine, doing just fine. The low hum of misery wasn't difficult at all to live with. Most of the time, he wasn't even aware of it.

But to see her again. Too many memories, and maybe his discipline had gone to hell because right now, he couldn't bury them.

He remembered the first time he wanted her. Felt like they'd known each other forever, and forever she'd been so damn skinny he had teasing names about it: Twiglet. Lucky Legs—*lucky they don't snap.* Junior year of high school though, things started to change, and she became a gentle light in his dark life that continually grew, until by senior year, she was brighter than the sun. He never wanted to be apart from her. If he hadn't been deployed, he probably never would have been.

Connor flipped the file open and started reading. Gradually, discipline returned. "Jeremy Olawale," he murmured. Three visits by Child Protective Services, prompted by concerned teachers. Repetitive absences at school. Caught stealing shoes from a discount shoe store at fourteen. Same year, he was interviewed by police over a suspected threat to shoot up his school. He denied it, no evidence. Juvie at fifteen for assaulting a kid at the park.

As he read the charge, it struck Connor that the boy he assaulted said a hell of a lot about how innocently he'd been hanging out when Jeremy attacked. Jeremy, on the other hand, said not one word in either offense or defense of his actions. While at the detention facility, it was noted by an officer during processing that when Jeremy changed into the corrections uniform, severe bruising was visible on his back, legs and arms. During his time in detention, his behavior was exemplary.

Then there was his father, Ronald Olawale. An upstanding citizen. Reliable employee at UPS. Respected member of the congregation at church. Only one little flag, a complaint by a female twenty years prior for stalking, which she dropped.

Finishing the file, he leaned back in his chair, and then rocked forward, using the momentum to get him out of it. He could walk fine, could even run, but something about sitting for extended periods aggravated the wound that had taken him out of the army. Sometimes, he wished like hell he could slip back into the brush in some remote place and zone into a technical mission, seemed to him his body could handle that more than it could the endless hours of sitting.

"What's the mother say?" Connor said, strolling up to Fernando.

"Dunno. She's in a psych ward, on a fifty-one-fifty hold." A forced psychiatric hospital stay for mentally unstable individuals. "You read the whole file already?"

"I read quickly. You should have told me about the fifty-one-fifty before we went to see the family therapist." Maybe this morning he'd been fine to sit back and let him drive, but this was flat bad form.

"You mean your ex-girlfriend?"

Connor briefly clenched his back teeth, an old habit he'd tried to break because the flex of muscle in his jaw gave away his aggravation. He was still working on it. "I wonder if you're an asshole to be funny or if it's personality."

"My wife wonders that too." His gaze turned to his computer, as if he'd lost interest in the conversation. Starting to type with hard stabs of his index fingers, he said, "Dr. Jones isn't the family psychologist. She was assigned Jeremy when he was released from the detention center."

"Where's that info?" Connor held up the file because it wasn't in it.

"It's right-- ohp, hold on." Some hard hits on *backspace*, followed by a slow search and tap of the keyboard. "Yep, it's right here." He squinted a little as he moved the mouse, followed by the sound of paper printing.

"You just wrote it down?" Connor said.

"Actually, I just printed it. Right before that I wrote it down."

Fernando had been in homicide for ten years and had a good reputation. Somehow, he must have earned it. "When's she due to be released?"

"Should have been five days ago, but then they extended it."

"Then she's on a fifty-two-fifty."

"If you want to get technical."

"I'm partial to it, yeah."

Fernando tapped keys, saying slowly as he did so, "Technically bribable." He flashed Connor a bland smile. "Making notes on you, partner, just so's I remember how to know you quicker."

Mirroring the smile, Connor said, "I'll follow up on Mrs. Olawale's condition."

* * * *

Connor was sixteen the first time he heard of Pandora's Box. He remembered with odd clarity that moment: the classroom with yellow fluorescent lighting, the girl with curly hair sitting in front of him, the way his teacher made a slight emphasis on the *Pan* in Pandora. All of it provided an enduring backdrop to the sensation of uneasiness he'd felt over the story. Not one to pause to wonder why he reacted to it, nevertheless he suddenly understood why he had. Seeing Liv again flipped the lid on his box, and all the years of his discipline with her was suddenly, irretrievably gone.

There were laws against peace officers using their privilege of information to find out details about civilians without due cause.

He broke them. It could be argued that reviewing Dr. Livia Jones' personal records was a valid pursuit considering her connection to a murder case. However, privately, he knew he wanted her address, marital status, and any other tiny bit of information he could possibly find out about her, because he was like a starving man who'd just been told where to find the only source of food.

With that information, he finished out his day and drove to her house, pausing to grab food before parking on her street like a stakeout. A shock of memories came flooding in as he sat there, and all the years of suppressing them meant they were like a traffic jam, fighting for a way out through the tiny lane he'd inadvertently cleared.

Five houses. She lived five houses from where they'd grown up. Together, as kids, they'd walked past the one she now owned a hundred times. He even remembered the time she'd pointed it out saying '*It has great bones*', and he hadn't known what the hell she was talking about but agreed anyway because why not. Not once since he'd left home at eighteen had he been this close to their neighborhood.

A shadow of movement behind Liv's barely cracked blinds made his heart rate speed up. A deep, profound longing to be able to walk through her door and settle in for the night disconcerted him.

Swiftly starting his truck, he pulled away, to the condo he'd just moved into. When he left narcotics, he made a complete change, scrubbing any connection to that life, partly out of necessity. New condo, new truck, new clothes, all of it good. Scrubbing his life wasn't hard. Starting over wasn't hard, he liked movement, liked change.

As he dropped down onto his new, dark grey sofa, he settled in to watch a game.

He couldn't settle. Grabbing his phone, he scrolled through the news then old texts, but he'd deleted most, and his contacts. He went through his photos, all of them of his new truck in his garage.

He did have one contact he hadn't deleted.

"Hello?" Shona answered on the second ring.

Seemed like no one answered their phone anymore, except Shona. She always picked up. "Hey, it's been a while, hasn't it?"

"Connor? You get a new number?"

"Yeah. Work got crazy, so I made some changes."

"So that's why you never replied to my texts. What are you doing?"

"Not much."

"Let's get together."

Easy as that, he had plans.

Practically jogging out of his condo to his truck, he drove the twenty minutes to Shona's place, relieved when she moved quickly from idle chatting to brushing her body against his, which he swiftly responded to.

She had medium length hair and a round face she didn't like touched, but she liked his hands in her hair, so he sank his fingers deep. She was uncomfortable with her body, sucking in her thick belly and frequently moving away if his hands strayed near it, so he carefully ground his hips against her and focused on her hot spots.

Pulling her hair to arch her head back, he trailed hot kisses up her throat, and she moaned, her hands clutching at his shirt as she widened her stance, spreading her legs so his cock could rub against her. She was quick to go off, and he wasn't surprised when she started panting and shaking, her hands grasping his ass to press him harder against her.

As she stilled, Connor drew back. She tried to follow, looking for his mouth but he pulled away.

She laughed. "I forgot."

Grabbing his hand, she dragged him to her room. Decorated extra feminine, with lots of ruffles and soft pinks, it was pleasant. He always enjoyed the moment when she pushed him back onto the soft bed and stripped him. Tonight was no different.

The sweet scent of her perfume drifted around him as her fingers unraveled his belt and buttons. She was surprisingly strong, able to strip his pants off with a hard, swift tug, and then she climbed onto the bed, onto him, and pulled his shirt off.

As usual, she'd dressed for the occasion, a specific kind of dress with spaghetti straps and no bra, so she could expose her breasts, hike the skirt up and ride him. As usual, she dropped one strap, then the other, tugging until her breasts tumbled out, the areolas large and pink, the nipples a tiny nub she leaned down to rub against his lips.

Connor nibbled one, gently licking, because that's what she liked. She'd told him years ago and he'd never forgotten.

Moaning, panting, she reached down between her legs, finding his hardness, fondling him from root to tip. She released him briefly to wetly lick her thumb and then grasped him again, rubbing her thumb on the tip, over the slit and he sighed with pleasure.

"I'm ready for you," she said, reaching under her pillow where she always kept the condom. *Sheepskin, ribbed for her pleasure.* She knew what she liked.

Smoothing it on him, the feel of her strong hands rolling it down his length was one of his favorite moments with her. With a small shimmy, she settled over him, easing down his cock until he was in all the way and then started a bouncing, rolling rhythm.

Connor played with her breasts, gently pinching, lightly fingering the tips and her rolling bounce increased. She usually went off in a few minutes, and she did, gasping, crying out, snapping her hips as she clenched and spasmed around his length.

Her eyes lifted slowly, and she smiled. "Your turn."

Connor leaned up, clamped his mouth around a nipple, filled his hands with her ass and yanked her down hard on him. Lift and slap of their hips as his shot beneath her, until he groaned around her tit as he came.

CHAPTER THREE

"We need to see your doctor girlfriend today," Fernando said as Connor walked in, right on time. "How the hell is it you're looking more tired than when you started? You're not visiting your narc buddies at night, are you?"

It took effort to maintain stoic. He looked tired? How he looked wasn't a fraction of the exhaustion he felt. After Shona's, he'd had a hell of a time getting to sleep. Not exactly unusual for him, but maybe he was getting old because he couldn't shake it off like he used to.

"Why are we going back?" He never wanted to go *back*. Just wanted to go forward and not think about the past, which was fucking impossible to do if he had to fucking go back to her.

Fernando's demeanor changed, from needling to calm, clearly a reaction to his foul mood. The guy noticed too damned much.

"We received an anonymous tip that Dr. Jones can speak about."

"Are you going to tell me the tip or withhold information again like it's the funnest game you ever played?"

"I have a teenaged daughter and she talks just like that." His tone oozed, *that's amazing*. "The tipster claimed Ronald Olawale was abusive to Jeremy. Doc Jones should have some insight if it's true. I already called her...secretary? What would you call that body builder guy?"

"Sssecretary," Connor said slowly.

"Really? He doesn't look like one."

"It's a job not a gender description. They don't call it she-cretary or re-she-ptionist."

"Jesus. Have you been actually talking to my teenaged daughter?"

"If she knows basic word definitions then maybe you should."

"Ow." Fernando clutched his chest. "Straight through the heart." He chuckled. "Turns out she has a tight schedule today. Doc Jones, not my daughter. Her he-cretary said she could see us in a half hour or not at all today. So, let's get you coffee'd up and go."

"Already had coffee."

"You're not going to hit your narc buddies up for something stronger, are you?" Connor gave him a dark look, and Fernando said innocently, "Just jokes, partner."

Fernando chatted the whole ride to Liv's office, but none of it registered. Walking into her building, adrenaline buzzed, and seeing her felt like a kick to the chest.

She wore slim black pants and a fitted black top, her long blond hair braided over her shoulder in a style she sometimes wore in high school. The structure of her face seemed both more delicate and fiercer to him with the gentle arches of her light brows, the sharp slashes of her cheekbones, the full softness of her lips.

Inviting them to sit, she looked calm and in control as she waited for Fernando to speak. Only her fingers gave her away, linked tightly and half-tucked under her crossed leg.

"Good to see you again, Dr. Jones."

With a polite smile, she said, "How may I help you?"

"You and I both know your non-disclosure rules go out the window when there's a threat to the life and safety of an individual, particularly when it comes to kids."

"Not particularly, actually. All threats to all individuals are of equal importance."

"Glad to hear you say that. Now, we've come to find out Jeremy's father has been accused of abuse. Did you know about this?"

"That he's been accused? No."

"Did Jeremy ever say anything about being abused, or witnessing any kind of abuse?"

"No."

"Was there anything that gave you any suspicions that abuse was happening?"

"I always consider abuse a possibility when I have a kid with Jeremy's record, Detective."

A vague answer. Fernando went silent, waiting for her to continue, but she sat, unwilling to.

"Did you know Mrs. Olawale was put on a psychiatric hold following Mr. Olawale's death?" Connor said.

She looked at him. Finally, she fucking looked at him! Her gaze was guarded but having her blue-brown eyes on him felt like being handed a prize.

"Yes."

"Any attempts to visit her?"

"That's not possible," she said with a dismissive shake of her head.

"Find out information then. Any attempts?"

A brief hesitation, then, "Yes."

Connor could feel Fernando perk up beside him from the slight shift in the couch.

"Now, why would you do that?" Fernando said.

"Out of concern, Detective."

"Do you always follow up on the parents of your patients?"

"I don't always have patients accused of murder."

"So that's a no?"

Connor was impressed with her boldness in staring down his partner, and it took him by surprise. She'd been more timid the way he remembered her.

"I still have nothing I can share that can help you in your investigation," she said finally. "I've got a busy day, so I'm afraid this meeting needs to end."

Again, she refused to shake his hand as they left. As they drove back to the station, Fernando said, "I can't decide if she's combative because her issues with you, or if it's because she knows something."

"Or if it's your charming personality."

"It's like Beer Pong, I'm not really sure where the ball is going to land. But with your particular knowledge of her, any reasonable guesses?"

"No. Like you, I think it could be any of the above."

Not true because he still recognized her tells, and she'd been lying about the abuse. She knew something, but why would she lie about it?

A call came in from dispatch. A body had just been discovered, described as a delivery man with a wound to the head. Connor plugged in the address as Fernando radioed back, "We're on it."

It took three days before they caught their guy with the murder weapon in his possession. Three days catching naps on cots at the station as they followed the details. Connor loved it, reminded of his missions, the intensity of focus, the movement. At the end they were both exhausted, but before they drove off, Fernando said in a craggy voice, "You did good. Rest up this weekend, partner."

At home, he crashed. Slept until late Saturday, almost evening. After ordering Chinese food, he took a hot shower and then dressed in joggers and a t-shirt just in time for the delivery guy. A game was on, he watched it while he ate out of the carton with wooden chopsticks.

An image of Liv's hands, clenched in her lap, popped into his mind.

Grunting, he shifted forward and concentrated on the tv.

He'd gotten into her personal space when she'd walked them to the door, his arm brushing against her. A flush had climbed her cheeks and her lips had parted slightly.

Damn it, he didn't want to think about her.

It had been three days—make that four—since he'd hit the gym. He'd go soon as his food settled.

The first time he met Liv's parents slipped into his mind. Her dad had asked him about a trick play in football, and Connor had known exactly what he was talking about. There'd been an instant bond of camaraderie. Mr. Jones had been an important part of his life, and he'd treated him almost as shittily as he'd treated Liv.

Fucking *Liv*.

Connor threw his chopsticks down in disgust and hauled himself to his feet, to his truck, to the gym. Muscle-shredding reps should do it. He lifted harder than he had in a while. Four hours in, satisfyingly exhausted, he knew he'd be in pain the next day, mind-numbing pain.

* * * *

"You've been avoiding me." Holly held up a bakery box and two lattes. "So, I brought magic of an irresistible nature. No one turns away coffee cake and lattes. Least not anyone I want to know."

Liv opened the door wider for Holly, surprised by the Sunday morning visit. "I haven't been avoiding you, Holls."

"Arguable." Setting the items down on Liv's kitchen counter, she turned with a triumphant smile, and hugged her. "And see? The magic worked."

"Your magic always works. You're the most successful wannabe-witch I know."

"It's because I know where my source of power lies and use it religiously."

Laughing, Liv gathered plates, utensils, napkins. Her backyard was small, but she'd filled it as full of trees, flowers, and swaying greenery as she could, with an iron dining set and bench swing amidst it all.

"I love it back here," Holly said. "It's been too long since we've done this." Settling into a seat, she leaned back with a sigh. "I should never have gotten married. We could do this all the time."

"We didn't do this all the time before you got married, " Liv said, amused. "You always liked to go out for breakfast."

"Stop trying to prevent me from pretending like my single days were the glory days. I'm determined."

"You're determined to avoid the potentially awkward friendship space when one friend is part of a couple, and the other is not."

Holly bit into the cake Liv set before her. "It would be a fair psychoanalysis if you were single."

"I am single."

"You mean unmarried, right?" At Liv's expression, Holly pretended to take a whiskey-shot of her latte, and then slapped the cup back down again with a hissing *ahhhh*. "Let's do this. Why were you avoiding me this week?"

"I had some cleaning up to do."

"Please tell me you didn't do anything rash since seeing Connor. Please."

Liv took a thoughtful bite of her cake. "I don't think it was rash. Greg kept talking about moving in together, and I felt dread every time. If I dreaded living with him, not exactly ideal for a potential marriage partner. So, I told him I enjoy his company but think we should no longer be exclusive."

Holly groaned and briefly buried her head in her hands. "We've talked about this! You have the dread with every man because of your hang ups about Connor. And lo, he shows up and you dump another great guy."

"I know. I do, but truly, before this last week I've been thinking about ending things with Greg."

"Because of your hang ups, Liv. You need to work through this, or you'll keep ending things out of fear that someone else will disappear first. I know you don't want to be alone."

"I was never excited about Greg, I just liked him. I accepted long ago that the...intensity...that Connor made me feel, I wouldn't feel with anyone else. I've hoped maybe I'd find a tiny bit of it though with someone. Since I liked Greg so much as a person, I really hoped that spark would come, but..." Liv held out her hands. "Honestly, Holly, it wasn't even an intense conversation when I told him. Says a lot about the quality of feeling we have for each other."

"Maybe." Holly rubbed her temples with a grimace. "I'll see if we can get a refund on our trip."

"No, we're still going."

"On a couple's trip to France and Italy? You'll be sharing a room with him. It will be the four of us in one of those tiny European cars."

"I remember the details," Liv said dryly. "I told you. It was terribly un-intense. We're—" *air quotes* "casually uncoupling."

Holly snickered. "Okay, I can maybe see how this could work, but if there's any awkwardness with you two, I'm cancelling. Sorry, not sorry."

"No cancelling. I'll order an escort before I cancel."

"*An escort?* That's ridiculous, bring Patrick."

Liv laughed before carefully steering the conversation away from her. Yes, she had been avoiding Holly, because she wasn't ready to deal with the *now*, let alone the past.

Maybe Holly understood, and that's why she let it go, or maybe it was her tightly packed schedule of clients that increasingly left her distracted from what was happening in the moment. Liv mentally told herself she should talk to Holly about her workload—when she had more to give, because right now, she barely managed the conversation.

"I need to go," Holly announced, standing.

"What?"

"This was just a drop over. Sorry I can't stay longer." She leaned down to give Liv a kiss on the cheek. "I'll see myself out. Enjoy the rest of the magic."

Holly closed the front door behind her, the low gleam of metallic orange-gold paint on a shiny new truck catching her attention. It was the same color she'd wanted her husband to get when he went for his truck. Instead, he'd gone with the most boring color of them all, *silver.*

Throwing a smile at the driver she could barely see through the too dark tinted windows, thinking, *he could get a ticket for those,* she got in her silver sedan, unaware that Connor watched her until she drove out of eyeshot.

As soon as she disappeared, he got out of his truck and strode to Liv's door. Not part of the plan. Not that parking outside her house on a Sunday morning was either, but at least only he knew about it.

He kept asking himself why in hell he was walking to her door, which graduated to demanding he turn his sorry ass around and get back in his truck, and finally culminated in a silent *What the fuck are you doing?!* to his hand as it knocked.

Liv was already talking as she answered, something like, "...d you forget—" Her abrupt silence as their gazes locked, made his heart pound.

"Hi," he said.

No response, other than a near imperceptible shake of her head.

Before she could tell him to get lost, he asked, "Can I come in?"

It worked sometimes, Fernando had said, to just ask the subject politely. Still, it shocked the hell out of Connor when she opened the door wider and stepped back. Then it confused him when she again did that near imperceptible shake before she turned and walked somewhere else in her house. Guess he'd just, ah, close the door then. And lock it in case she tried to throw him out. Anything to slow her down.

Each step inside was a revelation of how she chose to live and every bit of it he absorbed, ferociously taking in each detail. The outside of her house was charcoal grey with white trim and a light wood door, bold, but inside looked softer, with cream-colored furnishings and pale wood. Muted green walls drew his eye to the wide-open French doors that highlighted the green leaves of the trees and made it seem like the outside was in.

Following the direction she'd gone, he saw pictures he wanted to examine, paintings and knick-knacks he wanted to look at, just to know what she liked to see day after day.

At the French doors, he found her sitting at a little black table that looked artfully messy with flowery plates, soft lavender napkins, crumbling cake and a recycled paper coffee cup.

For the longest time he simply stood there, staring at her. The quiet as he watched her, the soft sound of fluttering leaves moving in the light breeze eased a weight on his chest he hadn't known he carried. Peace. Over the last ten-plus years of his life, he'd never felt as much peace as he did in this one moment with her.

"I remember when we were kids, you said that if you weren't so sure you wanted to do psychology, you'd be a decorator. You would have been a great one, Liv. Your place is beautiful."

Her eyes filled with tears that she tried to hide, blinking quickly, looking away. Then she seemed to grow still, accepting, not hiding. He was struck again by the strength he didn't remember her possessing.

Moving to the table, he cautiously took a seat. No more words came to mind, nothing that was *enough*, and so he sat, and experienced being with her in a way he'd never once let himself imagine.

Her eyes closed and she took a measured breath. When they opened again, glistening their unique blue-brown in the dappled light, she looked directly at him, without reluctance. The first time, he realized.

"I'm sorry about your mother," she said.

Connor may have jerked in his seat. It certainly felt like he'd been punched in the chest, so unprepared was he to hear that from anyone at this point, much less her. "It was a long time ago," he managed to say.

"I remember."

"I know." Lame. God, he didn't want to talk about this. Yet he'd brought himself here, unplanned though it was, he only had himself to blame. "A lots happened since then, so I'm... I didn't come here to talk about that." *What did you come here to talk about then?* A more perfect opening he couldn't have given her and *damn it!* he didn't want to talk about this.

She took another slow breath, her golden skin exposed by the baby blue V-neck sweater looked smooth, beautiful as her chest rose and fell, and the urge to draw nearer grew intense.

"The first day in my dorm, I put up a collage of photos of us." She smiled slightly. "Practically a shrine."

Again, words he wasn't expecting, and the one-two punch of surprise left him uneasy. He *knew* her, and yet he didn't, at all.

The Liv of his memory would have tiptoed around a conversation he didn't want.

"I must have driven people crazy," she continued. "I loved to talk about you, my boyfriend in the army. 'He's so good looking. We're so in love.' I used to say it on repeat. I even set up a whiteboard with big black marker counting down the days until you returned home. I talked about it *constantly*." Another brief smile. "My poor roommate.

"The first time you didn't call, I was in a near panic, thinking something must have happened to you. Everyone said, 'sometimes these things happen'. But your mom had just passed away two days before, and I kept thinking that the shock and grief had left you vulnerable to the danger you were surrounded by. When you didn't call again, I cried, convinced you'd been hurt, or worse. My dad said to give it another week, that maybe your group of trainees kept getting in trouble. Third week you didn't call, he tracked down Uncle Mark. God knows where he was, some classified location with shoddy reception, but you know him, he heard what we wanted and took care of it. It was another week before we heard back, but he found out you were doing outstanding, and that you didn't ask for leave to see to your mom."

Connor felt a dull heat rise up his chest and neck. To hear it said that way, he sounded like the coldest bastard of a son. "I"— he cleared his throat—"There was no funeral." There wasn't much about his decision making so far in life that he would defend, but he would defend this. "I found out the day after it happened. When Keith called," his drunk, asshole stepfather, "he told me he was having her cremated and a realtor was going to be putting the house up for sale, along with all her stuff. He said he wasn't doing a funeral and he didn't want me around, getting in the way as he got rid of stuff. So, I didn't come."

Her mouth opened as if to respond, but she closed it quickly and again that minute shake of her head.

"I couldn't make sense out of why you never called. If I had done something, or your feelings had changed, you'd at least call me, or even," she laughed without humor, "even a text message.

Something to let me know. If my parents hadn't been assured by Uncle Mark that you were in perfect health and doing extremely well, we all would have believed you'd died."

Another dull burn swept over him, but there was no defense for this.

"I had stopped changing the number on my 'Days 'Til Connor Comes Home' board, but I didn't put it away. I left it out with the number forty-eight still written with an exclamation point. On the day you were supposed to be home, I kept hoping that you were going to surprise me.

"That night, I erased the number and put the board away. My roommate gave me a sympathetic look that was humiliating, because I'd gloated about how good I had it, how amazing my boyfriend was, and I knew other girls were mocking me and making fun of all the things I'd said while my super amazing boyfriend was silently dumping me."

The cadence of her voice was even, meditative in the way she spoke, even as she continued with the details of the pain he'd caused her.

"I'd struggled my whole life with self-confidence. After that, I had none. None," she repeated, barely making a sound. "Not once did it occur to me to protect myself from you doing something like that, because I wore the heart you'd had *Forever* engraved on, around my neck.

"I felt grief for five years. I think the humiliation made it worse, and the doubt from being so wrong about all that I'd believed about us. Every day it felt like I was buried underground, trying to dig my way out. It was some of the hardest years of my life. Every kernel of confidence I had to *fight* for."

She looked away, and he wasn't sure what to say. Once, her face had been so expressive, she'd been easy to tease, and they'd laughed and joked constantly. Now, she was so controlled, he could hardly imagine it.

"I'm sorry," he murmured. He wanted to hold her, the impulse so strong he had to force himself to be still.

"I have nothing to tell you about Jeremy," she said.

A moment of confusion, before he remembered he was the cop investigating her patient. It had been a long damn time since someone had knocked him off-balance, yet she kept him in a constant state of it. His brows drew tight. "I'm not here about the case."

"Yet you're here because of him."

He started to refute it but strictly speaking, it was accurate. Had it not been for the investigation, he would never have sought her out. He was an asshole. Minutes in her company and he was right back where they'd left off as kids, where she was the brightest light he'd ever get close to in his dark life, and he wanted as much of it as he could get.

"I came to see you," he said.

Their gazes locked together. *Intensity.* But she quickly slipped away again, and he wanted to demand she return to him. He held his tongue. If he waited long enough, she would.

"From the time I began my practice, I've seen patient after patient that believes they aren't cared about, that their lives don't matter, that no one would notice they were gone, or if they did, not for long. I tell them that their one life matters and has an impact in ways they often can't see."

Finally, she returned to him, but her gaze had changed, disconnected.

"Take your one life," she said. "I cared about it every single day, *long* after you were gone, and the impact your life had on mine was so profound, it changed the person who I was—"

"Jesus, is this some, 'thank you for making me stronger' bullshit?"

Barely a reaction to his outburst, which only agitated him more. But he managed to hold his damn tongue long enough for her to continue.

"No. My gratitude is for myself, that I did the work to become someone I still like."

"Then why the hell are you telling me this?"

"I always wondered if you had any idea how you affected me. Or if somehow, you hadn't known how important you were to me."

"Did you figure it out?" he bit out.

"Did you?"

His words locked down.

"You should go." She stood.

"We're not done, Liv."

"I am."

Standing, he drew closer to her and took unholy pleasure in the way he towered over her. She was taller than average, always had been, but she'd stopped growing in high school. He hadn't. Being this close, his greater height was new to her, and he enjoyed seeing her reaction to it. Finally, she was the one off balance.

"I'm sorry for what happened," he said gruffly. "You were always too good for me. I told you that even when we were kids."

"It was never true." He made a dismissive noise, but she continued, "It's not true for anyone. You're as good as you make yourself. No matter what your stepdad did, what your mom or dad didn't do, it was always up to you to make yourself as good as you wanted to be. It was never that I was too good for you, it's not possible. It was that you never did the work."

"Some of us have a helluva lot more work to do than others."

"Yes."

His agitation soared. When she turned toward the front door, he wanted to demand she sit and keep talking, but she said, "I'd like you to leave now."

His back teeth clenched. He felt the flex of his jaw and tried to loosen it, to hide his reaction, but he couldn't manage it, and that just pissed him off. Jerking his head in a sharp nod, he strode out of her house, snapping the door shut behind him as he went.

CHAPTER FOUR

"Boy, you were supposed to sleep all weekend, not come in like we worked too many hours last week." Fernando set a steaming coffee cup on Connor's desk. "Here, help get you going."

Fernando oozed *middle-aged* as he walked away. Hefty paunch to his belly that made his shirt pull at the buttons with pants that drooped deeply under it. Soft, fluffy cheeks and greyer than not hair. He was… Hell, just a few years ago Connor would have called him old. Now, the age difference seemed negligible. All it did was highlight how meaningless Connor's existence was in comparison. No family. No marriage. No home.

When you got right down to it, nothing he'd done in his life had meant anything. Lock a drug dealer up? A new one stepped in to take that spot. Wipe out a terrorist? Watch ten more become radicalized in their stead. So why the hell did he even bother?

The most alive he'd felt in years had been with Liv, that pointless sensation fading, his whole self engaged. It lasted right up until she asked him to leave, and he'd had to go back to his condo, his nothing-worth-noting existence.

Aware he sounded a lot like Liv's 'patient after patient' she'd talked about, he nevertheless couldn't see a way around the truth of it. With how he'd arranged his life, if he died, no one would know. His coworkers likely the only ones who'd attend his funeral, if someone arranged one for him. Who would? Probably no one. He lived practically as a John Doe.

Drinking the black coffee, he grimaced at the bitterness.

"Let's go see the mom," Connor called over to Fernando.

"Last I checked, Olawale's still on a hold."

"Let's check again. In person."

Fernando took his measure before looking skyward. "Why not."

On the way to the hospital, Fernando said, "What set the bee abuzz under your ass? Couldn't have been my office-grade coffee, so let's take that idea off the table. Go."

"Go."

"Yeah, go, as in: start talking. Or, go ahead. It's all the rage, all the kids are saying it."

"Like your daughter."

"She's still getting the hang of it. I say it better. Go."

"Just trying to get us some news on the missing kid."

"Trying to win a cake that says, *You're the Best New Detective Ever* on it?"

"If there's a cake like that to be won, then hell yeah I'm winning it." Fernando snorted and Connor's lips briefly curved. "What happened to the bee under your ass for Olawale?"

"Too much time has passed," Fernando said. "The buzz starts to hum pretty low at this point."

"So you give up?"

"I give in. Been doing this too long to fight how I know it is. It becomes a sludge walk."

"But the kid's so young, he's bound to turn up."

"Unless he was murdered too," Fernando said.

When they arrived at the psych ward, the attending doctor refused them an interview with Mrs. Olawale. "She doesn't respond to anyone. Frankly, it's a waiting game at this point." And so they left, with Fernando grumbling about what a waste of time it was.

"Pointless," Connor said.

* * * *

"No, Greg." Liv strained away from him into a back bend over his rigid arm, while his other hand clumsily stroked up her ribcage to her breast. The moment she'd walked into his house for dinner, he'd clasped her tight, kissed her and pushed his tongue in her mouth. What the hell? "We just broke up." She tried to sound nice about it, even though she was pissed.

"No, we didn't." He smiled but it didn't hide his confusion. "We're having an open relationship."

Huh. She hadn't said 'open relationship', but by his use of that phrase did he think she wanted more sex? Liv almost laughed. That was part of the problem with him. She didn't want much of his sex at all. She didn't want much of anyone's sex, except Connor's.

That was undeniably one of her biggest regrets—she'd always kept things PG. *I'm just not ready;* she could practically hear herself saying it, and she curled her lip in disgust at her seventeen-year-old self, wishing she could tell her to give it up to the only guy she'd ever feel lust over. If she had though…God knows how she would have handled his disappearing act. She'd barely handled it without the intimate knowledge.

"*Greg!*" she snapped, shoving at his shoulders.

"Why?" As if to remind her of his superior strength, he was slow to release her. Slower than he should have been given her resistance. "Have you met someone else? Giving a trial run with the new guy before you completely end it with me?"

"What are you talking about?" she said sharply. "There was no drama about breaking up the other night."

"First of all, we didn't actually break up. We're no longer exclusive, free to explore other options. Your words, Liv. Second, I was a little off kilter by that sudden announcement, so I went with it. I'm not feeling so easy about it now."

"So, you want to completely break up."

"*No!*" he shouted. They'd been together long enough she'd noticed his tendency to raise his voice, but shouting was new. "*I wanted to move in together not break up!*"

"Why are you yelling at me?"

"*Don't use your doctor voice on me!*"

"Sorry." Automatically she eased back, putting space between them. She just didn't feel any kind of intensity to mount a verbal protest. He wanted to yell? Alright. She'd give him the space to do it.

As he shouted about the future he'd thought they were headed toward and what a shitty thing it was to blindside him like this, she just thought about how glad she was she escaped moving in with a yeller. She hated yelling. Especially how yellers' faces turned a dark shade of red, and the eyes bulged a bit, became a little glassy even. Sometimes spittle really did spray from shouting lips and the glistening quality mixed with all the other facial changes was really pretty off-putting.

"*LIV!*" He bellowed it this time. "*You're not even listening to me!*"

"Whoa, Greg, I'm really sorry I made you feel this angry." Her psych hat settled firmly in place. She needed to calm him down. Appeasing him would be the quickest route. "I never intended to cause you so much rage." Manly, manly rage. Of course, she couldn't say hurt feelings because that just wouldn't do to appease his masculine pride. That had to be what this was all about.

"Damn it, Liv, I wanted to marry you!"

He did? *Why?* They were so boring together! To be fair, she hadn't necessarily noticed until Connor showed up and scorched her attention, burning her up inside.

"You know what your problem is, Liv? You're so busy helping other people you don't stop to get help for yourself. You stay too busy so you can't even look in a mirror. We had something good here. For you to throw that away for no damned reason, without a single shred of feeling about it shows just how messed up you are. You need help. I wondered, with a woman your age, no marriage no kids, beautiful and smart, how could you have made it this long not married? Now I know. You're messed up. Get some help from one of your psychiatric friends and save us all from your trouble."

Liv recoiled.

"I'll take your advice, Greg." Her voice sounded hoarse from the restraint it took to not tell him how profoundly dull he was and no way in hell would she cry over getting away from that, and that he was almost forty, no marriage no kids, and what did that say about him? She told him *all of it* in her head.

Leaving silently, she went to the coffee shop she'd gone to since she was a kid. She opened her laptop on the same table she'd had her first date at. The guy had maybe liked her, but mostly wanted in her pants. Connor had crashed that date. The memory made her smile.

Dimming her screen, she opened a new message.

To: Lea Nonme
Subject: Health and Wellness

Hello,
I'm looking for food and location recommendations.
Dr. Jones

CHAPTER FIVE

"This is a record for us."

Connor grunted. As soon as Shona locked the door behind him, he sank his fingers in her hair and buried his face in her neck. He just wanted to fuck, and fuck, and fuck and not think about anything but the pleasure.

The same parts they always played unfolded—the grinding, her gasping—and he didn't want to think about how typical all of it was, so he abruptly dropped his pants and pulled her dress up.

She laughed and gasped as he ran the tip of his cock against her wet lips, but he stopped abruptly to say, "Condom?"

"In my bedroom," she said breathlessly. "You sure you want to wait?"

Huh? He yanked his pants halfway up his legs and dragged her to the bedroom.

He wanted it different, didn't let her put the condom on, instead did it himself, and then gently pushed her back on the bed where she opened her legs wide for him to see her glistening pussy. She kept herself waxed like a child and he didn't like it, although it felt nice when she was on top of him.

Focusing on her wetness, he sank a finger into her, two, pumping and rubbing until the slight bit of soft belly exposed by her raised dress trembled with shivers. Grabbing her legs—no she didn't like her legs touched—grabbing her knees instead, he pushed her legs wider, spread her further and sank in swift and deep. She let out a guttural cry and clenched all around him. He rocked deep and hard to keep her going. Before her spasms stopped, his started, and his hips jerked and slapped against her as he came.

Immediately he pulled out, discarded the condom, and washed up.

She continued to lay on the bed, watching him as he left the bathroom. "I dyed my hair," she said.

It was strawberry something or other, he thought. "Looks nice. Do you like it?"

"Yeah."

He went back to the bed and lay down beside her. He never stayed the night, but he didn't want to go home yet.

"I started seeing this guy," she said.

"You want me to go?"

"No, we aren't a thing yet. It's new."

"Let me know."

"Okay." It was silent for a while. "I want to have kids."

"With your new guy?" He wasn't freaked out. Her question about wanting to wait for the condom made sense though.

"I don't know. I'm starting to think with or without a man in my life honestly. I haven't met any man that I wanted to be with or if I did, they didn't want to be with me."

"If I knew someone to hook you up with I would." She laughed and said thanks. Connor smiled and did a rolling sit-up off the bed. "I'll see you soon?"

"Anytime."

He saw himself out, back to his truck, back to his condo—except his damn hands drove his truck down the wrong streets that somehow led him to Liv's house. *Shit*. He wasn't a stalker. He *wasn't* stalking. He just wanted to see her, maybe just seeing her would...

Angry at himself, he made a sharp turn, driving to his old house around the corner from Liv's, without thinking. He stopped at the curb, staring at the front door he used to get beaten behind. To this day he hated his stepfather with a consuming rage.

Too much.

He U-turned and went by Liv's parent's house. The memories, the lightness he'd felt every time he walked through their home eased through him as he drove slowly by. Until Mr. Jones came jogging out to his truck.

Connor's breath froze as Mr. Jones threw a hand up in a casual greeting, like he'd always done to passersby. There was no way Mr. Jones knew who he was, likely hadn't even seen him, it was his old habit that was all. Yet to be acknowledged by him, after all these years made his chest feel like it was splitting in two.

Since he'd been discharged from the army, he'd never wished as badly as he did now that he could reenlist. The entire drive home, he debated stopping for a drink. The memories of his drunk stepfather had always made him avoid alcohol, but maybe tonight, a drink would help relax him. He almost made it home, but right on the corner of his new street was a liquor store.

He went straight for the hard stuff. Whiskey he hated. Brandy he'd never tried but he didn't want to find out if it was like whiskey. Vodka, no. Tequila, no. The sweet shit, no. Feeling a stupid sense of defeat, he grabbed a bottle of wine with a demonic image on it, went home, and threw it in a cupboard.

On the sofa, he turned on a game.

Five minutes passed before he looked at the clock.

He flipped over to a documentary.

Three minutes passed since he looked at the clock.

Why was time moving like that? What the hell else could he do with his time until he could go to work? It was too early to go to bed, probably wouldn't be able to sleep again regardless.

Connor pushed off the sofa. Why was his life so fucking *pointless?* Was this relentless ticking of watched time his future laid out before him?

No one would miss him if he were gone. The thought grew as relentless as the slow movement of the minute-hand.

Connor thought of all the addicts he'd seen when he worked narcotics. He'd known how they'd gotten there, but sudden clarity had him really understanding why. Awareness was such a heavy burden and being drunk or high lightened it.

He almost wished he could do it. But why reach for a slow destruction of his life until death? Why not do it fast?

His pistol lay holstered on his dining table. The handle of the plain black Glock caught the light, seeming to shine. *No one would miss him if he were gone.*

An image of Liv's earnest blue-brown gaze filled his mind, from when they were kids. He'd been beaten up by his stepdad and she'd told him not to blame himself. He'd always mocked her psychology shit. But look at him now.

The gun gleamed in invitation, and he took it. Bringing it to the sofa, he sat with it cradled in his hands.

Forever. He'd given her a heart necklace with that engraved on it, and he'd meant it. He still meant it. So why had he let his claim on her slip away?

No answer came to him. How pointlessly he'd lived, if the single greatest mistake of his life, was one he had no idea why he made. What had he been doing instead? Killing terrorists, that only resulted in more. Getting drugs out of one hand that only pushed them into another's, all while thinking about nothing, caring about nothing, feeling nothing. Pointless.

He tilted the gun up and cocked it.

What the fuck am I doing? I'm not suicidal!

He stared at the black hole.

Liv's voice whispered, *Somehow you hadn't known how important you were in my life.*

His jaw clenched at the sudden memory. If they were kids again, she'd tell him to find a counselor, to get help because everybody needs help even the people who seem perfect. That sounded just like Liv.

He really fucking missed her. How had he not known that for thirteen years?

Connor reengaged the safety lock. Very slowly, he set the gun on the coffee table and braced his elbows on his knees.

When he'd been discharged from the army, they'd given him a card for a counselor who was a veteran himself. Not once had he thought he'd need it.

Did he need it? He wasn't really going to kill himself.

The memory of throwing the card at the back of his underwear drawer was clear.

Yeah, why the fuck not.

Connor found the card for Peter Hutchinson, MD. His office was just up the road from Liv's. Before he could think too much about it, he dialed, intending to leave a message but there was a 24-hour answering service that set an appointment for him tomorrow. He didn't need to be seen immediately, but there was an open spot from a cancellation. Lunchtime, no one would even notice him gone.

* * * *

The next morning, he got ready and grabbed his gun like he hadn't thought about using it on himself just a few hours prior. At work, he looked over files of other unsolved cases assigned to him while he waited for lunch. The urge to cancel his counselling appointment rode him all morning, but the thought of flaking on a fellow vet held him fast.

When he met the doctor who looked too young to be as bald as he, wearing Dad-jeans and Costco generic athletic shoes, Connor decided he didn't want to be there long.

"I stared down the barrel of my gun last night. I wasn't going to pull the trigger, but it was the thought of my high school ex-girlfriend that made me think I should talk about it." His response to the doctor's, *Glad to meet you. How are you doing?*

"She must have been very important to you. What happened to her?"

"I hurt her. I don't even know why. I ghosted her, before that was a thing, but her whole family was everything to me, and I ghosted all of them."

"Why did you?"

"Fuck if I know. Fuck if I know anything. I've lived my life following orders. Maybe I can't think for myself."

"You said her whole family was important to you. What about your own family?"

"Jesus, get right to it, huh?"

"By the way you introduced yourself, I'd say you're not looking for slow and delicate."

Connor briefly smiled. "Truth." He started to lay out how his dad, also a military man, left them for another women when he was a teen. How his mom met Keith, an alcoholic who abused him while his mom stayed medicated in bed, but somewhere along the telling, he stopped laying it out there like a report, and started fighting a rasp in his throat, a constriction in his lungs.

"Did your dad know?"

"He had a new life."

"How much did your mom know?"

"I dunno." It came out mumbled. "I didn't help her either. I was a strong kid, but I took off when shit started happening."

"How could you have helped her?"

"I...Yeah, I could have tried to get her away from Keith."

"Was he abusing her too?"

"No." The rasp was worse. Annoyed, he cleared his throat. "But he drove her to addiction. I could have..."

"Stopped an addict? Even I can't do that, Connor, and I'm licensed. Love doesn't stop an addict. Tools for coping with stress, anxiety, whatever burden they bear, is what empowers overcoming addiction. Could you have given your mother those tools?"

Connor scowled at him. "Next up, let's talk about how it's not my fault."

The doctor laughed. "Intellectually you know that."

"Emotionally I don't?"

"Emotionally, why did you consider suicide last night?"

Connor's lids flinched at hearing *him* and *suicide* put together. Sounded so fucking weak. "I didn't." Mumbled worse this time.

"Okay. I can tell you why a lot of vets go down that road," Dr. Hutchinson said. "They feel disconnected. They lack a network, be it friends, family, church group even. They feel pointless—"

Connor's gaze sharpened on Dr. Hutchinson, and he noticed, nodding at whatever was in Connor's expression.

Fuck it, I don't want to be here long, remember? "Everything I do *is* pointless, and no one would miss me if I was gone."

40

"Did your high school girlfriend miss you when you were gone? Her family?"

He had to clear his throat again. "Yeah."

"How do you know?"

Phone calls. Emails. Care packages. Liv's tears as she told him what she went through when he never contacted her again. "Hard evidence."

"But you chose to disconnect from them."

"I don't know why."

"We'll get there, Connor. But it matters if you can see that you made a choice there. Which means you can make a choice here, now, to connect, because when you were connected, you knew without a doubt that you were missed, that your life wasn't pointless. People cared."

A very still moment as that resonated for him, but then he surged to his feet. "I've gotta get back to work."

"Connor—"

"I've gotta—yeah I forgot to tell you I have to go—

"Connor—

"Look, Doctor Hutchin—"

"Call me Hutch, if you like."

"Yeah, okay. Look, don't worry about me. I'm sure you get a bunch of people that say that, but I'm not going to pop myself. I've just had enough for today. I'll come back—"

"In two days."

"Sure, yeah, two days."

"At 5:30, Connor, I've got an opening. In two days, at 5:30. I'll text you a reminder. I'll be looking for you."

"Yeah, okay, thanks doc—Hutch."

Connor strode out to his truck, looking devoid of emotion, powerful in his stride and confident in his physicality. Inside, he was shaking like a damned Chihuahua.

Back at the station, he hardly spoke to anyone, clearly annoying Fernando when he simply wouldn't respond to his needling. Soon as the clock ticked to off-time, he left, grabbed a burger and parked by Liv's house. Just being near where she lived eased some of the heaviness.

It was a creep move, parking outside her house, he knew that, and his truck was distinctive. If she hadn't figured it was his yet, she would soon. If she asked him to leave, he would. Until then, if she was the only drug he had that worked to lighten his burden, he was good with becoming a junkie.

Only she didn't show. He didn't see her the next night either. When his appointment with Hutch came, before a greeting could even be finished, Connor said, "I didn't think about her for over a decade. If a thought popped up, I shut it down, easily. Now, nothing works. She's all over my mind, all the time. What the hell is happening?"

"Your high school girlfriend?" At Connor's sharp nod, Hutch said, "So what tore the scab off that wound?"

Connor snorted. "Okay, I get it. I'm bleeding out."

"That was some hard ass crusty black scab you had, would you say?"

"Hell, I don't know. I didn't know I had one."

"Serious wounds can go numb. What tore it off?" Hutch said.

"Seeing her again."

"When?"

"Couple weeks ago."

"How was she with you?"

"Hurt." First thought that came.

"Then she still cares."

"Not in a good way."

"Is that what she said?"

"Not…no."

"Do you have any ideas yet why you ghosted her?"

Connor blew out a breath. "I don't even want to think about her, let alone why I hurt her."

"Not thinking is what landed you with a deep wound, bleeding all over the place."

"You using the wound analogy because I'm a vet?"

"I'm using it because I think it'll make sense to you. You saw combat?"

"Yes, sir."

"Were you ever wounded, or saw a comrade seriously wounded?"

"Both."

"Then you know."

"I know."

Hutch nodded his head in a slow rhythm that made Connor think that Hutch had lived knowing it too.

"Why would your high school girlfriend be such a wound for you?"

"Losing her was," he said quietly.

"Then why do it to yourself?"

"I didn't deserve her." Again, first thought.

"What did you deserve then? To be hurting?" Connor's lungs constricted again. "Keith hurt you."

Connor gave him a disgusted look. "Not the same."

"You didn't deserve to be hit by your stepfather, Connor."

"Fuck, I know that!"

"Then it shouldn't bother you for me to say it."

"I'm not bothered!" Hell, even he could hear he was. "Okay, fuck, fine I'm bothered. But I'm really fucking bothered that you're saying I ghosted Liv because of Keith."

"Your mother hurt you when she didn't protect you. Your father hurt you when he left you."

Connor rocked back and then jumped up. "Been sitting too long, Hutch. My wound aches when I do. Need to call it a day. I'll see you in a couple."

"Two days, Connor. Same time."

"I don't think—"

"Two days, same time, I'll text and be looking for you."

He should have never come here, never opened his damn mouth. "Yeah, fine. See you Saturday." With a swift salute, Connor left. Powerfully, confidently, shaking like a two-pound puppy inside.

Following the same protocol as two days before, he did his job and left as soon as time cleared, but he went to Shona's instead, brought his own condom this time too. "You never bring your own," she said as he smoothed it on.

"Turning over a new leaf." Did she have to talk?

"A new leaf is bringing condoms?"

He almost kissed her to get her quiet, but he didn't like to kiss her, didn't like how wild her tongue went, or the flavor of the fruity lip stuff she'd used for years. After the first time or two, he told her he didn't like to kiss, and didn't want to undo the parameters they'd long set.

"It's a small leaf," he said.

Shona laughed. "But a big, huge cock, thank god."

He smiled but didn't feel like it. He didn't find talking about the size of his dick appealing. Tweaking her nipple a little harder than he knew she liked, her sharp gasp quieted her long enough for him to position himself and drive deep into her wetness. He liked her wetness there. She went off even quicker than usual, but he kept pumping, driving his hips into her, and leaned back to watch his cock sink beyond her pink lips. She wouldn't go off again, there was no point in dragging this out. Cupping his own balls to softly fondle them for added stimulation, he finally released, and pulled immediately out of her.

In the bathroom, he cleaned up quickly and returned to Shona, still lying down, having covered herself as usual.

"You've been different lately," she said.

"How do you know?"

By the way her jaw tightened, she didn't miss his implication that she didn't know him well enough to know if he was different. "We've been doing this for years. You've been different lately."

"Maybe things need to be different."

Abruptly she sat up. "I agree. It's probably a good time to end this."

"Alright." He grabbed his stuff. "Thanks, Shona. It's been great."

He saw himself out, automatically drove to Liv's. That wasn't an ugly ending, a relief. It called to mind the last time he'd left a girl to go to Liv's. That had been a hell of an ugly ending. He wondered briefly how Anna was these days. Better than him, he hoped. He'd been a dick to her too.

CHAPTER SIX

"I figured out my first steps to get better," Liv said, beaming at Holly. She'd been in Ojai for two days, to unwind. It had only taken a quick call the day before to get Holly to drive up and meet her.

"All on your own? Without me?"

A cute waiter set two coffees on their café table, and they smiled at him before Liv continued, "Not on my own, entirely. I met this woman and her dogs on my hike yesterday. I spent hours with them, and I fell in love. So, it's official. I'm going to be a doggy mom."

Holly stared at her. "You're going to have a puppy."

"I should throw a puppy shower, now that you mention it."

"I didn't."

"Only because I said it first."

Holly stared some more. "This was not the outcome I was expecting from your Ojai retreat."

"Can't deny it's progress though."

"Sure can."

"Not if you think about it. I have a fear of being emotionally vulnerable—"

"With *men*."

"My biggest fear lies with them, yes, but I'd argue a fear of all situations that make my emotional stability vulnerable. I haven't had a pet since I was a kid, and I love dogs. Dog is God spelled backward, you know." The words came out so easily, but it made her thoughts go straight back to Connor, when they were kids walking her dog Darcy, and him saying those exact words.

Liv could feel the smile fade from her face, and she told Holly of his visit, finally. "I'm starting to accept I may never recover from him. That somehow, he's as much a part of my heart as I am. So maybe I never get married, never settle into a relationship. This woman I met yesterday, Julie, she was so lovely, so joyful and caring, and she was unmarried, no kids, lots of dogs. That could be me. I could be that and be happy."

"My cousin likes psychics, did I ever tell you that?"

"Holly, I'm being serious."

"It's relevant, I promise," she said earnestly. "I went with my cousin a couple years ago after she'd been through a terrible heartbreak. She wanted me to understand that no psychology could circumvent spirituality.

"The psychic said her boyfriend was the love of her life and she was his, but that he'd been too damaged in this life to love fully. So even though he was her true love, it would be better for them both to live without each other, because he couldn't help but cause her pain, and that pain they would take with them into the next life."

"That's a sad, crappy story, Holls."

"But there's notable information in it. If Connor is too damaged for love, you're better off without him."

"Still a sad, crappy story, but I appreciate the point. Did you end up going to the psychic for yourself?"

Holly leaned forward. "*Not a word about this to anyone,*" she whispered.

"I can't believe you never told me!"

"I can't believe I went. But, she told me I'd be married to Jake and have to work on my interests. So here I am, a bored wife and she was right about my humdrum stuff."

Liv said after a moment, "I think my love-life peaked in high school. I don't think I'll be better off with anyone, and I'm realizing that I don't want to try to anymore either."

"You're only thirty-two. That's pretty young to declare yourself a spinster."

"But a spinster of good fortune is always respectable," Liv said with a grin.

Holly's gaze went to the heavens. "Thank you, Jane Austen, for making Liv's dreams of quoting you legitimately a reality."

"Just, thank you, Jane Austen, for being you," Liv said, her own eyes to the skies.

"My cousin ended up marrying a nice guy, but I know she thinks about her first love, a lot."

"Maybe she should have stayed single."

"I don't think he would have left her alone if she had."

"That's not been my problem, has it?" Liv heard the edge of bitterness there, and muttered, "If only it had been, we'd be married and living happily ever after." No point in fighting the tears. This was meant to be a cleansing. "We would have been so happy, Holly."

"Maybe," she said gently.

"There is no one else. I know it in my soul. I've always known it."

"You know the saying 'It's better to have loved and lost, than never to have loved at all'?"

Liv used her napkin to wipe her eyes. "That saying doesn't cover the pain of the loss. How you have to live like you don't love to cope."

"Would you undo the love you had with him?"

"No. God, no." Liv appreciated the silence as she collected herself. "I won't love anyone else like that again. But I can love a dog. Hopefully it will never leave me. I'll buy a bunch of collars and trackers and dog tags to make sure." She had to laugh at herself, even as it was true. "There's a litter planned. In about a month the engaged doggies will do the deed."

"What kind of dog?"

"Silken Windhound. It's a sighthound, so they do racing. I'm going to go to some of the events, I think."

"You're going to become a dog show person?"

"Maybe you should too, it will help work on your interests."

"Funny," Holly said, but then she sighed, "I'm totally game to try. I've actually been thinking about a puppy. We could get siblings and have sleepovers."

"Operation Can't Leave Me is a go, Holls."

Holly fist bumped her. "All supporting parties are in."

* * * *

"I keep thinking about her and it's driving me fucking nuts." *Hey Hutch, actually glad to see you because now that I've started running my mouth off, sometimes I look forward to it.*

"Good to see you, Connor," Hutch said. "How have the last two days been? All Liv?"

"How do you know her name?" Connor frowned, wondering suddenly if Hutch knew her. Did they move in the same psych circles?

"You said it last time you were here. Is it okay with you if I use her name?"

Strangely he didn't like it, but he knew it was strange. "It's fine."

"Alright then, all Liv for two days?"

"About sums it up. I don't want to talk about my family."

"Your family is precisely what you need to talk about."

Connor stood up, paced to the window. "Shouldn't this go where I want it to? If I don't want to talk about something, that's the end of it."

"I get the feeling you're in a hurry, Connor. Which makes me think you may not spend as much time in my office as I'd like, so if I can help you—which I can—then I've got to get to it in a hurry. You start every time sharp and blunt, so let's get to it then."

"I don't want to talk about my family."

"Shutting Liv out of your life was like a form of self-harm, from what you've told me so far. Why do you think you did that?"

"Self-harm, like cutters, right?" He'd seen a few of those, always baffled the hell out of him, but he'd never asked *why*.

"Self-harm happens as a form of control. By cutting Liv out of your life, you controlled her ability to hurt you." Hutch paused a beat. "Why do you think you did that?"

"I don't know anything, remember?"

"Not in a hurry anymore?"

Connor turned back to him. He looked too damn young to be this hard-assed, but then those Dad-jeans and sneakers... "Do you have kids?"

"Yes, two, both in college. I'm a proud father."

He looked proud, Connor thought. "Ever hurt them unintentionally?"

"I've hurt everyone I love unintentionally, as they have me, but recognizing it helps ease the sting of it."

"Every word is loaded with you, isn't it?"

"Only when we're in a hurry."

Connor snorted.

"Sometimes we hurt ourselves unintentionally," Hutch continued. "Recognizing it helps lead us to the why of it, which helps us stop doing it."

"We're back at my parents, aren't we? It's always 'blame the parents'."

"Our most important formative years are early childhood. The single greatest source of formation comes from parents, either by what they did, or did not do. So yes, let's blame the parents for now, at least until we can get to recognizing how it has shaped us. Once we get there, then we can start talking about blaming ourselves."

"What do you blame yourself for?"

"I gave my clients more attention than my kids." No hesitation. "I'm fully to blame for that and I see how it has shaped my kids."

"What do you blame your parents for?"

"I don't anymore." Hutch sighed. "I really hope you give me more time, Connor, because not blaming them is some of the best parts of this walk we're on, but it's a long walk to get to that destination."

Connor dropped back onto the sofa. "You think I ghosted her to stop her from hurting me, thing is I wasn't hurting. She sent me so much love in those care packages I felt high from it."

"Can't have a high without a low."

"I was never low with her."

"*With* her. But you weren't with her when you ghosted her, were you? She was far away, other side of the world, right?"

Close enough. "Since I decided to join the army, I've been disciplined. Nothing could shake me. Now I'm a fucking wreck, staring down the barrel of a gun, obsessing over my childhood girlfriend." He pinched between his brows.

"What is it that you want, Connor? Do you know?"

"I want to be who I was when I handled shit and thought suicide was for the fucking weak."

"Do you still think that?"

"I don't know." He hadn't actually *been* suicidal. But, staring into that black hole, he hadn't felt weak. He'd felt…no hope. Meaningless. "No, I don't still think that."

Hutch reached for a paper on his desk, held it out to Connor. "I play basketball with some of these guys. You should join us."

It was a flyer for a veteran's group. He'd always avoided them, couldn't see why he'd change that now. "I don't do groups."

"Just play then, every Tuesday night by the pier."

Connor realized he'd seen them; he drove by it often enough he remembered the groups on the courts. "Basketball isn't my game."

"Most of us are pretty mediocre at it. Come anyway."

"Maybe. Two days 'til our next meeting?"

"Right. Same time."

Connor left, aware he'd made it through a whole session without bailing. His insides were shaking a lot less than the last couple times too.

With nothing to do beside drive by Liv's house—she wasn't there—he hit the gym and worked out harder than usual, then wasted more time by using the communal jacuzzi

A woman in a dark red swimsuit smiled shyly as he waded in. She was attracted to him from the way she kept glancing at him. He caught her doing it and grinned, making her blush.

"What's your name?" he said.

"Josephine."

"You work out here often?" The buzz of going after a woman began to hum inside him.

"I just signed up. I'm new to the area."

Perfect opening, yeah? "Where'd you move from?"

"LA. My job brought me here."

"What do you do?"

"I'm a pediatric nurse."

So sweet. He liked her. He said maybe he could show her around the area, and she said that sounded great. He told her to leave her number at the front desk and she did, so he texted her when he got home and set up a date for the next night.

The hum felt good. Gave him renewed energy.

He took Josephine out for dinner, one of those sidewalk places with great food the locals knew about. Her dark hair reached her shoulder blades and had been dyed long ago from the way it faded yellowish at the ends. She wore little makeup except for red lipstick-stain—something like that, where it wasn't sticky or wet looking. She was shorter than he'd thought, her body compact, sturdy. He liked all sizes.

His usual routine rolled out, light questions, teasing comments. It was so easy for him, had always been with women. At the end of the night, he kissed her, and she eagerly opened her mouth. Her tongue was soft, a little timid. She tasted good, like mint, she'd hoped he'd kiss her.

Running his hands down her compact frame, she slid her arms around his neck and pressed closer. Not a lot of ass to grab, but her nipples were hard enough to poke through her shirt and he liked that. It was a surprise when she pulled back and said goodnight, with no invitation to come inside. "I hope I'll see you again, Connor. I had a nice time."

"Yeah, I'll call you. Good night."

He drove to Liv's house, and noticed her lights were on differently than the last couple nights. Few minutes later, he could see her in the kitchen. The strength of his response took him by surprise, the urge to get out of his truck and go to her so strong his hand was already on the door handle. But then his phone buzzed with a message.

> Thanks again for dinner.
> I had a great time with you.
> Talk soon. J

Connor remembered the way Liv had looked at him as she asked him to leave. Guaranteed, the same look would be on her face if he knocked right now. He released the door handle in slow degrees and texted back.

> Same. Do it again
> Friday?

> I work Thurs, Fri. and
> Sat. No seniority! Weds
> or Sunday?

> Wednesday. Pick
> you up at 7.

> Looking forward to
> It. Gn.

One last look at Liv through her window, then he left.

The next morning, he said to Fernando, "Let's go see Mrs. Olawale."

One side of Fernando's face scrunched into a tight pucker. "Great idea. Let's go." On the drive, Fernando gave him a couple side-eye glances before saying, "Get your meds sorted out?"

"S'cuse me?"

"It was a rough week for you last week."

Connor barely twitched but his mind roared, *How the hell did he know?*

"You're more—" another side-eye "—with it so far this morning."

Connor stayed silent.

Fernando continued, "'Course it's the beginning of the week, so if we give it time it'll probably go to shit. It's all demons and unicorns with you."

Connor gave him a hard, unflinching stare that Fernando met a couple times in between glances at the road. Eventually he snorted thickly through his nose. "You're a tough sonofabitch to stare down. Mighty scary looking soldier I'd bet. I can see it in you. I never did thank you for your service. So, thank you."

He was too pissed to do more than give a sharp nod.

"My daughter loves saying, 'it's all demons and unicorns with you'. I hear her saying it to her little boyfriend all the time. Funny stuff. He's a good kid though. I think she's the one with the demon and unicorn moods. My five sisters all had 'em too so I know it's normal, but it should not be normal."

Connor didn't respond, Fernando gave him some more side-eye. "So, you get your meds sorted?"

"What the fuck is your problem?"

"Whew! Good. Glad a person's in there. I was really starting to wonder with that blank face of yours."

"This won't go well if you keep trying to make me lose my cool." Connor was no kid to be pushed around. Not any longer.

"Hell man, I was trying to make you lose your cool all last week and it was like you weren't even in there. Know what a relief it is to have you back with us?"

"Stop trying to dick with me. We're not friends. You know nothing about me."

"Not true. I know *now* that you're a vet. Finally looked info up about you—I've got stuff happening in my own life, so sue me, it took a while. I have more respect for our veterans than anyone. I also know you were a valued part of the team in the narc division. I respect that too. I *also* know both those things are hard on a man."

Connor stayed silent.

"Most of my friends didn't like me until they did. Do not worry, buddy, it will happen for you too," Fernando drawled. "What I want to know now is if you're good. Are you good?"

"I'm good."

Side-eye. "Okay." Fernando took a drink of his coffee. "You definitely look good. Pretty sure my girls would be unicorns over you. Maybe you should show me some gym stuff, help me whittle down this sexy belly rolling onto my lap."

Amusement slipped through the tension. "Wouldn't want to take anything away from you."

"My wife would love it if you did. She's still in decent shape. I'm the tubby in the family. She buys me donuts to mock me."

"Did your last partner quit because you drove him to it?"

"Ah, been too busy to look me up too. I feel you, brother."

More amusement. Fernando was a pain in the ass, but not all the time.

At the hospital, Mrs. Olawale was lucid enough to tell them she didn't want to talk. Fernando promised just a few questions, but she began weeping, the skin around her bulbous eyes looking bruised as tears streamed over it. She was so frail, incredibly thin and weak looking as she choked out, "He's not what you think. He's a good boy, officer."

They left her still weeping.

"Let's stop by Dr. Jones' office. See if she can squeeze us in," Connor said.

Side-eye. "Were you reading my mind?"

Connor doubted that's what he'd been thinking, alerted again to how sharp Fernando was.

They went to her office. Patrick was on the phone while a patient sat waiting. As they stood there, Liv's door opened and she stepped out, a warm smile on her face.

Her gaze speared to Connor's. The smile froze. She said to the patient, "Just a few more minutes, Joann. I need to speak briefly with these gentlemen."

Motioning them to follow, Connor appreciated the way her wine-red pants cupped her rounded bottom as he trailed behind her. In her office, she turned on them. "It is not okay for you to just show up in the middle of the day."

"Morning actually," Fernando murmured, and she blasted him with a glare. "Detective Peltier prefers to be technical," he added.

Connor almost laughed, and he thought she knew it by the way she swiftly glanced at him. She took a deep breath as if striving for patience, and he recognized the habit from all the times she'd done it with him when they were kids.

"I have patients with extreme social anxiety. I promise them the office will be clear of anyone who doesn't expressly work here. There are actual risks to you showing up without scheduling it with me first."

Fernando looked at Connor like he was a punk. "*Told you.*"

Liv glanced between them. "Is this a joke to you?"

"About as much as Jeremy Olawale is," Fernando answered, but Connor interjected, "Mrs. Olawale is lucid. We just came from the hospital."

"Does she know where Jeremy is?"

Connor wondered if Fernando could see through her as easily as he could. The way she asked seemed near theatrical to him, with her too-rounded eyes. She knew something.

"She wouldn't stop crying to ask," Fernando said. "She did say he's not what we think. Do you know what she's referring to?"

"Police files on him, I'd imagine." She nibbled at her full bottom lip, distracting Connor with its plump softness. "Were you able to speak to his friends? Have they heard anything from him?"

Now that was authentic, Connor thought. "We spoke to them, but if they heard anything they wouldn't share it."

"Not even with you?" she said softly, but then seemed to catch herself. "Or were you both there like enforcers?"

"Enforcers, definitely," Fernando said, nodding.

A reluctant smile curved her lips. "I want Jeremy safe, hopefully as much as you do. He *is* a good boy. Whatever happened had to be traumatic for him and he's suffering for it."

Connor noticed the way she switched tenses, *he's suffering*, as if she knew it. "We want to help him, Liv. If you know anything about how we can do it, we're here."

Their gazes locked together.

"Yep," Fernando said, breaking the moment.

"If I can think of anything, I have your card." She went to the door and opened it. "And I'm serious about calling first."

"Respectfully noted, Dr. Jones." Fernando tipped an imaginary hat to her as he walked out.

Connor paused before the door and held his hand out, but she ignored it. "You won't shake my hand, Liv?"

Her mouth opened, closed, and then slowly her palm slipped into his. It lit him up, sent his thoughts to the next step he wanted to take, sliding his free hand across her cheek, into her sunlit hair, down her soft neck. "Have dinner with me."

"I..." That little shake of her head came back, and she dropped his hand. "We both know that would be inappropriate, Detective Peltier. If you'll excuse me, I have a client waiting."

Fernando waited outside with his hands shoved deep in his pockets, his shoulders slightly hunched. He looked round as Connor walked out and gave him a brief, assessing glance. "You've been out for a bunch of years?"

"Eight." Felt a lot longer than that since he'd been discharged.

Back in the car, on the way to the station, Fernando finally replied, "Eight years you've been living around here, and you never looked her up in all that time?"

Here we go, Connor thought. Now that Liv's shock, or anger—maybe both—had eased, the chemistry between them was tangible. Of course Fernando wouldn't have missed it. "Never wanted to."

Fernando half laughed but then quickly sobered. "Well partner. I don't think it's necessary yet, but if anything with the Olawale case gets complicated, we'll have to be reassigned."

CHAPTER SEVEN

"I met someone."

Hutch's brows barely lifted. "Someone that puts Liv out of your mind?"

Was that a loaded question? "We've only been on one date."

"Going on more?"

"Yeah." Connor thought this topic would be an easy road to travel. He wanted an easy road today, so why'd he get the sense this was a minefield? "She's nice, a nurse for kids."

"Dating one woman when your mind is occupied by another often has unfortunate consequences."

"You think I shouldn't date anyone?" Connor snorted. "I have needs, Hutch. I'm not going to wait to stop thinking about Liv before I take care of them."

"What would happen if you didn't see to your needs?"

"I don't know, stare down the barrel of a gun?"

Hutch's brows shot up. "Is that why you think you did it?"

Hell. He hadn't meant to be so flip about it, but he wanted to shut this down. "It was a stupid comment, that's all."

But Hutch had a thoughtful look on his face as he said, "The constant pursuit of sex, going through women, sex addiction—"

"Fuck, I'm not a sex addict!" Connor stood and went to the window, remembering suddenly how Liv used to call him a slut in high school. "I've been with women since I turned fourteen. It comes easy to me and I'm always happy to have it. That's all."

"Distractions," Hutch said mildly. "What happens when they're not there?"

Connor didn't answer. Hutch continued, "The last time you couldn't find a distraction, you were willing to do almost anything to escape it."

"*Almost.* Fuck, I don't like this session today." Connor scraped his palm back and forth along the side of his head. "So I've got mommy issues, daddy issues, women issues, and sex issues?"

"I'd call it fear of being hurt issues. Did it hurt when you cut Liv out of your life?"

"I didn't feel anything. Maybe I never would have if I hadn't seen her again."

"Seeing her unburied the feelings, Connor, it didn't create them.

"I liked them buried," he muttered.

"You liked the life you were living?"

His pointless existence? "John Doe," he said silently to the window, a faint outline of his reflection in it.

"I don't like this, Hutch. I'm done." Turning from the window, he headed to the door.

"Two days—"

"Yeah, yeah. I got it."

"Come to basketball tomorrow."

Hand on the door, he threw an annoyed look at Hutch. "Probably not. I'll see you." Not shaky at all this time as he left, but aggravated as hell though. What the fuck, *sex addict?*

Driving to the gym, he popped his earbuds in and didn't make eye contact with anyone. He worked out for hours before he quit to grab some Chinese food and park up outside Liv's house.

Her blinds were tilted in such a way he could still see her well, yet they hindered his view enough that he wanted to go in there and yank them open. She stood at the kitchen sink, cleaning dishes. Probably she cooked herself dinner every night.

His Chinese food went down tastelessly. Finished, he guzzled and swished water, carefully wiped his hands and mouth, and got out of his truck. He went to her door, and when he saw the shadow of her through the peephole, flashed his badge.

Immediately the door opened, but then she took a swift glance at his gym clothes and temper snapped in her eyes. "That's *illegal*, Connor, and you know it."

"I'm just showing you my badge. I always wanted to." Her head sort of twitched at the suggestive remark, but she didn't respond to it. "Can I come in?"

Eyes narrowed, there was a longer pause than last time before she finally opened the door wider and walked away.

Flipping the lock, he went to the sofa where she sat with her legs curled tight under her, her thin black shirt almost slipping off one smooth shoulder. He sat in the chair opposite her, bracing his arms on his knees, and stared at her as she tried not to squirm or look away.

"Thirteen years without a word, and now you're all over my space," she said. "What changed?"

"I saw you again."

Abruptly, she uncurled her legs and went to the kitchen. Taking her time, she made one cup of tea. Back in the day, she would have asked if he wanted one, every time.

Returning to the sofa, cup in hand, there was a definite therapist vibe about her. Would she try to counsel him? Whatever angle it took to get to her, he'd take. Yet she didn't ask the therapy questions. She didn't say anything at all.

"Why aren't you talking to me?" he said finally.

"You're the one who came here."

"You talked all the time when we were kids."

"About things that didn't hurt."

Here we go, this is what he wanted: her, laying it out there. But again, she said nothing at all. *Damn it.* Why wouldn't she cooperate? "I'm here, Liv. You liked to talk about everything, even stuff that hurt."

"Is that what you want me to do?"

He spread his hands like, *what does it look like.*

"Alright, Connor. Tell me, what's your most important memory from the army?"

What? He even gave her a look, but she remained stoic.

"You're here, that's what I want to talk about."

Fine. He started to say the time his team took out a terrorist cell with a high-ranking leader on the FBI's most wanted list and rescued a dozen hostages at the same time.

"Makayla," came out instead. "She was from Hawaii, we were at the same base. She was a cool-ass woman. Tough. Great soldier. We became pretty good friends. Couple guys on base raped her, the higher ups did nothing. She was changed by it. Like someone completely different took her place."

Liv's gaze dropped to her tea like she couldn't look at him any longer. "I tried to help her, Liv. But what the hell did I know about that post traumatic shit you always warned me about? She didn't want anything to do with me anyway."

"Why is that your most important memory?"

"I don't know. It's the one that stays with me the most, I guess. Why did you ask?"

Looking at him again, she said calmly, "Why are you here?"

"I…" *want to pick up where we left off when I ghosted you, thirteen years ago.* What an asshole. He could hear it clear as day. "…want to be friends again."

"*Friends.*"

There, that got a reaction. Good. "Be my friend again, Liv."

She stood, setting her mug down with a hard thump before striding from the room. He could hear her moving some things around and then she came back holding something in her fist. "Here."

He opened his palm and she dropped something into it. "Recognize it?"

Reluctantly he looked. Weight compressed his chest at the silver necklace with *Forever* written on the heart-shaped charm. "Turned out to be less than a year. I don't keep fickle friends I can't trust."

"I was *eighteen*, Liv. Give me a fucking break—"

"Stop *cussing.*"

He smirked. "Still a goody-two-shoes."

"I always have been!" she almost-yelled, pressure building up so that he could see a delicate vein throb in her forehead. She turned, moving away from him until the coffee table stood between them. "If me being *me* bothers you so much, why would you ever want to be my friend? Why did you ever? Or was it all just pretend because you liked my family so much?"

"It wasn't." Everything he thought locked up inside him, words disappearing into a vault he couldn't think how to penetrate.

After a beat of silence, she shook her head. "I don't want to be your friend, Connor. I want you to leave."

"I don't want to leave." Why couldn't he think of anything worth saying!

"Well too bad! You lost the right to stay when you cut me out of your life without any explanation. *Nothing.* As if you'd died, Connor. You exited my life as if you'd died. You don't get a resurrection."

"Well I didn't die so I don't need a fu—damned resurrection. I was messed up, Liv! I still am!"

"And I can't fix you, so it would be better if you left."

"I'm not done."

"Aren't there laws against detectives—"

"Don't fucking start that! This isn't about the case, it's about *us*. Our history, *ours*, so stop using my job as an excuse to run away from dealing with it."

"Me, run away? I never ran! I was always here! And so were you for *years* apparently and you never once tried to deal with it. I don't understand you! Nothing makes sense to me, and I'm too tied up in you to think clearly. How could you do what you did?" Her voice quivered and she tightened her jaw.

"It was easy. I just didn't think." What he'd told Hutch, easiest thing to say. Wrong fucking thing to say to her. What the hell was wrong with him? He could see how his words hurt her, and he didn't want to hurt her anymore!

"Did you feel *any* of what I felt? You know how much I loved you. I didn't hide it at all."

"Yeah I felt it. I felt it too damned much and I couldn't live with it."

"So you just shut it off."

"No—I don't know, I was far away, I didn't see you, I didn't have to think about anything."

Had he hurt her again? It looked like it, but he didn't know what he'd said.

After a moment, she said quietly, "My heart never healed right from what happened. I have no idea what my life would have been like if I'd never met you, but I don't think it would be this." She gestured to her surroundings. "I'd probably be married, have children. Very traditional." A sad smile. "Like my parents. I accept how my life has turned out, the shape my heart is now, I accept it. It's mine. But, I don't want more of what you're capable of doing to it."

Was it wrong he felt a thrill at hearing her say she was still vulnerable to him? Fuck it, he'd run with it. "Then let's just be friends."

"I could never look at you as simply friendly. No. You still haven't been clear about why you're really here. I can't believe it's because you want an old friend. My best guess is that maybe you feel bad now about how you treated me and my family, so maybe you want to be absolved of any guilt. Or make amends for it."

When he said nothing, she continued, "I can't offer you any of that. I accept but I still hurt. Maybe my parents can offer it to you. I'd suggest you go see them and find out for yourself. You know where they live."

"Yeah, I know."

"Then go. Please."

Words locked up in his impenetrable vault again, and he couldn't find a single way to get to stay without her having legitimate cause to call the cops on him.

"Why did you ask what my most important memory was?" The only thought that came to delay leaving.

"Because you gave everything away for the army, and I wanted to know what you got out of it."

No words.

He stood, and with a last long look, silently left.

CHAPTER EIGHT

Liv watched him go, wanting to demand he leave the necklace. *Why had she given it to him?* For better or worse, she wanted the memories it brought of when he'd acted like he loved her as much as she loved him.

Friends. Ugh, why? What angle was he working? It couldn't be Jeremy Olawale, his off-record meetings with her would compromise the investigation. Guilt was the only thing that made sense.

Taking a calming breath, Liv grabbed her laptop. She couldn't control Connor, could hardly control her own emotions where he was concerned, but she could control what she did. After scanning for upcoming classes at her community center, Liv dialed Holly. "Want to take karate on Wednesdays?"

"Wednesdays are bad. Jake and I are trying to pump some excitement into our life by playing tennis every Wednesday." Holly snorted. "Karate seems random."

"It makes me nervous thinking about doing it." Which would hopefully occupy her. "But since I'm planning to be a spinster of good fortune, it would do me good to have some self-defense techniques in my repertoire."

"It's a good plan, but I'll have to support you from afar, I'm afraid."

"I'll report back on Wednesday the degree of my natural talent."

"I sense an inner karate genius in you, Liv. I really do."

Liv managed a dry, "Thanks," and they hung up.

One of the things she'd learned from her dorm-room-Connor-ghosting-years was that no one liked to hear incessantly about your joy or your pain. Holly was her best friend, had been almost from the start, but even she after a while had told her that if she didn't stop talking about Connor, crying about Connor, obviously thinking about Connor, she couldn't keep hanging with her. *A lot is happening in the world, but your whole life is all about this one asshole who treated you like trash. If you're going to give everything you've got inside you to that, all I can give you is pity and that's not friendship.*

Clawing her way out of the hole started with reading the news. She hadn't ever been terribly interested before, but Holly talked a lot about *all the shit going down in the world*, so Liv downloaded a news app and started paying attention. Shortly after, Wimbledon championships kept appearing in her news feed, coinciding with a flyer going around campus for tennis lessons. Thinking it would give her something to *be* besides pitiful, she signed up. The simple act of doing an activity and concentrating on something besides Connor, helped her. So she kept doing it. After a while, she tried art classes. Then feng sui classes. After a while it became habit to take classes because it helped in more than just not thinking about Connor, she noticed it helping her confidence too.

Holly had been all in, she loved going to stuff she just didn't like planning it. Liv planned. Then Holly got married and it almost instantly became a chain that held her back from doing all the things they'd done before. Once she had kids Liv knew it would be even worse.

Shying away from the thought, she finished enrolling in karate and then opened her email.

To: Lea Nonme
Subject: Catering

Hello,
Status update?
Dr. Jones

* * * *

"Might be we have a teeny weenie break in the Olawale case," Fernando announced the next morning. "Not to be confused with your ego—teeny weenie."

Connor slow-blinked.

Fernando smiled with owlish innocence. "Teeny little weenie."

"How long does this usually go on before you get to the point?"

"Depends on the mood. Today it's pretty good."

"I wonder what a bad mood looks like to you."

"You, last week." He dropped the Olawale file on his desk. "Already added the latest. Have a read while I take a piss."

A call log, all typed out like a report from an A+ student lay at the very top of the file. One of Jeremy's friends they'd talked to previously had called. He had some information he wanted to exchange.

Fernando came back, patting a crisp paper towel. "Ready?"

"You failed to record the time of the meeting."

"I didn't." He leaned in to scan the document. "Well hell. I was aiming for untouchable too."

"That's a B-student move right there."

"You finally looked me up?"

"So deep I know your grade point average."

Fernando chuckled and clapped him on the shoulder. "C'mon. Meetings in an hour. Let's get some good coffee on the way."

A cup later, they pulled up to a hiking trail in the middle of a neighborhood. Connor eyed their suit trousers and polished shoes. "How far are we going in?"

"About a minute."

They walked for a minute and stopped and waited. Fifteen minutes later, the kid showed up. He had long bangs that were so deeply side-swept he continuously jerked his head to move them out of his eyes, and wore artfully trashed clothing that said, *punk, but privileged-style.*

Jeremy's family barely kept up with the Jones's; this kid was the Jones. The two groups didn't often run in the same circle, so how was this kid in Jeremy's?

"Hey, whutsup," the kid said, jerking his head. His gaze skittered around but mostly met Connor's. "I know some stuff about Jeremy, but I need some help too."

"Oh yeah, what kind?" Fernando said.

"My brother got arrested for drugs."

"How old is he?"

"Sixteen."

"Was he caught with them?"

"Caught selling."

Connor sucked air through his teeth. "Shitload of trouble, kid. What kind?"

"Meth."

Connor barked a laugh. How many times… Poor, privileged, didn't matter. "He's looking at jail time unless your family gets him a good lawyer. What do you know about Jeremy?"

The kid jerked his head. "I think his dad beat the shit out of him. He would talk about wanting to take off to live in a trailer his mom's friend had."

"Why do you believe his father beat him?" Fernando said.

"He legit hated him, for real. And anyway, my brother used to get beaten up by this kid at school all the time, like in the stomach this kid always sucker punched him. I kinda remember Jeremy moving like how my brother would when he'd been beaten up."

"Jeremy never stated his father beat him?"

"Nah, dude."

"Did you ever ask?"

"Psh." The kid rolled his eyes. "Nah, it's none of my business. Could you help my brother?"

"Nah, dude," Fernando said with a middle-aged smile.

Connor almost sighed. "Do you know anything else about Jeremy? Observations or otherwise?" Another jerk of the head, this time with a mutinous stare.

"Alright, thanks for your help. Sorry about your brother. I hope he gets help because it's a dangerous road he's on. I've seen it first-hand."

"You sold drugs?" the kid said.

"I put dealers in prison. It's an ugly life. I hope for your sake you don't get into it like your brother."

Another mutinous stare before he sprinted off with a jerk of his head.

"Think he'll have neck problems?" Fernando mused, watching him go.

"Nah, dude."

Fernando grinned. "That approach did not work for the kid."

"You thought it would?"

"What do I know about teen boys? I've got girls, and I'm too old to remember how I thought way back in the day." They began the short walk back to the car.

"We got a lead though," Connor said. "His mom's friend's trailer."

"Let's pay a visit to Mrs. Olawale."

CHAPTER NINE

At his desk the next morning, Connor went over his interview with Jeremy's mother. She'd been clear-eyed, nothing resembling a patient who'd just undergone a psychotic break. But with each question they asked, she'd say to leave her alone until they found her son.

"I've been thinking about Mrs. Olawale," Fernando said as he strolled in, looking unusually unkempt with his five o'clock shadow twelve hours past shave time.

"What the hell happened to you?" Connor said.

"Don't want to talk about it."

"Like that would stop you."

"Getting to know me, partner." Fernando's brows had a pulled back quality, like the muscles around his face were clenched so tight they couldn't let go. "Let's talk to your girlfriend about Mrs. Olawale."

"She's not my girlfriend," he muttered, like a teenager.

Fernando grinned. "I already called her guy and made an appointment for six this evening. Busy schedule apparently." Then mumbled, "Lots of people messed up these days."

"I can't at six. I have—" a therapy session. "A date tonight."

"Well hell, I'll call the he-man back and reschedule for her next available." He threw a hand over his shoulder as if to say *see ya later.*

A half hour later, Fernando passed him to go take a leak. "In keeping to my schedule," he said with a salute. On his way back, hands patting a crisp towel, he said, "He-man said her four o'clock appointment canceled so we can see your girlfriend then."

Connor glanced at the clock: 8:37 a.m. His day just became a long one.

At noon, Fernando strolled back over. "Want to get lunch?" This was the first lunch invitation. All other shared meals were from necessity.

"Mexican food," Connor said. The tedium of the day must be getting to him. Any other time he would have said no.

"I know a great place."

It was in a little outdoor shopping mall that no one would notice driving by. Inside had a row of tables against the far wall, leaving space for a snaked line of hungry people to place their order.

"Weekends and evenings, this place is a nightmare if you're claustrophobic. Lunch is the only time I come. Get my fix, get out before a panic attack."

Connor laughed, but Fernando said, "Seriously."

Once they'd ordered and sat waiting for their food, Fernando continued, "I was in the academy first time I had one. They had us running all together like a herd. I was right in the middle, bumping shoulders with the sweaty guys all around me, tripping over boots, actually noticing how much we all stank. Man, I felt like I couldn't breathe right all of a sudden, my heart started going so fast I started thinking it wasn't even beating." He shook his head. "I was in good shape then too."

"What did you do?"

"Nothing. My poor mom would get them all the time, so I knew what it was. Shocked the hell outta me to actually get one myself though. Figured it was a one off because the stress of the academy, but I had another one when we graduated, all sandwiched together again in our uniforms. It was hot, I couldn't get up or move, I was right in the middle of the row." He shook his head again. "Every time after that when I got stuck pressed in with a bunch of people it would happen. It wasn't until I met my wife that she told me I'm claustrophobic. I have to take a pill to get on a plane."

70

Their food came. Connor didn't feel the need to say anything as they ate and neither did Fernando. Into the silence, Connor noticed again how unkempt he looked and the heaviness of his lids.

An alert went to both their phones. Fernando sighed and wrapped up his food, and then they went to the car.

"Just because I'm glad we have a new case on our hands doesn't mean I'm glad someone died," Fernando said. "Even though I'm glad someone died so that I have a new case."

Connor snorted with amusement. "You just said all that I couldn't."

"We're like a match made in heaven."

"Demons and unicorns are working for you today."

Fernando shook his head, driving with one hand while the other fumbled with the wrapping on his burrito, shoving in the last bites with his mouth working around the paper.

"I've done the Iron Man triathlon couple times, but I haven't heard about one for an Iron Stomach."

Fernando glanced at him. "Of course you've done Iron Man. I'll nominate you for the annual Hot Cops calendar." He belched into his fist. "Food not sitting right for you or something?"

"Great place, great food. I'm thinking more along the lines of wolfing down a beef burrito on the way to examine a homicide."

"Ahh the rookie has made an appearance. I've been waiting for you. You get extra credit for taking longer to show up than I expected."

"I've been waiting to get extra credit for doing nothing my whole life."

"I'm glad I could step into that role for you, son."

Connor grinned and turned his attention to the six-floor building they'd just pulled up to. He recognized the distinctive rounded corner on one side that was made entirely of windows, as if it wore wraparound sunglasses.

Inside, it had dated peach walls, fake plants, and blue hued pictures. A man sat crouched on the floor next to the reception desk. His elbows were braced on his knees, his thinning sandy brown hair woven through his fingers as he held his head in his hands. Beside him stood the first officers to the scene.

As they approached, the man lifted his head revealing a pasty complexion. Fernando introduced them, but the man could hardly focus his gaze. "He's in there. First—first office on your right. I walked in and it smelled and—" He clamped his lips together, his cheeks puffing slightly. "I just want to get out of here. When can I go?"

"Wait here please," Fernando said and then he and Connor went to the first door inside the corridor.

The smell was distinct, and it made the back of Connor's tongue press against his soft palate, as if he could restrict the scent from fully entering him. Brain matter lay splattered like confetti against the back wall from a bullet that went from the man's mouth through the back of his head, indicative of a self-inflicted gunshot. By appearances, a suicide.

The sight made Connor pause. It's how he would have looked if he'd done it. The memory of staring down the barrel of his gun flashed through his mind, and he shook his head to get it away from him.

"Y'alright, rookie?"

"Better than this guy."

"Remind me later to call your girlfriend. We won't make it in time."

They examined the scene. Just because it looked like a suicide didn't mean it was and they carefully assessed for evidence of foul play.

"I can't find anything," Fernando muttered. "I'm gonna call it, the guy popped himself. No suicide note though."

Connor wouldn't have left one either. "Maybe he's got no one to leave it for."

"We'll find out. Alright, let's get this wrapped up."

After the coroner arrived, they interviewed the witness, had the building notified for cleanup, and retrieved the security tapes.

They finished up with just enough time for Connor to be five minutes late to his appointment with Hutch.

"Late call on a homicide. I apologize for being tardy."

"At ease, soldier," Hutch said with a ghost of a smile. "How are you after that call?"

"The call today? It was a suicide. Nothing out of the ordinary."

"Have you seen a lot of them?"

"No. I've seen a lot of death though." Hutch didn't say anything for a moment, and Connor found himself filling the silence. "What I saw today. Part of me wonders how the hell I ever got close to that point, the other part doubts I did. Last night was a long ass night though, I was alone with nothing to do, and I felt fucking pointless again."

"Do you keep in touch with your buddies in the army?"

"No. I never keep in touch. And no I don't know why."

"Leave first before you can be left?"

Connor gave him a dark look. "Is that what it is?"

"What do you think?"

"I think I've got a date in an hour, and I don't know why I keep coming here." He rocked back and out of the chair. To the window again, he stared out at the parking lot debating leaving, for good. How was any of this doing anything besides bringing up shit he didn't like to think about?

Turning from the window, he said, "I gotta go."

"On your date with Liv?"

"No. With Josephine, the nice baby nurse."

"C'mon Connor, stay. You've got an hour before you meet her."

"I don't want to talk about this shit!"

"What do you want to talk about?"

"I—" Scraping his hand back and forth along the side of his head, he turned and then turned again and sat down. What the fuck was wrong with him? Was he dancing? "I don't know, Hutch. Nothing. I want to talk about nothing."

"Okay. What's nothing to you?"

His mouth opened, snapped closed.

"Liv," Hutch said quietly, "can we talk about her? She's not nothing but she's something good in your life."

"She was. I wish she still was. Yeah. I saw her the other day. She gave me my necklace back."

"Your necklace?"

"The one I gave her in high school. It was like a promise she could trust that I loved her." Shame over breaking his promise came over him. First time he'd felt it.

"Why was she worried about that then?"

"Because she was awkward. We were friends for ages, and she was a toothpick, I made fun of her all the time. Not mean, just teasing. I hooked up a lot, and she was not the type of girl I did that with. But we were friends, I always wanted to be near her."

"Why?"

"She was everything that's good in the world." Connor thought about the way she'd look at him when he teased her, like she found it funny but didn't want him to know it. "She was nice to everyone. Even people I knew she didn't like she'd still treat nice. She laughed at my stupid jokes and made the best cookies I've ever had. She took care of me when I was sick once. Her family protected me from my stepdad. Being with her, being a part of their family, was like heaven.

"She asked if I faked everything because of what her family did for me. They took me in, you know. Like I said, protected me from Keith."

"I could understand why she might wonder that."

Connor didn't respond.

"What do you think? Is it possible your feelings for her even now could have something to do with it?" Hutch pressed.

"I cared more about her than anyone, even when we were just friends. So, no, it has nothing to do with it."

An expanding ache began to fill Connor's chest and he stared down at his pointless hands that had worked so hard to accomplish nothing. "I wish I'd never done what I did. I wish I could beat the shit out of my eighteen-year-old self for being such a waste of fucking space."

"A waste of space, or really young with a lot of troubles you didn't know how to work out?"

"I haven't been really young for a long time, I still never fixed what I messed up. I wouldn't be thinking about this if I hadn't seen her again. And even that—why the fuck wouldn't I fix this? I want her, I've always wanted her, even when I didn't think about her, somewhere in my head she was there. Seeing her only one fucking time ruined me."

"It brought everything back, Connor. All that you shut down for a dozen years, suddenly at the forefront again. Sounds like somewhere in your head you knew that and were protecting yourself from facing the avalanche of what you'd buried."

"My parents again, right?" he said quietly. "I don't see the point in talking about any of them."

"Sometimes, the simple act of acknowledging the hurt their behavior caused you, is enough to begin healing from the wounds they left."

His phone vibrated and he automatically looked at it.

Hey, I'm 15 mins
behind. Sorry!
J

Connor looked at Hutch. "We're past time?"

"For the first time," Hutch said with a smile.

"You shouldn't keep your other clients waiting on my sorry ass." He rocked up to stand. "Thanks for today. I'll see you."

"Two days, Connor."

"I'll be here."

He drove to Josephine's and waited the extra minutes before knocking on her door.

"Hi!" she said brightly. "Thank you for waiting. I got held up at work and couldn't leave on time, so I've been running around."

She had a flushed look to her face as if she'd been running, literally. "I wouldn't have minded waiting longer, if you needed more time."

"Thanks." A relieved smile lit her face. "I appreciate you understanding."

He took her to a chain restaurant this time, it was louder than he wanted and the lighting too low, reminding him why he didn't like chain restaurants. She chatted easily, the conversation never slowed, but he could hardly focus on what she said and the minutes until the date ended were long ones.

As he dropped her off, he said the right things, gave her an automatic kiss with his tongue in her mouth and a slow stroke down her body, but he expected it to end there. Instead, she grabbed his hand and tugged him into her apartment. So he kept going, kissing, stroking, getting into it. Sex was always a welcome distraction.

She yanked her top off, revealing a black lace bra that her nipples strained hard against, and he reached for them, tweaking them both, enjoying her reaction when her eyes half closed, and her red-stained lips parted on a gasp. "You like that?" he rasped.

"Mm-hm," she moaned.

He kissed her again, enjoying the mint flavor on her tongue, how gentle she was with it, not getting his face wet. Her hands stroked under his shirt, and she pushed it up, pushing until he took it off, and then to his belt, undoing everything until she had him in her hand.

Connor groaned, low and deep as she stroked, his jeans pooling around his ankles. Dropping to her knees, she took him into her mouth, and he hissed in surprised pleasure as she sucked and stroked, cupping his ass in her hands while her head bobbed back and forth.

She released his dick after a long pull, and stood, pushing her skirt down her legs as she did so. "Let's go to my bed. There's more room."

Kicking his shoes and jeans off, he grabbed a condom out of his back pocket. "You sure about this?" he remembered to ask. He wasn't going to call her tomorrow. Or ever.

She half laughed. "I want a night with you before this is over."

That meant she knew, right? If she knew he wouldn't call again and still wanted this, hell that just made everything easy.

Grinning, he followed her to her bedroom, and she swiftly took her bra and panties off and got on her bed, patting the space beside her with a sexy smile. "Lay down on your stomach. I need to squeeze that amazing ass of yours."

A little awkward, but he did it, and she petted and stroked the curves of his buttocks before stroking all over his body, finally urging him to turn over where she slid her whole body over him. He used his own hands on her now, stroked her curves, her breasts. When she squeezed her smooth thighs on either side of his dick and rocked against it, he tweaked her nipples, making her gasp. She rocked harder, jerking her hips wildly and he lifted her enough to get a nipple in his mouth. Clamping it between his lips, he stabbed the tip with his tongue, and she practically squealed.

Pushing her onto her back, he swiftly rolled the condom on and pressed into her. She went quiet, hardly moving. "Is this okay for you?"

"You're big."

"Do you want me to stop?"

"Yes."

Fuck. Gritting his teeth, he pulled out and backed up, but she stopped him by grabbing his arm. "This way," she said as she flipped around and presented her ass in the air, her spine arching deeply so that her nipples hit the sheets.

Carefully he spread her lips and gently worked his length into her with slow, short pumps until he was in her fully. "Better," she breathed. Arching her spine even more, she worked herself on his cock, but when he tried to drive deep, she rocked away.

What the hell did she want? A gentle rock? But she was undulating and swishing her ass like crazy with her butt cheeks spread wide, her tight little hole puckered and exposed. Licking his thumb, he gently pressed it against her hole, and she instantly shrieked, rocking wildly on his cock and he plunged deep, pressing his thumb into her, and she went off like a rocket.

Slapping his hips against her, he worked his thumb in and out in time, feeling her clench all around everything inside her, and his cum rose fast, spurting out of him making him groan long and low.

Immediately, he eased out of her, went in search of the bathroom, washed and disposed of the condom and washed his hands. Damn, that was better than he'd had in a while, he'd needed that release of pressure.

Walking back into her room, he returned the lazy grin she gave him from her boneless position on the bed.

"If you lock the bottom handle on the door, I won't have to get up and lock up after you leave."

Nodding briefly, he said, "Thanks. I enjoyed that."

"Me too." Her eyes closed.

"I'll see myself out. Goodnight."

She smiled and rolled over, snapping her light off.

Connor dressed quickly, called out he'd locked the bottom handle and left.

It was late, he could go home now and go to bed, and not watch time ticking by until he had something to do with himself.

CHAPTER TEN

"I suck at karate, and my teacher's a little bit scary. It's basically like she's stepped out of a movie and moves too fast for anyone to even know that she hit them ten times."

Holly paused with a forkful of salad an inch from her lips. "I want to see an action hero in real life."

"It's not too late to join. Please join."

"It's too late to get unmarried so I've got to stick with our exciting tennis night."

"I love tennis."

"You wouldn't with Jake. He kept missing the ball last night and I ended up yelling at him to run after it, like he's a bad dog that doesn't get his one job." She whimpered. "Why did I get married?"

"Is it really that bad, Holls?"

Biting into her crispy salad, she said out of the side of her mouth, "Yes it's that bad with Jake. You know he's always been not-exciting, but now it's like being married to a lump of dead weight. I just want out."

"You seriously want a divorce?"

"Yes, but not, no. It's…it hasn't been long, you know, and I don't want to be a quitter, but he's way worse than I ever imagined he'd be." She took a sip of her latte. "And then there's this guy I met who makes me light up when we're together."

"Actual light up?"

"Everyone keeps telling me I'm glowing, and I stopped using my glow serum."

Liv snickered. Holly continued, "I keep finding ways to be around him, and I feel like he's doing the same. It's like we're drawn to each other."

Something in her voice had Liv going still. "Holly, that's got *Danger! Cheating Ahead!* blinking to light in my brain."

She looked away miserably. "The worst part is that I want to."

"It's that far into things already? Who is he?"

"A colleague of mine, you don't know him, he's new to the practice."

"Has anything happened?"

Holly grimaced. "Some things that I would not be okay with Jake seeing, but nothing strictly bad."

"Is it flirtation stage or making plans to see each other after work stage?"

"Close to option two. Why aren't you eating your sandwich? You only stop eating when something's bothering you. What's bothering you?"

"I don't want you to cheat, there's nothing but misery down that road, for several people. Is the guy married?"

"No, and I know, but it's not miserable right now. It's the only bright part of my life right now so I don't want to put a stop to it even though I know I should. I don't truly want to cheat though. I'll stop before it gets that far."

"Not reassuring last words, Holls."

"What's bothering you?"

"You should stop now, and figure this out with Jake."

"There's what I should do, Liv, and what I want to do. I'm giving each side of my brain a little more time to come to an agreement on it. Until then, what's bothering you?"

Liv fiddled with her veggie wrap, dreading saying it. "Connor." Holly instantly groaned and Liv said over the noise, "You asked! I wasn't going to say anything."

"Okay hold on, I want to hear what's going on, and I also want to be vocal about what a douchebag Connor is."

"You don't want to hear. Nobody does. He's my poor-me story that I keep repeating and everyone's sick of."

"That's not true, and I don't think you're 'poor me' still."

"It feels like it. Every time I see him, I'm like a kid again, wanting him so badly. Even with the broken pieces of my heart stinging from being near him."

"They're not broken anymore."

"I still feel the cracks."

"You're healed. It's just the shock of suddenly seeing him again that's getting to you."

Holly hadn't ever loved with her whole heart wide open and unprotected before, Liv knew. She'd never fully understood what it meant that Liv's heart had been shattered.

"He said he wanted to be friends again."

"No! Oh hell no."

"That's what I essentially said. But I'm thinking now I should take him up on it." If her heart were a mosaic piece, being with him would shine light on the cracks, because no matter how hard she'd worked to repair herself, she knew only exposure would make clear her strength.

Thirteen years, and he hadn't thought about her at all in that time. How profoundly weak to have been altered so severely by someone who didn't even remember her.

No. Not weak. She knew it wasn't that, would counsel others it wasn't.

Powerless.

"I'm seeing the *Danger Ahead!* signs now, Liv. There's too much there."

"Like you, I'll stop before it gets bad."

They held each other's gaze.

Holly quietly cleared her throat and steered the conversation away, to their couple's trip they didn't know what to do with but didn't want to cancel, before heading back to their respective offices.

Minutes after she returned, Patrick knocked on her door before poking his head in, one muscular shoulder bulging in with it. He'd worked for her going on three years and each year got bulkier. He was the son of her father's employee who hadn't wanted to work on a construction site, lest he injure his physique in any way. Mr. Universe was his goal, while he went to college to be a physical therapist. She'd hired him to help a family friend, going in with low expectations but he'd applied that same intense focus from the gym to running her office. When he left someday, she'd regret the loss.

"They're walking up. You ready?"

"Yes. Thanks, Patrick." After Connor's last visit, she'd given him the synopsis.

A moment later, he brought them in.

Trying to hide the way Connor's hazel eyes drew her in like a love song was hard.

With a soft sigh she said, "To what do I owe the pleasure of this latest visit?"

"I appreciate that you enjoy our visits, Dr. Jones," Fernando said, making her lips curve.

Offering them a seat, Fernando promptly tipped heavily to one side to dig in his pocket for a notebook. He looked tired, distracted, a very different mien than what she'd grown accustomed to.

"How much interaction did you have with Mrs. Olawale?" Connor said.

She met Connor's gaze again. "Hardly any. The first appointment, she came into my office to drop Jeremy off. She never did it again."

"What about phone conversations?"

"I discussed Jeremy with her on the phone occasionally, yes."

"Did she ever say anything at all that might hint at abuse?"

"She didn't."

"We received a tip from one of his friends," Fernando said, flipping pages. "Turns out his friends' brother is involved in drugs." He recapped the meeting they'd had. "Now, that's a couple different rumblings we've heard about abuse. Did you see or hear *anything* that would support these claims?"

"I never saw obvious marks."

"What we're trying to determine," Connor said, "is whether Jeremy ran when his father died, or if he was murdered along with him."

Startled at the idea, she nevertheless noticed Fernando's glance skyward.

"I'm afraid I can't help you," she said.

"The kid we spoke to said Jeremy talked about running away," Fernando said. "Do you have any knowledge of a location he had in mind to run to?"

"Jeremy's friend didn't know?"

"No." Connor answered.

"C'mon doc, we're coming up empty here," Fernando said. "You know there's some flex to that confidentiality agreement when abuse is involved. We keep hearing about it, gives Jeremy a motive but also a defense."

"You want me to point to where he's hiding?" she said with exasperation. "He was not prone to violence or rage. If I were in your position, knowing what I know, I'd be looking at everyone else connected to the family."

"At this point in the game that's what we're looking for, some guidance. Whether he did it or not though, we need to find him. He had an idea before his father died where he wanted to run to. Any guidance where that might be?"

"The homes of his family members. Consider past vacation spots that might shelter him. Friends are unlikely, though not beyond the realm of possibility."

Fernando exhaled loudly, but Connor said, "Jeremy's mother isn't cooperating. In your professional opinion, is that suspicious?"

"I'm not a criminal psychologist." She hesitated. "However...if she was in an abusive relationship, I'd perceive her behavior as scared."

"If her abuser's dead, what does she have to be scared of?" Fernando asked.

"It takes time to unwind from living in constant fear, and shame. There's a host of emotional complexities that would explain her resistance to opening up to you."

Fernando barely stifled a yawn.

"There's some coffee in the waiting room."

He nodded and stood, prompting them all to their feet. "Thanks for your time. We'll try not to bother you anymore." Pointing to the door, he said, "I'm gonna grab a cup."

* * * *

Connor stood there, looking at her. The urge to see her outdoors, with the sun reflecting off her tumbling hair, brought an image of them camping in the woods, with just a tent and a shared sleeping bag.

She fidgeted under his scrutiny, self-consciously tucking a lock of hair behind her ear. He tracked the movement, recognizing the girl in her that used to do that when they were young. "You're remarkable, Liv. You accomplished everything you said you would, and then some." She blinked at him, and he noticed a flush of warmth turning her cheeks to rose. "I wish I hadn't been such a dumba—fool—and missed all the years of you becoming this."

"I…" More fidgeting, looking away and back again before finally meeting his gaze. "Me too, Connor."

He held his hand out and slowly she took it, her soft palm nestling into his. "Have dinner with me."

"I…"

Knocks *tap-tap-tapped* on the open door, and Liv sprang away.

"Patrick!" she said a little breathlessly. "Oh good."

"Yeah, doc, there's an urgent message for you."

"I'll see myself out," Connor murmured.

Fernando waited outside and yawned a couple more times as they went to the car. "Moonlighting in my old job?" Connor said.

"Couldn't sleep last couple nights. That's not to be confused with right now. I could sleep right now."

"Want me to drive?"

"Hell no." Fernando tossed the keys at him.

By the time Connor had adjusted the seat and mirrors to accommodate his greater height, Fernando was already stretched out and snoring on the passenger side.

Back at the office, Fernando promptly made a long trip to the bathroom while Connor continued working on the suicide report on Stephen Shek. His desk phone rang.

"Detective Peltier," he answered.

"I'm looking it up right now. If we get your entry form in by the end of the week—make that tomorrow—you could still make it in this year's Hot Cops calendar."

"Fernando? Where the hell are you?"

"Bathroom."

"Ever planning to leave it?"

A loud fart sounded in the background, making Connor laugh.

"Been saving that for this exact moment," Fernando said.

"Well now you're just making me feel special."

The rapid *tick* of Fernando texting sounded and then he said, "Check your email for the entry form. I want to introduce you as Detective July."

"What if I'm Mr. December?"

"I'd have to lie to my wife. She loves Christmas, add in Mr. Hot Cop partner and she'd start visiting the station every day to leave cookies and milk."

"I can't think of a single thing wrong with that."

"A year of Mrs. Claus leaving you cookies means you won't be Mr. December again, which would disappoint my wife. I can't have my wife disappointed."

"I don't know if I can handle this responsibility."

"Do not worry, I will be your handler." Another fart sounded.

Connor snickered even as he said, "Jesus, what did you eat?"

"Salad. Mrs. Claus put me on a diet. She's got a mean streak, but we don't talk about it."

"I'll leave you to it then, buddy."

"I do my best thinking in times like these, so do not be surprised if I come out with cases solved."

Amused, Connor hung up and returned his attention to the case file he'd been working on.

The look in Liv's eyes when he'd asked her to dinner flashed through his mind. She hadn't been angry. The guarded expression hadn't been there either. Something had changed.

He tried to focus on his work.

But…Liv had been lying again about Jeremy. Again about the abuse. Why would she hide that? *What* was she hiding?

"I have a premonition about today," Fernando said as he strolled by. "It will be tedious."

"Feeling better?"

"Touch and go. I need a burger to comfort me."

Hours later, Fernando passed by his desk again with a long-suffering look. "Go work out for me tonight, will ya?"

Connor snickered. "If you'll get some sleep for me."

"Not likely," he muttered.

It was time to leave, yet Connor didn't want to go home, aimlessly looking for ways to pass the time. Instead, he went to the gym, lifted weights, and ignored everyone. Afterward he picked up a burrito and ate in his truck as he drove to the beach. The sun still lit the sky as if it refused to retreat, clinging to the last vestiges of summer.

The sound of the ocean drew him, and he wandered onto the fine-grain sand, down to the edge where the sea turned it into a dense sponge that resisted the imprint of his every step.

Years ago, he'd gone to the jetty not far from where he stood now. He'd broken up with his then-girlfriend, Ana, and the scene when he left her house had been worse than he'd expected. The look on her face just before he'd closed the door behind him, the makeup in her tears, running down her cheeks like colored streams was still clear in his mind. Her reaction, his indifference to it, was one of the first times he'd become undeniably aware he wasn't good enough for Liv.

Afterward, he'd abruptly stopped going over to her house. She'd been worried, texting and calling him but it had taken him days before he could talk about it. They'd finally met up at the jetty, where he'd planned to say goodbye, basically. Instead, she'd hugged him. She hadn't judged him for what he'd done, even after he told her bluntly what happened. And then he'd kissed her. Their first kiss. Her lips had felt incredibly soft beneath his, the scent of her, so bright and fresh had filled him up. She was light.

The months following that kiss were the happiest of his life. They'd quickly become a couple, and he hadn't had a single doubt that they would be together, forever. Nothing could break them. Not the army, not time or distance away from each other. Nothing, except him.

Jesus, could he be any more of a loser? He'd had Heaven, and he himself had destroyed it.

Why the hell was he even here? Rubbing the back of his neck, he looked back at his truck, noticing all the people enjoying the beach even as night finally began to take over day. Many were smiling or talking to friends, some relaxing with their families. It felt as though he saw it from a great distance, so separate from it he couldn't imagine ever being one of them.

Blanking his mind to it, he walked back to his truck and sat in the still air of the quiet cab. He didn't want to go home. He had no right to go to Liv's and should do her a favor and stay far away from her from now on. If a reason came up to go to her office, he'd tell Fernando he needed to be reassigned.

Eventually, he started the truck and drove back to his condo, each movement feeling weighted, everything in him heavier. The walk to his front door had the soles of his shoes sliding like sandpaper against the stair steps. Once inside, he stripped and got into bed.

Staring at the ceiling, he thought about being in the army again, doing rescue missions. The planning, the extraction, the protection of innocents, it had felt good and occupied his every thought. Now, everything he'd ever pushed from his mind clamored for attention.

His mom. She'd been so medicated when he left for the army, Connor could still picture the slow blink of her lids as he said goodbye. She'd mumbled, "I lllove you." He hadn't responded. That was the last time he spoke to her, saw her.

What a shitty son he'd been. She'd been too weak to deal with his dad leaving them, and then she'd promptly married asshole

Keith who'd started beating the crap out of him. She'd medicated to cope. He should have done more to try to help her. He hadn't been weak—

Connor thought of the gun on his bedside table, pictured the black hole he'd gazed into and the near overwhelming urge to use it. Maybe he was that weak.

He should have come home when she died, if only to grab photo albums of when times had been good. As it stood, he didn't even have a picture of her. He'd refused to take one when he left, never thinking it may be his last opportunity to.

Keith… God, he felt so much rage when the memory of him pummeling his body rose to mind that he instantly shut it down.

He'd felt the same consuming rage when his friend Makayla had been raped, had wanted to kill the motherfuckers who'd done it. He knew who they were, had believed everything she'd reported, despite the men's denials and the army's acquittals. He'd gone after one of them, started a fight, and been immediately disciplined with the threat of far worse if he didn't get his emotions under control. So, he'd shut it down, did what he'd always done. Failed everyone he'd ever cared about.

Pointless, whispered through his mind. *Worthless, just like Keith said.*

Connor turned his head to shake loose the thoughts, but his gaze landed on the muted shine of his pistol.

No one would miss you if you were gone.

CHAPTER ELEVEN

"Hey partner," Fernando mumbled as he walked by Connor's desk the next morning. His eyes were particularly puffy, fatigue sagging the skin around his jowls.

Good, Connor thought. Whatever Fernando's problem was, hopefully it would stop him from noticing Connor's.

With his partner distracted and no one to stop him, Connor opened up the Shek file again. The need to find out what pushed him to pull that trigger haunted him. Was there an identifiable tipping point? If he discovered it, could he watch for it in himself?

Rocking out of his seat, he went to Fernando's desk. "What are you working on?"

Fernando reclined back and linked his fingers behind his head. "Everything. I'm the best employee. Nobody employee's harder than me."

"I want to follow up with Mrs. Shek to see if she found a suicide note. Anything."

"Okay," he said with an exaggerated cringe. "I'll live vicariously through your youthful enthusiasm. Did you enter for the calendar?"

"No."

"Failing me already, partner?"

"I'm more than just my body, Fernando."

"I know. You've got a pretty face to go with it."

Connor snorted. "Alright, I'll call."

"Be gentle." Not an ounce of humor. "Don't give her hope it was murder."

"Hope?"

"With suicide…" Fernando raised his hands a little helplessly. "From what I've seen, it hurts the loved ones differently. It's more personal, like they weren't important."

Connor nodded slowly. "Got it."

Mrs. Shek answered on the second ring. Connor identified himself and said, "I'm about to close out the investigation, but I wanted to confirm whether you've found a note or letter before I do."

"Oh, yes, I did," her voice sounded tired and crackling. "I'll send it to you. I almost threw it out, but I—I'll mail it. I don't want it."

He wanted to press her to read it to him, but knew it was wrong. Instead, he gave her the station's address, and then apologized for troubling her.

He'd have to wait to get his answers.

When it grew close to quitting time, he called Hutch's office and canceled his appointment: *A case came up I can't lose my lead on.* Such an easy message to leave.

He went to the gym, ate takeout on the way home. Process repeat, for days.

He wanted to be consumed by his work, yet it didn't exhaust him like the army or his narc job had, and each night he lay in bed, staring at the ceiling wondering why the hell he bothered with anything. Even if he discovered why Shek killed himself, what difference would it make? If there was some tipping point for suicide, and Connor got there, would he care if he recognized it?

The thought of saying that to Hutch made Connor blank his mind to it. If only he could blank everything inside him.

You can, his mind whispered.

How would Liv react if she found out he'd died? He'd done everything he fucking could not to think about her since the beach. He didn't want to go there, didn't want…anything. Nothingness, he wanted nothingness.

* * * *

Weeks passed with that a constant companion. Each day he forced his focus on cases Fernando suddenly seemed content to let him take the lead on, but the work was painstaking, like finding pieces in a puzzle as opposed to the relentless action he'd long been accustomed to.

Daily, he considered putting in a transfer request back to undercover, but hell, he'd gotten out because his injury started plaguing him at times it had been damned inconvenient to be showing any signs of weakness. More than that, he'd been weary of it. Deeply weary and thought a change of pace would let him have a life. He'd just need to get one.

Couple times a week, Hutch called him too, and each time he silenced it. Would he call the department and report Connor as a head case? Possibly. As the weeks went by, the less Connor cared. Maybe they found out, maybe they fired him. Maybe he'd lose everything. Each day, it mattered less until he found himself driving one night, without a destination.

The beauty of his truck was that it managed steep climbs and rough roads like a mountain climber scaling a hill. The problem was that it easily brought him to the edge of a cliff.

Keeping his foot on the brake, he sat in his truck overlooking the valley below for a long time. He'd once seen a fallen truck at the base of the cliff, bottom side up, windows blown out, the paint dull from scraping against rock as it rolled. At the time, he'd been young and stumped how a truck could have slipped off the edge of the cliff.

Staring out over the edge, he understood it hadn't slipped.

Easing his foot off the brake, he rolled so far to the cliff edge he couldn't see anything beneath him. Everything before him was open air, free to fall. He could slip over the edge. Could be he had inches to go, could be centimeters. One brief lift of his foot would settle the question.

Headlights on a car suddenly bounced around the cab of his truck. A small SUV took the curve of the cliffside slowly and slowed even more after it spotted him.

Connor watched it in his rearview mirror as it came inching by. Then the dark passenger window rolled down, and a guy leaned out, shouting, "Hey, you Instagram dumbshit! Back up!"

Instagram. Posing for a photo. That's what he looked like.

Jaw clenching, he put the truck in reverse. The SUV drove off, and he went home, hardly aware of it, vaguely surprised when he found himself in his condo, staring at the pristinely tidy space.

Bed. He should go to bed. Try to sleep. Get up and do it all again tomorrow. A lifetime of it.

In the morning he called out sick from work. By ten he stood at the kayak rental in the harbor, signing out a single craft.

"Done this before?" a young guy asked as he grabbed a paddle for him.

"Yeah."

"Alright, have fun then, boss."

The sky shone bright and clear, with the sun unusually warm. Sweat beaded Connor's brow as he maneuvered his craft into the water, but he wouldn't take his black fleece zip-up off. Instead, he concentrated on paddling out of the harbor in rhythmic, even strokes.

Boats rumbled slowly by him. One was filled with a bunch of twenty-somethings ready to party, and a couple girls on board leaned over the edge, catcalling him. Stoic behind his dark aviators, he continued paddling.

When his muscles ached and he was alone as far as he could see, he finally stopped. Setting the paddle on his lap, he unzipped his fleece and shrugged out of it, and then pulled out his gun from the waistband holster he'd situated at his back. He checked the chamber, disengaged the safety lock, then stared at it nestled in his palms.

Small hills of water rocked the kayak, creating an intermittent slapping sound against the plastic siding. He looked around him, at the rolling expanse of blue-grey water with the sun reflecting off the rippling caps, making it sparkle like diamonds in light. His blood and body would taint that, for a bit. Then the dark, still ocean beneath would swallow him up and wipe it all away.

It would be over soon.

Leaning far enough over the edge of the kayak so that it would tip when his body fell limp, he brought the gun to his mouth. The clank of his teeth against the metal vibrated like a gong in his head. Angling the chamber upward so that it would go unequivocally through his brain, he set his finger on the trigger.

Liv will never know what she meant to me.

The memory of her crying silently as she told him how he'd broken her heart filled his mind with stark clarity. The first time they'd really spoken after thirteen years, and that's what she wanted to share with him.

I should have told her what she meant to me. So why the fuck hadn't he when he could?

I still can.

"FUCK!" he yelled as he yanked the gun out of his mouth. Why the fuck was he doing this now? "Damn it!" He moved to put the gun back in his mouth, but…couldn't.

He yelled out, muscles straining, tendons bulging. His voice cracked and his shoulders began to shake, and he wept.

* * * *

After a while, his breathing evened out, the tension around his eyes eased.

The pistol rested in his hands, and he stared at if for a long time.

He reengaged the safety lock.

With unusual care, he replaced it in the holster and then eased his fleece back on. The paddle felt like nothing in his hands, even though the energy to hold it took almost more than he had. He dipped one side into the ocean, then the other. The kayak moved toward land. One side, then the other. One side. The other.

When he finally reached the rental dock, the same young man who saw him off came out, saying, "Man, I was starting to wonder if I'd have to call the coast guard. You've been gone for *hours*, man."

Connor struggled to get out of the craft, his old injury making him stiffer than usual from his sat position in the kayak. The guy offered him a hand, and he was forced to take it.

"Charge the extra time to my card," Connor said when he was out.

"No problem. Hope you had a good time."

"Thanks," he murmured, and walked slowly to his truck, fighting the impulse to favor his bad leg.

In his cab, he got his phone out of the center console and dialed Hutch. It went to voicemail, and Connor debated hanging up, but found himself saying, "It's Connor, I… I almost… Fuck." He hung up.

Was there a way to retrieve voice messages? What a stupid fucking message he'd just left—

His phone rang. Hutch.

"I'm free in an hour, Connor. Come to my office."

Connor was silent, relief crashing over him that he had somewhere to go, someone to talk to.

"Or we can meet for lunch. I can come to you, whatever you want."

"I'll come to your office. Tha—thank you."

"I'm really glad you called."

Connor hung up and drove to Hutch's office, watching the clock for all of the sixty minutes until he could walk through the doors.

At exactly time, he went inside. Hutch stood as he walked in, and the sight of his Costco sneakers and dad-jeans gave Connor a surprising sense of ease.

"I am really damn glad to see you," Hutch said, looking as though he wanted to shake his hand, but he hesitated as he scanned Connor's gaze.

Tipping his head in acknowledgement, Connor murmured his thanks for being seen so quickly and then sat rigidly on the sofa. It was as if an invisible straight jacket held him both tense and immobile, and he said through wooden lips, "Two hours ago, I had a gun in my mouth."

Hutch drew a slow breath, held it for a moment before slowly exhaling. "What stopped you?"

"Liv."

"Thank God for her."

Silence.

"She's…" Connor began. "She's all I've got and—" his voice broke, and he began to weep. "I don't have her. I don't have anything. Any…one." He pressed the heels of his palms to his eyes, trying to control what was happening to him. "I could die and no one would notice."

Silence.

Then Hutch said, "What about her made you stop?"

"I hurt her, and she still cares. I thought I could fix it, before I…go."

"You're alone because you've chosen to be, Connor. You don't have to be."

"I don't know how to change."

"It's a journey, that's for sure. It's getting to a place where you're okay with being hurt, because from the time your dad left you, and shortly thereafter your mom essentially did too, a deep wound was cut into you, and I don't think it healed properly. I don't think it's even scarred over.

"You've been protecting that wound since. Only Liv managed to get close to it because you were young, and you needed her. The moment you stopped needing her, you cut her off to protect that wound."

"I'd be dead right now without her," Connor intoned.

"We need to treat the wound, Connor, so it can heal. Then, you can go after her and let yourself be vulnerable with her, and not let fear of getting hurt drive you to cut her off again."

"How?"

"You need to be honest with yourself, and with me, and not run from talking about the things that hurt the most."

"My parents," he murmured.

"I'd like to start there."

CHAPTER TWELVE

Liv pulled up outside a small, single-story house that looked like it had been built in the sixties but tended well in that time, with light blue paint and pretty flowers blooming beneath the windows in white window boxes.

"I'm nervous," Liv said to Holly with a grin, making her laugh.

As they got out of the car, a woman came out of the house. Petite of stature with thin, greying hair in a perfectly shaped bob, she held her hands clasped serenely in front of her.

"Hi Julie," Liv said as they walked up, and then introduced Holly.

"Are you ready to meet the puppies?" Julie said with a smile.

She led them through a side gate that had a heart wreath hanging from it, to where seven puppies played in a little playpen on an old blanket on the grass.

"Based on your lifestyle and what you're looking for in a dog, there are three in this litter I think will be a good fit." Julie stepped into the pen, carefully balancing between the tumbling and curious puppies, and grabbed one and handed it to Holly, then two more and handed one to Liv before she climbed out holding the last one.

They all sat cross legged on the grass, and Liv's and Julie's puppies immediately squirmed to be free to play around the yard. Holly's puppy moved more cautiously and ducked its head when she pet it.

The puppy Julie had held soon trotted back over, and when Liv put out her hand, the puppy came to her. It had marbled coloring of both white and silvery black. The fur around the eyes had the darkest coloring, with a tiny strip of white bisecting it down the nose, giving the puppy an appearance of wearing an eye mask, like some superhero from early ten-cent comic books.

It climbed happily in her lap, and when she picked it up to cradle against her chest, it rest its head briefly on her shoulder.

"This one," she said.

Julie's eyes twinkled. "I'm partial to him myself."

"So it's a boy?" She assumed she'd pick a girl.

"If you have a name picked out, I'll start calling him that, so he'll know it by the time he goes home with you."

Holly cast Liv a teasing glance. "In keeping with your life coach, Jane, there's Austen, Willoughby, Knightly, or Bingly."

"To name just a few," Liv replied with a smile, still looking at her puppy who looked back at her with his little superhero mask. "I think…Leo."

"You're stepping outside a Jane Austen novel? Well this is a new you. I like it. Leo, as in Leonardo DaVinci?"

"As in Leonardo Ninja Turtle. It's his little superhero mask."

Julie chuckled. "Perfect. Leo it is."

"I'm partial to the one you handed me," Holly announced. Her little puppy was mostly white with a strip of silver down its back. It was certainly on the timid side, not straying far from them and when the other puppy started to play rough, it ran back to Julie.

"Do you have a name for her?" Julie said.

"How about Jane Austen?" Liv said.

Holly rolled her eyes. "I'd picked out the name Winston for a boy, but I couldn't think of a girl."

"Winnifred is in the same vein," Liv said. "Call her Winnie?"

"Oh, I like that. Leo and Winnie. We've named our kids."

Laughing, Liv snuck in a quick kiss to the top of Leo's head before he bounded off to play again, and she grabbed her camera, taking photos and recording videos. A couple times she looked at

Holly with a huge grin over the puppy antics, only to find her on the phone, texting constantly.

"Holly."

She glanced up. Guilt, and something like defiance flashed in her gaze. "I'm sorry, I have a client I need to meet. A bit of an emergency, I'm afraid."

"Oh dear," Julie said. "I hope everything's okay."

"Me too," Holly said as she stood.

They rounded up the puppies and Liv gave Leo one last kiss before handing him back to Julie.

In the car, Liv said, "We were going to have lunch."

"I know, I'm sorry."

"Is it really an emergency?"

"Yeah. Yes. I wouldn't—it's an emergency, Liv."

"With a client."

"*Yes!*"

Liv glanced at her, eyebrows near her hairline.

Holly immediately apologized. "That was…" she sighed. "Sorry. I've been under a lot of pressure. Sorry."

"When do you think you'll be under less pressure?"

Holly set her gaze out the side window. "I don't know," she muttered.

Liv wanted to press, but Holly radiated *don't press* so she held her tongue. As she dropped her off, Holly promised to call later. Afterward, Liv drove to her parent's house.

Knocking as she unlocked the door, she called out loudly, "Mom! Dad!"

Once, shortly after she moved into her own place, she'd let herself in without giving them any warning, and she'd discovered them frantically covering themselves. It had been profoundly awkward in the moment, funny as hell in retrospect.

"In here!" her mom, Mary, called from the den.

As Liv walked in, eager to talk about Leo, Mary looked her over and said, "Something happen with Connor?"

Liv instantly felt an inner coiling, and Mary winced, watching her. "I'm so sorry, sweetie. You had a look like something happened and so I assumed. I shouldn't have—"

"No, you shouldn't," her dad, Cal interrupted. He stood from the sofa and gave Liv a kiss.

Hugging him in return, Liv enjoyed his familiar scent of woodsy cologne and laundry detergent. He'd always had a beard, and as he grew older, it grew whiter. Liv imagined it becoming Santa-like someday, especially as he grew a little thicker in the middle. Even still, both parents had long stayed fit, but especially her mother. Always slim as Liv would likely be, she kept her now dyed-blond hair in a cute pixie cut and somehow unfailingly looked twenty years younger than she was.

"I have a lot of anger too, you know," Mary said, walking over. "And I want to have a word with him. Many words."

Liv sighed and released her dad, regretting—again—having told them about Connor's sudden return. In the last couple weeks since she'd told them, it had caused arguments she hadn't expected, with Mary wanting every detail that Liv wouldn't give.

"My relationship with Connor was between him and I," Liv had said the first time they argued. Which had incensed Mary, causing her to say how Connor's effect on Liv affected her because Liv was *her daughter*, and *furthermore!* they'd treated Connor like a son, and his behavior had wounded her own feelings.

In all the years since he disappeared, they hadn't spoken much of him. Liv supposed she shouldn't be surprised that all the things they'd never said would need to be said now; his return making the examination of the wound acceptable.

"Well, Mom," Liv said now, "I haven't seen him in a couple months, so I think it's safe to say he's out of my life again, but he works for the city PD in homicide. You can call him there and tell him everything you need to."

"Don't be flip, I'm still your mother."

"I'm not being disrespectful. I'm giving you the tools to take care of this need you have."

"Alright, enough," Cal said as Mary's eyes went wide with increasing anger. "She's not wrong, Mary. And it's damned ridiculous for there to be fighting in this house over that boy, when we never did before."

"I'm not fighting over Connor," Mary said, "I'm fighting over Liv's silence on a matter that affected us all."

"Me most of all, Mom. *Me* most."

"That doesn't—"

"He still knows where you live, so if you were as a part of this as you think you are, he could come here and talk to you. But he didn't! He came to me!"

"I don't care how old you are, don't take that tone—"

"Oh my god, Mom—"

"*Stop interrupting me!*"

"ENOUGH!" Cal shouted. "No more fighting over this!"

"I'm not—" Liv squeezed her temples and consciously worked to calm her tone. "I came here to talk about my puppy."

"What?" Mary said sharply.

"I told you I was getting one."

Mary made a visible effort to calm down. "You said you were thinking about it," she said in her normal voice.

"I guess all this conflict hasn't been conducive to talking about puppies."

"I can't believe you didn't tell me. We haven't *only* been fighting."

Liv sighed and looked at her dad. "I picked a boy. I'm going to name him Leo."

"That's great, honey."

"Do you have a picture?" Mary asked.

Liv didn't want to show her, afraid the anger and tension would shade the experience.

"I was so busy holding the puppies…" Misleading wasn't great, but it sat better than outright lying. "I can ask Holly if she grabbed some and text them to you."

"Is Holly still getting a dog?" Mary said, with a look Liv hated that settled somewhere between *how foolish* and *what could she be thinking?*

The unhelpful urge to tell her mom that she couldn't stand her right now had her taking a fiery breath to burn it all down. "I have to go," came out crisply instead. Returning to her dad, she said, "I've got to buy some food for a cause that I care about. Have any spare blankets I could donate?"

"I'll look for some and let you know," Mary answered.

Planting a quick kiss on her Dad's cheek, Liv turned to her mom with a fake smile, identical to the one she gave Liv, and promised to talk to her later. Then she strode from the house, closing the door just a little harder than she needed to.

As her parents watched her go, Mary said, "How is it—how—that *now* we're going through the pubescent fighting years I'd counted us so fortunate to have missed fifteen years ago?"

Cal sighed. "I wish you'd drop the Connor thing, honey."

She rounded on him, eyes outraged again. "How could I drop it?"

"For the sake of the family, that's how."

"You know what he cost her. What he cost *us*."

"Mary," he began with resignation, already regretting having said a damn thing. He knew better.

"We'd have *grandkids* by now if that—if he hadn't *destroyed her heart!*" Tears formed in her eyes, giving them a glassy glow. "Now she's talking about being alone for the rest of her life and being a—just having…*pets*."

"There's nothing wrong with that."

"There is when that's not what she ever wanted! She wanted a family!"

"It's not like she's out of time, honey." His eyes shifted toward the den, at the big screen flashing a football game about to start.

"*Cal.*"

"What? I'm not watching it!"

Throwing her hands up, she stomped away, and Cal just about slumped with relief. If this mess continued, he'd hunt Connor down himself and force him to do something to clean it up.

CHAPTER THIRTEEN

Connor went to counseling every single day that Hutch would see him. Like the soldier he was, he focused on the task of repairing himself with the singlemindedness of a life-or-death mission. Because for him, it was.

The simple act of speaking out loud to another person about what happened in his life was harder than it fucking should be. Each time, it felt like he had to take a crowbar to his soul and rip simple words out of himself.

He...cried. Again. Several times. And it made him feel shame. If his teammates could see him now. Yet that was part of it, wasn't it? He didn't have a team any longer. He didn't have anyone because he was too fucking scared to. Apparently. Least that's what Hutch said, and Hutch damn well knew more than he did about his head.

Weeks and weeks of this.

"When are you going to take time off from me, Hutch?" Connor said, lips quirked in a wry half-smile. "What's it been now, two months?"

Hutch's lips curved. "You've worked hard, Connor. Really hard. I've never seen someone work so hard on themselves. I can see the difference in you with what you're doing. Can you see it?"

He didn't want to talk about it. But that was always his first thought, the next: why else was he here?

"I—" he exhaled. "I do, but I still keep wondering when I'll be better."

"What does better look like to you?"

"When I can feel in control of myself again. Like I did in the army, when I had my shit together."

"When you had purpose, a goal, a community that looked out for you and cared about where you were each day. That's what I hear when you say that."

The summary made Connor realize he didn't have a single one of those things.

"If that's what I need to keep from feeling like killing myself is a better option, how do I get there?" he said quietly.

Hutch leaned forward, resting his elbows on his splayed knees, and clasping his hands. "Come play basketball with me and the guys tomorrow."

Connor opened his mouth to decline as he always did, but Hutch added, "And one gal. She's new tomorrow too, so you wouldn't be in the spotlight. I know she'd appreciate not being in the spotlight either. Well, less of a spotlight," he amended.

A woman, a vet, playing basketball with that bunch he'd seen the one time he'd driven by. "Are you sure she plays?"

"She liked to play in the downtime in Afghanistan."

"Is she good?"

"I don't know. We'll find out tomorrow."

Connor considered, he wouldn't be the only new one there they'd wonder about, contemplating how fucked up he was to be there.

That he was considering going made him realize he'd continuously refused because he didn't want to be the only new one. An old memory of a bunch of girls asking each other to go to the bathroom so they wouldn't have to go alone popped in his mind. He was just like that. Not a proud moment. Didn't matter. One of the ways he knew his sessions with Hutch were working was his ability to notice the truth about himself. He didn't want to do this alone. The vet who'd had the courage to do it first, he'd thank her later.

"Alright, tomorrow, I'll see you there."

Hutch showed zero reaction, but Connor still felt certain he was proud of him or something. A feeling of goodness came in response, and he wished he could ask to be sure. How fucking childish was that?

As if he knew what he was thinking, Hutch said, "The way you remember yourself in the army was with an impenetrable shield on your emotions, but that wasn't having your stuff together, that was you hardly living."

"I feel like a child right now, Hutch. Crying. Needing my hand held. Approval."

"That's great you recognize all that," he said with genuine sincerity. "Well, here's the thing, we all need connection, a lot of us have it and get the hand holding and approval and time to cry all our lives from those connections. You didn't," he said simply. "And you're not alone, there's many people who haven't. That's what some of this work is about. Understanding what we've been missing, accepting all that missing it means, which helps move past the anger into learning how to make successful choices in life and relationships. Notice I said successful, and not painless. There's always pain in relationships, no escaping that, but it should be that the pain isn't greater than what the relationship gives you."

"The only pain in my relationship with Liv was what I caused. She never hurt me. Ever."

Hutch sat quiet for a long while, before he finally said, "I don't know if she feels the pain was greater than the love you gave her. Someday, it is my hope to see you both in here to talk about it."

Connor jerked a little at the thought. "Why would she come in here with me?"

"You've said she's a psychologist. She'll come."

"She wouldn't need to. She can figure this shit out all on her own."

Hutch chuckled. "Everyone needs a good counseling from time to time. No one is so together that they don't need counsel, or advice, or an impartial ear. Used to be people lived in villages where everyone knew each other and there were elders guiding the community, now most people don't know their neighbors, lost touch with their friends and hardly speak to their families about things that matter. That disparity is where I come in. I wish all people would seek counseling because *we all need it.*"

"That's a good pitch," Connor murmured.

Hutch grinned. "Maybe the next time you see her, you could ask her to come."

"Hell no!" Connor near exploded, making Hutch laugh outright.

"Too soon," Hutch said, still laughing.

The last thing Connor could imagine doing if he ever saw Liv again was asking her to go to counseling. And he really wanted to see her again. Just see her. It had been almost four months since the last time. In the last couple weeks especially, staying away had felt near impossible, to the point he'd driven by her street—not her house, he hadn't broken that line he'd set—but he'd driven by her street, hoping to see her getting her mail, or pulling her trash bins out. Something.

The timer on Connor's phone pinged. "Time's up." He stood. "See you tomorrow."

Hutch tipped his head. "You're doing good, Connor."

* * * *

Late the next morning, Connor got a call to investigate a scene, due to his background in narcotics.

He gave Fernando the rundown, and said, "They're waiting on us."

"I just knew they were gonna use your junkie status as an excuse to throw us these," Fernando drawled. He'd gained a few over the last couple months, using his belt to try to hide the fact his top button now lived in the undone position. Connor figured he'd wait for the right time to point out it didn't work.

"What status has gotten you assignments?" Cases were doled out to those who had specialized knowledge, yet so far, their cases hadn't had any discerning similarities.

"Jack of all trades, master of exactly none. I get the: 'no one specializes so give it to Fernando' files. Now that I'm partnered with an ex narcotic vet—not in that order—I'll be in on all the

fun special stuff with very little to offer." His lips pursed and he
clasped his jaw in the universal *thinking man* pose. "Am I getting
pushed out by the young hot stuff?"

"Only time will tell."

Fernando looked to the heavens. "Alright, let's check this out
and hope to catch an early lunch."

They met the first responding detectives at the crime scene. It
was gruesome, yet not unfamiliar to Connor. The filth inside the
dilapidated house, the stained yellow curtains drawn to block out
the light, leaving only a depressing low-glow. Clothes, trash,
needles littered the floor, along with forgotten food, tipped over
beer cans, vomit in some places.

Two bodies lay slumped over a chipped and worn wood table,
needles still in their arms.

"Oh jeez the smell," Fernando said on a choked breath.

"Never gets old," Connor said.

"Can't believe you did this shit for years."

"It's what lead me to you, sweetheart."

"I'd laugh, but I'd have to breathe more."

Amused, because that's what you had to be to get through the
shit pile they dealt in, Connor examined the faces of the deceased
and the baggies spread on the table, looking for identifiable
marks.

"I recognize this guy," Connor said after a moment. "The
woman looks familiar but I'm not sure. He dealt, but not a big
player. He wasn't known as a junkie, so this," Connor gestured to
the couple, "doesn't fit. Unless he recently went downhill, could
be this batch is either a fuckup or he was poisoned by a
competitor."

If it was a competitor, they would need to get a handle on the
perp quickly. Coming in this strong stood as a warning.

They spent a while going through the house, and when it was
over, they both wanted to head back to the station to shower and
wash away the stink that permeated their clothes.

Lunch came and went with Connor following up on
information with the narcotics division.

At end-time, Connor threw a hand up in goodbye, and Fernando called, "You're positively chipper after the day we've had. I feel like I need to go home and sing myself a lullaby."

Connor walked out the door singing Twinkle Twinkle Little Star.

Fernando hollered after him, "And a weighted security blanket! Gonna need that too."

At the basketball court, he found Hutch already there, doing a slow warm up. Jogging over, he lifted a hand when Hutch spotted him and called out a greeting.

There were a handful of guys already there, all in long shorts and t-shirts, all with varying degrees of fitness. Two of the guys had permanent injuries, the one he'd seen before missing a hand, and another with scars running the side of his face and a mutilated ear. Bomb blast, probably.

Hutch introduced everyone, each said their rank and division, and then they sorted the team. It was all so ordinary as to be unremarkable. He couldn't believe he'd resisted this.

A woman of slightly above average height with dark hair pulled into a slicked back ponytail walked onto the court. She wore burgundy joggers and an oversized black tee, and firmly shook their hands with a direct gaze when Hutch introduced her.

"Vanessa, this is Connor's first time to the group as well," Hutch said.

Her dark eyes settled on him, and she said, "Now I know who to beat."

Connor snorted with amusement, feeling a sense of familiarity with her mannerisms and shit-talking.

They started playing, and she was good. They all were. Connor felt rusty and Vanessa was all over him, stealing the ball from him constantly and slipping around him easily when he tried to block her.

Half hour in and he finally started playing how he remembered, about as good as everyone else, though the guy missing a hand was undeniably the best. Made Connor feel damn proud because he was Army too. Of course it was his brother-in-arms who took a handicap and shut it the fuck down.

As the game came to its end, with Vanessa's team winning, she dead-stared Connor and said, "You've been beat, son."

"Rusty this week. Worry about next week."

Some chuckled and then they wandered over to a little Mexican restaurant that had Diego Rivera and Frida Kahlo art glued to the walls like wallpaper.

They sat around a long table, and the conversation was largely casual, talking about sports, and what some of the other guys' kids were keeping them busy with on the weekend. There was little of the 'getting to know you' chit-chat, other than what kind of jobs they each had. Vanessa seemed to settle in easily with everyone, talking, joking and laughing. Instead of the heart-to-hearts and the Here's Why I'm Fucked Up group therapy he'd expected, it was like being with a bunch of soldiers during downtime.

When the evening ended, Connor felt good, in a way he hadn't felt in years. He thought about that as he drove by Liv's street, and saw her garage open as she loaded some bags into her car.

Jerking hard on his steering wheel, he turned sharp enough onto her street his tires screeched briefly, making her look. With his headlights in her face, she couldn't possibly see him—if she'd ever noticed what kind of truck he drove anyway—but he didn't stop to rethink what he was doing. Just pulled right up to her house and got out of his truck.

"Connor?" she said blankly.

As he approached, he admired how she looked in black leggings and a fitted wrap around top that made her appear like a ballerina just home from practice. Her hair was even twisted into a bun atop her head, and he said with a half-smile, "All that's missing is a tutu."

Fire snapped in her eyes. She slammed the trunk and then strode into her house.

She didn't say he couldn't follow.

Following her, they collided just as he stepped through the door.

"What are you doing?" she demanded.

"You didn't say anything."

"So you took that as an invitation to come inside?"

"It wasn't?" He pasted on an open, innocent expression.

Reaching around him, she pressed the button to close the garage, and then went back into her house.

Since she'd just closed them in, he'd take that as a definitive invitation.

The door to the garage fed right into her kitchen where she filled a kettle with water and got out two cups. She didn't ask if he wanted tea, just quietly set about making it, and so he quietly explored her living space.

She had a lot of plants and books on her shelves, and black and white framed pictures on her walls. Some were of places: cathedrals, trees, an elephant. The rest were people, with one of her and a friend in front of the Eiffel Tower, one of her family, and one of her graduating university with both her parents and her uncle Mark there. Connor stayed with that picture a long while.

Liv noticed.

Bringing the two cups with her, she handed him one, saying, "When's the last time you spoke to Mark?"

"Thank you," he murmured as he took it. "About a year."

Liv inwardly winced. She'd never quite come to terms with her feelings about Mark's continued friendship with Connor. A part of her felt that family loyalty should dictate he not be friendly with the guy who'd shattered her. Yet Uncle Mark had the ability to compartmentalize, just as Connor did, and so she understood he didn't see things that way.

"You look like you just got back from ballet class," Connor said turning to her.

"Pilates actually." Liv put space between them and sat on the sofa. "So that's what you meant with the tutu."

Lips curving, he sat in the same chair facing her as the last time. "It's almost like high school with assigned seating," he joked.

"Why are you here?" She didn't want to be charmed by his lazy smile.

"I just finished playing basketball at the pier and happened to drive by and see you. Thought I'd drop in and say hi."

"So when you said you wanted to be friends again, this is what you meant?"

He took a drink of his tea, eyes locked on her the whole time. "I thought you said no friendship."

"It's been four months."

"You noticed."

The low burn on her temper lit again. "Of course I noticed. I've always noticed. I will probably *always* notice. And when you come here saying you want to be friends, after ignoring everything else I've ever told you, you'll forgive me if I'm a little surprised you didn't decide to ignore that too."

"I can forgive you."

Fiery fury beamed out of her eyes, she could feel it torching him, and he chuckled looking at her. "So easy to rile, Liv."

"This isn't funny to me." Dead serious.

After a moment he sighed, "I know. I'm sorry. I'm trying to find my way in this." He scraped his hand along the buzzed side of his head. "I have this…when I'm with you it's just like before, for me, you know? When we were kids, and everything was so easy with you. So comfortable and, right. But there's a lot of pain I caused you, I understand that, and I want to help you come to terms with it."

"What?"

"Is that the wrong way to say it? Come to peace with it? I don't know. I just want to fix it."

Her lips parted slightly.

"Do you want to hit me?" he said suddenly.

"Hit you?"

"Yeah, it's something Hu—I just learned about. Called bio..bioenergy I think, where you think about what's bothering you and hit things. Maybe it will work even better if you can hit the thing that's bothering you."

"That would be abuse, Connor."

"Oh. Yeah. Right."

Unbidden, a laugh rose, slipping out, and he looked at her with such surprise, it grew to a full belly laugh. A bashful smile settled on his face as he watched her, and it made him look so ridiculously appealing that she had to look away.

"Where did you learn about bioenergetic therapy?" she managed finally, wiping moisture from under her eyes.

He seemed to grow real still, and then slowly lowered his mug to rest on his knee. "I've, ah, been going to, ah, therapy."

"You have?" Now her genuine surprise. "That's wonderful."

He stared intently, mutely, but just when the staring silence started to get awkward, he said, "It's good. I needed to. I was..."

"Was...what?"

"Glad. Just, I'm glad to be doing it."

"Good. I'm really happy for you." Actually, she was reeling, imagining him doing something like that, because she knew how he had been about anything psychology related. Even as a teen he'd mocked it and shut down any attempt she'd made to talk about what his stepdad had done, even though she'd *seen* him get hit, and had cleaned him up afterward.

"That's where I've been," he said, "since I saw you last. I needed—wanted to, to get my shit, ah, *stuff* together."

Gazing into his hazel eyes, her lips gently curved. "That's really great. You know what an advocate I am for that."

"Well yeah, since we were kids, you've been."

She wasn't sure what else to say, especially with how nervous he appeared, his eyes darting in between long protracted stares. It occurred to her that if he'd been in therapy a few months, perhaps he was here because of that. "Is there something you need from me?"

"Forgiveness."

Everything went quiet in her mind, and she unconsciously sat straighter. "Are you recovering from addiction?"

His gaze turned blank and then he jerked as if in shock. "No. Why?" Then, "Oh, the steps, right? Ask forgiveness." Another bashful smile. "I didn't realize my being here like this would make you think that, but I can see it."

"Forgiveness for what?"

"Come on, Liv."

"I don't know what you want forgiveness for."

"I said before I'm sorry for hurting you."

"Hurting me how?"

"Come on," he said again with a half roll of his eyes.

"Truly, I don't know exactly what you want me to forgive," she said carefully.

The muscle in his jaw flexed. "You want to make this hard on me, is that it?"

"No, I don't. I'm being genuine." Trying to hide how vulnerable she felt, her gaze dropped. "Maybe you feel sorry for making me think things were one way when they were another. Maybe you feel sorry for changing your mind and not telling me." She spread her hands, her eyes drawing back to his. "I don't know what exactly you feel sorry for. And it matters, to me, to know."

His jaw flexed again. "Every single thing from the moment I left your side, thirteen years ago, I'm sorry about."

Desperately, *desperately,* she wanted to ask him what *exactly* happened, but fear of hearing rejection kept her quiet.

"You said your life wasn't how you imagined it because of me. It's worse, basically," he said quietly. "That I changed you. I don't expect that you can forgive me, but I can ask for it. I never wanted to hurt you. My mind—heart—doesn't work right. I'm sorry I messed you up because of it."

God, she didn't want to cry, but nothing could stop the tears that seeped into the corners of her eyes, and Connor didn't look away from her, clearly seeing her reaction. The urge to try to hide it, to be aloof and unaffected prodded her, but she knew hiding would only hurt her more in the end.

"Thank you—"

"Don't *thank me*—"

"Let me finish, please," she interrupted as well, raising her chin. "No matter where my life is at right now, I wouldn't change anything leading up to that day you left. And I couldn't have the one without the other."

"So the pain didn't outweigh the good times?"

Her brow rippled, sure he was getting at something. Choosing her words more carefully, she said, "I wasn't finished saying what I wanted to say. I know what you went through when we were kids. In hindsight it's not surprising what happened after you left. Having you here, understanding what you've had to do to get here, I do thank you for doing it. It's giving me some…it's helping."

He studied her for a long moment, his expression almost shrewd. "Do you ever just respond without choosing each word like a counselor?"

The remark reminded her of Greg's parting shots along the same line and she retorted, "Without acting like I know things about people and relationships, you mean?"

"I want a *real* response from you, Liv."

"It is real!"

"It's calculated."

"I have boundaries now, Connor. It's as real as I can be with you because anything more is too much for me."

Something gleamed in his gaze as if somehow her response satisfied him, and he said, "Be my friend again."

She groaned.

"Be my friend again, Liv."

"I don't want to," she mumbled.

"C'mon, Lucky."

Her startled gaze locked on his, and he grinned. "Has anyone called you lucky since you've been with me?"

Heat suffused her cheeks. She hurriedly took refuge in her cup, glad the mug was oversized so that it hid almost her entire face as she pretended to sip.

"C'mon, baby—"

Her head jerked up. "*Don't* call me baby. If we're going to be friends, it has to stay—you can't call me what you did when we were…" she trailed off at his triumphant expression.

"I'll keep it to Lucky then," he said, his gaze so warm she had to look away. "Now that we're friends again, we should snuggle to commemorate the event."

A surprised laugh slipped out with the memory of the time he'd invited her to snuggle, after he'd been so sick she'd had to bring him food. "You're not at death's door," she reminded him.

"That's what it will take? Noted." He set his cup on the coffee table and then rubbed his hands together. "For the first order of friendship commemoration business, what shall it be, a movie? Dinner? Dinner and a movie?"

It was too date-like. If she was going to do this, she had to keep it under the friend umbrella. Shopping popped in her mind, but then she remembered the time in high school when they were friends and she'd gotten him to go shopping for a homecoming dress with her. He'd been so sweet and playful that she'd been utterly infatuated, and she realized she couldn't even put shopping under the friend umbrella. Least not for a while. This was going to be difficult.

"My parents," she blurted, suddenly remembering they played a part in this as well.

Instantly, his expression shuttered. "I'll go there, on my own."

She debated warning him about her mom, but then decided it was for him to figure out. Giving a brief nod, she said, "I remember how good you were with Darcy."

"Your old dog?"

"I'm getting a puppy soon, so I need stuff. Maybe we could…" she trailed off, thinking that was pretty much shopping, and hadn't she just reminded herself that wasn't a good idea? But Connor jumped on it.

"We could go to the pet store and get supplies. Figure out a couple good walking routes too."

"That's a good idea. I hadn't thought of that."

He nodded. "When? Tomorrow?"

"I have karate tomorrow." The last class of the session, thank God.

"You?" His lips quirked. "I wouldn't have guessed."

She smiled wryly. "It's part of my 'protect myself' campaign."

"I could teach you to shoot."

She eyed him sitting there, strong and still, aware he'd been a very effective special ops soldier, according to her uncle. "That might be the perfect friendship starter."

A faint smile ghosted over his face. "We've already started. So, dogs and shooting. I can't Thursday, what about Friday?" She shook her head and he sighed. "Saturday?"

Liv agreed and then stood, taking their empty cups to the kitchen. She wanted him to leave now, needed some space to sort out what just happened and how to manage what would come with it.

Connor took out his phone and started typing. "What's your number?"

She cringed, and he grinned at it.

"Do you really need my number?"

"Need."

She sighed long and deep.

"I am completely comfortable dragging you kicking and screaming into this friendship, Lucky." He wandered over to the kitchen. "Just a few little numbers," he said in a cajoling tone. "I promise I'll leave after."

His insight into how she felt struck something within her. Fear perhaps. "Connor, I don't understand why you want this, but… Don't mess with me this time around."

"I won't. I promise."

Liv thought of the necklace she'd given back to him, the promise he'd broken, and it must have shown on her face because she noticed him watching her, noticed the muscle in his jaw flex before his expression turned obstinate. "Number?"

CHAPTER FOURTEEN

Two days later, he texted. Since she hadn't asked for his number, all that came through was an unknown one, and the words: *Looking for Lucky Legs.*

"Nope." She closed the text window.

She finished making dinner, ate, cleaned, and then sat on the sofa with a cup of steaming tea in one hand and her phone with the text lit up in the other.

Sip.

She didn't have to respond. She didn't owe it to him.

She just…wasn't ready.

Using the off button felt appropriate, definitive, and she pressed it, but when the screen asked, *Power Off?* she stopped. Being a woman alone with her phone off wasn't smart.

Being a woman alone shouldn't be risky. She made a face. *Shout it to the centuries, Liv, and see what it changes.*

Sigh. Sip.

Tucking the phone under a cushion, she read a book until bedtime.

In the morning, as she drove to work, her phone rang. She pressed the screen to decline the call but accidentally hit 'accept'.

"*Shiiii,*" she breathed through her cringe.

"Lucky?"

"Hi Connor." Still cringing.

"You didn't answer my text yesterday."

Well, out of the fire, into the burning hot molten scorching volcano. "I realized I forgot to give you the wrong number, so I thought I'd just make you think I did instead."

A low, rumbling chuckle. "The mean streak makes an appearance."

"Compliments of the chef." Liv glanced at the egg wrap she'd set in a cup holder that she hadn't eaten yet. "I've got to go."

"Promise you'll answer my text before you do."

"I don't want to."

"Do it anyway." At her silence, he said, "I'll find a variety of ways to bug you until you do."

She made a face. "A plethora."

"What you said."

"Okay," she capitulated. "Okay, okay, I'll *respond*."

"That's a good Lucky."

"Go away."

She hung up on his chuckle, an undeniable curve to her lips. *How is this happening again?*

Morosely, she ate the egg-wrap and washed it down with hot coffee.

"Call Holly," she told the car.

"This is early," Holly answered.

"I just spoke to Connor. We're hanging out tomorrow."

"Are you sure you're okay to do that?"

"Well, I keep thinking of a freight train at high speed that sees a solid wall and doesn't slow down."

"That's concerning."

She sounded distracted, the energy in her voice low. "Alright, Holls, what's going on?"

"I'm busy, that's all." And instantly defensive.

"Did something happen with your coworker?"

"For fuck's sake, Liv—

"Whoa—"

"Don't call me first thing in the morning with this. Go have fun with your high school boyfriend and tell me *all* about it later." *Click.*

Liv parked outside her office and just sat there. Talk about a mean streak. Maybe she should call her mom just to round things out. "My mom isn't mean," she said dutifully, opening her door. She was just really good at making Liv feel crappy lately.

Trudging to her office, lost in thought, she didn't notice the person hiding behind the dried-up fountain until she walked past them. They wore a dark cap, and a big coat. Not one single discerning feature was visible.

"Dr. Jones." The voice was gravelly and could easily be taken for a man or a woman's.

"Can I help you?" Feeling jumpy inside, Liv nevertheless looked calmly at the person who kept their head dropped low.

"You need to help Jeremy." Mrs. Olawale just barely lifted her head to peek under the rim of the ballcap. "I don't know how to help him. I need to get him out of there, but I don't know how."

"Mrs. Olawale, please come inside—"

"No." She backed up as if afraid Liv would try to grab her and force her inside.

Liv didn't move, careful not to spook her. "I believe if you told the detectives all you know—"

"No."

"About who *would* hurt your husband—"

Shaking her head now, backing away even more, she said, "I can't do that," and then turned and hurried away.

Finishing the trudge to her office, she muttered, "That went well," as she opened the door.

"What did?" Patrick said from behind his desk, greeting her with a smile while his thistle-print collared shirt strained at the buttons across his chest. He'd gotten a haircut, his brown hair trimmed short at the sides, longer on top. He looked very Clark-Kent-about-to-go-Superman.

"Nice," Liv said, gesturing around her head.

"The barber said I should try a cut instead of my typical buzz." He grinned. "I was feeling adventurous."

Liv returned the smile, and he asked again what went well.

"Jeremy's mom." She told him what happened. "The more time passes, the harder it will be for Jeremy. I can't rush things with her, but then this is urgent."

Her phone beeped and she saw it was her mom, reminding her in a vaguely snarky way to bring the Tupperware she'd borrowed when she came for dinner that night. "Nothing is going well these days."

"You should come to the gym with me. Sometimes you've got to work out your troubles with some good old fashioned muscle work."

"I don't lift weights, I look at them."

"You should try it, boss."

"If things get desperate, I'll take you up on it. But I may be sobbing as I curl my bicep."

"Whatever it takes, boss."

Liv half laughed. "Glad you're here, Patrick."

"Always glad to be here."

He was like a shot of happy espresso and as she closed the door to her personal office to prepare for the patients she had coming in, she appreciated the affect his goodness had on her. Not a single mean streak in him.

Opening her email, Liv was relieved to see a message from Lea Nonme. Little was written, just names of foods and books. She replied to the email, "I'll need an address." How long it would take to get a response was anyone's guess.

Her schedule was busier than usual, but several times throughout the day she thought about texting Connor. She had to, because she'd promised. But… It wasn't until the last patient left that she finally took out her phone.

She'd reply with what time to meet for their 'friends day'. She needed to pick a time that was after breakfast and well before any possibility of dinner. Breakfast had an air of familiarity to it, while dinner was too intimate. Lunch felt the most casual.

Meet at 10am?

He immediately responded, as if his fingers had been poised over his phone waiting for her.

9

I don't want to
meet at 9.

9:30?

I like 10

10 isn't lucky. 9
is lucky. 7 is the
luckiest.

10

Bad luck for 10
years.

11am then.

Pick you up at 10

Liv found herself smiling even as the image of a freight train and a block wall flashed through her mind.

The smile dropped. Closing up her office, she went home to get the Tupperware. Taking time to change, she thought about what she'd wear for her friendly day with Connor.

God, what was she doing? She couldn't be 'friends' with him. This was so risky. But she didn't want it to be. She wanted to be able to take whatever came with him without it altering her as it had before. The only way that could happen is if she put herself out there.

Let her see what he was going to do. Let him leave her again. Let her live it with the strength she had now. Surely experiencing him with her hard-won strength would give her the perspective she wanted but that she'd not yet been able to fully achieve. She'd had glimpses of it, but whenever she'd find a sense of peace and release, it only lasted a short while.

"Alright, I've got to go."

When she got her puppy, it was going to be nice having him there to say that to, instead of no one which every so often made her feel more alone than she ever wanted to be.

Walking to her parent's house, she let herself in with a loud, "I'm here!"

"In the kitchen," at the same time as, "Watchin' a game," came back.

No matter the state of her relationship with her parents, their routine was always a welcome comfort.

"Did you bring the Tupperware?" Mary called out, peeling garlic.

Liv jangled the bag, set it on the newly painted kitchen table, and grabbed a knife to slice the multicolored sweet peppers her mom had laid out beside her. They were nearly shoulder to shoulder as they worked.

"Did you have a good day?" Mary said.

"Yeah, it was alright."

"Anything new with Holly?"

"I don't know. I think maybe she's crossed a line with her coworker."

Mary turned to her, brows drawn. "She cheated?"

"I don't know for sure, but whatever she's doing it isn't good. She hung up on me when I asked her outright."

Shaking her head, the soft compassion Liv loved about her mom showed in her expression. "Poor Jake. Poor them as a family. That poor puppy if she gets it."

"Why are you so against her getting a puppy?"

"You know how I feel about cheaters." The lip-curled, judge-y part that she didn't love made a swift appearance. "Cheaters—"

"I don't know if she has actually cheated, but even if she has, no one is perfect, and it's not like Jake has done much of anything to keep a connection with his wife. He's not completely blameless in their situation because the number one thing he does in their relationship, is ignore her."

"I appreciate your loyalty to Holly, and you must know I feel it too, I love her like my daughter's best friend."

Liv snorted, Mary continued, "She's been acting irresponsibly for a while. Bringing a puppy into your family is a responsibility, and here she's bringing one into a family that she's breaking apart. It's a terrible idea. You should tell the breeder."

"Yeah, let me go tell on my best friend." Liv rolled her eyes. "Plus, who knows how the breeder will start to look at me if my best friend who I'm having puppy kids with is cheating on her husband and is too irresponsible to have a puppy child."

"Did you hear how bad that sounds?"

"When I say it like you do, it sounds terrible."

"I'm glad we're agreed."

Liv laughed. "I don't say it like you do!"

"Well you should, because it's the truth."

"Truth missing compassion and understanding. All people are flawed, all people make mistakes. I think what she's doing is terrible, but I don't think it's our place to judge her."

"I feel pretty comfortable judging a cheater for being a cheater. I'd bet you'd feel pretty comfortable too if it was you getting cheated on."

Liv's posture minutely slumped as she carefully seeded a bright orange pepper. "If I judge her, I lose my friend. We'll get together, pretending to be what we were when we both know that we're not. I don't want to lose my best friend. Really, my only friend."

Mary looked subtly at her. "Some of my friends at my game night are starting to bring their daughters. You could come with me, meet some of them, maybe you'll make a new friend."

"I hate playing Bunco."

"But maybe you won't hate the people that do."

"But they all have kids, right? And they're playing Bunco to get away for a while, right?"

"That doesn't matter."

"Of course it does. We'll have nothing in common. They'll be talking about their babies and husbands driving them nuts and the guilt and pressure they feel, especially balancing work and motherhood—does it sound like I've heard this before, Mom?"

"I know, you've got clients..."

"So I *know* how important it is to find someone in a similar lane as you. Most people have conflicting responsibilities, but not me. I'm a single professional, and getting a dog is the biggest commitment I'll have made in over a decade."

They chopped in silence. After a while, Mary said, "Maybe once you get this puppy, you'll enjoy having a sweet little creature to care for so much that you'll have a baby."

Liv's chopping froze. "Have a baby."

"I know. All on your own. But we'll be here to help."

Chopping resumed.

"Who should I get to be the father?" Now was *definitely* not the right time to mention Connor was coming to her house in the morning.

"I..." Mary shrugged with a beautiful, pink-in-the-apples-of-her-cheeks, smile. "I'm throwing it out there. It may not be the most ideal, but my grandbaby will never lack for love."

"I can't believe you want me to have a child out of wedlock, and out a baby-daddy. My prepubescent self is stunned I tell you. Stunned."

"Greg could have been your baby-daddy."

"I wouldn't want to be tied to him for the rest of my life." She'd never mentioned what he'd said, but the memory of it still grated.

"My friend, Becky's son is such a great guy. Smart, respectful, good looking. Shame I can't just ask for some of his DNA."

"Didn't he just become an adult?"

"He's nineteen."

"Ewwww, Mom! Just, ew! You want a teenager to be my sperm-donor. That is so inappropriate, and also what is happening to you?"

Mary laughed, her head tipping back with it. "I just recently realized that since we're in a new era of modern minded people, you could have all the things you want without all the traditional requirements."

"I've never said I want a baby."

"But you do, don't you?"

Silent chopping. "I want a puppy," Liv muttered.

Mary's pink apple cheeks popped again. "Start there and keep an open mind."

"I can't believe yours is more open than mine right now."

"It's always a good thing to surprise your child. Have one and find out."

Snorting, Liv said, "Clever. But I'm going to do you a favor and not mention the teenager sperm donor idea to Dad."

"He's an *adult*. Stop saying it like it's a vulgar news story."

"Borderline."

"Patrick!" Mary turned to her with excitement. "Oh he'd be perfect!"

"Kind of unethical to be asking your employee to give you their sperm."

"I bet he'd do it."

"He's my *employee*. No."

"Just think about it."

"*No.*"

Liv set her knife aside and went to the fridge to grab the chicken, shouting, "Dad, time to fire up the barbeque!"

"Alright!" he shouted back.

"Leo's a very cute name, by the way," Mary said as Liv left the kitchen. "Liv, Leo, and Layla."

Liv's steps slowed and she looked back. "Dare I ask?"

"Don't you think it's a cute name for a little girl?"

"Oh my gahhhh."

Liv went to her dad, head shaking but undeniably amused, and he looked relieved to see it. "Things getting back to normal?"

"Here or life in general?"

"With your mother."

Teenage sperm donor idea flashed in her mind. "I wouldn't call it normal, but sorta."

"Good."

He grilled and they ate, and it was normal.

The next morning, she dressed in athletic pants that had a dark geometric floral pattern, a teal tank and a black zip-up hoodie that had thumb-hole cutouts. She put her hair in a high ponytail, tied her athletic shoes, and then paced around her house drinking coffee.

Nine would have been better. She could have told him she'd eat breakfast beforehand.

At 9:30 she saw his golden orange truck park outside her house. She was absolutely going to give him crap about getting there so early when she'd been adamant he pick her up at ten. Except, he got out of his truck, walked around to the side facing her front window and leaned back against the cab with arms folded.

"You turd," she said aloud, amused.

She made sure he couldn't see her through the window and spent a few moments studying him. Slate grey athletic pants, fitted black zipped up hoodie, dark aviators. He kept his hair longer on the top than when they were kids. Now only the sides were as buzzed as he used to like it and the top had a styled side-sweep.

The dark glasses seemed to highlight the indents in his cheeks, emphasizing his strong jaw which she often didn't pay attention to because she was too busy getting lost in his beautiful eyes. He really was ridiculously attractive, had only gotten more so since high school.

She'd had a patient once that was a high-end escort who'd had her heart broken by a client she'd said was an FOTC. *Fuck of the century*. That wasn't the core issue with that particular patient, but Liv always remembered how she said, 'FOTC' in a low, liquid tone like just saying it made her relive it. Looking at Connor now, Liv wondered if he would be her FOTC that she would practically moan just to recall.

"Do not go there."

Connor glanced at his watch.

"Shut it down, Liv."

Grabbing her water bottle, keys, purse, she opened the door, shaking her head.

Connor grinned and walked toward her. "I would have bet money you'd make me wait until ten, and not a minute sooner."

If she hadn't been practically salivating at being able to stare at him, she would have. "Turns out I was ready at nine."

"Told you." He stopped in front of her. "Why'd you make me wait five minutes then?"

"So I could watch you from the window and enjoy seeing you wait."

His low laugh rumbled. "I am at your service, Lucky." He leaned down to take her water bottle and swiftly kissed her cheek. "Top o' the morning to you."

She frowned at him. "Friends don't kiss."

"You smell amazing."

So did he.

This was a bad idea. She even took a step back and looked to her front door.

"It's different than what you used to wear. I should have realized you'd change it, but I've always remembered you smelling like that purple spray from Victoria's Secret."

He gave her a lopsided smile and it made her heart ache. There was no backing out now. For better or worse, she had to walk this path with him again.

"I forgot to double check if I locked my door."

"You did, I watched."

He walked her to the passenger door, opened and closed it for her like a gentleman. Once they'd started dating, he'd always done that.

As soon as he got into the driver's seat, she said, "Since we're just friends—and I appreciate the thoughtfulness but it's not what friends do—don't open my door for me."

He looked blankly at her for a moment, then, "No."

Starting the truck with a loud rev, he swiftly pulled away from the curb as if afraid she'd say she wasn't going to go then.

Some boundaries were worth fighting for, this one wasn't one of them, so she shrugged. "You'll have to move faster than me then."

"Challenge accepted."

Her lips curved and she suggested the nearest pet store they could go to.

"I've got a better one in mind."

"Which one?"

"It's in an animal loving town."

"Which one?"

"It's the best pet supply store I've ever seen."

"Whiiiiiich one?"

"It's in Riverside."

"That's over an hour away."

He gave her a wolfish smile. "Nice day for a drive."

It was too. But being enclosed with him for several hours without any real distractions was not conducive to the friend-climate she was trying to control. Except, when had she ever been able to control Connor, or her reaction to him? *Never.* Maybe it was time to stop resisting how things simply were. Could the cracks in her mosaic heart withstand it though?

With a small sigh, she said, "You keep in touch with anyone from high school?"

"No. You?"

"No. I didn't want them to know what happened with us."

He glanced over at her then back at the road. "Same." At her obvious surprise, he continued, "I didn't think about it, or anything but the army. I told you that. But I'd get calls or emails from time to time, and I'd never respond. I didn't want to think."

Liv said, "I shut down all my accounts connecting me to everyone. I wish now I hadn't done that to Chelsea. She was a good friend to me. I wonder if her and Jayden Crane got married like she predicted."

They both smiled, remembering Chelsea's years-long *Unrequited Love of Her Life*, Jayden, that Connor had somehow managed to bring together at the end of their senior year. They'd been in love and enrolled at the same college when they graduated high school.

"I could find her for you," Connor said.

"Are you always so swift to break the law?"

"Huh?"

"Flashing your badge at my house, using government data to track down a friend."

"I was going to look for her online, civilian-like."

"Oh. Not that swift then."

"Did you ever run into anyone? You live practically in the same place where you grew up."

"I've seen a few people, but—" It was hard to say it, but *see what happens*. "I hid from them before they could see me. I was so deeply humiliated by what happened, I couldn't bear talking about it to the people who knew us."

The muscle in his jaw flexed and an awkward silence followed.

Liv half-laughed. "I decided if I'm going to be your friend, I'm going to be straightforward with you. Hopefully you'll tell me the truth with whatever we talk about too."

Nodding slowly, he said, "I've seen a couple people. One asked about you and I told them we broke up, that was the end of it."

Of course it was. She even knew it wasn't a big deal to other people, but it was such a profoundly big deal to her that she couldn't imagine talking about it without giving away what a massive vulnerability it was. "Twice I was even with a boyfriend when I saw someone, and I still avoided talking to them."

"Did you date a lot after me?"

"I've been in a couple relationships." That had been like eating bland food. "What about you?"

"No relationships."

"A lot of hookups?" He didn't answer. "Sorry. But really, no relationships?" In thirteen years? The significance of that slowly sank in.

"No."

"Not even after the army?"

"I was as busy in the narc division as I was in the army. I've only had time since I moved to homicide."

"When was that?"

"First time I saw you was my first week in the department."

"So if I'd seen you a couple years ago when you were in the other division, you wouldn't want to be friends again?"

He never took his eyes off the road, but she could feel a change in his attention. "I don't think I could have helped myself. Like now. I would have used how busy I was to fight it harder though."

Warm, thudding heart. "That sounds true," she said lightly.

"I've always been honest with you, Liv."

Her mouth opened to deny it, but then she tried to reign in her own emotions and evaluate. "How do you see that you've always been honest with me?"

"Because I have been."

Evaluate. Evaluate... *What the hell was he talking about, how could he say this to her?*

"Okay, I can see you disagree," he said after a glance. "Tell me how you think I lied."

Uh, *Forever.* Instead, "That you'd call me, for one."

"I intended to."

"Yeah, just like no one intends to cheat—"

"I didn't cheat!"

Strong reaction, he even looked pissed.

"Really?" Among the many scenarios she'd imagined that lead up to him dropping her, cheating on her and not wanting to have to admit it had persistently featured.

"I've screwed up a lot in my life, but I'm not a fu—fecking cheater."

The tiniest knot of pain dissolved. The corner of her mouth tipped up. "My mom would be glad to hear it."

"Your mom thinks I cheated?"

Strong reaction again, and she said, "I don't know what she thinks. Because of how hard I took it, they were careful not to speak about you. Dad even hired a guy named Connor at one point, and they'd always preface saying his name with 'the guy from work Connor'."

The muscle in his jaw flexed again and she ignored the urge to soothe it away with her fingers. "But, I was thinking about something my mom said last night about cheaters, that's why I said that."

The muscle stopped flexing.

"After I got that call from Keith about my mom," he said, "every time I'd look at the phone, I couldn't pick it up. It stayed that way for... I don't know. It was a long time. By the time I could, I'd... stopped feeling. And it worked great for me. I excelled in what I was doing, so it seemed right."

"You didn't think about me *at all?*"

"I kept myself too busy to."

"No thoughts popped into your head, even when you were busy?"

"I'd shut them down."

So they'd happened. "Well, I got my doctorate, and I couldn't not think about you."

"Was your doctorate putting you in life or death scenarios that required all your attention to survive?"

"This isn't a competition," she drawled.

"Because I won."

"What about narcotics? That couldn't have been life or death all the time."

"When it wasn't, it was bone deep exhaustion from the lack of sleep and keeping up the image I built."

"Well it's still not a competition."

"Because I still won it."

Amused, and marveling at being amused about it, she said, "What about in between the army and narcotics?"

"The injury. That was hell. There were days when I was laid up that I'd think about things I didn't want to. So I pushed myself to heal as fast as I could. I figured I'd either hurt myself and they'd knock me out with pain meds, or I'd get better. I got better."

"What injury?"

"A bullet took a chunk out of my thigh."

"How much is a chunk?"

"Gruesome enough I won't be on any hot lists."

"Doubtful."

He grinned at her. "We'd still make the hottest couple list." Referring to the title they'd been given in high school.

"Is this your subtle way of saying I've aged well?"

"Baby, you're more beautiful than I ever imagined."

Before, when they were just friends and womanhood hadn't happened to her yet, he'd say she *had the makings to be hot one day.* The funny thing about being *not-hot* during your formative years, was that when you suddenly became attractive at a late stage, being looked at as desirable never really quite stopped being surprising.

Flustered, she smoothed her ponytail, bending the ends into the sun to stare blindly at the golden strands reflecting in the light. "Don't call me baby."

He made a tsk-ing sound. "So many rules. Did you like how I checked my language for you? I learned the eck instead of the uck from an Irish guy I worked with overseas."

"I liked it. It toes the line nicely."

"Your mom still wouldn't like it."

"Gonna go talk to her?"

His gaze shuttered. "I need to. I know I owe them an apology, but every time I think about it, I can't think about it."

"Did Mark never say anything to you about us?"

"No."

"I have a hard time relating to a friendship like that, where nothing is really personal."

"I have a really hard time with relationships, so it works for me."

"And Mark apparently. He's never married either."

"Why haven't you gotten married?"

Her stomach tightened and heat rushed through her head. As much as she'd shared with him, admitting she couldn't commit to another man because of him, was unbearable. "No one felt right, so I haven't wanted to."

"Good."

Yeah, great. "What about kids?"

"Have I had any?"

He gave her a look of surprise like it had never crossed his mind, but she'd meant if he wanted any. She didn't bother to correct him.

"No, I'm careful. Uh, you?" he said carefully.

"Just a puppy, in two weeks."

"No 'oops' or accidentals with your boyfriends?"

"I've had a couple scares, but it was nothing. You?"

"No."

"Good."

He nodded.

"So are you dating anyone now?" he asked.

"I just got out of a relationship, a couple months ago."

"What was he like?"

"A yeller."

"You dated a yeller?"

"He wasn't at first, but when I broke up with him, he was."

Connor laughed. "You're going to tell everyone he's a yeller because he was upset when you broke up with him? That's cold, Lucky."

She crossed her arms. "No, I had already seen signs he was a yeller, and then he really yelled when I broke up with him. There's a difference."

"Doesn't seem like it but okay."

"What about you? Dating anyone?"

"Well I had a date this morning at ten, but she was early so—"

"You mean our friendship outing?"

"I set the date in my calendar, and it was for today at ten…"
One hand on the steering wheel tipped skyward.

"I see, so we're on *the* date set for our friendship outing."

"You and your rules."

CHAPTER FIFTEEN

Connor kept sneaking looks at her. God she was beautiful, hardly any makeup, hair shining like the sun, blue-brown eyes shyly sparkling at him. He had a relentless urge to pull off the road, drag her onto his lap and make out with her. He remembered the way it felt kissing her soft lips, the way he'd sink into them. He'd never been able to kiss her without thinking about sinking into her body while she gasped and arched beneath him. She never let him, they'd never gone anywhere near that far, and fuck if he didn't want to rectify that now. Right now.

Shifting in the seat, he subtly adjusted himself. How long would he have to keep up this friends act? He wanted all of her, all of everything. Right now.

He had to win her trust back. Earn it. Whatever, it would take time. Shit.

How exactly, though? He should ask Hutch. Wished he could text him and ask real quick, but then it brought to mind caricatures of people keeping their shrinks on speed dial. Like hell.

Maybe he should just ask her, put it out there. He snuck another quick look. There was a sweetness about her, in her expression, she'd always had it. Getting her heart broken clearly hadn't diminished it, thank God. That sweetness was probably why she was even now willing to be with him like this. Yet now she was also undeniably guarded, as she had never been before.

Teasing her, her responses were all a familiar rhythm he easily fell into, but she held herself back from fully engaging, he felt it clearly. But how to get back to *before*?

He had to get her trust back.

His mouth opened to ask how, but as she turned to him sweet and guarded, the words clammed up inside him, and he thought fast for something else. "You like my truck?" *Dumbass.*

A small look of confusion gently furrowed her brow. "It's nice."

"Thanks, I got it a couple months ago." Might as well run with it. "You like the color?"

"Yeah. It's bolder than the black truck." The first vehicle he'd ever had that her dad had helped him buy. He really needed to make amends with her family, he owed them everything, and what an idiot he was to ruin everything.

Stop. Damn it. He had to stop doing this. And he was going to fix this. He opened his mouth to tell her that, but again the words got stuck. "I wanted a green one, but they didn't have it."

"Why green?"

"Fit the image I had in my head of it parked at a campsite in the woods. The orange was next in my image lineup."

"You like camping?"

"I go a couple times a year. I'll like it even better when you're with me."

Color brightened her cheeks, but she didn't take the bait, transitioning instead to her puppy and how she'd be taking it to puppy class so that it didn't pull on the lead when she walked it, like her dog Darcy used to.

It was fine. He could push and retreat all day long.

When they got to the massive barn-turned-pet-store, he took his time parking. Then he yanked the keys out of the ignition at the same time he shoved his door open. He jumped out, slammed the door, locking it as he ran around the front end to get to Liv's door. Right as she'd figured out how to unlock her door, he pulled it open for her.

He pretended to tip an imaginary hat. "At your service, ma'am."

Laughing, she said, "Round one goes to you. I'll be ready for next time."

Throwing an arm around her shoulders, they walked to the store while he crooned, "You try so hard."

She elbowed him in the side. He tightened his arm and hunched toward her, face against her hair. "You'll have to try harder."

Even with her new perfume, the way she smelled was familiar, and so bright and fresh it made him want to gather her up in his arms and simply stand there, holding her.

Instinct nudged him it was time to retreat and reluctantly, he released her. "I've missed you bad, Lucky."

"No you haven't, you've been too life and death to think about me."

There was a teasing glint to her eyes, and he appreciated that she apparently wasn't going to make him suffer for his honesty. "Maybe my head wasn't thinking it, but everything else was."

Her gaze grew intense as it briefly searched his, but he knew his dark aviators prevented her from seeing his eyes. If he took them off, it would be cheesy? Retreat.

Wait, maybe his quip sounded like he was referring to his dick? She'd stopped looking at him. Should he mention he was talking about his…heart? Hell no. They'd never done much with his dick anyway, so she had to figure odds were he wasn't talking about it now. She wasn't acting like anything, so that had to be a good sign.

In the pet store, he helped her pick out a leash and collar. Or rather, encouraged her pick of a tan leather that offered free name engraving, after she nixed his pick of spikes and skulls.

"What's its name gonna be?"

"Leo." She took one of her quick glances at him. "Like it?"

He could see himself very happily coming home to Liv and Leo. "Love it."

Next, they grabbed puppy food and then Connor directed them to chew toys, dog bowls, piddle pads, a dog bed and a crate. "And treats for when Leo does things right," he said, adding a bag to the cart. Then toothbrush, paste, regular brush, nail trimmer, and dog shampoo all went in.

Liv had a vaguely uneasy expression on her face and Connor stopped and turned to her. "What's wrong?"

"Noth—" She took a breath. "I had in my head I needed a leash, collar and dogfood. I'm…dismayed I think is the exact right word, that I'm in my thirties and I'm completely ignorant about caring for a helpless little thing that I'm bringing home."

Liv was a little perfect, always doing well always doing right, so seeing her having a very inept moment gave him unholy pleasure.

"Don't give me that look," she muttered. "Why do you know these things? Do you have a dog?"

"No, but I had my team, and you don't go into a situation without making sure you have everything you need."

"Well *I* do, apparently. I've always thought I was a planner. Maybe I'm just a go to a class-er."

Chuckling, Connor hooked his arm around her shoulders again, and pulled her in to swiftly kiss the side of her head. "Don't you worry, Lucky. I got you."

They finished at the pet store, and then drove to a hiking trail not far from her house. As he parked, he said, "I figure you already know all the routes around your house and the harbor."

Swiftly, he shut the engine off and opened his door, pressing the lock button on his key fob repeatedly to keep her in, except Liv manually unlocked the door and opened it. Connor dove back in for her, grabbing her by the waist to haul her back. Liv shrieked and grabbed hold of the seat to pull out of his grasp.

Still holding her, Connor climbed over the center console and straddled her, getting right up in her face as she squirmed and cracked up laughing. "Round two is mine." He jumped out her door then held it open with his hand out.

"How injured were you again?"

"Bad, Lucky. Bad."

"Where exactly?" She slowly slid out of the truck, landing with a sly look.

"Not telling, not while you're plotting something you'd feel bad about later. I'm doing this for you."

"So generous."

"I'll happily show you in great detail at a later time of your choosing."

Her cheeks went pink again but then she said, "I choose now."

"A *later* time of your choosing."

He grabbed her hand and tugged to get her walking and didn't let go, but she casually wiggled her hand from his grip. They began the hike, trees making a canopy over the winding dirt path that inclined steeply. They kept a good pace so that soon they were both breathing rapidly.

The sun dappling through the leaves, cast the path in a mellow glow, and occasionally a bird chirped in short bursts while the breeze gently swished the trees. Again, Connor experienced that elusive feeling of peace he'd only ever known with Liv.

"The only time I've ever felt any kind of peace is when I'm with you," he murmured.

Her steps slowed. "Maybe it's what we do together."

"I hike when I camp." He paused to catch his breath and turned to her. "I don't feel it then."

"Oh."

He waited, but she said nothing more and he laughed. "All that education and that's all you got?"

"You want an evaluation? You *hated* when I'd psychoanalyze you."

"I'm older and trying to be a bit wiser."

With a soft groan she pushed the little blond wisps that had escaped her ponytail back from her face. "I can't, not really. I'm too personally involved to make an unbiased analysis."

"There, that sounded education-y."

Her lips slightly curved. "I've only been studying my whole life."

"Make a biased analysis."

"No."

"I'm going to ask my counselor then."

Her eyes rounded. "Every memory I have of you and anything having to do with psychology, is of you mocking it. It was the one concern I had about our relationship. I remember thinking that if you didn't grow to respect my field, it could damage us one day." She snorted.

"Now don't be like that."

"What?"

"Making that sarcastic noise. I blindsided you, I get it. I hurt you, and I'm sorry. I'm here with you now and hearing those noises, it…"

"It's passive aggressive," she said. "I'm sorry. It might be habit with our story, so I might do it again, but I promise to try not to."

Connor grinned. "That was the sound of the most functional person I know."

"I've got issues," she said wryly.

"What issues do you have?"

She started walking again, her gaze locked on each step she took. "Anything I could love that could leave me, I can't commit to for long. It's the long-term damage from what happened. I've just now started to try to fix it—me. Getting a dog is my first foray into repairing this piece of me that I don't like."

The piece that *he'd* caused. It unsettled him, hearing the scope of the fallout from *him*.

"I…" she began, only to cut herself off and stop walking. "Do you want to leave?"

He motioned with his head to keep moving and she fell into slow step with him.

"You got a look on your face like you wanted to get out of here."

"Really? Guys on my team always told me I had a stone face."

"Which team?"

"Army."

"Maybe I know you better." He grunted and she gave him a swift glance. "Or, maybe it's the life-threatening situation that does it. I could shoot at you and see if you go stone faced and let you know."

"Thoughtful."

"I'm just that way."

"I didn't do it on purpose," he said suddenly. "Hurt you, I mean. I was just—am—fu—uh, like I said, fecked up, from what happened, you know, with Keith and my mom, and, yeah, my dad too I guess. I didn't know it got to me the way it did. I thought— I didn't think about it, so it didn't seem like a big deal. I didn't know."

"If we're going to be friends, I'm afraid you're going to learn in lengthy detail how important you were in my life."

Something like…hope…flickered in his chest. "Lengthy huh?"

"I've got *thirteen years* of anecdotes."

Chuckling, he wrapped his arm around her and pulled her into him, causing her to stumble, and he stopped walking to hold her, front to front. Her arms lifted, but she held them suspended out at his sides. It was fine, he'd give her time. In the meantime, he breathed in the smell of delicate floral perfume, shampoo, and the light scent of sweat. God he'd missed her. How could he not have known it, all these years?

Gently, her arms settled carefully against his sides, and then her palms pressed against his back. Something in him eased, and he gathered her up tighter, held her closer, his face buried in the hair trailing from her ponytail.

"Friends don't usually hug like this."

Laughing softly, he lifted his head to look down at her. Mixed in with her wobbly smile, was worry.

Slipping out of his arms, she cleared her throat. "I can see this is a good trail. Maybe we should head back down now."

She wanted to run from him. Satisfied, Connor retreated.

CHAPTER SIXTEEN

Liv threw her keys on the kitchen counter only to immediately pick them up again and hang them dutifully on the hook by the door. Then she went to the kitchen and grabbed a chilled bottle of white wine.

"It's too early." She poured.

Taking the cold glass to the sofa, she sat in her spot, curled her legs under and stared at the wall.

"I should just sleep with him and get it over with."

She wanted to not be hung up on him, but that wasn't ever *ever* going to happen, now was it? So eff it, might as well sleep with him and get to experience every aspect of knowing him. If he'd even sleep with her. Whatever it was that he wanted, she couldn't guess. He hadn't tried anything outside the friend umbrella, not really.

Scenarios where she could try to tempt him into sex played through her mind. Yet insecurities of old whispered that she wasn't sexy and how could she possibly tempt him?

With no one to talk to about it, she sat alone, silently immersed in the memory of him teasing her, hugging her, finding absurd ways to open the door for her, even when he dropped her off. He'd only walked her halfway to her door, and then stopped, saying, "Until next time".

The confusion, the push-pull of him was so reminiscent of high school and it made her so...*frustrated*...that she as a woman now, was seemingly locked in an endless high school loop. The impulse to do something rash, uncharacteristic, like go out and try to pick up a guy came over her.

The impulse was an attempt to gain control of her situation, she reasoned. It wasn't what she really wanted to do.

"Thanks, degree," she said, raising her glass.

The truth of the matter was that Connor was her Achilles heel. Being strong and protecting herself simply didn't matter when she couldn't get away from the one enormous vulnerability that could devastate her at any moment.

"And I'm back to this."

Endless loop. So, she reminded herself the only thing she could control was what she did. Either A: Try to seduce Connor, or B: Protect herself from any and all damage he could possibly do to her, which for her, meant NOT sleeping with him.

Sip of cool wine.

Maybe he'd just disappear out of her life again and none of it would matter.

And like a prophecy, he did.

* * * *

Monday after work Connor went to Hutch's office with a dread he hadn't experienced in months. He felt uncomfortable, shifty, pulling at the loosened collar of his white button up dress shirt.

"What's up?" Hutch asked almost as soon as Connor sat.

"Not much. Eager to play basketball tomorrow."

"Good."

Hutch looked him over, making Connor tug at his collar again, which he promptly stopped when he noticed Hutch tracking the movement.

"How'd it go with Liv on Saturday?"

Connor wished now he'd never mentioned it. "It was good." The tick of the clock in the silence that followed seemed pronounced.

"What happened?" Hutch said finally.

"Nothing. It was good. Not much to talk about. We got her puppy stuff, went on a hike, I dropped her off." Connor noticed the slow, patient breath Hutch drew in and quietly released.

"Connor, I think we've been doing this long enough where I can say with some frankness here that Liv is important to you, so much so your life hinged on her. Having time with her again is a very big deal, whether you realize it or not. Even if you think Saturday was mundane, let's talk about it."

The clock ticked.

"Very well," Hutch said, "Why *don't* you want to talk about it?"

"There's nothing to say." But hell, he knew there was. "I don't want to think about it." He'd also been doing this long enough to know that was a sure sign he needed to think about it. "Hell."

Rocking back and up out of the sofa, he went to the window. Been a while since he'd visited it. "I don't know, Hutch. Before Saturday I would do anything to be with her, after Saturday, I don't want to think about it."

"Did the day go badly?"

"No," he said softly. "No, she's amazing. Beautiful and sweet. Fun to be with. But also, not. Stuff came up that was heavy. I fucked her up, Hutch."

"How?"

Tick. Tick. Tick.

With a heavy sigh, Connor returned to the sofa. "I'm fucked up that I'm reacting like this." When Hutch neither protested nor agreed, he pressed, "Aren't I?"

"Let's talk about what happened and then we can go from there."

Connor told him the things she'd said and how once he left her side, he'd immediately shied away from thinking about her.

"How could I want her so badly one minute, and then the next, not? Maybe it's all in my fucked up head. Maybe I don't really feel anything, I've just convinced myself I do."

"Think about her right now," Hutch said. "Don't shut it down. *Really* think about her."

Okay. Connor shifted and closed his eyes, but that felt weird, so popped them open with a glance at Hutch. Shifting again, he stared at the carpet and pictured Liv on Saturday. Cute in her little workout gear and ponytail, declaring rules he enjoyed breaking, and her shy, flustery amusement at his antics. The delicate furrow in her brow as she realized how unprepared she was for puppy shopping. The heartbreak in her eyes when she talked about her fear of committing to someone she could love.

"Are you thinking about her?" Hutch said a moment later.

"Yeah." His voice came out gravelly. "I'm thinking about her. I want to get the fuck out of my skin when I think about how her eyes looked when she said she couldn't love right because of me.

"She wasn't being accusing either and that makes it sit worse. She's so sweet and honest, and I'm the bastard that hurt her so bad I changed her. It's awful, Hutch, the way it—I just want to get the fuck out of here."

Several months ago, that's exactly what he would have done. The memory of the kayak, the way he'd felt slid through his mind like a ghost and kept him seated; the only relief he'd experienced had come from doing exactly what he was doing right now.

"You feel something," Hutch said.

"I—" His throat closed up, choked with sudden emotion. Pressure built in his eyes, and they grew wetter. Was he going to fucking *cry*? Over *what*? "I'm not suicidal, not...anymore. I don't understand what the fuck is wrong with me." He gestured to his face. Could Hutch see?

"You're doing good, you've made tremendous strides since we started this. It could be that this thing with Liv is simply too soon to delve into. You've got your own self you're working on and adding her hurts to work on as well might be too much right now."

"Why didn't you say something before I started this with her?"

Wry smile. "I tried. You can be hard to reach at times."

Fuck, he knew that. "Sorry. It's not your responsibility, it's mine." He pinched the bridge of his nose. "If I disappear on her now, it will be the last time. She won't let me in again."

"She might, if you let her know you need more time."

"No." He trusted his instincts with women, and his told him she wouldn't tolerate another move like that. "I started this. I can't run now."

"That's precisely what you wanted to do though, after one day with her."

God he sounded like a loser. "Why, Hutch? Why would I want to run? Why did I think I felt nothing when clearly—" He gestured to his face again.

"It's that deeply rooted fear of losing someone who could devastate you rising up to protect you, by making you want to run and numbing out to being connected to her. The roots go deep. It takes work and time to get them out."

"I want them out. I want them fucking gone. I don't want to live the way I've been living since I left her."

"That's why I think you'll win this battle."

When the session ended, Connor felt depleted in a way he hadn't almost since he'd started therapy. He still didn't want to call Liv, and that worried him because he knew he cared, even though he couldn't feel it again.

On his way home, he picked up some tacos and sat at his round glass dining table to eat. It was so quiet in his place. He'd never noticed it before. Probably because he typically had a game on, but he didn't want one on now.

An image of sitting with Liv around her own dining table, with a dog sat at their feet hoping for scraps filled him with such a sudden, profound longing, that his taco paused midway to his mouth from the intensity of it.

Jesus, feel nothing, don't want to talk to her and then abruptly feel every damn thing under the sun for her. He was all over the fucking place. God if his team saw him now, or hell, if Fernando knew the state of him, any one of them would wonder how the hell he hadn't gotten them killed.

"Calm down, soldier," he rumbled. No one knew what was going on inside him but Hutch, and even he had to pull it out of him to know. It wasn't obvious.

If all of this was fear, like Hutch said, he had to stop being afraid, but it didn't feel like fear as he knew it. So how do you fight something you can't recognize?

Maybe he should tell Liv what was going on with him. She was a counselor, she would understand. *She's also a woman.* His instincts weren't off on this, he was sure, and if he told her he may ditch her to deal with his shit—after everything else he'd done—that would be it. The end. So how did he fix this?

He had no answers.

Nothingness was a relief and it settled around him again like a comforting mantel of steel.

The next morning, he just remembered to grab his black gym bag before leaving for work and grunted at Fernando who grunted back when he got there.

"Nice tie," Fernando called out. "Orange. It's very gender neutral, according to kids these days."

Connor stroked a hand down the silver tie with orange stripes. One of the aspects of his job that he liked was the attire, he enjoyed sharp suits and interesting ties. "What's going to happen to you when I show up with a pink tie?"

"As my daughter would say: mind. blown. Which means my mind will be blown. There's an emoji for it."

Connor smirked and dropped into his seat, black pleather creaking. "Is there an emoji for brain matter cleanup?"

"There you go! Now you're thinking like you're in homicide!"

"Oh yeah? What was I doing before?" He knew he was walking into it.

"That's what we've all been asking each other."

Other detectives around them snickered. The oldest guy in the room, not far from retirement and not inclined to talk much said, "When are you going to move a desk, so we won't have to hear you two shouting across the room?"

"I am not a shouter," Fernando said mildly.

Connor tipped his head at the open desk Fernando's previous partner sat at. "Wanna…wanna move in together?"

"What I'm looking for in a roommate:" Fernando ticked off his fingers, "Clean, tidy, fun-loving and doesn't take long bathroom breaks because I do."

"Clean and tidy are the same things."

"They're not." Decisive shake of his head. "Short bathroom breaks with clean hands afterward is clean. An organized desk is tidy."

Connor stood and grabbed a pile of case files, strolling to the open desk. "I like good coffee and nice smells. I don't mind your long bathroom breaks so's long as you call sometimes."

Fernando stood. "My wife will be jealous, but welcome home!" He held his arms wide and Connor cradled in, curling over him from his greater height so he could rest his head on his shoulder, saying, "Papa."

Fernando rumbled with laughter and pounded him on the shoulder. "Alright. Bathroom break." And he moseyed off with his phone in hand.

Twenty minutes later, sat at his new desk, Connor's phone rang at his old desk, and he had to jog over to catch it. "Detective Peltier."

"I was thinking about Jeremy Olawale," Fernando said, his voice vaguely echoing from the tile surround in the bathroom. "He's too young to lay low for long. We should go for a look again."

Connor promptly thought of Liv. "You want to check with his mom?"

"And friends. Couldn't hurt."

"Agreed."

"Yeah." A short tinkling sound. "Now we're done. Meet you at the car."

They made zero progress with Jeremy's friends. The mom though, she made eye contact longer than she ever had, her brown eyes lucid. The curving tightness of her lips eased as she spoke a little more, asking for help to see Jeremy's name cleared, but she shied away from saying why she felt so sure he hadn't killed his father.

Afterward, as they sat in a booth eating a burger from, '*another great little place*' Fernando knew, Connor said, "Ever been dead wrong about one of these?"

Fernando snorted heavily. "I was such a hot little shit in the beginning—not unicorns hot like you. I was smart enough not to *tell* everyone my instincts were untouchable, but dumb enough to act like it, all the damn time. My luck on my assigned cases would not run out either. If there was a calendar for best new detective, I would have been Mr. January through December.

"Couple years in, I screwed up big. Got careless, didn't follow procedure and the perp walked free. I think about that every single day. Made me a little less cocky, but not enough." He took a big bite of his burger, lime-green lettuce squishing out the back.

"How much less cocky do you need to get?" He seemed pretty normal to Connor.

Fernando's chewing slowed and a look of sheer anguish filled his gaze. It made Connor uncomfortable because, hell, did he ask? His time with Hutch told him, yeah, do it. His years as himself told him not to. Taking a bite of his burger, he chewed, gaze fixed on the thick cut fries that had a reddish seasoning tinting the golden crisp.

"My daughter is pregnant."

Connor's gaze jerked back up.

"Sixteen years old. I thought I knew my kids. I thought I had raising them handled." He blew out a breath and took a bite. Around his food, he said, "I was too cocky."

"I don't think that makes you cocky."

"It does, because I thought I'd done such a fine goddamned job of parenting, that there was no way on God's green earth *my* kid would be a teen mom. I never talked about it with either of my kids because I figured, hell, they're too smart, and they've got too great of parents for something that dumb to happen.

"It's not your life now, buddy, but when you have kids, don't make that mistake. Because I'm about to have a grandkid that I'm also going to have to raise as my kid because my kid is too much of a child to raise a child."

"How long until she has the baby?"

"About two months. She'd been hell to deal with for months, I didn't know what the hell was going on with her. Figured I'd just leave her alone 'til she got over it." He sighed heavily. "She hid the pregnancy. I took her to her first appointment just last month. Six months pregnant and no doctor checks in all that time." His eyes shut as if to block out what was happening. "If my wife hadn't walked in on her changing and seen what was going on, what was she going to do? Have the baby in a public bathroom, drop it off at a 'no questions asked' drop box? I'm sick thinking about it. My wife won't even talk to her right now. A whole month later, and she still can't speak to our daughter. I swear my wife wrote the procedural manual on the silent treatment, but this is a lot, even for her, and hell, it can't be good for the baby. It's one big goddamned mess and my household is in unrest, when all my adult life I've been cocky as hell about being in control, having everything in order—" He shook his head and then took a bite.

They ate in silence for a while before he asked around a mouthful, "Why'd you ask?"

Sheepishly, Connor said, "I was talking about all these hole-in-the-wall places you say are great."

Fernando choked a little, coughed, and then laughed, wheezing through the food still in his mouth, face turning dark red as his eyes watered.

"Careful man," Connor said with amusement. "Heimlich and I aren't friends, so I'll have to beat that burger out of you."

Gradually Fernando wound down, crowing "Oh Jesus" as he wiped his eyes with a napkin. "I get it wrong a hell of a lot more than I even thought."

"I'm pretty sure that's true for most people."

He took a long drink of sweet tea. "That has a ring of psycho-babble to it. Get it from your shrink girlfriend?"

"Need me to schedule you a visit?"

"I feel like we just had a one-night-stand."

Connor's brows shot upward. "Not where I would have taken it."

"There's this sudden, deep knowledge between us that happened unexpectedly."

"Well, I just moved in with you so you can't leave me in the morning."

"We're the unlikely couple that somehow makes it despite the odds."

"I want chocolate for our first anniversary."

"I would have picked roses."

"Shaky start."

"We'll pull through."

They finished their burgers and then returned to the station. An hour before quitting time, Fernando tossed Connor an envelope he'd grabbed off his old desk on his way to the coffee machine. "Don't forget to put in a change of address with those government hacks downstairs."

"I'ma tell them you said that," someone called out, making them both grin.

Connor tore the envelope open and pulled out the suicide note Mr. Shek had left his wife. It must have gotten lost in the mail somewhere.

Scanning the brief note, the constriction around his chest eased.

Mr. Shek had done it because he'd lost all his money. That was it. They were nothing alike.

Connor filed the note, while Fernando ducked out a few minutes early citing 'a family thing' with a pained look. After work, Connor went to the basketball courts.

Everyone was already there and right away, Vanessa gave him a hard stare. She'd slicked her long, dark hair into a ponytail that she'd braided, and the broad angles of her face added to that tough-as-nails demeanor he remembered from last week. He looked away, ignoring her.

They mixed the teams up from the previous week, and Connor's lost again. Afterward, they went back to the same restaurant as before. A lot of banter had them all laughing, and Connor felt good at the end of it.

As he walked back to his car, he heard, "Yo, Connor." Turning, he watched Vanessa jog up to him.

"What's up?"

"It's still early. Want to get a drink?"

Since he felt good from the night, and with no one and nothing to go home to, he said yes.

"Let's try that new Ocean Café up the street," she said. "I'll meet you there."

He followed her low-rider hatchback to the restaurant, amused when she had to take speedbumps at an angle and slower than a baby could crawl them. He joked about it as they went into the restaurant where they were promptly seated at a bistro table.

The place had been designed to look like an old wine cellar, with stacked stone walls and dark wood built ins. It had a wine-rack wall with a gentle glow filtering through the bottles. Golden pendant lights and flickering candles at each table had Connor thinking this would be a great place to take a date. Not so much a buddy from therapy.

"I'll have to come here with my husband," Vanessa said.

Good. They were on the same page. "How long you been married?"

"Twelve years. Got married just before I deployed. We did a Vegas chapel, had Elvis marry us." She smirked like, *can you believe that shit?*

Then she said, "You have a rough day today?"

"Uhm. No."

"You remind me a lot of this guy I went through basic with. He never showed any emotion neither but when he had bad days, his face would like, not move. So, here I am, figuring we're all doing therapy, we're all here trying to deal with our shit. We know how to work as a team, so as teammates, let's work together to deal with our shit."

Eyes narrowed, he sighed deeply. "I don't have heart-to-hearts, but you're the second person today who's gone personal."

"It's like when you're out on patrol and ain't nothin' goin' right," she said with amusement. "C'mon, boy, let's deal with it."

Why'd she pick him?

Fuck it. "I've screwed up a relationship that's everything to me."

Her fingers linked behind her head, and she nodded. "I know what that's like. Can you do anything about it?"

The waitress came, saving him from answering.

"You go," Vanessa said.

Connor ordered a brownie and ice water. Vanessa ordered the same. Once the waitress left, she said, "You're a good friend for me."

"Why?"

"Because I'm a drinker and you're not."

"How do you know?"

"I can tell. You're not uncomfortable with strong women either. I can tell that too. Some of the guys in the group get all up in their own grill over someone like me."

Connor knew.

"Well, I don't know what the hell I'm supposed to say about your relationship. I suck at this but I'm trying to get better at it for the people I care about." She released the clasp of her fingers and leaned forward, resting her elbows on the table. "I figure you don't want to talk about what's going on, but I can tell you're a good guy. Bad stuff hits good guys hard."

"I'm not sure I'm a good guy."

"You are. I can tell. But that's why we're all here, we don't feel right. I don't know what right is, but whatever we're feeling ain't it. I want to say don't let it get to you, but we've all been told that and it don't work. Talking sort of helps, but I kind of think having someone notice it's hard and that we're not really alright sort of helps too. So I'm saying I notice."

"Alright. Thanks."

"Sure."

They lapsed into silence and it could have been a little awkward but it wasn't too bad. She had an alert yet relaxed quality to her as she looked around the place, the pads of her fingertips gently bouncing on top of the table.

The waitress returned with their brownies, warm and fragrant and Connor enjoyed the quiet as they both ate the soft, chewy chocolate. As they spooned in their last bites, she said, "You like good food?"

"Always."

"Good. My husband is a great cook. I'll have you over some time and he'll cook for us." She signaled to the waitress for the check and then pulled a wallet out of her back pocket. "I've got to run. I promised my kid I'd say goodnight before she fell asleep." Handing over a ten, she said, "Thanks for hangin'." She left, walking out of the place with chin up and a vaguely lumbering side to side gait.

"Hope you enjoyed your brownie," the waitress said as she set the check on the table.

Connor gave a half smile, dropped cash on the check and then left. It was so easy to blank his mind. Like old times. Even as he drove so close to Liv's house it would take him one minute to get there, he thought of absolutely nothing.

CHAPTER SEVENTEEN

Balancing two lattes and a box of pastries in her hands, Liv carefully used her elbow to open the door to Holly's office building. There were a couple hours left in the workday, but she knew Thursday was typically her slow client day.

She'd tried calling, but Holly hadn't picked up. Neither had Holly called *her* in the two weeks since she hung up on her. They'd never, in all their years of friendship, gone longer than a day without talking, or at the very least texting.

The sudden, harsh treatment, when Liv hadn't done a single thing wrong that she knew of, had her questioning herself and the true depth of their friendship. Also, why life seemed to hand out a pile of crappy cards all at once.

The receptionist had the phone to her ear but recognized Liv and motioned for her to go on back. At Holly's door, she tried knocking with her elbow, but it made a rustling thumping sound instead, with no answer. She pushed the door handle down with an elbow and nudged the door open. "Oh my God—"

"Shit!—" Some guy turned his back enough to block Holly, the sound of his belt jangling as he fumbled with his pants.

"Liv, *get out!*" Holly hissed.

Backing away while the frantic couple flailed, she strode out of the building, pausing at the reception desk to leave the latte and pastries. An after-sex treat, perhaps. The thought made her lips press in a grim line.

She drove to the harbor and walked. With the evenings drawing in sooner the sun had already slipped further down the sky, lighting up clouds with a dying glow.

Never had she ever wanted to see Holly having sex. Of course, they'd been mostly dressed, with parts concealed, but the motion, gasps and expressions in that second it took to process what was happening and for them to notice her were unmistakable.

Neither had she ever wanted to walk in on a cheater, but she supposed if she had to experience it, she should be glad it wasn't on someone cheating on her.

A flare of sorrow for Holly's husband made her chest ache.

Connor popped into her mind, and she took a meditative breath, trying to usher the thought back out. She needed to think about Holly and how to handle what just happened.

Having Connor's number made it harder to keep her thoughts anywhere but him. She kept going back to the fact that for the first time since he left for the army thirteen years ago, she had a direct way to reach him. The temptation to ask him what he was up to, you know, in a *friendly* way tormented her every other minute of the day.

If they were friends, that's what friends would do.

But they weren't friends.

The urge to do something out of character came over her again. An attractive man fishing from the rocks up ahead became the focus of her attention, enough so that he suddenly looked over at her as she walked nearer. She smiled. He smiled back. And then she looked away, because she didn't want him, she didn't want anyone but Connor and she didn't want to give that baggage to anyone.

Over the past days she'd had to face how little control she had of her own thoughts and feelings. She'd thought her education and the years of work to build her confidence had equipped her to handle how Connor affected her. Instead, it gave her humility, because she had those things and still felt all over the place emotionally.

The most memorable professor of psychology Liv ever had liked to say, "The human experience is a hard one." It had seemed like a throw-away comment, like *Have a nice day,* or *Drive safe.* Now, Liv grasped the weight of it. No matter how well set up you are, it's still hard. It's still complicated and difficult and you still have to work to figure out how to be. How to go forward in a way that you want to. And even when you figure out how you want to, actually doing it was hard too.

* * * *

The next afternoon, Liv escorted her last client of the day to the reception desk and found Holly sitting in a waiting room chair.

"Come on in," she said.

As usual, Holly looked cute, hair twisted in a clip, light dusting of pink hued makeup giving her a soft freshness. She wore paint-splatter print leggings and an oversized white t-shirt with NOT TODAY written in dripping hot-pink paint.

"Telling me something?" Liv said with a meaningful glance at the shirt.

"Huh?" Confused glance downward. "Oh, no, I just liked the paint theme."

Holly sat in a patient's chair and Liv sat across from her, saying, "To what do I owe the pleasure of this visit?"

"Ugh, I hate when you do that."

"Do what?"

"This." She waved her hand around. "Acting like you don't know when you do. You know why I'm here."

"Fine. I wish you were here to be a friend to me, but it hasn't felt like that for some time. From where I'm sitting, it looks like you've been too busy cheating on your husband to be anything—"

"So high and mighty," she interrupted. "That's why I haven't wanted to talk to you! I knew you'd talk to me like this."

Liv briefly thought of her mom's judgmental attitude and how much she hated it. Was she becoming that? But what about *her own* feelings? "How is it that *I'm* the problem when you've ghosted me the last number of weeks and have been barely available for months before that? And by the way, I'm getting my puppy tomorrow, are you?"

"What?"

"Remember 'Operation Can't Leave Me'? The irony that it promptly resulted in you practically ditching me." And Connor appearing and disappearing in an echo of the same. "We were doing that *together*, like we used to always do stuff together since pretty much the day we met. Even after you married Jake, we hadn't changed all that much. But suddenly, you start screwing your coworker and screwing the rest of us as well!"

Holly's gaze stayed fixed, her mouth tight.

"And Jake," Liv continued. "He's my friend too—"

"No, he's not. You'll never talk to him again once we're divorced."

"I've shared holidays and birthdays with him, Holly. He's not some random person I don't care about."

"But it's not like he's someone you really care about either."

"You *cheated* on your *husband!*"

"Say it louder, little Miss I Don't Do Anything Wrong, maybe it'll make you feel even more superior to the rest of us."

"I knew you had it in you. I knew. But it's still astounding that you're turning what you did into my failing."

"Nope, I'm turning what you're doing right now into an explanation for why I've avoided you."

Liv slowly shook her head and said, "I didn't need an explanation."

"Then why bring it up?"

"Are you kidding me with this, Holly? You're a *counselor*—"

"I know what I am."

"—and we're in a relationship that's in a bad place. You hurt my feelings. You've treated me badly, you've treated your husband horribly, and it looks to me that you're thinking so much about you, maybe you need a reminder that there are other people you should be thinking about too."

"I really don't want to deal with this," she said sighing. "I came here to talk about what you saw, but if I'm honest I really don't want to *be* a friend to you right now. I'm just trying not to drop you like Connor did."

A sharp knife slipped deep into her chest.

After a moment, Holly looked away. "Sorry. I didn't—I shouldn't have said that."

"And yet words cannot be undone."

She sighed again. "And yet, I still don't want to deal with this. I've got a lot going on, I can't be what you need—"

"A decent person?"

"Sure. Yeah. I can't be that. Sorry." She stood. "I'm sure I'm in the wrong. I'm sure I'll come crawling back to you regretting all the mistakes I made, but I'm not there at all right now. So let me do what I'm gonna do, and hopefully we can come together later when things have settled. Oh, and I've cancelled our couples trip. Contact them if you don't get your refund."

God that hurt. But Liv said pleasantly, "Fine. But one more thing before you go. Little-Miss-I-Don't-Do-Anything-Wrong won't keep your secret for you. Tell Jake what you've been doing."

"Or you will?"

"You've got a week."

The pretty pink lipstick on Holly's lips shimmered as her lips curled. "It is not your place to dictate what, how and when I speak to my husband."

"You mean Jake, my friend?"

"He's not your friend."

"Holidays and birthdays."

Holly's hard, angry gaze would have normally made Liv want to retreat, but a burning sense of injustice fused her spine into steel that would not bend.

"Fine." Holly didn't look back as she strode with fast, heel-pounding steps out of her office, ignoring Patrick's goodbye and slamming the door behind her.

Ow. That's all Liv could think as she sat there, the silence punctuated by the occasional creak or roll of Patrick's desk chair.

After a few minutes, he walked into her office with a gentle knock.

"Couldn't help but notice…" he said with a sheepish smile.

"Yeah." She rubbed her temples.

"You okay?"

"Well, my very small network of loving and supportive relationships is swiftly and possibly irretrievably fragmenting and I'm not sure what the quality of my future is going to be without them."

"Whoa." Patrick said it like he'd spotted a weight he'd have trouble lifting. "I'm really sorry to hear that, boss. Can I do anything to help you?"

Her mother's comment about his sperm popped into her mind and she almost laughed like a maniac. An odd choking sound came out instead and Patrick moved further into her office. "Oh, hey, you said if you were gonna sob, you'd come to the gym to do it. How about that?" He mimicked a couple overhead barbell lifts, making the corner of her mouth tip up.

"I have zero desire to weightlift, ever." She gave him a warm smile. "But thank you. I really appreciate you."

"I appreciate you too, boss. If you change your mind, you've got my number."

Thinking endorphins *would* help, she went to a Pilates class, deliberately pushing herself so hard she felt sore as she left. Good. Let that occupy her instead of her crappy relationships.

When she woke the next morning, her first thought, *I'm getting Leo today!* followed closely with, *Holly*, was interrupted as she groaned from her sore muscles.

Good.

When she got to Julie's, she took a moment to stretch out her muscles, but Julie came out with Leo on a leash, already so much bigger with his superhero mask a little darker.

"Ohh," she melted, squatting for him—and then toppled onto her butt, because her muscles hurt so badly that she tried to stop and stand back up, but was too weak to do it.

"Oh my goodness!" Julie cried. "Are you okay?"

Leo swarmed her, soft paws climbing over her chest while delicate whiskers danced over her face as he sniffed.

Laughing softly, Liv rubbed her cheek against his little face and held his squirming body against her. "I made the mistake of working out way too hard, and now I'm struggling with mobility."

Julie smiled with relief. "He's not an expert, but Leo just said long walks will help."

"I knew you were a genius," Liv said to him and kissed his head. She levered herself up, and with a groan, got to her feet. "Me, however, not so genius to do this right before bringing you home."

Julie handed Liv the leash. "Hopefully you and Holly do a puppy playdate soon. It's good for the puppies. And hopefully, we'll see you at the events coming up." Her voice wobbled a bit. "I don't do this part well. I have to do it quickly, so I'll say goodbye now and, I wish you joy." She waved and turned swiftly away.

Leo tried to follow her, so Liv carefully picked him up and eased him into the soft crate. There was an un-ceremoniousness to the moment that surprised her. This life-changing event she'd anticipated for months had all culminated in a few ordinary minutes.

Leo barely made a sound the entire car ride. Once home, she brought him straight to the dog door her dad installed. Julie had potty trained all the pups, so he went confidently through the flap and Liv swiftly rewarded him with a treat. *Thanks for the treat-tip, Connor.*

She showed him his water and food bowl and where his dog bed and crate had been placed. After about twenty minutes of exploration, he found a spot on the floor and lay down, stretching out long on his side.

"Tired?" she said with a smile.

The doorbell rang and his head jerked up, one ear popping upright like a soldier at attention, the other continuing to flop.

"Oh jeez that's cute." Still smiling, she opened the door to her parents.

"How's my grand puppy?" Mary said, barely acknowledging Liv with a half kiss on the cheek as her gaze swept the house until she spotted him. "*Ohh*," she said, her expression softening. "What a beautiful little sweetheart." She went to him and carefully picked him up and he lay soft and docile in her arms, peering at her and his surroundings through his superhero mask.

Taking him to the sofa, they sat while Mary cooed to him, and her dad kissed his head and tickled his face with his own whiskers. Watching them, Liv realized this is how it would be if she had a baby. It was a thought she'd never wanted to ruminate on before but now it happened without choice. Her, with a baby, and a family dog.

Had her mom planting the seed done that or was it this exact moment working on her? After a moment, Liv supposed it didn't matter. It was done. Christmas, vacations, school plays and sports and birthdays with her child and parents and dog.

Yes.

Not yet, but she abruptly determined that if life didn't sort her out by the time she turned thirty-five, she'd pursue life on her own.

Coming around to sit opposite them, she hissed and fell into her seat, making both her parents look at her sharply.

"I worked out too hard yesterday," Liv said. "I'm paying more than I knew I could for it."

Cal chuckled. "I did that once. Never did it again."

"That's going to be my story."

They smiled at each other, though it fell from Liv's face when Mary asked, "Did Holly get her puppy too?"

"I think so."

"You don't know?"

Mary's pointed glance instantly softened when she looked at Leo. It made Liv smile and not want to fight with her. "I'll tell you all about it when I come over for dinner tomorrow."

"Thank you."

Her attention back on Leo, a look of tenderness filled her expression, and Liv watched her parents becoming grandparents. If Connor hadn't disappeared on her, they would be actual grandparents by now, she was sure. With how much she already loved having Leo, the years of being alone stretched wide and long behind her. She'd battled feeling resentment before, and that old foe came at her again.

A host of '*if only's*' presented themselves and she swiftly had to talk herself away from them. *I chose to be alone, to never get a dog and to avoid deep relationships.*

Because what *he* did, Resentment replied.

But I still chose to let him affect me this way.

You didn't choose. You had no choice, you could barely cope.

But when I could cope, I chose not to work on those parts of myself.

Resentment scoffed and started to retort again but she shouted at it, *My God, he was* a high school boyfriend! *I need to get over my shit! This is all bullshit!*

Maybe it was the language, maybe it was Leo looking over suddenly and blinking his sweet puppy eyes at her, but Resentment abruptly went quiet, and Liv could finally live in the moment.

CHAPTER EIGHTEEN

"You still haven't talked to her?" Hutch said.

It had been nine days in which Connor successfully thought about nothing besides how increasingly detached he felt, again. "I don't know why. When I think about doing it, I go blank and do something else."

"It's not uncommon for there to be a regression."

"I don't want that."

"Then doing what you've always done isn't going to get you where you want to go."

"I don't know how to be different. I'm aware of this window I have with her closing but when I think about reaching out to her again, it's like...nothing. I'm nothing."

Hutch simply looked at him. After a prolonged silence, he said, "I have two books I'd like you to read." Getting up, he went to a tall bookcase Connor had previously assumed was crammed full of psychology books for effect. "The first one's about trauma, the second about self-esteem. I'd like you to read a chapter by the next time we meet. Can you do that?"

"Sure." It would probably rank at least equal with sitting in silence at home, staring blankly at a game, fighting the itch to hook up with a woman because the 'sex-addict' suggestion still rankled.

"Liv has my number too. She hasn't talked to me either." Just saying it made him think about the expression in her eyes the last time they were together. "There was this moment when we went out where I thought I could have her again, and I backed off. When I first saw her, after all the years, I couldn't stop thinking about her. All I wanted to do was be with her and erase everything that happened. But once I know I can have her again—" he looked around, not wanting to say what he knew sounded shitty. "I know you said it's fear," he continued. "But it doesn't feel like fear. It doesn't feel like anything. I've heard women say guys just like to chase, and yeah, that's sometimes true but I didn't think that was true with Liv. "

"Feelings for Liv saved your life, so feeling nothing now isn't a real state of being, it's more like a safe holding position, a survival instinct you've long relied on.

"When I first asked you how you felt when your dad abandoned you, you said you didn't know. When I asked you how you felt every time your stepdad hurt you and your mom did nothing, you said you didn't think about it."

"I remember."

"And I told you that you protected yourself by not thinking about it so that you didn't have to deal with the hurt. But one way or another, it still comes for you because it's a wound that either gets treated properly so it can heal, or not and becomes an infection that takes over your whole life. We've been working on the wound, opening it, and I think it's a good time now to work on the next step of cleansing it.

"Start with writing a letter to the ones who've wounded you the most. Write your stepdad a letter, even if you don't send it, telling him what you think of him and what he did to you and your mom. Write your mom a letter about how her actions after your dad left hurt you. Write your dad a letter and tell him what you think of a father who leaves his wife and son."

"I don't know where he is," Connor murmured. "Last I heard he was in Germany with his wife and kids."

"So you have half-siblings."

"Yeah. I thought about that when I was in Germany, I could be walking by my brother or sister."

Hutch nodded. "Write about that in the letter. I want you to *pursue* addressing the hurt. It's empowering to take control of the wrongs committed against you. To say 'this is what you did, and I've got the strength to say how much you hurt me and say out loud how wrong it was'. To open an old wound takes strength, to clean a wound always hurts, the healing takes time, but a properly healed wound no longer takes something from you."

"I think I'd prefer an antibiotic," Connor said wryly.

"A lot of people do. That's why we have a drug epidemic."

Connor thought of all the addicts he'd seen and dealt with during his time in narcotics. A surprising number had been good citizens that became addicts from the drugs doctors prescribed. "I'd prefer to do the work."

An expanding smile eased across Hutch's whole face and something like…joy filled his gaze and he blinked repeatedly.

"You like the sound of that, huh?" Connor said, amused.

Hutch laughed. "I like the sound of that."

Their session ended and Connor took the books home, pausing to pick up a poke bowl on the way. As he ate at his glass dining table, he grabbed whichever book happened to be on top of the stack. Trauma. Okay.

When Hutch gave him the book, Connor had thought it would apply more to the shit he'd experienced in the army, yet one chapter in and his thoughts kept going to when he was young. He read for hours, his attention heightened on the subjects of neglect, abandonment and helplessness. With each one, Connor felt a sense of revelation, of understanding of himself and his reactions from his experiences.

By the next evening, he'd finished the book. Then he grabbed a pad of paper and a pen:

Dear Sir,

I didn't think it right to call you 'Dad' since you haven't cared for me as a father would. My stepdad beat me when I was a kid. Mom hooked up with him after you left us. You knew she wouldn't handle you leaving her, it made her lose her mind, she stopped thinking clearly, and did everything she could to stop feeling. She took so many pills to numb herself it was easy for my stepdad to use me as a punching bag, and easy for her not to deal with it. Thank God someone found out. A family helped me, gave me a home to go to and fed me. The dad gave me a job so I could buy myself new clothes since mine had gotten so old they had holes in them. Someone else's dad cared more than my father. I've never been able to understand that. I'm not sure I want to, because I don't want to make sense of that kind of coldness. I don't want the son to see the sense in the father. I don't want to be like you. You failed in your duties. You failed your family. You failed your wife. You failed your son. You. Failed.

I don't really think this letter will ever be read by you, but just imagining it is something. I wonder if I have a brother. Did you treat him better? Part of me hopes so, the other part—what the hell makes him better than me? I was a good kid. I'm strong. I'm skilled, I've always worked hard. If I had a son like me, I'd be really fucking proud. So why weren't you?

Most of the time I feel nothing when I think of you, but right now I fucking <u>hate</u> you. As a soldier, your dereliction of duty disgusts me. You've proved yourself to be the weakest, most pathetic of men. I'm glad I never had to serve with you.

Connor

For a while, he simply sat there looking at the letter. What did he do with it? What was the point of it when obviously his father didn't care about what happened with him. If the letter ever made it to his hands, he'd probably throw it away.

The urge to crumple it made him aware of just how agitated he felt. He got up and paced around his condo, then strode out the door. He'd jog.

An image of Liv walking by with her puppy came to mind, but he automatically pushed it away. It was a beautiful image though, with the sweetness in her expression as she smiled at her puppy bouncing beside her—or more likely, running around crazily and pulling. Connor's lips curved thinking about it.

Wait, *now* he was okay to think about her? Why was he so fucked up? It was enough to make him want to punch his own damned head. Automatically, he tried to push his thoughts back to blank, but then doing what he'd always done wasn't getting him where he wanted to go. *Thanks, Hutch.*

With a sigh, he let his mind wander.

Was Liv freaking out about accidents in the house? She'd made her home so welcoming, a place you wanted to settle in to and feel good in. He bet she let the dog on the sofa. He wanted to sit on that sofa with her. Just thinking about being with her eased the tension riding him.

If he could have her, why the hell didn't he have her?

Because he didn't fucking deserve her.

There's no such thing, Liv whispered in his mind. *You just have to do the work.*

"I'm doing the work, Liv," he said under his breath. "So why the hell am I still so fucked up?"

The memory of them walking her dog when they were teens came again, with all the laughing, talking and teasing they'd done while strolling the neighborhood. He kept the memory foremost in his mind as he turned back home. He'd been a part of someone then. Not just one, her whole family. They'd brought him home like a stray dog, and the only thing that bothered him about that was that he wasn't as smart as a dog to know not to leave the family that loves you and cares for you.

CHAPTER NINETEEN

"Come here you little baby," Liv said, laughing as Leo pounced on the crocodile toy she'd bought him after puppy class. He wasn't the star in the class, but it was close, and she felt absurdly proud of him.

Gently picking him up, she nuzzled her face into his soft fur and hugged him while he went languid. It always made her laugh how he could be a busy little thing but as soon as she picked him up, he lazed in her arms like a pampered dame.

She yawned and his head perked up, gaze alert on her wide-open mouth and she laughed again. "It's almost time for bed, isn't it?"

Rather dramatically, he dropped his head back onto her arm.

Burying her face in his fur again, she murmured, "I'm so grateful for you."

A knock sounded at her door and they both perked their heads up. She thought about the camera she wanted to install as she went to the peephole to see who was there.

Connor.

She opened the door.

He simply stared at her and Leo.

"What are you doing here?" she said after a moment.

"Can I come in?" his low voice rumbled.

She stepped back. He walked in and closed and locked the door behind him.

He looked like he'd been working out, in orange athletic shorts and a thick black hoodie. His cheeks held a pink tint from the crisp air and the thought of going into his arms, against the coolness of his soft sweatshirt felt unbearably appealing. Instead, she rubbed her cheek against Leo's head.

"He's cute, Liv," Connor said, watching her movements. He moved closer and reached out to pet him. "Hi Leo." Gently he scratched the side of his neck and Leo leaned into his fingers, eyes falling to half-mast.

The proximity, the intimacy of the moment had her heart thumping warm and heavy in her chest.

"I just finished playing basketball with a bunch of vets," he said. "We play not far from here."

"Did you serve with them?"

"No, they're—" Connor dropped his hand. "My counselor put the group together."

It was hard for him to say it, she saw it in the hesitancy that began in his expression before becoming obvious in his voice.

Leo squirmed. After Liv carefully set him down, she debated moving to the sofa to continue whatever this was but then, she didn't want any more intimacy either. She stayed rooted to her spot. "I'm glad you found them. I wish everyone had someone to guide them as a counselor can, and a group of people to lean on."

A ghost of a smile passed. "I love it when you talk therapy to me."

A soft laugh escaped but she quickly sobered. "It's pretty late, Connor."

"I know, but I figured you always used to stay up late."

"When I was kid. I've got a lot of responsibilities now running my own practice."

He should say sorry and leave. Instead, "So this is when you go to bed?"

Liv sighed. It was only nine. "No." She went to the kitchen and put the kettle on.

"You drink a lot of tea," Connor said, following her.

"Yep." *Why are you here?*

He leaned back against the counter, watching her take a single cup out of the cabinet. She wouldn't ask, she wouldn't make him one, because it was too…

But it really wasn't her nature to refuse to share, so with a subtle glance, she took out another white glazed cup.

"Do all your cups match?" he said.

"If they don't I get rid of them."

He smiled and she couldn't bear how much she wanted to stare at him, share the smile, the moment. "Why are you here, Connor?"

He didn't answer for a prolonged moment, so she said, "If you wanted to see Leo, I could have texted you a picture."

"Why haven't you texted me?" he said quickly.

She stilled. "Why would I?"

"We're friends."

"Over the last months you've popped in and out of my life at random with absolute silence in between."

"You could have broken the silence by texting me."

"Were you waiting for me to?"

Connor looked like he was about to say something and then changed his mind, subtly shaking his head.

"I still don't know what you want, why you keep showing up and disappearing."

"I told you last time why-" he stopped to clear his throat, "I can't help myself."

And she remembered how he'd said he'd have fought harder to resist the draw, years ago. Logically, she reasoned if he thought that, the impulse to fight it was still there.

Finished making the tea, she set his cup beside him but decided to stay in the kitchen, easing back against the counter opposite him. Leo had curled up in his puppy bed next to the sofa and she simply did not want to add Connor to that cozy scene.

"This isn't working for me," she said. "I've tried really hard to adapt to whatever you throw at me—"

"I'm not throwing things at you, Liv."

She gave him a look, like, *Please.* "You come, you go, friendly, flirty, nothing. Signals—I don't even like to use that term, but yeah, signals all over the place and then dead silence. It's just, there's too much. I don't want to do it. I don't want to be friends. I don't want to be friendly exes. I don't harbor anger towards you, I just want this to stop."

"No."

She half laughed. "You don't get to decide. It takes dual participation, and I don't want to participate."

Connor shifted closer, the muscle in his jaw flexing. "You don't care about me anymore?"

"I don't want to do this, Connor," she said quietly.

"You don't feel anything for-?" He cut himself off, as if he couldn't say, *me.*

"I do. I'm sure I always will. But I don't want to be friends."

"I don't want to be friends either!" Agitated, he moved even closer until he stood directly in front of her. "I—" he began at the same time she said, "Then why are you here?"

"I can't help myself."

"That tells me nothing." She snorted. "Other than that you don't really want to be here, which isn't exactly surprising given our history."

He raked his fingers through his hair. "No, that's not—"

"Why is it so bad to want to see me?"

"It's not bad."

"Then why have you been trying so hard to resist it?"

"I don't know."

Exasperated, she said, "I'm just trying to understand why, because none of this makes much sense."

His mouth formed a grim line, his jaw flexing and releasing. "You want to know why? Fine. I'll put it all out there. When I'm with you I just want to pick up from where we left off when we were kids."

A tingling sensation surged up her spine and her hearing became sharp enough to pick up every little sound. "And that bothers you so you avoid being with me until you suddenly can't help yourself?"

"No. That isn't what bothers me."

He shifted even closer, the rustling sound of his clothes a resonant rasp to her ears. His hand came to rest on the counter beside her, and she had to tip her head back to keep eye contact. "Getting close enough to lose you again, does."

"Lose me," she repeated softly. "I was always here. You always knew how to find me." She blinked to clear the spell. "But I lost you. I couldn't find you. I had no way to even look for you."

"I did lose you. Do you think I wanted this? But there's this part of me that takes over and blocks everything I feel. It's like there's a demon inside me that shuts me down, and you're the...angel that brings me back to life."

Her heart felt like a flower unfurling to the sun, but she forced herself to stand unmoving. "So I'm in a tug-o-war with this demon inside you?"

"No, there's no fight when I'm with you. You're the light that takes away all the darkness. But when I'm away from you, the nothingness takes over where all that light had been."

"I can't be with you at every moment."

"And you can't fix me. I understand. I keep trying to fix it, me, because I don't want this. I don't want to be apart from you."

"Except when you are apart from me, then you don't want to be with me."

"That's not *me*. That's not what *I* want. *I* want everything with you, Liv. Everything."

Everything.

Stunned, her gaze lowered to her tea.

"Will you set the fecking cup down?"

"What? Oh."

As soon as she set it down, his free hand rose to her cheek, then the other followed to cradle her face in his hands, and he eased his body against hers.

What was happening? Her mind couldn't catch up with her emotions, as sensations rushed through her at the feel of him pressed against her. The weight of him, the warmth, God she wanted him. She'd wanted him for *so long*.

"Liv," he said softly, his gaze searching hers. Then he lowered his head.

The brush of his lips was soft, gentle and her lids slid shut at the feel of it. With a soft sound, she moved against him, hands gliding up his sides, around his back and her lips parted. The warm, languid stroke of his tongue into her mouth made her sigh and his fingers slid into her hair, angling her head to stroke deeper.

The taste of him, God his taste. So perfect. She wanted more. Sliding her tongue against his, she closed her lips around his tongue and gently pulled back letting it stroke all along the insides of her mouth. He groaned and his hands moved, dropping to her sides, stroking up under her shirt to her skin.

Hhhhh. It was so good. His hands. Rough and strong, sliding over her belly, up her sides, his thumbs brushing at the undersides of her breasts. Restlessly she shifted, arching into his hands and slowly his thumbs eased up the swell before giving firm flicks over the taut nipples. She gasped at the flare of intense pleasure, so unimaginably aroused, just the feel of him there had her close to coming.

Abruptly he lifted his head. He tugged her shirt up, off. Her bra disappeared and her aching breasts rose to his rapt gaze.

Reverently he caressed the plump fullness and then turned his gaze to her face as he stroked her nipples. Her eyes nearly slid shut again and he took her mouth, his lips slick and full, slipping against hers, clinging, tongues thrusting. She was so close. It shouldn't happen this fast, but just a little friction would send her over the edge.

Her hands grasped his sides and her leg slid up to his hip as her back arched to bring them closer. A growl sounded in his throat and his hands curled around her bottom. He lifted her, and she locked both legs around him.

He turned, moving down the hall to her bedroom.

Grasping his face in her hands, she kissed him without restraint, in a way she'd always been too afraid to. Licking his lips, she tangled her tongue with his, gently setting her teeth on his tongue when it retreated. He laughed and groaned, and she licked it again then nipped at his upper lip before their lips fused back together.

She didn't want to let go, didn't want to stop, but the soft cotton of his sweater chafed when she wanted skin. Dropping her legs, she pushed his sweatshirt and shirt out of the way, and he pulled it over his head.

"*Hhhnn.*" A sound of pure pleasure came from her throat as she pressed her torso against his smooth chest. She lifted her head, seeking his mouth and his descended on hers as he bore her back against the bed.

He tugged her pants off as she pushed herself further onto the mattress. He paused at her panties, eyes locking with hers. Curling his fingers gently around the thin fabric at the sides, he waited. "Yes," she whispered.

Sliding them off her, he stood back and stared at her bared before him; her long, sleek legs, narrow waist accentuated by flaring hips, and pert breasts tipped by little pink nipples.

"I've waited my whole life," he rumbled.

Hooking his thumbs into his shorts, he pushed them off, his thick arousal bobbing from its release. He was long and deeply veined, the hooded head broad and plump.

"So beautiful, Connor."

Emotion flickered in his expression, and he climbed onto the bed, over her, sliding his body against her and she felt…heaven. Her legs shifted to cradle his hips and she lifted her own to bring him to her, but he resisted, leaning on one elbow to free his hand to stroke down her body.

His fingers grazed her collarbone as his palm settled on her chest and then slid down over her breast, to her ribcage, belly, hip. His thumb brushed at the blond curls before sliding his whole palm over her. His thumb stroked downward, straight down her slit, against her clit, against the swollen wet folds. Everywhere he touched felt unbearably sensitive, swollen with arousal and she said thickly, "Connor."

His breath came out ragged and he gripped her thigh, opening her wide as he looked down at her, where his erection strained inches away to reach her.

"Are you—" he began but then stopped.

Gripping himself, he shifted those few inches and Liv felt the smooth head slipping against her lips, pushing them open, the exquisite friction feeding her nerves with unbelievable pleasure.

He pressed in, moving over her and their eyes locked as he pressed and pressed and pressed. When his hips met hers and he was fully, deeply in her, she gasped softly.

"This okay?" he murmured, pulling back.

"Ye—" he sank back in. "*Hhhnn.*" She almost came.

She fought it, didn't want it to end so soon.

With long, slow strokes she felt every inch of his thick fullness, stretching her, filling her. He pushed into her, tilting his hips to press himself high and deep, his gaze unfailingly locked on her as he watched her unravelling.

With his elbows braced on either side of her, his body rose over hers in a mesmerizing rhythm. His warm, smooth skin slid over hers and her hands stroked him, over his sides and back, down the hard contours of his buttocks.

Lifting her legs, she gripped the taut mounds in her hands, and he thrust hard into her. "Connor!' It was too soon, she didn't want it to be over, but he ground deep, and her whole body shrank to that one spot, that one point of connection, and then pleasure exploded, and her core clenched all around him as his deep thrusts built her ecstasy, making her back bow and her cries echo.

"I can't...*fuck!*' With a sudden growl, Connor jerked and shuddered, goosebumps chasing across his skin as he pumped into her, pumping and pumping, the pleasure going on and on like a flood of warm honey filling up every part of her body.

CHAPTER TWENTY

Connor slowly lifted his head, keeping himself pressed within the warm clasp of her. That was...the *pleasure*... He'd known it would be different with her, but that...nothing had ever been like that.

When they were young, he'd wondered how long it would be before she'd let him have her. He remembered the drive for her had been relentless, every moment he'd wanted her, but she'd been shy of sex, and he'd promised her he wouldn't push.

He'd gotten her top off only once, and she'd been trembling with nerves at just that. It had been a pleasurable kind of Hell, wanting and so close to having, touching but not taking, but if he'd *known* what it would be like between them, no way could he have ever kept his promise.

A lingering shudder of pleasure shook him, and he looked at her. Had she experienced it too? He wanted to ask, but no words came to him. The look of her, with heavy-lidded eyes, lips damp and red, and cheeks glowing with a flush had him kissing her again. Languidly, he licked through the seam, stroking her tongue.

Perfection.

Slowly, he pulled back to look at her again, and then gently kissed the tender space next to her eye, the flutter of her eyelashes tickling his lips. Dragging his lips softly down her cheek, he kissed next to her mouth and then skimmed across her lips to her other cheek, then high on her cheekbone, and back to her lips again.

Her hands eased down his sides and he reached for one, then other, sliding her arms up the bed over her head, linking their fingers together, clasping palm to palm.

He wasn't hard but still he pressed into her, unwilling to release their joining. He stared into her eyes, the blue-brown that had always intrigued him, and all the years of knowing her, of not having her, since they were *so young* played through his mind as their gazes held locked together.

Releasing a hand, he stroked the backs of his fingers over her cheek, savoring the softness of her. His gaze slipped to her lips again. Even when everything about her had been gangly, her mouth had been so damned sexy. Leaning down, he licked the plump bow of her upper lip then nibbled at it, testing the fullness between his own.

She made a soft sound, and he released her, trailing kisses along her jaw to her neck, nipping at the spot below her ear in a way he remembered used to give her goosebumps.

When goosebumps dappled her skin, he laughed softly, mouth still pressed against her. She shifted slightly, arching to press her chest to his and just that touch of movement caused the beginning climb of pleasure, and he began to thicken inside her.

She made a low sound and tilted her hips. Their gazes locked and he rocked against her. It was too soon for him to go again but he couldn't relinquish her, couldn't stop feeling himself inside her.

Her breasts trembled from his deep rocks, and he watched the tight pink tips move under his gaze. Lowering his head, he licked a hard peak, slid his tongue along the ridged sides and then dipped the tip of his tongue into the center of her nipple. Her hands slid over to the sides of his head, and she held him there, rocking her hips more insistently.

He glanced at her, and murmured so that her nipple grazed his lips, "Do you like that?"

She stared, seemingly mesmerized as his mouth toyed with her nipple, and then he rocked hard into her, angling his hips up and a guttural sound escaped her. "Are you close again?" he whispered.

"It feels so good," she whispered back.

He gave her a lazy smile. "So, not that close."

He kissed between her breasts and eased downward, feeling himself slide slowly out of her the further he went. The coolness of the air heightened where the wetness of her coated him.

Her belly felt smooth, the skin delicate, soft as he stroked his cheek against it, one side, then the other, and breathed her in.

Further down, he looked at the golden shimmer of her blond curls and rose to kneel between her legs, staring at her. She shifted slightly, as if self-consciously about to cover herself but then stilled and kept herself open, allowing him to gaze upon her.

The backs of his fingers stroked down her mound, his gaze focused on the pretty pink folds peaking out. Gently, he used his index finger to part her more, riveted by the glistening flesh, still wet from him. He slid his finger along the inside of the plump lips and watched a bead of his cum slide out of her. He stilled, seeing it. A ferocious possessiveness swept through him, and his gaze abruptly locked with hers. *Intensity.*

He went rock hard, his breath hissing. To see his seed, *in her*, made him burn. He rose over her again and slid his shaft thick and deep into her. His lips descended to hers and he kissed her hard, tongue thrusting and lapping as he plunged forcefully into her.

She cried out, her body clenching and he gripped her thigh, pulling it high and tight as his hips surged against her. Long, deep, hard thrusts. Every inch of him, clasped hard and hot by her body. The tight, wet squeeze. Bliss.

"*Liv.*" He gritted. His hips slapped against hers, his cock swelling. "I need to…" Her back arched, dragging her nipples across his chest and he gripped her head still, taking her mouth. She cried out suddenly, convulsing, head arching back and he held her lower lip in his teeth, not letting her go.

Her internal muscles suddenly clenched hard around him, forcing him over the edge and his seed spurted out, making him jerk and groan, his whole body shuddering.

Collapsing on top of her, breathing heavy, he tried to support his weight enough she wouldn't tell him to get off. He didn't want to move, ever. Ever.

Eventually, Liv began to shift. He ignored it. *Don't make me go.* He wasn't clear on how he got to be in this exact moment, but he didn't want it to stop. If he said nothing, stayed still, maybe she'd let him stay.

Her hands stroked up his back, and then she hugged him. He stayed still, liked how this was going. Her head lifted and she kissed his shoulder, and something inside him he hadn't known was tense, relaxed.

After a moment, he reluctantly raised his head, then reluctantly pulled his elbows in enough to brace himself above her. Almost hesitantly, he met her gaze, and then something else in him he hadn't known was tense, relaxed. Her expression was soft, her lips and cheeks rosy. She looked well loved.

I've waited so long for you, he wanted to say, but held it because he didn't want to shade the moment with what he'd done. *I love you. I never stopped loving you,* but his past problems would make her doubt it. So he simply thought it, felt it, as he stared at her. *I imagined my whole life with you.*

Her head raised and he kissed her, feeling so connected to her it was like they were one.

Then she pulled him back down on top of her, his head resting beside hers. He began to relax, pressing her body into the mattress so he subtly shifted to ease his full weight off her, and paid acute attention to the feel of his softened shaft slipping from her body.

They dozed.

Some time later, he felt her moving and he deliberately pretended to be too deeply asleep to notice. She got out of bed, and he cracked an eyelid to watch her smooth, lithe form as she disappeared into the hall, only to return moments later carrying Leo to his crate. She disappeared again to the bathroom, and he tensed as she came out, keeping his eyes solidly shut, careful to make his breathing slow and deep.

She was silent and unmoving for a long while, and the intense need to look at her nearly had him breaking his resolve to stay deeply asleep. Was she debating kicking him out? Thinking about how to politely wake him up and tell him to go? He knew she'd do it polite.

The lights snapped off and a moment later he felt her weight shifting the bed. She slid right next to him, and he waited what had to be a reasonable amount of 'still asleep' time before rolling over and pulling her back against him.

"Connor?" she said softly.

His mind tensed, *was she going to throw him out* now? Thinking quick, he made a sleepy sound and mumbled, "Let's snuggle."

CHAPTER TWENTY-ONE

The first time Connor cracked his eyes open, it was five in the morning. He lay on his back, Liv curled against his side. Cautiously lifting his head, he peered down at her, long lashes fanned the soft fullness of her cheeks, lips slightly parted as she breathed deep and slow. Then he looked over at Leo in his crate, sleeping pretty much the same way. That feeling came over him again, and he lay his head back down, closing his eyes.

When was the last time he'd actually slept with a woman? Possibly with her when they'd spoon on the couch when her parents weren't home; a couple times he'd fallen asleep. All the women he'd had sex with since, he'd left shortly afterward. It wasn't a rule, just something he did. It was the thought of waking up in the morning with someone. This was for sure the first time he'd slept all night with a woman.

Liv shifted, turning to her other side. She turned from one side to the other a lot. Her bed was a type of memory foam, so it wasn't the shaking that made him notice it, more his own movement to pull her back against him that did.

Turning on his side, he spooned her again. The feel of her soft skin against his had him exhaling long and low. That feeling.

Another came with it. The firm press of her taut bottom nestled against his hips had his shaft twitching, lengthening, pushing between her thighs. She was so warm and soft he briefly daydreamed about her being wet and ready, rocking into her, waking her up with his cock buried deep and a cry of pleasure coming from her lips.

His shaft twitched against her. He tried to think of math.

Easing his hips back, the pleasure of sliding between her thighs had his jaw going slack and he had to force himself to carefully disentangle himself. It was their first morning. She should be awake and able to consent to him having her again. Shouldn't she? She hadn't kicked him out last night, after. They were still in bed naked...

"Shit," he mouthed and eased himself out of the bed. Good time to take a piss, give his head a moment to win the argument.

It took a long damn time for his body to calm down enough to relieve himself. He washed his hands after, looking at himself in the mirror. She hadn't seemed to notice his injury last night, would she this morning?

He'd have to run home and grab fresh clothes before work, so he should leave in an hour. Maybe she went in later in the morning. Maybe she'd still be asleep when he left. Should he slip out like that?

Silently, he went back in the room. Liv hadn't moved. Leo sat up, watching him with one ear up, the other folded over. "Not yet," he said quietly and climbed back into bed.

Keeping a slight space between their bodies, he gave in to the pleasure of simply being able to touch her. The gold of her hair that had always drawn his gaze caught it again now, and he lifted his head to watch his fingers stroking through it. The smooth creaminess of her shoulder beckoned, and he trailed gentle kisses across her skin. His fingers wandered, sliding from her ribcage to the sharp indent of her waist.

A soft sigh escaped her, and he lifted his head higher to see if she was awake, but her eyes didn't flutter. His hand slid over her hip, shaping the gentle curve of it

Liv turned toward him, and he held his hand up like he'd been caught, but she was still asleep. Perfect opportunity to stare hard as hell at her. He gazed at the crescent fan of her eyelashes to make sure they didn't flutter at all before he turned his gaze to her breasts. They were little and round and firm with delicate pink nipples that he started to reach for but then paused. *Should he?* They were in bed together, naked! But…were there morning rules when you slept the night through together? And whatever he did to get here, he wanted to make sure he did again, but he didn't know what that was, so.

He lowered his hand. *Err on the side of gentleman.* He let out a harsh sigh and gazed at her stiff nipples. Not super stiff, about halfsies, the exact state where they seem to want to be stroked but aren't demanding it.

Forcing his gaze away, his eyes trailed down the contours of her stomach to the tidy mound of springy blond curls shining between her legs. He wanted to pet her there, just gently. It wasn't *un*gentlemanly to just lightly…?

His fingertips grazed her stomach and he paused, staring, debating. His pinky slipped lower—

BEEPBEEPBEEPBEEPBEEP!!!!!

Connor jerked so fast and hard away he teetered wildly on the edge of the mattress. Liv shrieked, bolting upright, and Leo let out a long, worried whine. Connor had to quickly find his feet before falling flat on his ass out of the bed, and Liv swiftly reached over to the alarm clock and shut it off.

They stared at each other, he still half crouched, his erection still standing at attention, her with her eyes wide as though she'd been stunned.

"I've heard bombs quieter than that," Connor said finally, and it must have knocked the stunned out of her because blood rushed to her face, turning her cheeks an exuberant pink and she blinked her gaze away to anywhere but him. And then, "Oh! I've got to go! I've got—" she scrambled out of bed, clutching the sheet to her. When it stayed tucked into the mattress, she leaned against it, trying to pull it with her but it wouldn't budge.

Connor stood there blatantly watching her, not covering himself at all as she tried to imperceptibly strip her bedsheet off and failing miserably.

Face flaming, she swiftly glanced at him then away, but then jerked right back to him, to his thigh. She stopped pulling the sheet and turned to look. "Oh." Her gaze softened with compassion. "That is bad. I'm sorry that happened to you."

"Liv," he said gruffly, and she looked in his eyes for a moment before her face flamed again and she dropped the sheet, dashing to the bathroom. Over the sound of the water running, she called, "Will you let Leo out?"

Connor looked at the little guy as he pulled his shorts on. He had one ear up and his head was tilted as he watched him. As soon as he opened the crate, Leo casually climbed out and gave a full body stretch, little paws finishing the movement with a small shake. Then he sat and looked up at Connor, so Connor said, "Bathroom?" Nothing happened. "Uhm, pee? Need to pee?" What did she used to say to her dog Darcy when he needed to go out? "Outside?" Leo yawned. She wouldn't say the john, toilet or piss. Did she used to say potty?

"Potty?"

Leo stood and started walking out the door. "Pretty good," Connor murmured, following him.

Leo let himself out the little dog flap to the backyard and Connor stood there watching him, thinking about how Liv was clearly freaking out. The thought made Connor grin and filled him with a calm sort of relaxation.

The sound of her moving around in the bedroom had him wandering back to it. She'd already dressed in a business suit with her wet hair wound into a high bun.

"I'm going to have to run out of here," she said, hardly looking at him. "I have an early meeting and I forgot to set my alarm to compensate for it."

Connor shrugged into his hoodie and then sat on a tufted bedside chair to get his socks and shoes on. Finished, he stared at her, waiting for her to be still and look at him. It took a minute, but finally she did. "I'm sorry," she said awkwardly. "I have to run."

He stood. "I'll call you."

"Okay."

She gave him a wan smile and he fought the urge to grin. Striding over to her, he cupped his palm to her cheek and leaned down to give her a hard kiss. Then he left quickly, resisting the impulse to hang out down the street to see if she really was in such a hurry.

* * * *

Liv deflated once the sound of his truck driving away faded to nothing.

Last night. How was she going to *cope* if he disappeared on her again? Was she going to be worse off, or better, now that she'd had him? Her very own, "FOTC," she groaned.

It was. Oh it was.

She'd never get over this. *And she had no one to talk to about it.*

"Eff," she muttered.

Leo came trotting in, and she swooped down to pick him up and bury her face in his fur. "I'm so glad you're here." Liv kissed his head. "If I was alone, I might be going a little crazy right now."

Setting him down, she swiftly got his food and refreshed his water. She still hated leaving him every morning, but she really had to run. At the door to the garage, she paused to glance at him, and he stood there watching her. Maybe she should get him a buddy so he wouldn't be lonely.

"Yeah, go *years* without any real commitments and then switch to full on family explosion mode." Shaking her head she said, "Bye, sweet boy," and left, and then muttered, "It's not out of the question though."

At her office, she hurriedly flipped on lights before swiftly opening the back door to her office. Outside it, a dark figure buttoned up deep inside a hooded trench coat stood waiting.

"Mrs. Olawale?"

The hooded figure slowly moved toward her. Once inside, she lowered the hood, and Liv noted the dark rings under her eyes and the frizzy hair she typically kept severely restrained.

"I don't usually wake up this early," Mrs. Olawale said, patting her hair self-consciously. "But I haven't been sleeping much lately either." She dropped her hand and her shoulders dropped with it.

"Would you like some coffee?"

"No. My stomach can't take it." She looked at the seating area. "You don't look old enough to help someone like me."

Not the first time she'd heard about her age. "Who's someone like you?" she said only.

"Old." She smoothed her hair again. "I'm only here for Jeremy. How do we get him out?"

"Can you come forward with who committed the murder?"

"Can't." She shook her head, closed her eyes, and whispered again, "Can't."

"If you turn them in, they won't be able to get to you anymore, Mrs. Olawale. You're safe if you turn them in."

"Easy to say."

Liv thought quickly about how to reach her. "I know you want to help your son. I know you don't want him to have to hide and be afraid. You've had the strength to carry on all these years, you have the strength now to protect him. Please, Mrs. Olawale. He's scared and alone right now."

Tears filled her eyes and dripped down the sunken hollows of her face. "I'm scared too," she whispered shakily.

"I'm here with you. I'll help you."

Her expression changed. The tears dried up. "What do you know about life? You can't help me. You can't even help my boy." She backed away, anger and accusation in her gaze. "You call me all the time promising help, but this ain't no help."

"Mrs. Olawale, you know exactly what happened to your husband. You can help your son with that knowledge and once you share it, I can help you get to a safehouse if necessary."

"No!" she hissed. "I won't be saying anything! I came here because you said you could help. Now you help Jeremy, testify for him, tell them what a good boy he is."

Mrs. Olawale had completely closed off, her expression defensive and obstinate.

"I already have, Mrs. Olawale. I will continue to, if given the opportunity. Once Jeremy is found though, I don't know how much good that will do."

"He's still a kid, he'll just go to juvie for a couple years."

She seemed to be reassuring herself, and it made Liv's heart clench for Jeremy that his own mother would rather him serve prison time than help him in his innocence. Yet clinically she also knew Mrs. Olawale was exhibiting behaviors of long-time abuse, and not only from Mr. Olawale, because clearly there was someone in her life that still scared her.

"This was a waste of time." Mrs. Olawale abruptly jerked her hood up. "*Never* call me again." She left, pushing the door open so hard it slammed against the outside wall.

Liv promptly went to her computer and started a new message.

To: Lea Nonme
Subject: Catering

Good morning,
Things aren't looking good. We'll need to meet to discuss the situation. Let me know when you can meet, and where. I'll bring food and books. Please get back to me soon. I need to see you.
Dr. Jones

Patrick unlocked the main door, and then popped his head in her office. "Morning, boss!" She started to return the greeting, but he said, "Have a long night?"

Liv could feel heat flooding her cheeks, and he quickly fumbled out an apology. "That's rude as hell. Sorry. You looked a little zoned out is why—yeah, sorry, rude as all hell. Make it up to you with a workout?"

"Oh, god no," she said, laughing. "It's okay, Patrick. I was zoning out. I do have a lot on my mind."

"Anything I can help with?"

Ah she loved him. He was such a great guy. If she were in the market for sperm, his really would be top notch. She swiftly looked away, because on the heels of that thought came the one of Connor's sperm, sticky between her legs just a few short hours ago.

"No, I really just want to zone out again at the moment," she said almost desperately.

Patrick gave her a long look and then nodded slowly. "You need anything, holler."

As soon as the door closed behind him, Liv closed her eyes and groaned softly. Just that one thought of Connor had her limbs going liquid, her body ready to accept him. She wanted to call him and ask if it had been as good for him as he'd hoped because it had been better for her than she'd ever imagined. She hadn't *known* it could be that good. Did he want to do it again? Forever?

Forever.

Her heart clammed up. Not again. She wouldn't.

Surging out of her chair, she went to Patrick's desk for the files he hadn't finished gathering for the day.

"Two more," he said, standing over the open file cabinet, fingers skimming over the manila tabs until he found one and pulled it out. "One more."

Liv scanned the list of clients coming in and read through the last couple session notes on her first client of the day.

"No more." Patrick handed her the last file.

Back at her desk, she checked her phone to see if Connor…anything. She powered it off after staring at the wallpaper of Leo lying like a sphinx on the grass in her parent's backyard.

At lunch, she still didn't turn it on. She went home and Leo stood waiting for her at the door. He wanted to play so she took him for a walk and then did a little tug-o-war with him while she ate a salad. It wasn't until she absolutely had to that she went to her bedroom to get workout clothes, even still, she avoided looking at the bed.

When it came time to go to Pilates, she followed the same protocol as before: she worked out way too hard. Halfway home, she fished out her phone and powered it on.

Why did it take so long to load? She was in her neighborhood by the time everything came online.

Three texts. All from Connor.

Overwhelming relief soared through her, but then she did a swift scan to make sure *mistake* or *sorry* wasn't written anywhere. It wasn't. *Lucky* and *Baby* was though.

That soaring feeling.

Her phone pinged with a voicemail and her face softened because it was probably him.

She pulled into her garage, eager now to know everything he'd said throughout the day. Before she'd even put her car in park, Connor pulled into the driveway.

CHAPTER TWENTY-TWO

Today had probably been one of the best days of his life. Every call she didn't answer, every text she didn't respond to, hit him as a minor blip because he knew her. She had to be panicking. They'd *gone all the way!* as she would have said with whispery shock in high school, which made him grin. And they didn't have a single commitment ironed out yet. Oh yeah, panic-mode.

He was patient. He could wait.

And wait he did, sat outside her house for over two hours. He hadn't known at first if she was home. Wanting to make sure she was before going to the door, he'd parked a little away and watched the window for movement. A single light shone while daylight faded but no other lights or shadows moved as night enveloped. So, he sat, patient.

Finally, her garage door went up, and so did everything in him.

Trying not to screech the tires this time, he swiftly pulled in behind her before she could shut him out and spend time debating letting him in again. He was out of his truck and grinning at her dumbfounded expression, when she took a shaking step.

"Why are you shaking?" He stopped in front of her and looked her over. "Did something happen at karate?"

"Oh, that ended. I just worked out too hard."

"Pilates works you that hard?" He could literally see her deltoid spasming and smoothed his hand over it.

"When I want it to. I probably won't be able to move tomorrow." She smiled wryly.

Perfect opening. "Poor baby," he crooned and turned her toward the door, hooking his arm around her shoulders. "Somebody will have to take care of you."

Her quick, uncertain glance made his lips twitch.

"I… I'm surprised to see you," she said.

"Why?"

They walked into her house and Leo happily bounded over to them, tail wagging so hard his little body wagged with it. Liv laughed softly and picked him up, snuggling him against her cheek.

Connor stood there, arrested by the moment. *This.*

His arms came around her and he gathered them up, burying his face in her hair and breathing her in. Leo squirmed between them to get to Connor, soft muzzle brushing his face as he sniffed.

This.

Liv tried to pull away, but he tightened his arms. "Not yet. Please."

She stilled.

After a while, he raised his head and met her gaze. "You ran me out of here this morning before I could get one of these in. And then you didn't talk to me all day. Pretty cold, Lucky."

She flushed.

He whispered, "Why are you surprised to see me?"

"You know why," she whispered back.

She tried to move away again, but he tightened his arms and lowered his head. Before his lips could find hers, Leo's fluffy head got in the way.

Liv laughed, and then set him down.

As soon as she stood, Connor cupped her cheek and pressed his mouth to hers. The softness of her lips entranced him, and he spent time pushing and retreating against them, nibbling the tender flesh, gently biting, sucking, licking.

She pulled away, saying shakily, "I need to shower. I'm sweaty from—"

Connor kissed her again, his hands sliding down her hips then up over her buttocks, palms stroking up her sides and back down again. Her tank top was damp, and he pushed it up. She pulled back to take it off, saying, "I'm sweaty. I should—"

He kissed her, tongue stroking over her lips, into her mouth to slide against hers. His hands stroked her back, down over her buttocks before he cupped them firmly and rubbed her against his erection.

With a soft sound, her hips rocked against him. He felt the fluttery brush of her fingers as she unbuttoned his shirt, making sexy noises in the back of her throat when he continued to thrust against her.

She pushed his shirt open, groaning in frustration at his undershirt, and then suddenly lifted her leg on his hip and grabbed his ass and ground her pussy against him. She keened a cry as he hissed his pleasure.

He wanted *in* her. Swiftly he yanked his shirt off and growled, "Take off your clothes," as he unbuckled his belt and dropped his pants.

"Here?" She looked at the countertop. "The—" His fingers hooked into both her pants and underwear and stripped them to her ankles, then he lifted her onto the counter and pulled them the rest of the way off. Parting her legs, he pulled her hips to the edge of the counter and watched himself feed his erection between her glossy, plump lips.

"*Mmhh.*" The hot, wet, clench of her body. With short pumps, he worked himself inside her until his hips met hers and then he did a long pull out, and a long sink in.

She was silent and still, her gaze fixed on where they joined. "This okay?" he breathed. Because it was fucking awesome for him.

Her heavy-lidded gaze lifted to his and she leaned back on her hands and brought her knees up, bracing the heels of her pretty feet on the edge of the countertop.

The angle, the clasp. His hips shot forward with long hard strokes.

Abruptly, he stopped. "Take your bra off." He wrapped his hands around her waist to hold her up enough she could work her sports bra over her head. She threw it to the ground and leaned back again and his hips surged. Her tight pink nipples, bouncing with each thrust made his mouth water and he stroked his palm over them. Cupping one breast, then the other, he flicked his thumb over the tip while pumping deep and she gasped, "Connor! Oh! I'm—" He pinched her nipple, ground deep and she screamed, her body spasming, clenching him, hard, and a guttural shout erupted from him as his seed came spurting out, going on and on until he finally shuddered and stilled.

It took a few moments before he came to some measure of awareness. They were both breathing heavy, and Liv's arms were trembling. Sliding his hands behind her back, he pulled her upright and kissed her. Gentle, tender kisses.

"Were your arms trembling because it was that amazing, or because they're overworked?"

Her lips curved and she arched up to give him another soft kiss. "It was that amazing."

"And the workout?"

"I was maybe about to collapse," she admitted.

Connor's lips curved and he eased himself out of her. She promptly scoot back on the counter, and he watched as his semen spilled from her. Meeting her gaze, he said, "I didn't use a condom."

"Well," she said after a moment of heavy silence. "If I get pregnant, I know where you work."

Blood rushed to Connor's head at the thought of her, pregnant with his child. Them. A family. Finally.

"Don't worry, Connor, I'm on the pill."

"Not worried." He stroked a thumb over the softness of her cheek. "It's how I used to picture us one day."

Her gaze searched his and she said softly, "Me too." Then she blinked and looked away. "I need to feed Leo and clean up."

She tried to lift her body up enough to jump off the counter but her shaking arms had Connor quickly grabbing her around the waist to lift her down.

"I can barely move already," she whimpered.

"Poor baby," he crooned and wrapped his arms around her. The feel of their whole, bare bodies pressed against each other made him sigh with contentment. "We should be naked together always."

The feel of her smiling against his chest made him smile in return.

"That could be awkward for unexpected visitors."

"Do you get a lot of those?"

"My parents. They live just down the street you know."

"I know." He stroked a hand down her hair. "Think they'll see my truck in the driveway and come over?"

"If they knew it was *your* truck in the driveway, probably, with a shotgun."

Connor grimaced. "I'm working on what to say to them, so they won't want to shoot me."

"Not the truth?"

"I'll tell them the truth, but if they still want to shoot me, I'm telling them you're pregnant." Liv slapped his ass. "Did it do it for you?" he teased.

Her hands smoothed over the round curves of his buttocks, and she rubbed her cheek against his chest. "I did dream of doing this when we were young."

"I can't tell you how many times I wish you had."

With a quiet kiss on his sternum, she eased out of his arms. "I *need* to *shower.*"

"Alright fine. I'll feed Leo and clean up the kids."

She looked at his sperm on the counter. "The kids." She snickered.

The dogfood was in a stylish metal bucket with DOGFOOD stamped on it. The cleaner took only a couple cupboard glances to find. Tidy and organized, she made it easy.

Scooping up their clothes, he went to the bedroom and debated joining her in the shower, but the water shut off. Instead, he put his boxers and trousers back on, but left off his shirt. He didn't want to give the impression he was good to leave.

Liv walked out wrapped in a towel, wisps of damp hair clinging to her skin while the rest was twisted up. She looked at him with surprise—did she really think he'd sneak out? But she said, "Do you often walk around your house in pants, no shirt? I'm a fan if you do."

He flexed subtly and she grinned. "Big fan."

"I'm a big fan of you walking around in just a towel. Bigger fan of when you take it off."

"I'm gonna crush your dreams when I put on loungewear."

"I'll be the judge."

As she disappeared into her walk-in closet, he said, "I didn't bring a change of clothes, so this is the way it's got to be."

"You might get cold."

"If I do, we can snuggle."

A moment later she emerged wearing a cream-colored long sleeve shirt and matching pants. He noticed how the material was thin and clung in nice places. "I'm a fan."

She walked right up to him and hugged him. The impulsive sweetness of it took him off guard.

"It's soft too," he murmured, wrapping his arms tight around her. "Not as soft as your skin though."

He could feel her smile again and then she pulled out of his arms. "I'm starving. I haven't eaten."

"Neither have I," he said quickly. "I came straight here so I wouldn't miss you."

"Are you trying to get me to feed you?" she said with amusement as she walked to the kitchen.

"Please. And also cookies. You still make them, right? Please say you still make them."

"Not as often and only on the weekends."

"That's in three days! I can be patient." She gave him a swift, uncertain glance, so he said, "But only if you want to." Then he chanted softly as if in prayer, "Please want to. Please want to."

She laughed as she pulled various containers from the fridge. "White chocolate macadamia nut still your favorite?"

"Always."

"How are we back to this?" she said, looking to the heavens.

Connor had no idea and didn't want to say anything that might mess it up, so he gave her a wide-eyed innocent expression and said nothing at all.

It worked, she continued to appear amused and swiftly went about making some sort of stir fry. Twenty minutes later they were sat at the dinner table eating, Leo asleep in his bed by the sofa. Almost exactly how he'd imagined it.

Reaching for her, his fingers curved around the back of her neck, pulling her to him for a soft kiss.

"I've got to say," she said with an appreciative look at his bare chest. "This is *not* how I pictured dinners at home with you, but this version is *way* better than the one I had."

He grinned and released her. "You like me half naked at the dinner table?"

"I'm pretty sure anyone who likes men would like you half naked at the dinner table."

"How about completely naked? I could be completely naked."

"You want more kids to clean up?"

"With you, baby, *yes.*"

After the meal they washed the dishes, working together in the kitchen. It was so easy with her, things were so easy with *them,* how could it have been so difficult all these years? Because of his damned head—*No.* He stopped himself. *I've had problems, but I'm here now and I'm getting better. I* am *better.*

When they finished, she turned to him, about to say something, but he said quickly, "Are you ready?"

"For what?"

One arm slipped behind her back, the other hooked behind her knees and he swept her up into his arms.

"Connor!" she gasped.

"Do you have that machine you can shout at to turn off the lights?"

"No."

"Not conducive to my needs right now."

"You want to stay the night again?" she said as he went around, flipping off lights, tilting her in his arms to do it.

"Yes, thank you for asking."

"I have to put Leo in his crate."

"C'mon, Leo!" Connor called, walking down the hallway to her bedroom. The little click of puppy nails on wood floor followed them.

He set her down and then went to the bathroom. He came out to find her brushing her teeth, and their gazes locked in the mirror for a moment. Such a strangely intimate thing. Brushing teeth, getting ready for bed. It gave him a vaguely uneasy feeling, like he didn't belong, he should go.

Like hell he was going to leave when she'd just let him in.

A new toothbrush rest on the counter beside the sink and he plucked it up. They brushed together.

Liv spit the last of the foaming paste from her mouth then used her toothbrush to rinse by repeatedly sucking water from the bristles. Interesting way to go about it.

And then, with a tight smile, she left him alone in the room.

He rinsed his mouth and then braced his hands on the counter.

I don't want to be fucked up anymore.

Hutch would probably tell him to be gentle with himself, or something like that. That it was fear making him lose his shit right now.

I'm not totally losing my shit.

So, good. Progress.

Don't fuck this up, soldier. I want everything with her.

With one last look at his stoic reflection in the mirror, he flipped off the lights and went into the bedroom. She wasn't in bed. She sat on her tufted chair, looking damned uncomfortable, knees pressed together, hands tucked between them.

'What's wrong,' almost slipped out, but he caught it. *Don't give her one damned opening to say this isn't a good idea.* Instead, he went to stand right in front of her, dropped his trousers, grabbed her, then launched her on the bed.

She squeaked when she landed, and he grabbed the legs of her pants, tugging them off.

Snickering, she scrambled back and slipped under the covers.

"I can't believe you don't make your bed in the morning," Connor said as he got in, following her under the covers.

"I usually do."

He braced an elbow beside her head and leaned over her. "In too much of a hurry this morning, huh?"

She gazed up at him, blue-brown eyes heavy. "And maybe I wanted to see the way we left the sheets when I got home."

His lower belly clenched. "I can remind you." He slid his hand under her shirt, up the soft contours of her stomach. He watched her expression as he thumbed her nipples. "So sensitive," he murmured. Tugging the shirt off, he teased them until they stood erect in high, tight peaks, then bent his head and licked them, dragging his tongue across the tips.

Liv moved restlessly, arching her hips up and he rolled on top of her. He kissed down her body, her stomach, her lower belly, her mound. She parted her legs wide and rose on her elbows to watch him. So fucking hot.

Using his index finger, he made a long stroke from the top of her mound, over her clit and down, sinking his finger deep inside. So wet. He dragged his finger back out, parting her lips wide to expose that shiny little clit pulsing for him.

Gently, he blew cool air on her, and she laughed breathily. Then he licked her. His tongue stroked up the side of her nub and down, under it, all around. She watched. Gasping, mouth open. He couldn't resist sinking his tongue into her opening, suddenly, deeply, lapping at her. Her eyes rolled back, and she made a guttural sound. He sat up on his heels, gripped her under her thighs and lifted her to meet his cock. Fuck, he loved watching it sink into her. The way her wetness sucked him in.

Bracing a hand on the wall, he held her thigh wide with the other and pushed into her with long, measured strokes.

"You feel so good," she breathed as he sank deep.

The way he held her there, she could barely move, could only receive, and the pleasure of stroking himself inside her was unbelievable.

She tried to hitch her hips up, to reach her spot, he knew. He had already clocked where she went off when he was inside her, but he didn't want to give it to her yet. Instead, he angled his hips just enough to *almost* reach it but backed off when she bore down on him.

"Connor!" Her hands reached for his ass, and she pulled hard on his hips.

"Not yet, baby."

Her back arched, nipples pointing at the sky, begging to be sucked. "Why," she moaned.

He stilled, taking his hand off the wall to thumb the tight peaks. She clenched down all around him, her hips rocking, and he groaned, "Fuck!"

Pushing high and deep into her, he pumped his hips, hitting her spot and she went off, crying out, throat arched and working as she shuddered and shook beneath him.

"Liv!" he bellowed, his own orgasm exploding like a fire through him, pleasure taking over every part. His whole body went rigid as he came within her.

CHAPTER TWENTY-THREE

He collapsed beside her, and she lay boneless, unmoving. After a while, he said, "Let's do that every night," making her laugh.

"I honestly never knew it could be like that."

"Neither did I."

She looked at him. "Do you really mean that? I know you've been with many women."

"It's different with you. You know it is. I told you I haven't been in a relationship with anyone since you."

"Or brushed your teeth with them?" she said with a slight curve to her lips.

He grimaced. "No."

"I was fully prepared for you to suddenly remember you had something you had to do and take off."

Sighing, he turned on his side to face her. "Why do you think I reacted like that?"

The surprise in her expression was unmistakable, and with her, he felt proud that he was now tuned in enough he could ask.

She turned on her side to face him. "There's something deeply personal about mundane self-care. Sharing it gives the feeling of exposure, I think, of our private moments."

He stroked a hand down her shining hair. "That's a good diagnosis. I think I know the cure."

"Oh yeah?"

"Doing it every night." He wiggled his brows. "After."

Her smile made his heart swell.

"I'm sorry for all the years we lost," he said quietly.

A glassy quality shimmered over her eyes, and she blinked repeatedly. "I am too."

"I wish I'd been your first."

A surprised laugh slipped from her. "Such a guy."

"No—well, yeah, but that's not what I mean. I meant that experience of being your first. That memory."

"I'm not sure how I would have coped once you ghosted me, if we'd gone all the way."

He grinned at *all the way*, but quickly stifled it at her look. "Sorry. It was—never mind."

"It wasn't funny."

"No, and I wasn't—Anyway, I don't know if I would have if we'd…" He sighed. "I probably would have. I was really messed up. I shut down."

Her gaze searched his for a moment, then she said, "It wasn't horrible, my first time. None of my boyfriends have been horrible. Just, not terribly stimulating."

"I think all I really want to hear is that I've ruined you for anyone else," he said, only half joking. Less than half. Not at all.

"I think that's been true for over thirteen years," she said dryly.

Be true for a lifetime, he thought. Saying it aloud though… what if she backed off, not believing him? What if he went dark again? She'd never trust anything he said. He had to make absolutely fucking sure he never did anything like that with her again.

"Now go on," she teased. "Tell me I ruined you for anyone else now too."

Connor gazed at her a long moment. "There is no one else for me."

Her eyes shimmered again and then she smiled so beautifully, it moved every part of her face. "That's the most perfect goodnight we could go to sleep to."

Hours later, with Liv curled against his chest, Connor jerked violently awake to the explosive *BEEP!* from her phone's alarm.

"Holy sh—" He jumped out of bed and charged across the room to tap her phone silent. She was still dead asleep.

"Liv!" Her heavy lids barely blinked open. "Sit up!"

Groaning, she slowly pushed herself to a sitting position. "Not a morning person."

"No kidding." He came to sit on the bed beside her. "My body exploding should have woken you if that blast from your phone didn't." Her eyes had closed again.

He pinched the ends of her hair and used the tips to tickle inside her nose. She jerked back and rubbed her nose aggressively. "Turd," she muttered.

"Wanna go for a run?"

"Never in a million years." She yawned and eased out of bed like a ragdoll on strings. "You know how women always joke about wine and coffee?"

"One of my buddies in Narcotics said every woman on this dating app he used had wine and coffee listed as one of their interests."

"Precisely." She groaned as she slipped into a robe. "I'm sore. And I don't joke about coffee." Puppet strings dragged her ragdoll body out to the kitchen.

"Should I let Leo out?" he called as he pulled on his boxers.

"Oh my gosh I'm a terrible doggy mom," he heard her mutter before she called back, "Yes please."

"She's so polite in the morning, huh buddy," Connor said, flipping the latch on Leo's crate.

The sound of coffee beans grinding had him wandering out to the kitchen.

"Did you work in a coffee shop after high school?" She had a pretty fancy setup for an amateur.

"No, my dad supported me until I finished University. I am aware of how lucky I am."

Coming up behind her, he wrapped his arms around her waist and dropped his chin to her shoulder. "You've always been lucky, Lucky Legs."

"Lucky they don't snap," she said with a small smile.

They listened to the coffee brewing, the scent another pleasure of the moment. "I've got to go in a minute to get clean clothes and get to work on time," he murmured.

"How long does it take you to get home?"

"Ten minutes."

"You live ten minutes from me?"

"You don't know where I live?" He leaned sideways to look at her. "You mean you can't hack the government system that tells you exactly where I live?"

Her eyes rounded and she turned on him. "I *knew* you broke the law—"

"Not badly!" he said, laughing. "You *are* a party in a case I'm on." Her expression went guarded and she turned back to the coffee. "Aw, c'mon, baby." He nuzzled her cheek. "I promise I won't throw you in the slammer."

She snorted and her elbow nudged his stomach.

Chuckling, he backed away to her room and finished dressing. When could he bring clothes over? Maybe he could sneak some in over the weekend. He looked in her closet. It wasn't rammed with clothes. It would be easy to hang a few things toward the back that she probably wouldn't notice for a while.

When he came back out, she was pouring coffee into a stainless steel to-go cup for him. "Do you have milk and honey?" he said, getting a sticky pad and pen from the drawer he'd seen it in earlier.

She set the items beside his cup. "I can't make any promises about parting the red sea though."

He had no idea what she was talking about.

"Bible joke," she said.

"That explains it." He slapped the sticky note on the counter and swiftly fixed up his coffee. "The bible isn't funny." He took a sip. "Neither is this coffee. Wow. I was gonna ease into this but forget it. I'm here every morning."

"Told you." She peered at the note. "What is this?"

"Directions to my condo."

"GPS won't take me there?"

"I wanted to make sure you could find me no matter what."

"Well," she drawled, "I could always stalk you at your work."

He drew her into his arms, each balancing their coffee cups away from their bodies. "I wouldn't complain." He kissed her, lips warm and soft. "I don't want to go."

Her hand stroked down his back to squeeze his butt. "You better before I do things."

"I'm always happy to put more kids on the counter." He kissed the column of her throat and then eased away from her, adjusting himself. "I'll call you. Answer this time, okay?"

"If I can. I won't turn my phone off this time though."

"More progress. I like it."

At his condo, he swiftly showered and changed. He didn't like being there. It was sterile and unwelcoming, amplifying the warmth he'd just left. Before he took off, he grabbed a couple changes of clothes and put them in his biggest camping bag. If she balked when he started slipping stuff in, he could pretend it was a camping mix up.

Like she'd believe that. He shook his head at his own absurdity. Wasn't going to change anything though.

At the station, Fernando sat grimacing at a little pot of breakfast food that had *iSlim* written on the side. His gaze flicked over him before returning to the mush he clearly didn't want to eat. "Why in the damned hell do you look like you're riding on sunshine?" He shoved in a spoonful of the sludge. "Walking on sunshine. That's what it is." He chewed and talked. "One look at you and that song starts playing somewhere in the background. It would be eerie if it wasn't causing a pain in my ass."

"Sounds like a personal problem." Connor grinned at his partner's crankiness. "Bad night?"

"Bad everything." More sludge disappeared. "Bad gag reflex I'm fighting right now." He picked up a couple files and waved them in the air. "Toxicology report came back on your junkies. OD'd from Fentanyl in their heroine. Everything else is pretty quiet, so I pulled a couple cold cases. Maybe your beginner's luck will find us all the answers."

"My beginner's luck isn't working with the Olawale case."

"Give it time. Give everyone time. Give everything time. Because everything's shit and time won't fix it but it's something to say to distract us while we eat shit." Another bite.

Connor blew out a breath. "Well. That's a heavy cloud to pass over my sunshine." He grinned at Fernando's glower. "Want to get coffee and talk about it?"

Fernando's head jerked and he looked at him like he'd grown three heads. "I want whatever you're having. Is it something I can take? Give me some, I want out."

Connor dug in his drawer and grabbed a *Cutie* mini orange he'd stashed there earlier in the week and tossed it to him.

"Sunshine grows oranges. Why did I never think of this." Fernando handed Connor a file. "I'll eat while you work. It will be the highlight of my life."

Fernando lapsed into a melancholy silence that lasted the whole day. It was bad enough it made Connor want to press him about what was up. He didn't do it though.

Several times, he texted Liv. When she didn't respond, he called but she didn't answer. Was she panicking? They still hadn't talked about where things stood, so he supposed it was possible once he was gone, she started putting her walls back up.

After their morning, he hadn't thought she'd ignore him again.

Her office wasn't far. Maybe he should. But she'd been very clear about dropping in. He shouldn't. *Calling her office* was allowed, however. Snatching up the phone, he dialed. He-man picked up.

"This is Detective Peltier." Maybe it would make Patrick cautious and put his call through. "I need to speak with Dr. Jones."

"I'm afraid she's unavailable, Detective. I can take a message."

"This is urgent." He'd play the card.

"She's not in the office."

"When will she return?"

"I don't know, she hasn't been in all day."

All day?

By the time he left work to go to Hutch's, agitation rode him hard. Again, he texted her, again nothing.

"How's it going," Hutch said.

"If you asked this morning, I would have said the best it's ever been." Connor dropped onto the sofa with a long exhalation.

"And now?"

"Now, Liv is pulling a me, and it's making me crazy."

"She's ghosting you?"

"Seems like it. She hasn't responded to my texts or calls. Found out she hasn't been in her office all day, but she didn't say anything about that this morning."

Hutch's brows rose. "This morning?"

"Yeah, Tuesday, after basketball, I went to her house. I've stayed with her the last two nights. First day after, she didn't respond either, but I expected it because the night had been unexpected. So, I went back to her house last night, and basically same thing happened. It's just that when I left, things felt clearer. I told her to respond when I texted and she said she'd try, but that was it."

"Unexpected how?"

"I told her I was trying to be better for her, and then we kissed and then, everything. It was our first time, and it was—" he shifted, uncomfortable at the shot of arousal in front of Hutch from remembering them together, "—incredible.

"I don't know what happened for her that she didn't try to get rid of me." Then he told him about the tooth brushing incident and her response. "She acted fine, but did I screw something up with my dumbass reaction?"

"Without talking to her I couldn't say," Hutch said. "In a broad view, what it sounds like to me, is you've got a woman afraid of getting hurt by you again and she's trying to protect herself. That you've taken things to a place you've never been before has got to be a little scary for her."

"So what do I do?"

"What do you think you should do?"

"Oh come on. Don't give me that shit—sorry, language. I'm working on it. But, come on, Hutch. Haven't we been doing this long enough you can give me some real advice instead of leading me on a journey to find my own answer?"

"I like the way you put that," Hutch said with an echo of a smile. "But I'll try to do both, how about that. When you want to disappear on her again, do you think you'll be able to stop yourself from doing that?"

"Yes. Especially if she lets me be with her on the regular. It's when I'm away from her that I get screwed up."

"What if she can't be with you on the regular? Or what happens if she goes away for a week on a work conference?"

"I want to move in with her. Even if she's away, there'll be no being apart."

"Think she'll let you move in?"

"She'd want marriage."

"Do you want to marry her?"

Connor thought, *yes*, but his insides froze. Hutch watched him closely and he tried to hide his reaction, but after a moment slumped his shoulders. "Okay, why am I reacting like this?"

"Can you describe what you're feeling?"

"I don't know. The thought of getting…hell, I don't even want to say it. Thinking it makes me want to get up and walk around."

"Getting married?"

Connor gave him a look. "That."

"You watched your mom get married and then essentially leave you."

Connor's eyelids flinched. "Because of an abusive asshole. Liv isn't like that."

"Have you written him a letter yet?"

"No."

"How about your mom?"

"She's dead."

"You could leave it at her grave. It's not uncommon, Connor."

"I don't know if she has one."

Fucking right. He didn't know. Like him now? He hadn't even *tried* to find his mother's grave and no way in hell was he going to ask that asshole Keith about it.

Hutch gazed at him, clearly trying to decide what to say. "Then burn it once you've written it. Turn it to ash, as we all become. It's an important step for you."

"Yeah. Okay. I'll do that."

They both knew he was blowing Hutch off, and Hutch let it go.

Once the session finished, Connor left feeling as agitated as when he got there.

As he got in his truck to drive by Liv's, his phone buzzed. "Liv."

"Connor, I'm sorry!" Liv sounded like she was cringing as she said it. "It's been a crazy day."

"Where've you been?"

"Running around on this donation project I've got going. I've hardly eaten today, it's been that crazy."

"Let's get dinner."

"What?"

"Meet me at Ocean Café, you know where it is?"

"Um, yeah. I…"

Did she not want to meet him? Connor's jaw flexed. "I just got done with work so I'm starving too." Be playful, he reminded himself. "C'mon, Lucky, let's eat."

"Okay. Okay, yeah. I'll meet you there in a half hour. I'm still driving."

Connor drove to the café and sat in his truck until she pulled into the parking lot. He went to her door and as soon as she got out, he snatched her into his arms and kissed her long and deep.

When he pulled back, she looked flustered but languid. Good. Taking her hand, he tugged her along to the restaurant. The warmth of the lighting, with the stone, oak and wine bottles felt exactly right with her.

"This is nice," Liv said with a tentative smile.

He nodded shortly. "Why didn't you answer my texts or calls today?"

"Jump right to it, huh?"

"It's been on my mind."

"Well, like I mentioned when I called, I was incredibly busy working on—"

"Don't BS me, Liv. I've seen surgeons and soldiers in situations that qualify for too busy to send a quick text. That's it. Why were you avoiding me?"

"Why do you get to be this direct and I don't?"

"Who said you don't?"

"It's the trust, isn't it? You trust I'll sit here and respond reasonably. Would you do the same if the situation were reversed?"

"Of course."

"So, if you suddenly disappear on me again and I'm able to find you now, you'll sit and listen and respond reasonably?"

"Are you going to respond reasonably?"

Her brows lowered. "I'm not being unreasonable."

"You seem defensive."

"I'm—"

"Welcome to the Ocean Café!" A waitress said in a sing-song voice as she came up. "Oh!" she said, looking at Connor. "I remember you from the other night. Your friend dropped her ID and hasn't come back for it yet."

"I'll let her know. Thanks."

She smiled brightly, took their order and then left to get them a beer and a glass of wine.

"The other night," Liv said. "Which night?"

Of course, Connor knew where her thoughts had gone. "Tuesday."

"You came over to my house after?"

"Yes."

"Oh God," she moaned, her head dropping. "We didn't use a condom. Oh my God."

"Stop it, Liv. She's just a friend."

Her head jerked up. "You don't *have* women friends. You always said, remember? 'Guys and girls can't be friends'. Did you come to me right after being with her?"

The waitress arrived with their drinks. Connor folded his arms and leaned back in his chair, gaze hard on Liv and told the waitress, "We'll both have your fish of the day with all the healthiest options for the sides."

Liv's brows faintly rose but she stayed silent.

Once the waitress left again, Connor said, "I didn't have sex with my friend, and I haven't had sex without a condom since before you and I dated."

"With Ana?" Liv said.

"Ana," he agreed. "She was on the pill. I was too young and stupid to consider other things to worry about. I started considering them after you and I broke up."

"We didn't break up."

"Were we together?"

"You mean physically?" Liv said.

"At all."

"No, we weren't."

"Okay, let's call it then."

"Fine, we were broken up. When exactly should we identify the date? The first day you never called me?"

"How about the day I got the call my mom died. How about that?"

Liv's gaze flickered. "Sorry."

Connor fought to unclench his jaw. "I didn't sleep with Vanessa before coming to your house and it pisses me off that's the first thing you thought."

"Why wouldn't it be? You've always slept around—"

"Still slut-shaming, Liv?"

"*What?*"

"Yeah. I remember how you used to call me a man-whore and tell me I'd been around the block so many times there was a path. There's a term for that—slut shaming."

Her face flushed red. "I... You're right. I'm sorry."

Connor's eyes narrowed. "I didn't sleep with her."

"Even if you did, we have no understanding, no commitment between us. You're absolutely right, I have no place to even ask if you—"

"For fu—feck's sake, Liv! I didn't sleep with her, and you do have a right to ask because we do have something here."

She was silent.

He felt like growling. "Hutch said you were probably afraid of getting hurt by me again, after how things have changed. Is that why you ignored me today?"

"Hutch?"

"My counselor."

"Oh."

He felt like throwing his hands in the air. Weird feeling for him. "Vanessa is a vet in my therapy group." When her expression eased, he said, "Yeah, you like that? You should feel bad for making assumptions."

"I do," she said seriously. "I'm an advocate for freedom of expression and choice, or I thought I was, I've always said I was. I was *convinced* I was. But if actions speak louder than words my actions towards you are the opposite of what I've championed."

"Your actions said you were ignoring me today."

Fire suddenly snapped in her expression, and she leaned over the table toward him. "Okay, yes, I'm panicking a little about what's happening. I don't think you understand how I felt like I barely survived you leaving me."

Connor's chest clenched, hearing that. His mother hadn't when his father left her.

"And now, even though I don't think you'll be able to utterly devastate me again if you take off, I'm not a fool either. It will harden me in ways I don't want to be hard, and I don't know how to protect myself while still being open to you."

"But you are open to me, and I am not going to do that to you again." A thought occurred to him. "Is that why you didn't answer all day? Make me feel what it's like to not be able to reach you?"

Her eyes widened. "A few hours cannot come close to even a fraction of what it feels like. You want to know what it feels like? Imagine me dying suddenly, right in the middle of the happiest, most perfect time together."

His jaw clenched.

"And then, find out that I faked dying just to get away from you."

"I didn't fake anything with you. It wasn't even about you!"

"I...*know*. I know that, now. That's why I can be open to you now, but I'm still shaped by what happened."

"Alright. How long 'til we can move past this? You can't want to hang on to this forever. You've never been the type to stay angry. Unless that changed over the last thirteen years?"

"No," she said softly. "It hasn't. But my heart has to catch up with what my head understands. I'm still scared."

"What can we do?"

"What *do* we have here?"

"I don't want to be apart from you."

"Even now? When we're fighting?"

"This is fighting?" He thought of the screaming his parents used to do, the punching his stepfather did.

Her expression changed, sorrow clear in it. She knew.

"How do you know you won't do that to me again?" she said suddenly. "You didn't know you were going to do it the first time. So why are you so convinced it won't happen again?"

"Because I'm getting help now. Because I can't run from myself anymore."

"Why can't you? How do you know?"

He thought about the kayak, the gun, the way the metal barrel clanging against his teeth reverberated in his head. His mouth opened to tell her, but he froze up again, the words sticking in his throat.

The waitress came with their food. Connor cut into his fish, but then said with a raspy tone that took him by surprise, "I was suicidal, Liv. That's how I know I can't outrun me anymore."

She stilled, her gaze intense. "When?"

He couldn't keep eye contact. "Not long after we saw each other again."

"Had you been before?"

"N—I don't know. All I used to have time to do was sleep. Once that changed, I realized how pointless my life has been."

"How far did it get?"

His throat closed up, so tight he could barely breathe. He had to take a couple slow breaths, gaze locked on the dark windows behind her.

"It's okay if you can't tell me, Connor," she said gently.

"Gun in my mouth, close. That's how far it got."

Then he had to see if she pitied him, thought him weak.

She gazed at him with aching eyes, as if she hurt for him, an expression he remembered from the first time she found him bloody and bruised after a beating. "I hate that I've always been a broken piece of shit you have to clean up after." Words he hadn't intended to say.

A faint, sad smile moved her lips. "It's thinking like that, that's made you believe you aren't good enough."

"I'm *not* good enough for you." Why the hell couldn't he shut his damn mouth all of a sudden? He knew she didn't want to hear this from him. But it was true. Pretending like it wasn't didn't change a damn thing. "Did you get suicidal when I stopped calling?"

It took her a moment to reply. "I wished I would die so the pain would stop, but I had no thoughts of ending my own life."

"See." He snorted. "You say you felt like you couldn't survive what happened with us. I've never felt that. I've always felt I could survive fecking anything, except my own damned self."

"Most people vastly underestimate the effect trauma has on the brain, and the connecting emotions," she said carefully. "You've experienced some serious trauma, and your reactions are in line with that."

"You sound like a counselor." He scraped his hand along the side of his head, fingertips digging in. "I thought I was through this. I didn't want to come to you with all my bullshit." He dropped his hand. "Language. Working on it."

"You're working through this with Hutch?"

"My problems, not my language."

"So you're working on it. That's the win, Connor. As a counselor, I would have no expectations that you'd be over what's happened in your life already. Really, ever. It's more that eventually you'll be able to recognize reactions as a result of what's shaped you and make a conscious choice to do otherwise for your own well-being.

"As a...whatever we are...I'm grateful you've had the strength to do what you've done so far. I just really hope you'll keep doing it."

"I plan to." Her smile, so warm and beautiful eased him and he could breathe again, his chest no longer bearing an invisible weight. Exhaling, he said, "This was supposed to be about you ghosting me today."

Liv laughed. "I promise I won't tomorrow."

"I'll hold you to it." He finally took a bite of fish. "Food's cold."

"Want to get it to go and heat it up at my house?"

Once they got back to her place, Connor only just stepped through the front door before immediately going on high alert, ears sharpening, gaze scanning. "Where's Leo?"

Liv glanced at him and then stopped messing with the food to kiss him. "I love that you're worried about my puppy. He's at my parents. I called them on the way to meeting you for dinner."

"They know we're together?"

"No. I haven't—no."

"Why not?"

She half-laughed. "Because I still don't really know what we are so I don't want to field the million questions my mom will ask. You say you don't want us to be apart but in Pride and Prejudice, that meant Darcy spoke to Elizabeth's father and then they began their life together."

"I have no idea what you just said. Pride and what?"

Liv laughed. "Only the most important piece of literature in my life."

"Oh."

She laughed harder at his baffled expression.

He came to her suddenly, wrapping both arms around her, behind her head, caging her in. His hazel eyes focused deeply on her, and she felt the intensity of their connection.

"I love you."

"What?"

"I love you," his deep voice rumbled.

Her heart clenched. My God, she was afraid to open herself fully to this again.

"You know I never stopped," he whispered.

"I don't know that." Tears sheened her eyes.

"Did you stop loving me?"

She blinked rapidly. "Things are changing fast all of a sudden and I'm afraid if we rush, you'll…"

The strength of his gaze never wavered. "I won't."

"If we don't see each other again for a week, you might. You said as much."

"Do you want to try it?"

Liv hesitated. No, she didn't. "Yes."

"Okay." Connor leaned down and kissed her tenderly and then released her, stepping back. "I'll see you in a week." One side of his lips quirked, and he moved to the door.

"Connor?"

"Yeah?"

He turned back, looking a little hopeful, and she had to force the words out. "Don't call or text either."

That bothered him, she could see it, but he nodded.

"Do it right. Alright. Goodnight, Lucky." The door clicked quietly closed behind him.

CHAPTER TWENTY-FOUR

Dear Mom,
I

He crumpled the paper. Then sat, staring at the steel frame supporting his glass dining table, thinking of…nothing. He loved it.

He wasn't supposed to love it. Try again.

Dear Mom,
I can't think of anything to say to you.
Connor.

"Stupid," he muttered, crumpling the paper.
Fine, try something different.

Dear Keith,
I fucking hate you.
Connor.

Actually, I'm not done, I FUCKING HATE YOU. You're the biggest piece of shit. No one should have to spend one minute with you, fuckface, but I had to spend my teen years with your sorry, drunk ass. HOW DARE YOU FUCKING HIT ME! You sick fuck! Fuck you for hitting me! FUCK YOU. FUCK! YOU! I HATE YOU FOR WHAT YOU DID! YOU RUINED MY MOM! YOU RUINED—

Me. He wouldn't write it

I hate you for making me feel weak I hate you for taking my home away from me. I hate you for TAKING MY MOM. YOU KILLED HER. She started popping pills BECAUSE OF YOU. Because she couldn't take YOU. I HATE YOU. I FUCKING HATE YOU. I FUCKING FUCKING FUCKING H A T E Y O U!

Connor abruptly shoved back from the table and stalked to his garage. The previous owner had left a hanging punching bag there. Connor never used it or wanted it before, until right now.

He attacked the bag, grunting with each punch, the sound strangled and furious. His hands ached, but he kept thinking about Keith, about how it felt when Keith hit him, how scared he'd been, how hurt, and the shock that an adult would do that to a kid. How helpless he'd felt, how alone. And hurt. Helpless. Afraid. Hurt. *Punch. Punch. Punch.*

He beat the bag with his throbbing hands, kept going when the skin on his knuckles began to shred.

Abruptly, he stopped. Sweat drenched his clothes and dripped from his face, his breath so far gone it felt like he might never catch it. He'd known this was there, none of the feelings a surprise, but the ferociousness in releasing it was.

Roughly pulling his shirt off, he used the dry edges at the bottom to wipe down the bag and then returned to his condo. He felt both energized and weary, the burning intensity gone. A relief. Automatically, he moved to the shower, but noticed the letter out of his periphery and stopped to look at it.

Finish it.

Almost cautiously, he sat, the rage in his erratic handwriting evident and already uncomfortable to see.

Finish.

With a sigh, he picked up the pen.

I'd like to forget about you. I'd like to remember my high school years without you in them. Actually, I'd like to go back in time and fucking kill you, but since none of that is going to happen, when I think of you, it will be as an example of all the things not to be.

So fuck off. Fuck you. I hope you die alone, with no one to mark the end of your sick existence. You earned that.

Connor

Flipping the letter over, he took a long shower, limbs heavy. After, he treated his knuckles with an antiseptic. When he'd stopped punching, they were obviously raw, but they looked worse than raw now.

Hunger gnawed at his belly, but he didn't feel like scrounging up anything to eat. The urge to text Liv, to say something like, 'Make sure you eat my leftovers', was harder to ignore than his hunger.

As he went to bed, the week before him stretched long and lonely.

* * * *

The next morning, his knuckles were stiff and looked black with crusted blood. When he got to the station, Fernando gave him a baleful look as he ate the *iSlim* sludge.

"Still at it, huh?" Connor gestured to the container.

"Only until I can button my pants again. What's on your hands?"

Connor held them up for inspection. "Boxing."

"Bareknuckle? Is Mr. December a prize fighter?" He looked skyward. "Oh my gawd. My wife will squeal. My daughter would too, if she wasn't... pregnant," Fernando finished a decibel louder.

"Did I hear pregnant?" Detective Peter Santucci at the next desk said. "I know I heard you say your wife."

Sound dwindled in the room. Fernando slumped, his brows drooping so heavy it looked like opening his eyes required effort. "My daughter." Fernando scrubbed his face with his hand. "My sixteen-year-old daughter, due in a few weeks."

"Holy shit," three desks down said.

"Not holy, but definitely shit."

An uncertain silence, until the detective who'd just returned from paternity leave said, "Well, Grandpa, I think this is where we congratulate you."

"I've got some stuff I can give you," Peter said. He had two kids, the youngest a toddler. "My wife just gave me the green light to—" he made scissor snipping motions with his fingers. "Which means I can finally get my garage back." He smiled. "Once I give you everything."

"A whole garage worth?" Connor said.

"Son, you have no idea," Peter said.

"How's your wife taking it?" The soon-to-retire detective asked. He'd known Fernando long enough to know his wife too.

"There is zero chance any baby items will be coming through her network," Fernando said.

"She's not telling anyone?"

"She's not talking, period. At first it was only aimed at my daughter, but it's spread to all of us. Haven't heard from her in weeks, and she's right there when I wake up!"

There was a quiet chuckle or two, but most alternated between nodding or shaking their head. The whole scene reminded Connor of times in the army when his team would hear from their loved ones and share some of the hard news. Then, he'd felt separate from them with nothing ever to report. He'd find a way to slip into the background and not participate, not be seen. Now, for the first time, he felt a part, connected.

"Take her a picture of Connor, tell her she can see Mr. Calendar as soon as she starts talking," Peter said.

"Careful," Fernando warned, "He's a bareknuckle fighter, he could beat you."

Connor felt heat suffuse his face, and the thought of blushing while everyone was looking at his injury from attacking a Keith-bag flustered him so much he froze up inside. And then he laughed. It was all so bizarre.

Fernando observed him for a moment. "Shirt off with a Santa hat would probably do it."

"This is getting weird now," Connor said, folding his arms around himself.

"I volunteer to do the shirtless, Santa hat pic," the detective with the biggest gut said. "It's been my life-long dream."

Fernando pointed a sharp finger at him. "Done."

Plans on how to stage the shot followed, more joking. It was good. Connor felt good. He wished he could tell Liv about it, and later, as he left for the day, he reminded himself that no matter how many reasons he might find to text her, he wasn't supposed to.

On Saturday, he nearly failed. What if he just dropped something off for her? Like those tea lattes she used to like? That wouldn't be breaking the rules, right? But what if she thought it did and wanted to reset the clock? Instead, he went to the gym and worked out for hours, until dinnertime, and then went to a sushi bar, so he could eat not facing anyone and not be alone in his condo.

Sunday.

He paced around his condo. What the hell did he used to do with his time? Sleep. Hike. Work out.

Hike. Okay. Too bad he couldn't take Leo.

He grabbed hiking boots and sat at his dinner table to lace them up. The letter to Keith still lay on the table, though he'd flipped it over. Staring at the blank back page for a moment, he reached over and looked at what he wrote.

The extreme emotion all over it made him want to slap it down again, but he forced himself to look at his writing, his words, his feelings.

Thank God he'd had Liv's family when all this was going down. They'd saved him then. So why hadn't he talked to them since? Liv's Uncle Mark still talked to him. Liv was talking to him now too. Surely her parents would.

Swapping out boots for running shoes, he went to their house before he could think too much about it.

As he pulled up, he noticed how tense every muscle in his body felt. Even his vital organs felt tight, and each step to their door made them tighter. He'd been less wound up patrolling the middle of a warzone than this.

Through the cottage-style door that looked newly painted a blue-grey, he could hear the sound of the television going in the background. Pausing to take his sunglasses off, he pressed the doorbell.

"Cal!" he heard Liv's mom call out.

"I'm getting it!"

The door opened without hesitation, an old-school way of trusting who stood outside your space that Connor rarely experienced these days. The compulsion to seem official in some way disappeared the moment his gaze locked with Liv's dad, and the man Connor believed himself to be shriveled away with it, leaving him feeling like the kid he'd been when he'd stood bloody and beaten, waiting to see if he'd be let in.

"Well I'll be," Cal rumbled. His face flushed a little, his eyes going glassy. "It's about damn time."

He motioned him inside and Connor felt almost separate from himself as his legs moved him into the house.

Over the threshold, Cal wrapped him in a bear hug.

Connor stood taller than him now, yet he lacked the width of Cal and felt near consumed by the girth of him.

Emotions flooded Connor. He could barely manage the riotousness of it, and he had to clear his throat repeatedly as he held on tight to the best man he'd ever known. "I'm so sorry," he rasped.

Cal gently pat the back of his head before releasing him, stepping back to look at him. Tears trailed over the puffs beneath his eyes, and he wiped across the wet tracks on his cheeks and down over his bushy beard. "It's not good to surprise an old man. You never know what will happen."

He motioned him further into the house, half-turning to lead the way, yet keeping an eye on him as if afraid he'd disappear if he took his eyes off him. "Mary's gonna kill you in a minute. We heard you'd been coming round again, but," he exhaled, "I'm glad you're here."

They went to the den, where Connor had spent countless hours, watching football games with Cal, or movies with Liv. They'd made out a few times in there too, but they'd always been afraid of getting caught.

"New sofa," Connor commented as he sat.

"We've had two sofa changes since you left." Cal sat in his La-Z-boy recliner that looked identical to the one Connor remembered from years ago, though this one was clearly a replacement. "New paint and kitchen since then too. Everything has to be duck-egg-blue or go with duck-egg-blue. I told Mary I've never seen her like ducks so much in all our years together."

Connor smiled, unsure what to say. Should he begin? Without Liv's mom here?

"Are you thirsty? Want something to drink? Guess you're old enough for a beer now." Cal's beard rolled with amusement.

"I'm alright, thank you. Is Mrs. Jones here too?"

"I'm here."

From behind them, she stood slender and stern, hair cropped an edgy blond. She wore a red striped tee and jeans, both appearing to stop short of being long enough for her. She'd aged, but barely.

Her gaze fixed hard on him, her lips a tight line, and Connor felt a sinking inside. She wouldn't forgive him. The thought of her kicking him out made his gut clench and he stood. "I shouldn't have come. I'm sorry."

"Don't you dare leave. You better sit back down because we are going to talk." She pointed a hard finger at Cal. "Don't let him move."

She strode out of the room and Cal gave him a somber look. "Told you. Just ride it out."

She came back carrying an old wooden dining chair and set it across from him, almost like how Hutch would sit across from him, or how an interrogator would. As she sat, looking as unwelcoming as he'd ever seen her, he wondered if she had nothing but hate for him now.

"You broke our hearts, you know that? We loved you like a son. We used to say that even if things didn't work out with you and Liv, we wanted to be a part of your life no matter what. But you, you just cut us out, without so much as a word. To have you do that to us, when we hadn't done anything but support you, it was like a knife to the heart."

Her words started out slow, but the more she spoke the quicker they clipped out. "We trusted you. We trusted you with our home, with our time, with our *daughter*." Connor flinched, which only seemed to incense her more, words running over themselves now. "Our daughter who wants to have *puppies* instead of *babies* because of you! Our beautiful daughter! Who's too afraid to live life fully because you broke her heart so badly, she was never the same again!"

"Mary," Cal murmured.

"No! He should know!"

"Maybe Liv doesn't want him to."

"But he *should know what he did*."

"I do know," Connor said quietly. "She's told me, and I understand how badly I've hurt everyone."

"Do you? Do you really? How could you? You have no idea what we've been through, what we've *lost*—"

"We haven't lost anything," Cal muttered, and Mary's head just about popped off as she rounded on him.

"I'm trying to convince her to get some man's sperm to have a baby *on her own* so her life isn't totally ruined because of him!"

"What?" Cal said.

"Don't look at me like that. You don't know what it's been like watching her lose her dreams of having a family, because all you really watch is football. And you," she turned back to Connor, "don't know what it's like to watch your own dreams of having grandchildren dwindle away because of some guy that destroyed your family!"

"He didn't destroy our family," Cal said, his own voice raised.

"He *changed it*, in a way I never—" her voice broke.

Silence suddenly charged the room while she visibly collected herself, her struggle to do so difficult for Connor to watch. The full draw of air he needed to take made the rise of his chest feel like an offensive expansion and he tried to hide it by slowly, slowly releasing his breath.

"All he did," Cal said, anger still hard in his voice, "is dump her, Mary. That's it."

Mary's mouth dropped open, her eyes sparking with fresh outrage.

"He didn't murder her, he didn't beat her, he didn't harm her. He-dumped-her. That's it. That we are here right now with all this stuff you're saying, with you finding…sperm…for fuck's sake, Mary!"

"Cal!"

"I'm not apologizing for my language!" he roared suddenly. "He dumped her! So what! You girls need to get over it! I've sat quietly by for years while you two have acted like he murdered the family dog!"

"We don't have a family dog anymore!" she yelled back.

"And he never murdered it either!"

The sudden urge to laugh had Connor looking at the floor. None of this was funny. But that was funny.

"You shouldn't have done what you did," Cal said to him. "It was cowardly. And you did break her heart worse than anything I've seen. That's all true. But you *did not* break her, despite how Mary is making it sound. Maybe Liv is saying it too. Women—" he threw a hand up like, *who knows*. "But *I* can tell you what I know to be true because when I wasn't watching football—" a dark glance at Mary, "—I watched my daughter closely. I can tell you, she suffered, but you bet your ass she got up every day, got straight A's in all her classes, and built a career that makes me damn proud to tell anyone who will listen. Life carried on. Liv carried on—"

"With a *puppy*," Mary interrupted snidely.

"Cute little guy too. Have you met him?"

Cal looked near cheerful now.

Had Connor simply forgotten that Liv's parents had this side to them or was this something that had developed during his absence?

"I have. He is cute." Connor leaned forward, propping elbows against knees and clasping his hands together. "I came here to apologize for what I did. I never called Liv to break up with her because I never wanted to break up with her. I think I couldn't deal with living after my mom died. I wasn't a very good son to her. I haven't been good to the people who care me. I'm sorry. It sounds stupid, but I never meant to hurt anyone."

Cal nodded and said gruffly, "It's okay. You're okay, you're here now."

Mary shook her head, arms folded as she leaned back in a petulant slouch. "I hate how men can just move on like *years* haven't passed with all this trouble."

"Didn't have to be trouble if you girls hadn't acted like—"

"—he killed the family dog," she said with him.

"Well, Connor." Mary pinned him with a laser gaze. "What are your intentions with our daughter?"

All the moisture in his mouth dried up and his head went numb. "I never want to be apart from her again."

Her gaze softened minutely, but swiftly hardened again. "What does that mean exactly?"

"Whatever she wants it to mean?" Did his voice sound like it was coming from a distance?

"Are you asking me or telling me?"

"Mary," Cal muttered. "Jesus."

"It's Jesus, Mary and Joseph, Cal. Remember it for next time." She air-kissed at him.

Connor's brows rose.

Cal gave him a long look. "Ever since the change…"

"Don't you dare say it," Mary warned.

Cal held both hands up in surrender. "Not another word."

"Is the change when I stopped calling?" Connor said carefully.

"Nope," Cal said. "It's the lady change—"

"*Don't say it.*"

Hands up again. "Didn't."

"Where do you two stand?" Mary said to Connor.

"I want to be with her. She wants me to stay away for a week to make sure I mean it."

"See," Cal said, a proud look on his face. "She carried on."

"When's the week up?"

"Thursday."

"Oh!" Mary's gaze darted around. "Then you've got to go. She'll be here for dinner soon." She stood.

Connor didn't. If he lingered and wrangled an invite that technically wasn't breaking any rules.

Cal seemed to catch on to his line of thinking, kicking up the footrest on the La-Z-Boy and flipping on a game.

"Cal!"

"What's that, love?" He winked at Connor. "I think he should stay."

"She said a week!"

"And he's staying away from her. He didn't know she'd be here in," he glanced at his watch, "a half-hour."

"No." Mary stood in front of the television, her gaze ferocious again. "We'll honor her wishes."

With no other choice, he stood, Cal following suit and they all walked to the door. When he turned back to say 'goodbye', Mary hugged him. Cautiously, he hugged her back and she felt small in his arms, different than the last hug he'd given her, the day he'd left for the army. Strange how clearly he remembered that day, down to the way she felt in his arms.

She stepped back and the warmth he remembered was suddenly there in the way she gazed at him. "Please don't ever do that to us again. We *care*, Connor. We always have. We always will."

CHAPTER TWENTY-FIVE

Through sheer force of will, Liv stayed away from her parent's house after seeing Connor's truck in front of it. She'd spotted it by accident after wandering outside to check on a plant, and lo, the glint of golden orange drew her gaze like a falling star.

She missed him. But she had to see.

"Stay away. Stay away." Hurrying into her house as she chanted, she paced, and periodically plastered her face to the window to see if he were still there.

Not a good look.

"C'mon, Leo!" She clipped on his leash and then went for a long walk, away from her parent's. When she returned to her street, Connor was getting into his truck. He looked toward her house, but the sun hung low at a blinding eye-level, so he missed seeing her just beyond it.

All she wanted to do was run to him, jump on him, wrap her legs around his waist and devour him. Suck his whole tongue into her mouth and clamp his head in her hands and not let go until he was in her bed.

Jeez. If he did disappear, she may not take it lying down this time.

As his truck drove away, she walked to her parent's, Leo happily trotting beside her. Their house had quickly become as comfortable and familiar to him as her own, so when she went, he went.

For the first time in ages, she didn't knock. Letting herself in, she called out, "What did I just see?"

Mary came charging at her—well, at Leo, bending down to scoop him into her arms, kissing his little face. "He just showed up, honey. We had no idea he was coming."

"What happened?"

"Why didn't you tell me he's the one you've been seeing?"

"I couldn't think what to say about it. I wanted to wait and...see."

"You should have told me. I know we've had some tension lately about him, but you have to know it's because I love you and I'm here for you. I want to be here for you, but I need you to *come* to me so I *can* be here for you."

All Liv wanted to talk about, was what happened. "I love you too, Mom. What happened?"

"Oh good lord, I lost it on him! I just lost my head, I was *so angry!* But really, good lord, too, he's so handsome. He always was a good looking boy of course, but as a man. Wow, handsome."

"Yeah. I know. How'd you lose it on him? What did you do?"

They wandered into the kitchen and Mary set Leo down to give him a couple treats she kept stocked in the pantry.

"I yelled about babies," she said with a cringe.

"*What?*"

"I know! It just, it just happened! I was *so angry!*" Then she whispered, "Don't tell Dad, but I think he's right about it being menopause. Out of nowhere I'm a fire breathing dragon."

"I heard that!" Dad hollered. He came into the kitchen. "Hi honey." He gave Liv a kiss on the cheek and then ruffled Leo's fur, chuckling a little when he pounced playfully, tail wagging. "So you're finally admitting to the lady change," he said to Mary, and then with a wink at Liv, "Today has been a good day."

"Wait," Liv said, "I'm not sure I'm okay with you yelling at my high school boyfriend about me not having babies."

"Oh honey," Mary said, "he's so much more than a high school boyfriend. All of us know it, even he does and he's the one who's squirrely."

"Was he squirrely?"

"No," Dad said. "He was a man about it. I was proud of him."

Liv let out a long breath and grabbed some crackers and cheese and sat at the kitchen table painted to match the duck-egg-blue cabinets. "Tell me everything he said."

"That's my cue," Dad said and sank his hand into the cracker box, fingers wiggling through it like tentacles. Liv shaved off a few cheese slices and handed them over before he disappeared to the den to watch a game.

"I never had a problem with the *relentless* sound of the announcer in the background until recently too," Mary remarked.

"You cut your hair shorter," Liv said. "It's a little rockstar, I like it."

"Dad says it's too short." She ran her fingers through it. "I like it though, and when I'm feeling the fire breathing dragon stir inside, I feel like telling him he can suck it."

Liv laughed. "I'm both entertained and uneasy."

Mary smiled and pulled out some steaks. "I wanted Connor to stay but he told us about your weeklong separation." She glanced at Liv over her shoulder. "I just want you to know that we're respecting your wishes."

"Thanks," Liv said with a grin. "Now tell me everything."

Mary told her how emotional Cal had gotten—she'd watched them from the other room without them noticing. How uncomfortable, but accepting, Connor had been when she'd raged at him. And how much she'd realized she'd missed him. "Having him here again made me realize how much I personally felt the loss but hadn't dwelled on it because I was so upset at what he'd done to you."

It had never occurred to Liv they might grieve losing him too.

Mary gave her a cautious glance as she slowly unwrapped the steaks. "Your dad made a...strong point, when we were arguing." Another careful glance. "That maybe we, uh, we made too much out of what happened. That. That he just du—um, broke up...no, well, dumped you."

When Liv showed no reaction, Mary finally spoke easily, "It didn't seem like it at the time, but suddenly it doesn't seem like such a catastrophic thing."

"Because he's back in our lives, Mom, being the guy we knew and loved. It was the shock, and for me the humiliation of it that made it such a big deal." Liv sliced off some cheese, wanting to perform the process more than the eating. "Now that we understand what happened, it's taken that away."

"I think you're a better person for living through it. You wouldn't have taken all those classes if you hadn't been trying to recover."

"I'd like to think I would." But the motivation, the need wouldn't have been there. "Probably not as many."

"See. Think about how much more interesting you are with all the things you've tried. You're an interesting person, you can talk on a lot of points. If you'd never had to fight for your sense of self, you probably wouldn't have done all the things that make you so fully formed now."

Liv grinned. "I think we're eager to see the bright side because he's back and we want it to be good."

"It is good. He said he never wanted to break up with you but that he didn't know how to live after his mom died." She teared up, and then suddenly came to give Liv a hug, bending down to embrace her. As she pulled back, she said with a warm smile, "It's time we let it go, don't you think?"

"We?"

Heavy, heavy sigh. "*You*. Geesh, everything I say sets you off."

"Sets *me* off?"

"See?"

"Oh my gosh, Mom. I'm not set off. I just don't understand why you keep insinuating my relationship with Connor is a 'we' thing."

"Maybe because it is? Because *we* are a family and that means *we* are involved."

"Certain aspects, yes, but my--." Liv heavy-sighed herself. "You know, we could go to counseling to help us work this out."

"What's there to work out?"

"Boundaries, for one." Liv gave her an exasperated look. "C'mon, Mom. This is my field, I think I know what I'm talking about."

"I just don't think we need to." She backed away toward the steaks. "But I know, I know, you're the expert here. If we continue to have difficulty talking about *your* relationship with Connor, then we can go."

A tense calm settled in the kitchen while Mary pounded and seasoned the meat.

Liv grabbed her phone to zone out on social media, even though she hated when she wasted time on it. But then she remembered she wanted to find her high school friend, Chelsea.

Within minutes, she found her, with her high school boyfriend's last name now.

"Chelsea from high school is married to Jayden and they have three kids."

"Let me see." Mary hurried over. "The oldest looks about twelve. Goodness! Can you imagine having a twelve-year-old right now?"

"I've only just imagined having a puppy."

Mary grinned. "You know, now that Connor's back in your life, maybe we don't need to find you a sperm donor anymore."

"We."

Mary laughed. "Now that one I'll give you. Creepy mom moment." She went back to the counter. "Are you going to say hi to Chelsea?"

"Just did."

Chelsea immediately messaged her, saying, *You're alive!!!!*

They had a lively exchange before Chelsea had to run. Soccer practice.

"Are you going to meet up?" Mary asked.

"She's in Northern California now. When they visit though."

"Did she ask about Connor?"

Liv nodded. "I told her we broke up but that we're seeing each other again. She said she's shocked we ever broke up, but that was about it. She's busy with her kids." Then she mused, "Sometimes I feel like my life is stunted and has no meaning when I talk to women my age with families."

"Don't make me start talking about sperm again, sweetie."

Liv snickered. "Maybe somewhere deep, deep down I actually like these intrusive and vaguely inappropriate conversations."

"If ever you wonder how well I know you, remember this conversation."

After dinner, her dad walked her home.

"What do you think, Dad? Will he take off again?"

Cal's beard shifted and he gave her a quick side-eyed glance. "Livvy honey, there's only one way to find out."

CHAPTER TWENTY-SIX

"This has been the longest week of my life, Hutch. Makes me wonder how I managed to cut her out before and not feel anything about it." Connor scraped his hand back and forth along the side of his freshly barbered head. "It's extreme, you know? The difference."

"What worries you about what you're feeling?"

"I wouldn't call it worry. But…the extreme difference is what makes me…"

"Not trust yourself?"

"I suppose. I can't sit with the thought of going numb on her again, but I didn't ask to be like that before. It happened. And I'm, okay yeah, I'm worried I'll do that again, and the thought of treating these people I love like that again, really fucking worries me."

"From what I'm hearing, Connor, with both your past and your present with Liv, the love is your natural state. The numb was your traumatic state. *If* you ever go numb again, that's the feeling you can't trust, that's the one where you go," he put a finger to his temple and donned a concerned look, "'this isn't right, I should go talk to someone about this'."

Connor nodded slowly.

Into the ensuing silence, Hutch said, "Your knuckles look better." They were shiny and pink. "Any progress on that letter to your mom?"

"I can't think of anything to say."

"Start with your best memory. See where it goes from there."

The session ended. Connor picked up fish tacos for dinner, figuring he could eat them slow while thinking about what to write to his mom. The best memory. He knew exactly the one. Ironically, it involved fish.

Since the taco place was close to Liv's, he decided to do a subtle drive-by on the way home. Maybe he'd catch a glimpse of her. If she saw him, he could still argue he followed her rules.

As he rolled up to Liv's house, her garage door opened and he snorted at himself with the way his heart rate kicked up.

She pulled out in front of him. Would she stop when she noticed his truck?

She didn't seem to notice him. It was starting to get dark, so, okay. Still, she drove with unusual speed, for her. He remembered she drove like a grandma when they were kids, but now she zipped and wove around cars going nearly twenty miles over the limit. Since they were headed in the same direction, he kept track of her until he reached his exit to his condo.

Last minute, he didn't take it. Where was she going so fast? Was it wrong to follow her? Free country. Maybe she was late to a Pilates class. He'd make sure she got there okay and then have a talk with her later about safe driving practices when she'd see him again.

Ten minutes later, still going over the speed limit, he started eating a taco, carefully angling it over the plastic bag in his lap. Pilates couldn't be this far. Maybe an urgent client situation?

Twenty minutes later, dinner finished, Connor figured it definitely was not a Pilates class, and very likely not a client because they were soon to be in Los Angeles County.

What the hell was in LA she had to rush to? She liked shows, maybe she had tickets to a theater event?

Forty-five minutes later, she exited the freeway onto a dumpster of a street. Streetlights served only to highlight how dilapidated and impoverished the area looked. After a while, he was careful not to follow too closely in case she finally noticed that the car not far behind her was the same size as the one that had been silhouetted behind her for over an hour.

Dark, shredding tarps draped over junk mounds and reflected overhead lamplights as they drove by homeless encampments with two people blatantly smoking crack on the sidewalk. Further down, a man yelled at a lamppost, eyes bulging with his rage.

"I swear if Liv is coming down here to drop off supplies to these people at this time of night…" Muttering did little to ease his mounting tension. If she got out of her car in this kind of place, he'd lose his shit. How often did she do stuff like this? He knew she was naïve when they were young, but was she still, that she actually felt safe enough to take her little fuel efficient four-door into the slums of drug addiction and mental health disorders and go strolling through the darkness with her cozy bags of goodies?

The urge to call her and yell at her for being reckless and, fuck it, *ignorant* about the dangers that awaited her right outside the glass of her little car near overwhelmed his reason.

A few minutes later, she slowed to a crawl. Connor pulled to the side of the road and killed his headlights. She crawled down the street a little more, and then stopped in the middle of the road before easing onto the driveway of a property that had warped chain-link fencing surrounding it.

"What the hell?" Connor murmured, taking a quick scan of the area. He could see someone walking up the street behind them and palmed his gun while he waited to find out what the hell was going on.

Cracking his window so he could hear anyone moving near him, Connor almost wanted to laugh when he heard the blaring sound of Liv's car dialing a phone number, the ringing like a beacon that, *something out of the ordinary was happening right here and now.*

A moment later, someone came running up to the fence and Liv got out of her car. Connor swiftly scanned for the person coming up the street, but he couldn't see any movement. Scanning all around them, he didn't see anything and focused back on Liv, handing over a couple bags to a long and lanky male. The face, highlighted by her headlights, looked familiar.

The kid was young, fifteen maybe, and so skinny his clothes hung like paper bags on him. "Jeremy Olawale." Fuck. This put him in all kinds of shit. Here was his number one suspect, and here was the love of his life harboring him. If he called it in, he'd be calling *her* in, and then she'd be charged with obstruction and harboring a suspect and she'd lose her medical license, her practice, her job, her house, her whole fucking life. And he'd lose her.

Fury burned inside him, his chest lit with embers as he watched her talk earnestly to Jeremy, standing in the spotlight of her headlights, oblivious to all the fucking risks.

Eventually, she got back in her car. Jeremy waved and trudged back toward an old camper with weeds growing all around it. And then Liv drove off, perfectly safe. Lucky.

Uncaring now if she noticed she was being followed, he flipped on his lights and stayed right on her ass, all-the-way-home. When she pulled into her driveway and opened her garage door, leisurely waiting for it to slowly roll up and just as slowly ease into her tidily organized parking space, Connor yanked hard on his parking brake, killed the engine and stalked up her driveway, right into her opened garage door as she got out of her car.

"Connor!"

"Inside," he ground out, walking into her house, hitting the garage door button to close the damn thing as he did.

Leo sat in the kitchen staring at the door as he walked through. His tail wagged side-to-side, sweeping the floor and then he did a leaping jump toward him before trotting the rest of the way to his legs. Connor bent to scratch his neck but when Liv walked through the door, he straightened slowly, his gaze pinning her to the spot so that she froze in her steps to the kitchen.

"I'm..." she began slowly, "pretty sure this isn't a week."

The embers in his chest sparked to full fucking life. "I could have you arrested *right now*."

"What are you talking about?"

"Don't play innocent with me, Liv!"

"Did you follow me?"

"How the hell could you *not know* you were being followed? How the hell could you drive into a dangerous neighborhood like that and be so goddamned oblivious? I stayed on your ass the whole time you were driving home, and you didn't notice a goddamned thing!"

"I wish you wouldn't cuss."

"*LIV!*" he roared.

"What? Jeez!"

"*Jeez?* You could lose *everything* by harboring Jeremy. Do you have *any idea* the kind of trouble you're in?"

"Yes, obviously I do."

"Obviously? No, it's not obvious! You stood in a damned spotlight in the middle of a drug zone in a pretty pink sweater with a shiny blond ponytail as if you haven't a care in the world! Do you have any idea how dangerous places like that are? Because *I do.* You might as well have held up a sign saying, 'I'm vulnerable and I don't know what I'm doing!'"

"I know what I'm doing."

"No, you damned well don't! You could go to prison for what I saw today! *Do you understand?*"

"Don't talk to me like that!" she snapped. "I'm not an idiot. I know what could happen if the cops found out—"

"*I am a cop!*" he yelled.

"I know!" She folded her arms. "Why are you even surprised? We did it for you!"

"What are you talking about?"

"Your stepdad. We broke the law to help you! Would you change that? Arrest Uncle Mark for what he did? A decorated soldier who's served our country with honor. Would you throw him in jail for breaking into your house and threatening your stepdad to get him to stop his abuse?"

"It's not the same."

"It is the same!"

"I was a kid—"

"So is Jeremy!"

"*I* was a kid so *I* wasn't responsible for the letter of the law. I am now."

"Well Jeremy is a kid and *I'm* responsible for getting him the help he needs for the health and wellbeing of his own mind. Putting him in prison, defending himself against accusations of *murder* is not in his best interest."

"If he's guilty—"

"He's not!"

"It's not up to you to determine his innocence."

"I don't need to determine it. I know he's innocent."

"Then there shouldn't be any issue of turning him in!"

"There is when the family is threatening him! They want him to take the blame, but I *know* he didn't do it."

"How? Be. Specific."

"Alright! This is everything that happened, okay? He called me, he was hiding in the closet in his house, his dad was in a rage, I could hear him yelling in the background, and it sounded from far away so I know he wasn't in the same room with him. Jeremy was scared to call the police in case his dad found out. His mom all of a sudden screams for Jeremy to run, and then someone else shouted, I think a woman, and then there's the sound of a gunshot and Jeremy starts chanting, 'Oh my God, I'm scared, Dr. Jones, I'm scared.'

"He was sobbing, and there was all this noise, and then I hear that voice shouting, 'Who are you talking to!' And he told her, and she said, 'If she calls the police you're dead.' Then the line clicked off.

"So, I called the police, anonymously, and then waited to hear from Jeremy."

"Liv, you just told me you're a witness to a murder I'm investigating, after you've spent *months* concealing it. Do you have *any idea* the position you've put me in?"

"I…Why did you follow me?" she said in a small voice.

Connor's jaw flexed. He stepped away from her. His temper was too volatile, an unfamiliar state for him.

"You're leaving?" she said, as he went to the door.

"I need to figure out what the feck to do about this."

"Are you going to arrest me?"

"I'm supposed to!" He left, wanting to get the hell out of there before the pull of just being with her clouded his judgement beyond reason.

As he drove home, he thought he shouldn't be surprised at all that she'd done something like this, because as she said, she'd done something like it before, for him. He remembered that night well. He'd been scared out of his mind, tied up, mouth taped shut by some man in black clothes and combat boots. The man had prowled through the house, to his parent's room, tying them both up before threatening his stepdad with a violent death if he didn't stop beating the shit out of his stepson.

The next morning, he'd gone to Liv's house, where the entire household was clearly exhausted. When Connor told them what happened, Liv had reacted so dramatically it was comical, while everyone else asked if he thought his stepdad got the message or not. Connor felt sure then they'd organized it, and when Mark had hugged him and murmured *De oppresso liber*—free the oppressed—he'd known who wore the combat boots too.

So, no, he wasn't surprised. Now he just had to figure out how the hell to fix this situation so that none of them went to jail.

CHAPTER TWENTY-SEVEN

"Dad, I screwed up."

"Not you, honey. You're perfect."

"Dad, I'm serious." She'd spent the whole day at work unable to think of anything other than what happened the night before. So much guilt weighed on her, breathing felt difficult. "I've done something—" Liv clenched the phone harder in her fist, "—illegal."

"How illegal?" Cal said with dead seriousness.

"I think it could be classified as harboring a fugitive—"

"*A fugitive!*—"

"No! I mean a suspect."

"You're harboring a suspect?"

"Or maybe it's obstructing an investigation, maybe that's what it is. I'm not technically harboring anyone, but I do know where the suspect is located, and I pretended like I didn't."

Cal groaned. "Livvy… You better start from the beginning." She explained all that she could.

"You've been lying to Connor this whole time about it?"

"At first I did because I couldn't trust anything with him, and then he stopped asking when I did start to trust him. So if we split hairs here, I didn't actively lie this whole time."

"No one in any legal capacity would see it like that," Cal said dryly. "And as your father, I'm telling you I don't see it like that either."

"What should I do, Dad?"

"Start with turning Jeremy in."

"Dad—"

"I can call in a tip about his location."

Liv blew out a breath. She didn't want Jeremy to be arrested and experience that, but without his mom stepping in to help him, it was now a matter of time until he was found. "Do I need to turn myself in too?"

"No!" Cal barked. "Let me talk to Joe." An old friend whose daughter just so happened to be an attorney. "I'll let you know what he says."

"Thanks, Dad."

"How'd Connor find out about this?"

After Liv explained, Cal said, "I really mean this, honey…*Never* do this again."

The urge to say she's a grown woman who can make her own choices barely made a blip. "Sorry, Dad."

He grunted. "I'll call you back. Love you."

"I love you too."

Another grunt, and he hung up.

Liv called Connor.

"You're not supposed to call me," he answered immediately.

"Because of the one-week thing or because I'm in trouble?"

"Both." Then he muttered, "Hell."

"My dad is calling in a tip about Jeremy's location."

"He's in on this too?" he said with astonishment. Then muttered, "Shouldn't be surprised."

"He's not, I just called him and told him about it. Connor, I'm sorry I lied, but I genuinely was just trying to help what I know to be an innocent and mistreated boy." She paused. Into his silence, she added, "If things had been like they are now between us, I would have told you." She paused again. More silence. "How *are* things between us?"

"Angry at the moment!"

She exhaled, relieved at the qualifier. "I'll fix this."

"Don't you fecking call in a confession—"

"I'm not!" Then she mumbled, "I was going to, but my dad told me not to."

Connor groaned. "Woman, you're going to kill me."

"I'm sorry," she said in a small voice.

The sound of his truck pinging a seatbelt warning sounded in the background. "Did you play basketball?" She didn't want to hang up. If they kept talking, maybe the feeling that everything was okay would come.

"Yeah, thought it would help clear my head."

"Are you going out to eat with them now?"

"Right now, I'm getting brownies with Vanessa."

"Oh." Her stomach dropped.

It was silent a moment before he said, "She needs a sober friend and for some reason she's picked me. She wants us to come for dinner at her house soon. Her husband's a good cook."

"I'd like that."

"If we're not in jail."

"Connor—"

"I know you're sorry. I'm still trying to figure this out, Liv. I've got to go. I'll talk to you later."

"Bye." Her voice was near soundless.

How could she fix this? Reaching for the rope Leo brought her, she tugged. *What could she actually do?* She'd never intended to end up here, the progression of her involvement a series of quiet steps that had each seemed small, but taken as a whole, stretched with devastating severity.

"Careless, Liv," she whispered, burying her head in her hand, the other jerking from Leo's tugs. If she went to prison, she wouldn't see her puppy again for who knew how long. It could be years if the judge wanted to make an example out of her. And this thing just starting with Connor again, would be destroyed. And then there was the threat to his own existence. He was breaking the law for her now. A decorated soldier and peace officer, violating the laws of the land he'd spent his adulthood defending and honoring.

"I'm such an idiot. Oh God, I'm such an idiot." *I'm so sorry. Please forgive me. I didn't mean to cause harm. Please help me. I'm so sorry.*

Snatching up her phone again, she swiftly scrolled for Mrs. Olawale's number.

"I told you not to contact me again," she answered.

Liv almost cried. She hadn't thought she'd answer, and this was her last chance. "Your son will be arrested in the morning. If you care about him at all, *show him*, by speaking up for him."

"I can't!"

"He'll be sent to an adult facility, Mrs. Olawale, and what the other inmates will do…*please* don't let this happen. Speak up for him! You're his mom and—

"I have to go now." She hung up.

Liv's arm jerked from Leo's sharp tug on the rope. Leaning down to pick him up, she buried her face in his soft neck while he swung his head side-to-side, the rope still clamped in his mouth, the ends smacking Liv in the head as she started to cry.

* * * *

Fernando gave Connor a horrified look as he dragged himself in the next morning. "Did you find out your daughter is pregnant?"

"What?" Connor dropped heavily into his seat.

"You have the same look I had when I found out all my happiness would be gone."

"You're going to have a grandkid soon. You shouldn't talk like that."

"Let me finish. *For the foreseeable future.* So what happened, kid? Why do you look like my worst morning?"

"I'm back to being a kid?"

"My daughter said my belly is bigger than hers, like any good grandpa's should be, so here we are."

Connor didn't respond.

Fernando continued, "Although, my daughter hardly has a baby-belly. Due in a couple weeks but you could easily not notice that she's carrying a child. I told my wife she could pass the kid off as ours. Pissed her right off."

"Why?"

"Her words," he made air quotes, 'You think I can pass as carrying a baby to full term with the way I look right now?' I said our daughter could so why not her? Completely reasonable, right? Didn't change a damn thing. She's not talking to me again."

"I didn't know she'd started."

"Yesterday was the first day. I promptly put a stop to that."

Connor reluctantly smiled.

Fernando started to say something, but his phone rang. "Detective Velez." He abruptly went alert and still as he listened to the caller. "We'll be right there." He stood and adjusted his belt over his unbuttoned pants. "Mrs. Olawale is here. Let's go."

Connor surged to his feet, adrenaline rushing violently through him. "Did she say why she's here?" What if she told them about Liv's involvement? Did she know?

"Rookie question," Fernando said.

Mrs. Olawale waited in an interview room. She sat facing the door, grooves in her frown-lines running deep. Her protuberant eyes were dark circled, highlighted by her salt-n-pepper hair slicked back into a tightly wound bun. She wore a black turtleneck under a dark trench coat, buttoned and tied tight. She looked ready.

Connor wasn't ready. Trying to hide how on edge he felt, he took his seat across from her, and consciously tried to keep his jaw unclenched.

Fernando introduced them, and Connor had never been happier about being outranked in his entire life. Any question he asked could incriminate him if his part in keeping their prime murder suspect concealed ever came to light. *Jesus.*

"What can we do for you today, Mrs. Olawale?" Fernando said.

She gave Fernando a prolonged look and then turned her attention to Connor. "I need to say what happened."

Cold sweat dampened his armpits as he held her bleak gaze, but she said nothing else. Was she trying to communicate that she knew he knew? Stress pounded through his body as he sat there, waiting to find out if she would destroy everything he cared about.

"You remind me of my husband when we were young," she began. "Handsome, strong. I felt so lucky when we started dating, that he picked me. I loved being on his arm, and how all the other girls were jealous." She trembled suddenly. "My son will be handsome like that. But he'll be a good man. He didn't hurt his father. He was scared of him. We both were." Her shaking worsened and her gaze dropped to her lap.

Time ticked by in silence. Fernando had told Connor early on that silence often worked to get someone to keep talking. Waiting to hear what she would say felt like waiting to find out if he'd ever be able to walk again.

"I..." Mrs. Olawale's gaze briefly flicked to Connor's again then back to her lap. "My husband—he choked me. He'd get angry and he'd choke me. And...slap me. I always knew one day he'd kill me. He'd go too far and then...then I'd...he'd kill me."

"This happened more than once?" Fernando said. "More than the night he died?"

"Yes. Sometimes he'd seem to get better. Once, he went over a year without doing anything, but it always came back, worse each time. I was starting to get scared of the times it stopped because I always knew when it was over it may be the time he killed me."

"Did he hit Jeremy too?" Fernando said.

"I don't know. I think he would after I passed out, but Jeremy never said and I...I was afraid to ask."

"Do you—" Fernando began, but Mrs. Olawale held up a hand and then quickly fisted it back in her lap when it shook.

"I killed my husband."

Fernando gave her a long stare as she sat there shaking in her chair. "Would you like to speak to an attorney?"

"No."

"Alright. You were found passed out, unresponsive at the scene while Mr. Olawale lay dying with a gunshot wound to the back of his head several feet in front of you. How does that happen?"

"I killed my husband before I passed out."

"How?"

"He was over me, choking. I had taken to carrying a gun. Before I blacked out, I shot him."

"You don't have a gun license. We saw no records of a gun, of a purchase, of any type of firearm associated with your family whatsoever." He tapped his fingers on the table twice. "I can't help but think you're in here doing this to protect your son."

Mrs. Olawale showed no reaction. "I purchased the gun through backdoor channels."

"How?"

"I know someone who could get me a gun that I paid cash for."

"Who?"

"I'm not saying. I'm not here to get anyone in trouble."

"Just yourself."

"I'm taking responsibility."

"Okay, so you have an illegal firearm you're carrying that your husband doesn't notice. He's looming over you, choking you, you're scared, pull out the gun, he still doesn't notice, and you wrap your arm around his back and angle the gun from a couple feet away to go through the back of his head."

"I kneed him in the balls. I'd never done that before because he would have killed me. I wasn't afraid of that this time. I kneed him and I pulled the trigger."

"And then you passed out."

"Yes."

"Alright, Mrs. Olawale. That all happened, then where did the gun go? Where did Jeremy go?"

"I screamed at Jeremy to run when his dad started choking me. I never did that before either. I saw him running away before I pulled out the gun."

"Then where did it go? You're passed out. Jeremy is gone. Your husband is dead. Who took the gun?"

"Thieves."

"Thieves?"

"Maybe the person who sold me the gun. I don't know. I don't live in the best neighborhood. Even in good neighborhoods, crime happens all the time. My door was unlocked, we'd made a lot of noise, it probably attracted attention, and someone came to steal our stuff."

"Have you noticed anything else missing from your home since you returned?"

"Just my son," she said quietly. "But he didn't do nothing wrong. He shouldn't have to hide, scared he's going to pay for something he didn't do."

"Do you know where he's hiding?"

"I'm not saying anything about that."

Fernando gazed at her for a long stretch of silence, but she didn't fill it this time.

"Would you like some water while you wait?" he said finally, standing.

"Yes."

Connor followed Fernando out, feeling almost as if he floated with the release of the pressure he'd felt.

"I don't think she killed him," Fernando said as soon as the door closed behind them.

Connor compressed his lips, afraid to say anything to sway the outcome.

"But we don't have anything tangible tying Jeremy to the murder either." Fernando rubbed the back of his neck. "And if by some chance she did manage to pull off a shot like that, hell, an abused woman having to go to prison for defending herself is a miscarriage of justice in my book."

"Her medical records showed bruising on her throat," Connor said.

"If she gets a halfway decent attorney, she has a good defense." Fernando sighed. "If she didn't do it, we've still got nothing else to go on. Even her psychiatric hold makes sense if she killed her abusive husband."

"Or if her son did," Connor said, saying what he knew he should.

"We'd have to find him and the gun for that to stick." Fernando rubbed the back of his neck again. "Let's take her into custody."

"Fernando!" Their chief walked over. "Olawale's in there?" He handed over a piece of paper. "Funny timing, with this coming in."

"Jeremy's location," Fernando said, scanning.

"I took the liberty of calling in a pickup." He slapped Fernando on the back and looked at Connor. "Good luck."

They went back into the room, Connor remembering to grab a water for Mrs. Olawale who sat still and quiet at the table.

"We found your son," Connor said, handing her the bottle. She showed no reaction.

"Why was he hiding if he hadn't done anything, Mrs. Olawale?" Fernando said.

"I told him to hide and not come out. I don't want him paying for my problems. Not anymore. He paid enough having to grow up with what he did."

"So you're protecting him," Fernando said.

"I'm taking responsibility for what I did. Jeremy is innocent and I don't want him to pay."

"Will we find the gun when we pick Jeremy up?"

She took a sip of water, hand still trembling. "No. He ran before it happened."

Fernando looked at Connor. "Do you have anything?"

Nodding slightly, because he fecking *would* have questions if he weren't toeing the line of corruption, he cleared his throat and said, "Is there anyone else who was there that night?"

A long silence stretched, making the damp perspiration under Connor's shirt begin to drip. He'd been thinking of the other voice Liv had heard, but what if he'd somehow brought her attention back to naming Liv?

"No," she said finally, but Fernando's gaze had sharpened. "Are you certain?"

"I was being choked, and watching for my son to run away from what was about to happen, so maybe it's not all clear." The first sign of testiness she'd shown.

"We're trying to make sure you're not taking the blame for something you didn't do, Mrs. Olawale," Fernando said.

"Well I did it! And my son is exactly where I put him, and he followed my rules. I'm his parent, I'm responsible for him and I'm responsible for him hiding so don't you punish him for it.

You're always so quick to throw kids in jail and it only makes things worse."

"You realize he's not going to have a home if you're convicted?"

"You can't put him in jail just because he doesn't have a home. My son is a good boy, and he is innocent of any crime. Ask his doctor, she knows he's good. She can help him now more than anyone. You can take him to Dr. Jones, she'll make sure he's alright."

Connor's heart stopped beating in the silence that followed. Looking over at Fernando to gauge his reaction, was damn near the scariest thing he'd ever had to do.

Fernando had a poker face on, and Connor stared, waiting, not beating.

"Mrs. Olawale, you're under arrest—"

"I want an attorney now and I won't say or do anything else until I get one."

Fernando gave Connor a dry look. "Alright." And he began to recite the Miranda Rights.

Connor felt numb through the droning words. Getting her processed for booking allowed the numb to fade by gradual degrees, but when Fernando alerted him to Jeremy's arrival, the numb flipped back to blood pounding stress.

"Maybe we should call your girlfriend in for emotional support," Fernando said as they went to the interview room Jeremy waited in.

"Funny."

Fernando gave him a shrewd look. "I'm not totally comfortable with this case, to be honest. Should've asked to be taken off it a while ago, but hell, I've had a lot on my mind and you're the noob who could believably say he didn't know better.

"To be downright stupid honest, I didn't even think about your girlfriend's connection in there until she brought her name up. What a cock-up. I'm usually by the book, rookie. Don't take this snapshot into one of the worst times of my life as an example of what I'm like."

Was he joking? Should Connor laugh? The stress of what would happen with Jeremy obscured everything.

As they entered the holding room where he sat, Fernando said, "Jeremy Olawale?"

The boy looked exhausted. Defeated. And so young.

"Do you understand your rights?" Fernando said when Jeremy just looked at him.

At his nod, Connor said, "Do you want an attorney?"

"Don't matter," Jeremy said. "Don't matter what I say or don't say. Never does."

"What do you want to say?" Fernando asked.

"I know why I'm here. I didn't kill my dad."

"We know," Fernando said.

His body twitched. "You do?"

"Your mom just confessed."

"*My mom*? But she didn't kill him."

"If she didn't, then who did?"

Jeremy looked away, lip curling but then as if he made some decision, he turned back to them. "She's like an aunt or somethin'. Helped raise my mom. They talk on the phone a lot. She's mean but she keeps on with my mom. I don't know why she was there that night. She musta come in when my dad was choking mom and she shot him and I ran."

"How do you know she shot him?"

"I could hear her in there. She had the gun. Plus she said it a lot since.

"Do you know where the gun is now?"

"Should be her house." His lip curled again. "But she said if I told she'd put the gun in my trailer and say it was me. That's why it don't matter what I say."

"Was that trailer hers?"

"Yeah, her trailer, I mean."

Fernando nodded. "Do you have any grandparents, or next of kin you can call to come get you?"

"Come get me? You're not putting me in jail?"

"No reason to."

His lips parted.

"Do you have anyone?" Fernando said again.

"My dad had a sister. She stopped talking to him a couple years ago. She's the only family there is."

It took Connor an hour to get in touch with her while Fernando went to the courthouse to get a search warrant. At first the aunt said she couldn't help, but then she changed her mind and said she could for only a little while. Before she arrived, Fernando returned with the warrant.

"Let's go, rookie." Fernando paused to tell the desk officer to go slow on releasing the kid. "We need time to do this before he gets his hands on a phone."

CHAPTER TWENTY-EIGHT

As they pulled up to the fence where Liv had stood like a beacon, Connor's jaw clenched anew at the danger she'd put herself in, made clearer in the light of day.

"What a shithole," Fernando muttered.

Flanked by a small fleet of armed officers, they got out and cut the bolt on the chain. No dogs came charging at them, but Connor had a taser ready.

At the door, Fernando rang the bell, saying, "June Lewis! This is the police, we have a warrant!"

Seconds ticked by, no answer, no sound of movement.

He pounded the door.

More seconds of silence.

"June Lewis, this is the police! We're coming in!" They drew their weapons and Connor motioned for the ram another officer carried. He came to the door and bust it open.

Fernando entered first, shouting, "June Lewis! We have a warrant—"

Gunshots hit the wall behind Fernando, and he dropped to the ground, firing his revolver. Connor flattened against the door for cover. He peered around the edge to fire, and saw a person crumpled on the ground.

"Fernando!" Connor barked.

"I'm good."

Connor moved stealthily into the room, gun aimed and ready as he scanned for movement. Officers swarmed the house. He approached the body. Elderly, with frizzy, thin hair, he was sure it was a woman. Blood pooled beneath her.

"Mrs. Lewis!" Connor said loudly.

No response. He crouched and checked her pulse.

"Anything?" Fernando said, limping over.

"No."

"Shit," Fernando muttered.

"The house is clear, she's the only one here," an officer said, walking back into the room.

Fernando sighed deeply and looked at the gun the woman had dropped, resting several feet away from her now. "I've got odds this is our murder weapon."

Connor called for crime scene investigators while Fernando told the officers not to touch anything.

"C'mon. Let's check out the kid's trailer," Fernando said.

Inside was rank, the stink of an untreated septic tank permeating every particle of space. The bed and seat cushions were mottled with filth, with the walls bulging in spots where yellow water stains oozed down it.

Littered around the space were stacks of books, mostly sci-fi and space stories. There was a plastic building set on the peeling dinette table that appeared to be in the process of becoming a spaceship. An old tablet rested on the dinette bench. Connor pressed the power button, relieved to see a password required. They wouldn't apply for a warrant to get into it, but if it were unlocked, looking at who Jeremy had been in contact with would be fair game.

Fernando opened the cupboard and whistled softly. "Nice groceries."

Fruits, vegetables, organic seed crackers and organic, non-gmo Pho noodle bowls were stacked neatly inside. All-natural popcorn, steel-cut oats with real maple syrup, and tins of wild-caught salmon rounded out the stash.

Connor wanted to shake his head, scrub a hand over his eyes, laugh, and yell. *Liv.*

"Hide him in a shithole but feed him like this," Fernando mused.

"She cares about his health."

"I wish my mom cared about my health like this. I'm lucky if she shares her donuts when I come over."

Connor went back to the books, flipping through pages. Nothing incriminating fluttered out and the strangling knot of tension began to unwind.

"Might as well take him his stuff," Fernando said, finding a wadded trash bag tucked into the corner of the pantry. He shook it open but paused to pull something out.

Connor looked over and tension shot right through him again. A note from Liv. He'd recognize her handwriting anywhere.

You are loved, Jeremy.

Fernando read it aloud before flipping the note over and back again. "A lunchbox note." Fernando tossed it back in the bag and then loaded it up with the groceries. "My wife used to do that with our girls. Maybe she'll do that with our grandkid."

Numbly, Connor gathered up the books and tablet, and hoped like hell to get out of there without having a damned heart attack.

Once they were clear to leave, they went back to the station and pulled Mrs. Olawale from her holding cell into a meeting room.

"We spoke to Jeremy," Fernando said. "He told us who shot your husband, and it wasn't you. So, we went to the house of June Lewis—" Mrs. Olawale visibly blanched, "—and she fired a gun that matches the type of bullet found in Mr. Olawale. Officers returned fire, and she was hit. She passed away at the scene."

"June is dead?" Mrs. Olawale whispered.

"Yes. Who was she to you?"

"My aunt." Her gaze slipped slowly around the room as if she were trying to think but couldn't make any thoughts connect. "She's really dead?"

"Yes. I'm sorry for your loss."

"You saw her—you're sure?"

"Yes, ma'am. I saw her and I am sure."

"She's really gone," she whispered. Her eyes closed and then a look like pure relief crossed her face.

"Did she kill your husband?" Connor said.

Blinking her lids open, a suggestion of tears clumped her lashes together though her cheeks remained dry. Faintly, she nodded.

"Why?" Connor pressed.

It took her a moment to collect herself. Hesitantly, she spoke, "She couldn't control him anymore. I tried to leave him, early on, but she would never let me. He would always give her money, until recently."

"What happened that night?" Fernando said.

"I called her. I knew he was in one of his moods and I was scared because the last time I'd passed out, I thought that was it for me. She told me to stop making trouble and hung up. I didn't know she was going to come. When he was—" she touched her throat, "—I saw her, but I thought maybe I was hallucinating.

"It's not so clear in my mind. I remember feeling like I was dying and I wanted Jeremy to run away and not see. I think when she shot my husband, his hands were still...around my neck, so it...that's the last thing I remember."

"If you didn't see her do it, why are you so sure she shot him?" Fernando said.

"Because she told me not to tell anyone or she'd kill Jeremy next. She had him with her. She said we'd all die before she went to jail."

"And your confession earlier?" Fernando said.

"June wanted Jeremy to take the blame, but I...it was wrong."

Silence settled in the room, and Connor felt like climbing out of his skin, willing her not to fill it.

She didn't.

Fernando finally said, "Alright, Mrs. Olawale. We're going to need a witness statement before we can discuss your release. Are you willing to give one, or do you wish to wait for an attorney?"

"I think...probably wait for an attorney, in case I... I'm sorry."

"We understand," Connor said. "You can wait here until your attorney arrives."

"Can I take Jeremy home after this?"

"You can. He's still here in fact. I'll let his aunt know she doesn't need to get him now."

They turned to leave, but Fernando paused. "We brought the groceries you bought him."

"Groceries?"

Confusion furrowed her brow again and Connor instantly felt like he couldn't breathe. *Damn it!* Before Fernando could say anything else, Connor said, "Not just the groceries, we brought his books and the few articles of clothing we found as well."

"Oh. Thank you."

They left, and after the door closed behind them, Fernando snorted. "I'm starving. All I can think about is food. Kid you not, I hoped she'd say she didn't want his stuff so I could have one of his Pho bowls." His phone rang with a unique ringtone that sounded like an evacuation alarm. "My wife," he said as he palmed his phone.

"That's her ringtone?" Connor tried like hell to sound lighthearted.

"I like to set the ringtone to reflect my feelings." He grinned in a baring-of-teeth way before answering the phone, "You're speaking to me?" A moment later, "Okay, calm down, I'll—I know! Sorry, I know 'calm down' doesn't help anythi—" Another pause. "I don't know why I do it. Maybe it helps me, okay—" He closed his eyes and shook his head. He took a deep breath, and when next he spoke, his tone was soothing. "She's going to be okay. I'll be there in twenty minutes."

He hung up.

"*Shit!*" he exploded. "My daughter's in labor! I have to get to the hospital."

Relief nearly made Connor sag. "Go, I'll finish this up." And tie up every end so they could close the case and put away any risk to Liv.

"Thanks," Fernando said, already walking away.

Quitting time came and went, but Connor stuck it out until Mrs. Olawale gave her witness statement and then reunited with Jeremy. Watching her face as she saw her son, no joy or happiness showed, but shame, sorrow. It made Connor think of his own mother, and the way he'd judged her for letting him suffer because she was too weak to do anything about it.

Jeremy showed no judgement. He ran to her and hugged her, held on tight, his head buried in her shoulder as his own shoulders began to shake.

After they left, Connor followed up with the LA-CSI team, but their final report would take a few days. He'd closed as much of the Olawale file as he possibly could.

Place mostly deserted, he said goodnight to the few officers he passed on his way to his truck. Inside, he sat, trying to think about where to get food, but then started the engine and drove straight to Liv's, boldly pulling into her driveway. He knew the height of his headlights would beam right into her windows.

As he walked to her front door, he imagined again, coming home.

The door opened before he reached it and she stood there in that same cream loungewear set he'd seen before, blond hair piled on her head in a loose bun, face clean and bare of makeup. Home. He was home. *She* was home.

She said nothing, but he easily recognized the sadness in her expression.

Until Leo came bounding through the open doorway and a sudden flurry of activity and panic made them both bolt toward the little streak of fluff.

Connor was apparently his destination, and he swept him into his arms while Leo bumped his cold nose all over his face in happy greeting. "Hey buddy," he murmured, walking past Liv, into her house without a word.

At the quiet click of the door closing, Connor set Leo down and then stood to face her. She'd been crying, the puffiness under her eyes reminding him of the days leading up to when he had to report for duty. He'd thought to make her uncomfortable, pay a little for the trouble she'd caused him, but the memory and the realization of the opportunity he had now, brought him to her.

Six steps, he took her in his arms and held tight. Her body shuddered as it always did when she cried, and he held her as he had done then. He pulled back a little, hand cradling the side of her face and kissed her forehead when she kept her head down. "It's okay, baby. Don't cry anymore."

Her arms went tight around him, and she cried harder, so he simply held her. This time, not having to rush, not having to say or do anything.

As her shuddering slowed and she sniffled through a nasal passage so blocked it sounded like her nose was suffocating, he murmured, "If you get snot on my shirt, I won't tell anyone."

A small laugh, and she pulled away from him, wiping her cheeks and under her eyes. "I'm so sorry."

"For the snot?" He looked at his shirt. "I don't see any snail tracks."

She laughed again and then moved away to discreetly blow her nose into a napkin before turning back to him. Her gaze searched all over his face as if to determine his thoughts, so he deliberately kept his expression blank.

"I didn't tell anyone about that phone call," she began, "because I thought if I could just keep him safe until you found the killer, or until his mom came forward, it's what I *should* do. And I told myself that call was privileged information, shared with me from an innocent victim."

He nodded, having already deduced her thinking but he figured she needed to say this more than he needed to hear it.

"When Mrs. Olawale wouldn't say anything, I tried getting Jeremy to come forward and say what happened. The night you saw me, I hadn't seen Jeremy since our last session."

"How have you been communicating with him?"

"The day after his dad died, the woman I heard before made him call to tell me he would die if I did anything. Before he hung up, I told him to create a fake email account and email me for help.

"I got an email from Lea Nonme, asking for food. Jeremy had mentioned a couple times before how his mom would sing that song 'Lean On Me' all the time, so I knew it was him. I ordered groceries and books for him to pick up at a market he wanted, but I didn't know his address until a few days ago. He wouldn't tell me before that, I promise I didn't know it."

"I had to go when his aunt was asleep. That's why I went there so late. I needed to make a connection with him again, to bolster him about coming forward. I got an email later that night saying he was going to go to the police this weekend."

That sharpened his attention. "You're saying if I hadn't followed you, the problem would have resolved itself."

"I'm not saying that. I don't know that he would have gone. But I am trying to say that once I knew what was happening, I tried to fix it. I never, ever would have intentionally put you in this position."

"What about the position you put yourself in?" He said, incensed.

"I was afraid if I did anything he'd be killed, as promised. I'd already heard that woman kill one person, so I knew she was capable. And I had no information about her I could share, so Jeremy or his mom had to do something to keep him safe. I kept thinking if I could just maintain until that happened, that it would the right thing in the end."

"You can't do that anymore, Liv."

"Because I'm going to jail?"

He hadn't told her. He almost said, 'Not this time," but her swollen eyes made him rethink it. "No. You're clear. Mrs. Olawale and Jeremy both gave statements. We found Mr. Olawale's killer."

Her eyes slid closed. "Oh thank God," she breathed.

"But not ever again, Liv. I'm the cop. I'll handle things from now on. Or, option two, you become a cop."

"Would you give me a good reference?" she said, all dewy-eyed sweetness.

"Hell no. You've been breaking the law since we were kids."

She laughed, the sound joyful and he went to her again, not willing to resist the draw. Cradling her face in his hands, he leaned down until their lips almost met. "Promise me."

"I promise," she whispered.

Gently, he settled his lips on hers. The way they sank into the pillowy softness of her mouth made heat race up his spine.

Swiftly, he pulled back and stepped away. The need to have her rode him hard. "I have to go."

"What?"

"A week is tomorrow."

"But. We haven't. It didn't work."

"The hell it didn't. Keeping your sweet aa--arse out of prison notwithstanding, I've honored your test." He walked to the door, while she continued to stand there looking like the last thing she wanted him to do was leave, and he paused with his hand on the handle to take it in. "You never said you love me." It almost surprised him how easily he said the words she could so deeply hurt him with.

Her mouth opened a little and she seemed to freeze up.

"Watch out for those bugs, Lucky." He grinned as her mouth snapped shut. "We'll talk about it tomorrow." Then he left. Last fucking thing he wanted to do. The thought of her saying they needed to stay apart another week forced him out.

When he got home, he wandered around the place, hoping it was the last time he'd ever have to stay there. He knew exactly where he wanted to be. The camping bag still sat in his truck, and tomorrow it would be in Liv's house, his clothes in her closet. How long 'til he could move everything? Would it be when he proposed?

The thought made him uncomfortable, and he brushed it off, but then didn't. Hutch had said it was because of his mom's marriage to Keith that he reacted badly to the idea.

His mom. She hadn't shown shame or sorrow, like Mrs. Olawale had. She'd popped pills so she didn't feel anything. He could practically hear the judgement in his own thoughts and remembered how Jeremy seemed to have none.

Sighing heavily, Connor took out a piece of paper and pen, and sat at his dining table.

CHAPTER TWENTY-NINE

Dear Mom,

Do you remember the last time Dad left for deployment? You said, This time I refuse to be miserable, and you took me to Bishop to fish. I had to handle the pontoon boat after you almost crashed it because you couldn't stop it quick enough. That was my favorite day. Do you remember it, wherever you are? Would you remember it if you were here?

I wonder what you would think about me now. If you would think about me. People who do what you did become junkies before long. Maybe you were and I didn't know it. I've always believed you took so many pills so you wouldn't have to deal with what Keith did to me. But maybe you were already a junkie by then and didn't care. I wish that you cared. But I almost killed myself because I didn't want to live with the way I felt, so maybe I would have been the same if I were in your position.

Things are different for me now because of Liv, again. In some ways I think about how I've had her in my life because of you. In other ways I think about how I let her go because of you too. Would I have had her in my life if you hadn't been the way you were? Would I have missed out on being with her if you had been okay? It's a little hard for me to think about how the best thing in my life came to be because of the worst.

I don't honestly know what I think about you. Angry, no I don't experience that when I think about you. Hurt. Yes, that's there. But not a lot. It seems far away now. When I think about you, for the most part, I think about you dying and me not coming home. I think about how I carried on doing what I was doing like nothing happened. Thinking about that now, makes my chest hurt. I'm sorry, Mom. I should have come home, no matter what Keith said. He may have not let me into the house, but I've never been able to stop thinking about the fact that I didn't even try.

I don't know where you are now. I'm not sure what I believe about Heaven or Hell, but I hope if they exist, you're an angel flying around and happy. If you are, I hope you'll watch over me, because no matter what's happened, you'll always be my mom and I'll always love you.

Connor

He became aware of the stillness inside him as he looked over the letter. How different everything was to the other two he'd written.

If he knew where his mom's grave was, he'd have liked to leave the letter there. The first time he'd ever experienced the urge. The first time he hadn't resisted thinking about her. What a waste so much of his life had been.

"I'll do better, Mom," he murmured.

Carefully tri-folding it, he found an envelope and sealed it in, writing simply, 'Mom', on the outside. With nowhere to take it to, no pictures of her to place it with, he dug out the old bible Liv's parents had given him when he left for deployment and put the letter in there.

The next morning, he looked repeatedly to see if Liv texted him, because no way would he do it before dark, marking the official end of the weeklong decree. But nothing came from her, making him want to growl and laugh at her stubbornness— another thing he didn't remember her possessing, at least when it came to him.

Before he left, he made a piece of toast and grabbed the chain he'd draped over his bedside lamp that gently sparkled in the light.

At work, Fernando sat at his desk, eating his slop. "All good?" Connor said.

"It's a boy. Six and a half pounds and healthy."

Connor set a wrapped-up paper towel, stained with buttery grease on Fernando's desk.

"What's this?" Fernando unfolded it to reveal the toast.

"A toast to you, Grandpa."

Fernando grinned and looked up at him. "Clever." His eyes went a little watery, as if he held back tears, and though Connor didn't understand what was going on, he grinned back and squeezed his shoulder. "Congrats, partner."

"Thank you," Fernando said gruffly.

Connor went to his desk as Fernando cleared his throat. The loud sound of a crunchy bite made Connor laugh.

"Olawale," Fernando said around a mouthful. "All buttoned up?"

"Looks like. Just waiting on Forensics to confirm the pistol matches."

"Good. Case Closed is one of my favorite songs."

"The one only you can hear in your head?"

"It'd be a smash hit if I ever went public with it. Post it to YouTube, instant star." Another bite of toast.

More detectives came in, as they normally did, but one came in with a 'BIG PAPA!' sign and a six-pack of beers wrapped in diapers. Eventually, Fernando took out his phone and started showing pictures of the baby, including one with his wife holding and smiling at the tiny bundle.

"Looks like a happy ending," someone said.

Fernando scrolled to the next photo. "I'm calling it a happy beginning."

* * * *

At exactly five, Connor stood, saluted Fernando who looked at him with a raised brow and took off to Liv's. He knocked with anticipation buzzing beneath his skin, listened to Leo bark in response and thought, *good boy guarding the house.*

Leo quit barking, Liv didn't come to the door.

Over to her parent's house he went.

"Connor!" Mary greeted him with genuine warmth and held out her arms. Feeling a little silly, but mostly not, he went into them and hugged her.

Cal came walking out from the den. Mary released Connor and then Cal gave him a bear hug. His first time seeing them, it wasn't the most unexpected thing to happen, this time was.

"Still so damned happy to see you, son," Cal said, releasing him.

"Thank you, sir. I… same."

A cautious look suddenly changed Cal's expression. "There's no more official business, is there?"

"Official business?" Mary made a face up at Cal. "What are you talking about?"

Cal kept his attention locked on Connor.

"No, sir," Connor said. "Case is just about to be closed."

"You let me know when it's officially closed. Can you do that?"

"I can."

Cal gave him an approving nod, making Connor feel like a kid, proud of his accomplishment.

"I guess we'll be talking about this later," Mary said with syrupy sweetness to Cal before rounding on Connor with fake brightness. "Are you hungry?"

"Actually—thank you, but I'm looking for Liv. Do you know where she is?"

"She's usually at her office until seven on Thursdays. Would you like to stay for dinner?"

"Thank you, Mrs. Jones." He smiled, remembering the way she always fed him as a kid. "I'll take a raincheck." Leaning down to give her a kiss on the cheek, he said goodbye and then drove to Liv's office.

Mindful of her rules, he waited outside until he felt certain her last client of the day would be enclosed with her before he opened the door to the waiting room. Patrick sat behind his desk and looked up from his computer with a quizzical expression.

"How can I help you, Detective?" Patrick said.

"I'd like to wait here for Liv."

He nodded slowly. "Sure. It's about another forty minutes."

Considering his lack of surprise, Connor guessed Liv had told him something about their relationship.

Five minutes in, Patrick said, "Dr. Jones said you found Jeremy Olawale. That's a win! Great job!"

A smile caught Connor by surprise, and he quickly blanked his face. "Thanks. He's with his mom now so hopefully the family can heal."

"Absolutely, that's everything. That's the best thing you could have done for that kid. Good job!"

The guy was so *positive*. Connor thought if there was a Self Esteem Superhero, this guy would be the prototype.

Over the next half hour, they connected over weightlifting, with Patrick saying Connor should come by his gym sometime and work out.

When Liv's patient walked out of her office, Patrick said to him, "You can go in. Mind, body, man."

Connor grinned.

Inside, he found her stood beside her desk, wearing a long hunter green skirt with matching heels and a white sweater that looked soft as a cloud. Her hair fell in satiny waves around her shoulders and when she looked at him—*connection*.

He snapped the door shut and then he stalked to her. "The week is officially up."

As he reached her, he took her face in his hands and swept his lips along hers, back and back again before his tongue sank into her mouth.

Hands roaming, they slid over the silky skirt covering her taut bottom, over her hips, up her sides before wrapping her in a crushing embrace. She wriggled against him, hips canting to cradle his hardness, and she rocked, breath coming in gasps.

Abruptly, she jerked back, out of his grasp. Cheeks pink, lips rosy and wet, she said, "I can't." And his heart stopped.

"What do you mean?"

"Patrick is right outside, he could walk in. And I totally judged Holly for having sex in her office, it's so cliché I just can't."

Heart beating again, he laughed softly. "For a minute I thought you were saying you can't," his hand gestured between them, "us."

"Oh! No! I mean, yes, yes I can, us, just not the inappropriate cliché stuff."

"You and your rules, Lucky."

"I can't unsee that moment in Holly's office."

"I thought as a counselor you aren't supposed to judge."

"I'm a work in progress."

His lips curled and he stepped toward her again. Hands sliding up her back, he murmured, "I want to make progress with you."

"Then we should go," she whispered.

Stepping away from him again, she grabbed her office bag and they left together, Patrick saying a cheerful goodbye on their way out.

When Liv veered toward her car, Connor took her hand and towed her to his truck.

"I need my car," she protested.

"I'll give you a ride in the morning."

As he opened the passenger door for her, she said, "I suppose if it gets stolen, you'll be on hand to take my report."

"Something like that." He grinned and shut the door.

On the drive to her house, he took her hand, and she linked her fingers through his. "Do you forgive me?" she said.

"For what?" He glanced at her, frowning.

"For putting you in a legally questionable situation. I could have ruined your career. The one thing you've consistently tended to that I caused you to risk."

Connor was silent a moment, thinking about what she said. "The one thing I've tended to… You mean care about. Baby, I only cared about it because I didn't have to care for it. It's always been the thing I did that I didn't have to feel anything about." He squeezed her hand. "Do *you* forgive *me?*"

"Yes," she said without hesitation. "I may still feel a little worried you're not going to show up one day, but I do forgive you for the past."

"Is that why you didn't call me this morning?"

"That may be why I didn't call you."

He lifted their joined hands and gently kissed the back of hers. "I think we're in a position now where neither of us can leave. We can both blackmail the other with the Olawale case."

She gave a muffled laugh. "A commitment by blackmail. That's not promising."

"Oh we have the commitment. The blackmail is the insurance tap to the head." Liv's Uncle Mark used to say that about shooting bad guys to make sure they were dead.

"You're more romantic than I remembered," she said dryly.

Connor chuckled as he pulled into her driveway, but when she moved to get out of the truck, he hit the lock and said, "What are you doing?"

"Getting out."

"You can't. You have to wait."

"We're not on a date. And anyway, you know I hate waiting. When we get in the car, opening the door is always the right choice. But when we arrive, I want to get out and I don't want to wait."

"I remember."

"Then?" as she delicately pressed the unlock button.

He promptly locked it. "I don't want you getting too comfortable too quick."

She grinned. "More romantic insurance taps to the head?"

"You're speaking my language, baby."

He got out and kept pressing the lock button on his keyfob, though she sat still and ladylike, utterly prim. She'd always been cheerfully straightlaced and he was as charmed by it now as he'd always been.

Opening the door for her, he noticed right away she'd pulled her skirt high up her thighs. She gave him a seductive look as one leg slid long and lean out of the truck, leaving her legs spread wide with her skirt dripping between her thighs, before slowly moving her other honey-toned leg out of the truck.

Arousal shot so hard and fast through him, he growled low in his throat and closed the space between them, hands at her thighs to stop the edge of her skirt from slipping back down. Then his hands slid under, rough palms sliding over her soft buttocks, fingers trailing along the cleft of her ass to tease the lace of her thong. "Did you wear this for me?" he rumbled deep in his throat.

"No," she said breathlessly and then smiled. "I wore it for me."

Dipping his head, he licked the smile from her lips and then her tongue as it met his. Abruptly she pulled away. "My parents could see."

"Hgh?" Arousal clouded his mind. Her parents? "We're not kids—"

"But they could see from their house. They could even *video*."

He shook his head as if to clear it. "Why did you buy a house a few doors down from them?"

She shifted slightly, smiling sweetly up at him and suddenly he felt the gentle drag of her fingernails over his shaft. He sucked in a sharp breath, and she laughed, then she practically bolted away from him, into her house. If he turned and her parents *were* videoing, his hard-on pressed like a beacon against his light grey pants. Taking a moment to breathe, to ease, his eyes fell on his camping bag, and like a trophy, he grabbed it and held it in front of him all the way to her door.

She'd closed it behind her, and he pushed it open to find her crouched on the ground, silky green skirt a puddle around her as she hugged Leo.

Connor dropped his bag, eyes locked on her. "You're mine, woman."

She stood and walked backward to her bedroom, and he followed, stalking her step for step. She stopped next to the bed, and he went right to her, gaze fastened on her heavy-lidded blue-brown gaze, with her sexy mouth soft and ready. Savoring every moment, he slid his hands over the satin mounds of her buttocks to the zipper. The sound of it falling down her legs a tantalizing whisper. His palms slid up, up the side of her ribs, pushing the sweater over her head. The way her hair fell around her lace covered breasts as the sweater came off made his cock pulse.

With one hand, he unclasped her bra and stared at her peaked nipples, peaking through her hair. Gently, he dragged his thumb across the tip and watched her lips part on a soft breath.

Her hands moved languidly to his tie, removing it slowly while he stroked her nipples. She unbuttoned his shirt, and he slipped his hands beneath her panties pulling them down. She pushed his suitcoat and shirt off, and he bent his head to tease her neck with his tongue.

He could feel her trembling, and as she unbuckled and opened his trousers, his fingers slid to her soft, damp heat. Her lips were plump and wet, and as she pushed his pants and boxers down, he pushed his finger up into her.

She stepped her legs wider, her breath growing heavier. He watched her as she rocked on his hand, tightening around him as his finger dragged along her delicate tissue. "You're so wet for me."

She bit her lower lip, swelling even more and he moved her back using his hand, keeping it in her as she eased back onto the bed, legs open wide to accommodate it.

He moved her until her head met the pillows and then he loomed over her, staring at her spread, trembling, glistening before him. Pumping slowly, deeply in and out, with his other hand he spread her lips, exposing the delicate pointed nub. Very gently, he stroked it and she made a guttural sound of pleasure. He fucking loved that sound. Leaning down, he licked it, lapped it at, while his finger worked her.

"Connor! I can't—I'm going—" Her head arched back, her whole body shaking, and he plunged his finger deep, curling, as his tongue flicked back and forth over her clit. *"Connor!"*

Her whole body spasmed and she clenched down so hard he could barely move his hand. Chuckling softly, darkly as he tasted her pleasure, he watched her breasts trembling from her orgasm.

His hand stilled as she came down, but he didn't want to stop tasting her. Like a cat cleaning up the cream, he licked patiently all around her delicate little nub. "I love the way you taste," he said, mouth still on her.

Her languid gaze watched him. "I never thought I liked this," she breathed.

Slowly, her breath grew heavier again, tension shifted her legs, and she slid her hands to her breasts and stroked her nipples. Her hips canted, wanting more and he rose up to fill her, but she sat up and shifted their position, pushing him onto his back.

"Look at this," she whispered, staring at him before her. She trailed a hand down his stomach as she moved between his legs. Connor felt the faintest brush of sensation beneath his balls before her nails very gently dragged up them. He groaned and she smiled. Their eyes locked and they were connected, deeply.

The hand on his stomach slid to his shaft and he held his breath. Her eyes flicked down, and then her head lowered. Soft, warm lips pressed against the head, and he watched as her hot fucking mouth opened and sucked him in.

"*Mhhn,*" he groaned deep, his head rolling back.

Her cheeks hollowed as she suctioned around him. Her head bobbed slowly up and down. He loved when she lifted so high the head popped out of her mouth, her teeth flashing in a bashful smile, before swiftly sucking him hard to the back of her throat.

He had to touch her face, her hair. He slid his fingers through it, holding it back so he could see her taking him in and out of her mouth. When she sucked him deep, he lifted his hips just a little, pushing it into her throat, making her eyes water.

He murmured, "Sorry," and she snorted. He chuckled and did it again. "So fucking good." He did it again. "Fecking, sorry." She did it this time, pushing back against his lifted hips with the back of her throat. *"Mhhn!"*

Abruptly he pulled her mouth off him. The sight of it popping from her lips nearly made him lose control. Before he could move, she climbed up him, straddled his hips and grabbed his cock, feeding it inside her. Hot, so wet, tight, squeezing him all the way down. The skin of his flesh glistened as she lifted, and he grabbed her hips, driving up into her again. She lifted and he drove up, yanking her down, again and again. The tight clasp of her drove him out of his mind, and fire raced up his spine, pleasure tightening his belly. He couldn't last.

Locking her against his hips, he set his thumb on her clit and rocked deep, pumping himself in her wetness. Goosebumps raced over her skin, her breasts bounced, and she quivered and shook and vibrated as high cries squeezed through her throat.

The rhythmic clenching on his cock milked his release, and his hips shot wildly beneath her, bouncing her on him as he groaned long and low. Yanking her down, plunging deep, his hot liquid spurted as pleasure consumed every part of him.

CHAPTER THIRTY

As Connor's breathing evened out, he tugged Liv down until she lay on his chest. He loved the feel of her soft skin against his and periodically stroked a hand over her, just for the pleasure of it.

"Do you think it would have been this good if we'd done it when we were seventeen?" Liv wondered in a voice so relaxed, it brought to mind hot days and poolside drinks.

"Doubtful. I lose my mind when I'm inside you. It probably would have taken me four tries before I could hold it long enough to do any good with it."

He could feel her smile against his chest.

"Did you lose your wad often?" she asked.

Barely lifting his head, he took in her serene expression. Guess it was okay to talk about? "No, but I probably would have with you."

"Have you always been good at it then?"

Lifting his head again, he studied her to make sure the serenity was real. "I can't speak for my past partner's experience, but it seemed like they liked it."

"Ooh, very diplomatic." She rolled off him. "I'm starving."

He sat up and watched her walk to the bathroom, enjoying the way the globes of her ass shifted with each step. She glanced at him before closing the door and then paused and smiled. "You have this look on your face…"

"In my head, I still see us as teenagers. Then all of a sudden, you're strolling naked in front of me as a smoking hot woman."

Laughing softly, she closed the bathroom door.

Connor lay there a moment before suddenly remembering the bag he'd left at the front door. Swiftly pulling on his boxers, he silently jogged to the bag, willing her to take her time. He'd stow it until he could hang his things without her knowing. He didn't want to talk about what he wanted to do. Didn't want her to even know about it until it was too late. No debating, just done.

Jogging back, he came to an awkward stop. She stood in the middle of the room, wearing a little patterned robe tied in a bow at her waist. Leo sat beside her, one ear perked up, head angled as they both stared at him curiously.

"Why are you both looking at me like that?"

Liv glanced at the dog and whispered, "You're so cute." Then to him, "Why are you jogging in your boxers around the house?"

"How did you hear me jogging?"

"I've got perfect hearing."

"Of course you do. Why were you so quick in the bathroom?"

Her eyes narrowed. "Why are you acting like you're hiding something?"

"I'm not hiding something. I'm *trying* to hide something. It's different."

Crossing her arms in front of her, she said. "I'd argue that's arguable. What are you trying to hide?"

Connor very deliberately moved the bag to hide behind his legs. "Nothing."

She scanned his expression, down to his legs and then leaned sideways as if to peer around them. Standing upright, she said, "Well then, please continue trying to hide nothing."

Uh, *what did he do now?* He started to walk toward the closet, aware of her pivoting to watch him, so he paused to say, "Hiding nothing works best when you're not watching."

"Oh. Right." She turned and left the bedroom.

That…that was it? She was going to leave him to it? Connor went to the bedroom door and peered down the hallway. He could hear her in the kitchen getting food out of the fridge.

Swiftly he went back to the closet, took all his clothes out of the bag, most still on hangers and hid them behind her stuff. Then he went to the bathroom and situated his grooming supplies in subtle places he hoped she wouldn't notice. Finished, he put his pants back on but left his shirt off because she'd liked that last time.

Walking into the kitchen, her eyes lit up when she looked at him, hands holding two bowls of chicken salad. She motioned to the table with her head and he sat. She set the bowls down on their place settings and then straddled him.

"Oh hello," he murmured.

She laughed with her mouth closed and then said out the side of it, "I've got food in my mouth." Her hands stroked his chest, over his shoulders, up his neck. She swallowed and then kissed his cheek, following it down to trail kisses along his jawline.

"You smell like wantons," he said, stroking his own hands up her back. Did she need the robe on?

She hugged him, held still with only the slight movement of soft kisses on the side of his neck. Heaven. Sweetness.

"I love you," she said softly.

Reflexively, his arms tightened, and he squeezed her, possibly too much but she didn't resist. "Thank God," he muttered, and felt her smile against his neck before she gently kissed him again.

She leaned back, twisting to grab the salad and then fed him a bite. "Now we both smell like wantons." Then she kissed his flexing jawline as he chewed, his temple and then his lips after he swallowed.

He pulled back to gaze into her eyes. "I want to do this with you, forever."

Her brows minutely lifted. "Making a forever statement didn't work out so great for us last time."

"I think it did. I promised I'd love you forever, and I have. I've never stopped."

"We just need to be more specific about defining it this time?" she said with a half-smile.

"You could write it in our vows."

Her mouth dropped open. He hadn't intended to say it, hadn't even been actively thinking it—though of course it had been on his mind. He'd thought talking about it with her would be a huge hurdle he'd have to fight himself to get over, but no. The only one feeling uneasy appeared to be her. "Too soon?" he said, then, "There could be a bug in here, you might want to—" Her mouth snapped shut.

Connor chuckled and smoothed a golden strand of hair behind her ear. "Best get used to the idea, Lucky. Let it settle."

"This isn't a proposal," she said, more statement than question, but he answered, "No. When it is, I'll be so romantic you'll pity all the women in those old books you like to read."

"Now that I think about it, I don't think Darcy or the Colonel had devastatingly romantic proposals."

"Thanks for making it easier on me, baby," he said, softly kissing her.

"I can't believe we're talking about this," she whispered.

"We're not talking about this yet." He leaned around her to get another bite of salad. "Why does this taste so good?"

She tried to get off his lap to eat her own salad, but he held her hips in place. They settled on her holding a bowl and taking turns having bites. When she took the last bite from the second bowl, he said, "When can I move in?" making her choke a little.

"You just moved some of your clothes in," she said.

"How do you know? I did it stealthy-like."

"I've had boyfriends move some of their stuff in before."

"Really? I've never lived with a woman, in any way."

"Really?" They studied each other curiously. "Oh, I almost forgot." She started to get up, but he held her hips again. "You're going to want to let me go for this, I promise."

She gave him a quick smile-kiss and stood, going into the kitchen to grab a medium-sized container with a lid. Straddling him again, she leaned back to settle the container between them and peeled the lid back like she was removing packaging from a priceless artifact.

The scent of white-chocolate macadamia nut cookies hit Connor's senses at the same time his eyes understood what they were seeing. These had always been his favorite, he used to regularly beg her to make them. Groaning, he took one and bit in with reverence. He'd never had better cookies than hers. They'd been perfect in high school, and they were perfect now.

"I made them after you left last night," she said, looking both pleased and abashed at the same time.

He finished chewing and then said, "I need to rephrase, I'm moving in."

"Ah, the cookies made it official, huh?"

"No, they highlighted the urgency."

"Of more cookies," she said with a smile.

"Of all of it. I want all of it with you."

"I don't want all of your furniture. Or any of it, probably."

She wasn't getting it, how serious he was, and he didn't know how else to say it. Leaning his head toward hers, not shielding the depth of his seriousness in any way, he locked their gazes with a new intensity. "What about the garage?"

"What about it? You want a parking spot?"

"I've got tools and a bench. I'd rather have that set up than a parking space."

She blinked.

"I don't care about any of my furniture, we can sell it all, but the tools and the workbench; I like my garage space."

The way she looked at him—as if he were a stray dog that she wasn't sure would welcome her or attack her if she put a hand out.

"Normally there's a little bit of joking, or teasing, but you're not doing any of that," she said slowly.

"No."

"No." She blinked again. "You're really serious." She looked at the cookies nestled between them. "You used to joke about marrying me for my cookies. I thought that's what this was. But garage organization, selling your furniture, that's planning, with details. What's… happened?"

There was not one minute more he wanted to waste on uncertainty or disconnect. He'd lay everything on the table to get them to where they should have been for the last thirteen years.

"I look back at my life, and every moment without you in it is empty. What we have between us is rare, I know it is and I don't deserve it. I don't deserve you and I *never* will but for some reason you love me and I'm not going to waste any more time."

He cupped her cheek, stroking the softness with his thumb, mesmerized by the warmth and emotion in her gaze. "What do you want? Do you want kids still?" She jerked but he held her in place. "You used to say you wanted a couple. I can give you babies."

Tears swam in Liv's eyes, and she laughed self-consciously. "Do you want them?"

"I want one with you."

"Just one?"

Shrugging, Connor couldn't resist kissing the bow of her mouth. "One or two."

She sat bemused on his lap, looking up at him with wide, enormous eyes. "What brought all this on?"

He couldn't resist kissing her again. "I've worked really hard on my life," he said, a mixture of pride and embarrassment tangling within. "I even wrote a letter to my mom, to change the way I disconnect. I am actively working on being the best version of me there is, because of you. I don't want to wait anymore to do what we always should have done."

His voice rumbling low, he told her how it would have been. "We would have gotten married after you graduated, because your dad would have insisted we wait til then. I'd work the graveyard shift as a new officer and wake you up in the morning when I got home with hot, sweet loving. We'd buy a house, and you'd finish getting all your degrees, and we'd talk about having kids someday when we were on the same work schedule and you had your practice." He stroked his thumb over her cheek again. "All that's in place now. So let's pick up from there."

Tears spilled down her cheeks, catching on his thumb and he gently wiped it away. "Say yes, baby, to all of it. Let me have all of it, with you, starting now."

Her lips trembled as she smiled, and then she laughed, tipping her head back in joyful release. "Yes, Connor. Yes."

Freed of the tension he hadn't been aware of carrying, his mouth swooped to hers and she laughed into the kiss as she hurriedly set the cookies aside from between them.

He stood, lifting her with him and she wrapped her legs around his waist as he carried her to the bedroom, to *their* bed. Laying her down, this time it was slow, tender, hands linked, mouths fusing, bodies moving in harmony together. She came with a soft cry, and he watched while the pleasure consumed her, adding to his satisfaction, amplifying his orgasm as he groaned and shook from it.

Afterward, she lay curled against his side, head on his chest, one leg tangling over his.

"We could wait to tell my parents you're moving in, maybe let them discover it on the day."

"Afraid to tell them?"

"They'll ask a lot of questions."

"I'll talk to them, I don't mind."

She slid her palm over his chest. "I wish your parents had known what they had in you."

Instinctively, his arm tightened around her, and he kissed the top of her head. "I wrote something a little like that in my letters to them." He described the three, amazed at how easy it was to tell her.

"What did you do with them?"

"My dad's and Keith's are in a drawer. I put hers in a bible because I…" he got stuck on having to say he didn't know where her gravestone lay. "I don't know where else to put it."

"A bible's a good place. If you want it with her, you could always put it with her urn."

Connor tensed. "She's in an urn?"

"You—" She sat up and looked at him wide-eyed. "Oh God," she breathed. "You don't know, do you? I'm so sorry. It's been so long I think we all forgot that you didn't— my parents didn't give you anything when you were there?"

Mutely he shook his head.

"Oh Connor, I'm so sorry we forgot—"

"Tell me," he interrupted.

"I'm— Keith didn't have a funeral. Did you know that?"

"No."

"Okay—God I'm sorry—but Keith had an estate sale after she died. The house was sold, and he pretty much opened the doors, said everything was available to buy. My parents went and they were—you can imagine how they were. He literally was selling everything, your family photos, photo albums, he even had her urn out on a table that made it seem like it was for sale. They told him who they were to you, and he said they could take your photos but to leave the frames. Before they left, he gave them her ashes that were in a little baggie inside the urn. So my parents bought another urn and have kept it for you."

"She's with them?"

"Since the day you didn't return home on leave. Keith had the sale the same day."

A piercing ache sliced through Connor's heart. All that he'd lost by shutting down, disconnecting. Never—again. Tugging her back down onto his chest, he held her crushed against him. "I don't have any photos of her. Of my childhood. Nothing."

"You didn't take any with you?"

"I didn't want to."

Softly, she kissed his chest. "You have pictures now."

Connor slowly stroked a hand up and down her back as his mind wandered. He was aware when her breathing deepened and her body lay heavier with sleep, but still couldn't stop thinking about his mom, and how Keith set up a sale of all that should have been his, just for him to see when he came home on leave. What would he have done if he'd pulled up to the house, probably dressed in his army fatigues, to see strangers rifling through his childhood memories? His mother's ashes? It made him so angry he wanted to punch something.

Lying there with Liv was exactly where he wanted to be, but the urge to find a punching bag and beat the shit out of it rode him hard too. The sound of Leo scratching at something in the other room gave him the excuse to move. Carefully, he eased out of Liv's embrace, but she didn't stir at all. The sound of something falling to the floor had him jogging to the living room.

"*Hey!*" he snapped in a harsher tone than intended.

Leo immediately cowered, tail tucking between his legs as he backed away from the container of cookies he'd knocked to the ground. The sad, sorrowful look made Connor soften, and he crouched to the ground, carefully picking up the cookies that spilled out. "Guess we didn't seal the lid all the way. And once you could smell them, I can't blame you for trying, buddy." Leo walked back over and sniffed gently all around Connor's hand and arm, anywhere the cookie smell lingered. "I'd do the same."

Leo sat and looked up at him with his dark eyes, one ear popped up with the tip flopping over. Smiling reluctantly, Connor scratched his neck. He was soft as a bunny. After a moment, Connor's leg started to ache from the crouched position, so he scooped Leo up and held the softness against his chest. Happy with this new position, Leo draped his head over Connor's shoulder and went to sleep.

"I'm putting everyone to sleep tonight," he murmured, stroking the puppy. The anger burning inside him dwindled.

With the love of his life and the softest little puppy under his care, he wanted no part of Keith shadowing this. Another time he'd talk about it, probably with Hutch when he saw him, but right now, he could *see* the blessings in his life, touch them. They were the light, and he wouldn't let anything darken it.

* * * *

Connor nearly fell out of bed the next morning when Liv's alarm went off like a bomb dropping next to his head. Yelling, "Holy shit!" he lunged at her alarm clock on the side of the bed he'd ended up on, and yanked it out of the wall. He turned to look at her with crazy eyes, further incensed when she barely had one eye cracked. "*Liv!*"

"G'morning." She smiled sleepily.

Holding the clock, he demanded. "Did you turn this thing *up* since last time?"

"Had to," she yawned and shook as she stretched. "Wasn't getting through."

"You're going to go deaf, woman! That's at a decibel that damages ear drums!"

Her eyes scanned his body, lingering on his cock. "You look good in the morning."

Still incensed while his semi grew to full attention, he tossed the clock on the ground and climbed onto the bed, pushing the covers off her and settling between her thighs. Her legs drew up beside him and he nudged her dampness, not quite ready for him. "No more alarm clocks," he said, rocking against her.

"Somebody has to get the job done." Her hips canted as she drew him in, wet now. Slow, deep slide in, slow slide out.

She drew her hands over her head and arched her back, bringing attention to her hard little nipples. Irresistible. He curled his head over her to lick, nibble, and she bucked against him, gasping at the sensation.

Her hands abruptly went to his ass, and she squeezed his cheeks, grinding him against her as her hips pulled him in. "Connor, I'm about to," she breathed.

His brows rose as he gazed down at her rosy skin, flushed with need. "So soon?"

She pulled a leg up higher, grabbed his ass tighter and worked herself on his length as he pushed into her. He felt her release gripping him and the sight of her ecstasy aroused him beyond reason, and he came in hot spurts, shuddering and trembling as the pleasure consumed him.

Laying heavily on her, breathing deeply, one last shudder took him before he levered himself on his elbows and kissed her swollen mouth. "I'll be your alarm clock from now on."

A languid smile moved her lips. "We're still talking about that?"

"It took a year off my life this morning."

"If you're up for the challenge of waking me then I accept."

Easing out of her he got up and let Leo out of the crate. "If I have to dump icy water on your head to get you up, the job will be done." He grinned at her expression. "I've got a new title for us on the Hot List," he said, referring to the notorious list that had been passed around their high school, the one Liv always wanted to be on that he'd *always* been on. Her dream finally came true their senior year when they'd been named 'Hottest Couple'.

"Oh yeah? You think they'd still let me on it?"

His gaze raked over her golden skin, her taut curves, her satin hair. "There's no letting. No one could keep you off it."

Her smile beamed and he chuckled, remembering her same reaction when they were teens. "No one but me could know about this title though."

"Uh oh. I'm not sure I like the sound of this." She got out of bed and walked toward him. His gaze heated when he saw his seed slicking her thighs.

"But it's *the list,*" he said snagging her into his arms as she tried to walk past him to the shower.

"Will I like it?"

The feel of their naked bodies sliding against each other had him saying huskily, "I love it." He kissed her pouty little mouth. "Hottest Couple in Bed."

Her lips curved and she stretched against him, sighing with pleasure at the way he felt. "That's exactly the list I want to be on in your head."

Unwilling to part from her, he joined her in the shower, but it ended up frustrating the hell out of him because they couldn't be late to work. He wanted to *linger.* As they both dressed and got ready, he had a couple moments of pause where he marveled at watching her put makeup on, do her hair…but it was more like awe that he got to be so close to her, not the stupid reaction he had to brushing their teeth the first time.

When he dropped her off at work, he grabbed her by the back of the neck and kissed her hard, thoroughly. With her gaze heavy-lidded and her lips dewy, he said huskily, "I'll see you at home."

Her lips curved. "I'll get a key made for you today."

As he strolled to his desk, Fernando closed a case file and held it out to him. "LAPD is in top form. Already got confirmation on the June Lewis bullet matching the one found in our very own Mr. Olawale. That's another case officially closed."

Thank God, Connor thought fervently.

Later, he went to Hutch's, and went in knowing he looked the happiest he ever had.

"Everything going good?" Hutch said, eyes warm behind his glasses.

"She said she loves me, Hutch. I'm moving in. I talked about getting married and having kids and it's all good."

His brows rose. "I'm tempted to caution about moving too fast but then I know your long history. You brought up getting married, and didn't feel uncomfortable?"

"No, I wanted to." And since he knew he'd ask, "I wrote that letter to my mom. I realized as I wrote it that she cared, she just didn't have strength. She'd lost it, or maybe she'd never had enough to handle life getting tougher, but she had cared about me, I know she did. Even my dad, he did too. I figure he shuts down any thought of what…hurts. Like I did.

"I remember the last time he called me, my mom answered the phone and screamed at him for breaking our hearts. I remember clearly her saying that every time he called it was a reminder of his betrayal of us. I didn't say anything about it when I talked to him after, and he didn't either, but that was the last time we spoke.

"They were messed up. So was I, I just happened to be lucky enough to not have a kid of my own get caught up in it. I wish things had been different for me growing up but there were a lot of good times too. When I think about them, I want to remember that. I still fucking hate Keith though." Connor told him about the estate sale and urn.

"He's earned your anger. We'll work towards indifference," Hutch said.

"I don't know if I want to feel indifferent."

"You will, because the anger takes energy from you, energy I know you'd rather put into your life with Liv. You have a chance at happiness with Liv again, why give any bit of energy you could be putting into that, into a man you want no connection to? Your anger keeps that connection. Indifference breaks it."

Connor thought how his shutting down had looked a hell of a lot like indifference and how effectively that had broken his connection to Liv. "So we've still got work to do," he said. "And here I thought you and I were moving to a more casual thing."

Hutch chuckled. "I think we can drop down to once a week. Plus, you've got a lot of changes coming up, and even when they're good and what you want and everything is going great, having someone to talk to, advocating for your best mind-frame is always a good thing for your whole self."

"Considering where I've come from, you won't get much argument out of me."

After the session ended, Connor went home, to Liv. She met him at the door with a kiss, and he held her, forehead to forehead. The glint of her necklace caught his eye. "You found it." He'd hung their *Forever* necklace around a solitary hanger the night before, between his clothes and hers. "I wasn't sure what you would think about it."

"I wasn't sure if you wanted me to leave it there," she said. "But," she gently gripped it, the heart held in her fingertips. "It's mine."

"It's always been yours. It will always be yours. Forever, Liv."

FOUR MONTHS LATER

The doorbell rang, but even before Liv went to answer it, she knew who it was. Connor had installed safety cameras all over the perimeter of the house and mounted a monitor in the kitchen that kept a live stream of the camera rolls. It added an air of Situation Room ambiance, that she'd quickly discovered she liked.

"Do you know who that is?" Connor said, looking at the screen, sipping his morning coffee while Leo barked in his best guard-dog voice.

"Holly." She held a pastry box and two lattes. "Looks like she wants to talk."

"Oh." He had a *get me out of here* look on his face as he leaned down to give her a kiss. "Good luck. Don't let her upset you. If you start feeling unhappy, kick her out."

"Okay," she said with amusement, but he wrapped an arm around her back and held her still. "Promise me."

"Really?" He nodded. "Okay, I promise."

Connor told Leo to 'come', and they disappeared into the garage, while Liv opened the door with a pleasant expression on her face. Or she hoped it was.

"Hi," Holly said with a tense smile that didn't move beyond her lips. "I was hoping we could talk." She glanced down at all she carried. "I brought breakfast."

Liv stepped back and held the door open.

As they went through the house to the garden, Liv suddenly remembered the last time Holly had come by, sat at the very same bistro table with coffee and pastries. It struck her how greatly her life had changed since then.

The sun shone warm and pleasant despite the early hour. Birds chirped readily, and the air held a crisp freshness that felt unique to Spring. Weeks prior, she'd potted over a dozen spring blossoms around the garden and they bloomed in happy hues of peach, red and purple. She'd tried to keep her flower color choices cohesive and chic, but she kept getting swept up in the beauty of the variety of blooms, so she had pink, orange, yellow and black-burgundy flowers dotting around too. Connor finally told her to give up on designing her garden and just enjoy it. She'd agreed outwardly, inwardly: *designing never stops.*

He'd laughed, he knew what she'd been thinking. Thank goodness he understood her, because if he'd insisted on bringing any of his profoundly boring furniture to the house when he moved in, there would have been some tough talks. Thankfully, he'd done as he said and sold it all without any problem. The garage was the only place he wanted to plant his flag, and the day he sold his condo, she had it clear for whatever he wanted to do with it. If he wanted to turn it into a mancave, have at it.

He spent *days* getting it set up so that it looked straight out of a magazine for tool lovers and craftsmen. Her dad came by when it was done, and she'd have sworn he almost got teary-eyed. As it was, her dad hugged him and said, "You make me proud, son." Since Connor had learned construction working for him as a teen, she wasn't surprised by the sentiment, but she was by the depth of emotion.

"You've done stuff to the house," Holly said now, voice subdued as she sat at the bistro table. "The pergola looks great. I know you've been wanting it done for a while."

"Connor just finished it." Liv belatedly remembered to get plates and napkins. When she returned, Holly said, "So you're back together with him?"

"We've been living together for the last few months. My mom was a little outraged about it, but he talked to her." Liv smiled. "She won't tell me what he said but things have been really nice between her and I since."

"That's great, Liv. I'm happy for you. I hope it all works out this time." Holly's gaze cast down to her cup and held.

Liv couldn't stand the silence. "What's been going on with you?"

"Jake and I are divorcing." Her gaze returned. "Final in about two months. I told him after we talked. You never called him, did you?"

"No...I didn't know what the right way was, so I hoped you'd...do the right thing."

Holly slowly nodded. "I said to you last time maybe I'd come crawling back to you, but I'm not. I'm not here to beg your forgiveness. I still feel that what I did with Matt was between me and him, and Jake, and that honestly, you have no place in it."

"Really?" Liv could feel the muscles in her face tightening. "I thought friendship meant something else then."

"Liv, you *judge*, too much. You're not *God*. I'm figuring things out, I'm messing up, and I don't need you sitting in judgement. That's not what friendship means to me."

"I know I'm not God," Liv said quietly. "But I do know we're supposed to do all the good we can do, as often as we can do it. Betraying your spouse is not that."

Tears welled in Holly's eyes. "I know. I know I messed up." She wiped at her face. "But I still don't need your judgement. I did this to Jake, not you."

"I don't know how to be a friend to someone who's doing something I feel is very wrong. I'm truly trying not to judge you, but I can't in good conscience stand by and watch.

"And you keep saying I had no part in what was going on, but the hurt I feel stems from it. Your friendship meant so much to me, and it felt like you so easily discarded it for a fling. Maybe you didn't want to hear from me that it was wrong, but if I didn't care about you, I wouldn't say anything. Again, that's not friendship. Even though you didn't like it, I was still looking out for you when I was sounding the alarm about the path you were on."

"I didn't discard our friendship. I was trying to quiet it for a while, because I didn't want to hear you sounding the alarm. I wish I hadn't done what I did, but it was a mistake I felt worth making, at the time. I've learned from it, and I want to move forward with what I've learned from it."

When she didn't continue, Liv said, "Move forward how?"

"I want us to be friends again. I'm asking for your forgiveness for making you feel discarded, and for the words I said in your office, but I'm not asking for your forgiveness for what happened leading up to it."

Boundaries, Liv thought. She was setting them. Had Liv violated them at some point or was this simply the evolution of their friendship that came with the complex layers of life over time? Either way, she loved Holly and valued their friendship. "I forgive you for your words and making me feel discarded. I'm sorry I was judgmental. I don't always know I'm doing it, but I'm trying to be better."

"Thank you," Holly said softly. A moment later, she smiled wryly. "I'm not really sure where we go from here."

"Ah," Liv's face brightened. "I've got just the thing. There's a fencing class I just signed up for. Two more spots are open."

"You and your classes," Holly said with a small curve of her lips. "Fencing sounds better than karate."

"I was so bad. So, so bad." They smiled at each other, and the sense of peace and camaraderie Liv had missed with her seemed to wind around them like a ribbon. "Are you in?"

"I'm in," Holly said. "Will you help me sign up, so I don't miss the spot?"

Liv held up her phone like it had the answers. As she got Holly enrolled, she asked, "How's your puppy?"

"Oh, well." Sad smile. "Jake kept her. He was nuts about her, and I felt so bad about everything I said he could keep her. I wanted to keep her though, she was really sweet."

"That's hard, Holls. I'm sorry."

"Maybe I'll be the spinster with lots of dogs."

"You've got to start with getting one."

"I'm on the list again with Julie."

Liv finished the enrollment. "But you'll never be a spinster. You're too cute."

"I never thought you'd be either. I just didn't expect you'd be with Connor. When I meet him, I may still punch him and probably won't like him for a while after all the years I watched you recover from him."

"But I did recover, and I like me better for it. I do also still like your loyalty in wanting to punch him however."

They laughed.

"He's here," Liv said. "I think he's in the garage, giving us privacy. I can go get him. Do you want to meet him?"

Holly drew back slightly. "Really? I..." She looked around. "Honestly, I'd rather not right now. I feel raw, and I don't want to meet the love of your life like that. I may punch him, but I want to do it on the right foot." They both smiled again, and Holly stood. "I should get going actually."

Liv walked her to the door, and they shared a hug.

"I'm glad you came," Liv said.

"I'm glad you opened the door."

Feeling relieved and happy as she closed the door behind Holly, Liv went in search of Connor. He was drawing up plans for a wooden dog crate she'd found online that he'd said he could make better than anything she could buy.

"Went well?" he said, searching her expression.

She went into his arms and brushed his lips with a kiss. "Very well."

"Good." He kissed her again, their lips sinking into each other in that way she found entrancing. When he pulled back, she sighed.

"Your parents want us to come over."

"Right now?"

"Yeah, now." He curved his arm around her shoulders and steered her from the garage, down a few houses to her parent's.

They went inside and Mary greeted them, her face bright with overly rosy cheeks. She looked flustered and Liv wondered if they'd interrupted something, but her blue floral print shirt was fully buttoned, so she'd clearly had time to dress.

"How'd it go with Holly?" Mary said as she kissed both their cheeks.

Connor must have told her, Liv thought. "Wonderful." And she really meant it.

"Good! It sure was unexpected!"

Liv gave her a concerned look at her overdone enthusiasm.

"Think she'll be your maid of honor?" Connor said.

Liv gazed at him with something near alarm. If he talked about anything related to marriage in front of her mom, they'd NEVER stop hearing about it.

"Well, you'd need to get engaged first," Mary said over-bright.

"Oh yeah," Connor said, and then he snapped his fingers, "Leo!"

Leo?

The clickity-click of dog nails tapped along the floor and lo, there came Leo running right to them. How did he get there? Did he escape and her parents caught him and that's why her mom was so flushed?

Then her uncle Mark came walking out of the den, followed by her dad. *Uncle Mark?*

"Uh—" Liv sucked in a breath as she realized what this was. Eyes *huge*, she looked *down* at Connor, because he'd gone on to bended knee.

He quickly pulled a chain from around Leo's neck, where a ring lay dangling from it, and said, "Liv, I've loved you from the beginning and I will love you until the end of my days. Will you marry me?"

She was trembling all over, happy tears leaked from her eyes. "Yes!" she laughed and cried at the same time.

He surged to his feet, sweeping her up into his arms to spin her around while her family—*their* family, celebrated. Even Leo barked from the happy excitement.

Setting her down, Connor kissed her and kissed her, and Liv heard her dad say, "Let's give 'em a minute."

"Just don't make any babies in the receiving room," Mary said.

Mark snorted. "Nice one, Mary."

Dad's long-suffering sigh faded to silence as they disappeared into the den.

Connor slowly lifted his head, breaking the kiss. "I'll put babies in your receiving room."

Laughing quietly, Liv gazed up at him with all the love and joy she felt in her soul. "I love you. I'm grateful for you, for the man that you are. I'm grateful that you're mine."

His eyes, his beautiful hazel eyes, so full of warmth and light held hers and made her feel like they were in another universe no one could reach.

"There's only you," he said softly.

The palm of his hand slid along her arm, bringing her hand between them. The ring he'd bought sparkled in the light as he held it to her finger. It was an antique with a large center diamond with detailed platinum fillagree and sapphire marquis stones surrounding it in an art deco style.

"I had it sized," he said with a sweetly bashful look as it slid perfectly onto her finger.

While she stared at it on her hand, he pulled something from his back pocket. A flat black-velvet box.

"I wanted to get the ring engraved but the band is too little," he said, carefully opening the box. "So I thought this would be the next best thing."

Inside lay a necklace in a similar art-deco style, round with a center diamond surrounded by sapphires. The backside was solid white-gold made to lay flat against her skin and on it was engraved, *Forever and Ever.*

"Just like those Disney movies you loved to watch," he whispered teasingly.

Laughing, Liv launched herself at him and covered him with tickling, laughing kisses. "Oh Connor, we are going to have so much fun."

And they did, forever and ever.

THE END

NOTE FROM THE AUTHOR

I started Liv and Connor's story over ten years ago, when they were teens. I had planned to write a snapshot of their high school years together, before catapulting us into their adult lives, but I couldn't. I had to write the evolution of their early relationship, and it was a heck of a lot of fun. Their younger years will make you laugh more than cry, but as you can imagine after reading Connor's journey, he went through some tough experiences.

If you haven't read their years together before *Liv, Again*, I hope you check out the beginning of their relationship in *Liv, in the Moment*. It's special. They're special, and I'm glad you've gone on this journey with me, with them.

~Tracy

ABOUT THE AUTHOR

Tracy Dale lives in California with her awesome husband, kids, three wonderful dogs, and one horse... so far. She graduated with a degree in Psychology, but when the stories in her head enthralled her more than the stories in real life, she happily jumped into the world of writing and has never looked back.

* * * *

Find more great reads at https://flyingfeatherpublishing.com

Or find me on Amazon at
https://www.amazon.com/stores/author/B00MYU0M16

www.ingramcontent.com/pod-product-compliance
Lightning Source LLC
Chambersburg PA
CBHW020258200626
46816CB00001BA/346